a slater brothers novel

NEW YORK TIMES & USA TODAY BESTSELLING AUTHOR

L. A. CASEY

Brothers
a slater brothers novel
Copyright © 2018 by L.A. Casey
Published by L.A. Casey
www.lacaseyauthor.com

This book is licensed for your personal enjoyment only. This book may not be re-sold or given away to other people. If you would like to share this book with another person, please purchase an additional copy for each recipient. If you're reading this book and did not purchase it, or it wasn't purchased for your use only, then please return to your favorite book retailer and purchase your own copy. Thank you for respecting the hard work of this author.
All rights reserved.
Except as permitted under S.I. No. 337/2011 – European Communities (Electronic Communications Networks and Services) (Universal Service and Users' Rights) Regulations 2011, no part of this publication may be reproduced, distributed, or transmitted in any form or by any means, or stored in a database or retrieval system, without prior written permission of the author. The scanning, uploading, and distribution of this book via the Internet or via other means without the permission of the publisher is illegal and punishable by law. Please purchase only authorized electronic editions and do not participate in or encourage electronic piracy of copyrighted materials. This is a work of fiction. Names, characters, places, brands, media, and incidents are either the product of the author's imagination or are used fictitiously. The author acknowledges the trademarked status and trademark owners of various products referenced in this work of fiction, which have been used without permission. The publication/use of these trademarks is not authorized, associated with, or sponsored by the trademark owners.

Brothers / L.A. Casey – 1st ed.
ISBN-13: 978-1731228314

To those of you who love the Slater brothers, and their ladies, as much as they love their ladies. I will never be able to correctly put into words—and words are my job!—how truly thankful, grateful, touched, and blown away I am by the support for these characters from each of you over the last four years. The Slater brothers were never just mine, they were always ours.

PART ONE: DOMINIC	1
Chapter One	2
Chapter Two	28
Chapter Three	34
Chapter Four	39
Chapter Five	44
Chapter Six	55
Chapter Seven	61
Chapter Eight	74
PART TWO: ALEC	85
Chapter One	86
Chapter Two	106
Chapter Three	114
Chapter Four	125
Chapter Five	134

Chapter Six	158
Chapter Seven	163
PART THREE: KANE	174
Chapter One	175
Chapter Two	185
Chapter Three	194
Chapter Four	200
Chapter Five	220
Chapter Six	229
Chapter Seven	249
PART FOUR: RYDER	261
Chapter One	262
Chapter Two	271
Chapter Three	278
Chapter Four	286
Chapter Five	291
Chapter Six	319
Chapter Seven	333
PART FIVE: DAMIEN	340
Chapter One	341
Chapter Two	357

Chapter Three	363
Chapter Four	379
Chapter Five	393
Chapter Six	398
Chapter Seven	415
Acknowledgments	422
About the Author	424
Other Titles	425

PART ONE

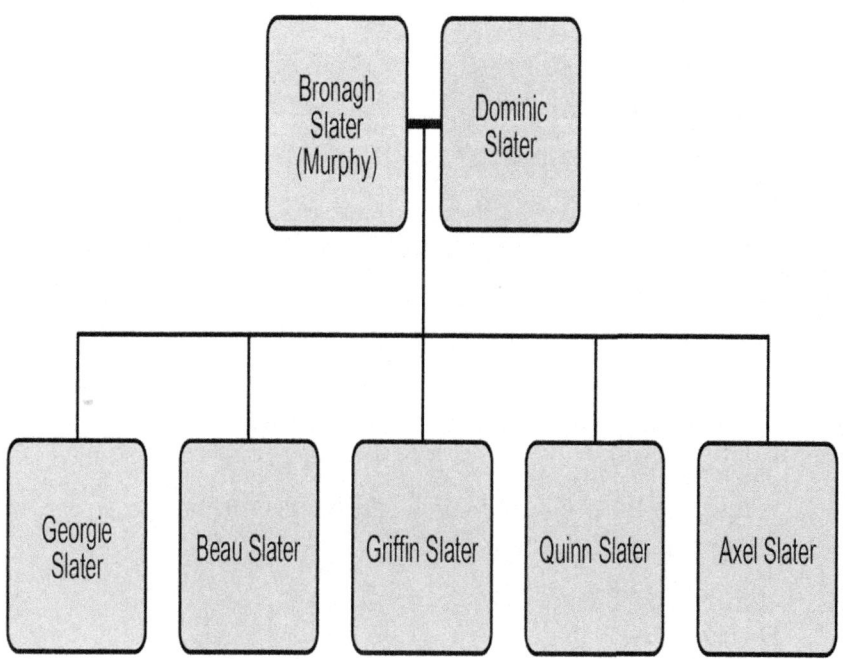

DOMINIC

CHAPTER ONE

Present day ...

When you had five children, sleep was very hard to come by. And sleeping in on the weekends was practically unheard of. I was a trier, if anything, so ever since I became a father fifteen years ago, I attempted, every single weekend, to catch a few extra minutes whenever I could. My know-no-boundaries offspring made it their personal mission to make sure I didn't.

"Daddy?"

I refused to lift my eyelids as I grumbled, "Go away."

"Come on, Daddy. Get up."

I snored. Loudly.

"Daaaaaaddy?"

I groaned but kept my eyes shut, hoping the kid harassing me would give up and leave.

"I know you're fakin' it."

"Go bother your mom," I half pleaded, snuggling into my pillow. "Please."

I felt tiny, soft hands touch my bare back, and that was when the let's-pretend-dad-is-a-drum game started.

"I don't wanna play with a *girl*. I wanna play with *you*. You're stronger than Mammy."

I chuckled gruffly before I rolled onto my back, halting the drum game my son had started. I reached up and rubbed my eyes before I opened them and stared at the ceiling of my bedroom. A ceiling that had multiple stickers of stars and moons stuck to it from when Georgie was a baby. I turned my head to the left and came face to face with my actual baby. I reached over, gripped under Axel's armpits, and heaved him onto the bed, making him squeal with laughter. He was the youngest of our five, our last child. My baby. He was spoiled rotten because of this.

"Your mom is plenty strong. Why don't you want to play with her?"

"I'm not talkin' to 'er anymore."

He said this as he sat directly on my chest, making me grunt.

"Why not?"

Axel scowled. "She keeps callin' me a *baby*."

My lips twitched. "You don't think you're a baby?"

"I just turned *seven*," Axel said, puffing his chest out with pride. "I'm not a baby, Daddy."

I grinned at him. "Your mom doesn't mean anything when she calls you baby, son. It's just a habit from when your brothers and sister were little. She even calls *me* baby now and then ... Do you think *I* look like a baby?"

Axel considered this, then giggled. "You're *definitely* not a baby."

He spoke as he poked at my abdominal muscles. Muscles that at thirty-eight were still tight, toned, and *very* defined. My love for working out never faded as I got older and neither did my wife's adoration for my body, so I made sure to keep it in peak physical condition because it made her moan on sight.

I *loved* hearing that woman moan.

I yawned. "Is Mom still in her pjs?"

"Yup." Axel nodded. "She said she's gettin' a shower when ye' wake up."

"I better go downstairs and relieve her then. What do you say?"

Axel cocked an eyebrow. "Are ye' goin' to kiss 'er again?"

"Do you not like when I kiss her?"

He shook his head. "She's *my* mammy."

"And she's *my* wife," I countered, grinning.

"I was in 'er belly," Axel deadpanned. "Beat that."

Easy.

"I *put* you in her belly."

He stared down at me. "How?"

I hesitated, wondering if he was too young for the talk that I had given to all my other kids at various ages, but Axel's attention switched to flicking my nipples and laughing when I flinched. He crawled off me when I playfully swatted his hands away, then jumped off the bed and ran out of the room shouting, "I woke 'im up, Ma!"

I shot into an upright position. "You said you wanted to play!"

"I lied," Axel shouted as he reached the stairs. "Mammy said I'd get the *biggest* cookie ever after dinner tonight if I woke ye' up. Sorry ... not really, though! Cooookkkiieeee."

I kicked the blankets off my body, then turned and hung my legs over the bed. I snorted as I heard my wife praise our youngest at the bottom of the stairs for waking me up. I wasn't surprised that she enlisted our kids' help; she always had them scheming when she didn't want to do something. She said it was one of the perks of having children.

"Beau!" Georgie suddenly bellowed. "Give it back or I swear to God I'll—"

"Hey!" I shouted, getting to my feet and walking out to the hallway to see what was going on.

Georgie, my eldest, had Beau, my second eldest, in a chokehold with her arm hooked perfectly around his neck. She had her right leg wrapped around his left to angle his body so she could get a firm grip in a better stance. He couldn't attempt to break her hold on him without hurting himself in the process, and she knew it. I had taught her how to protect herself and how to hold her own, but she wasn't supposed to practice her self-defence moves on her brothers.

I stared at my firstborn son, and a flashback of his birth suddenly entered my mind.

"He's perfect, baby," I said to my exhausted partner as she cradled our newborn son against her chest. "He's so perfect."

"He looks so much like ye', Dominic." Bronagh smiled. "We have a mini me and now a mini you."

"How did we get so lucky?" I asked, amazed. "How did I get so lucky?"

Bronagh smiled up at me, so I leaned down, closing the distance between us, and brushed my lips over hers.

"What will we name him?"

"I love the name Beau."

I raised a brow and leaned back. "How do you spell that?"

"B-E-A-U."

"That's pronounced Bo, baby. I like that, though. Let's name him that."

Bronagh blinked. "No, it's pronounced Beau as in beau*tiful*."

"In the States—"

"We aren't in the States," she tiredly interrupted. "I like Beau bein' pronounced like the word beautiful. Bo can be his nickname, if you're so pressed about it."

"Okay." I chuckled. "His name is Beau like beautiful, and Bo will be his nickname. I'll inform my brothers of this to avoid your wrath."

Bronagh smiled. "What will his middle name be?"

My heart warmed when I said the name, "Damien."

My girl beamed up at me. "Beau Damien Slater. I love it, I love him ... I can't wait for Georgie to see 'im. She's a big sister now."

"Alannah will bring her up when I call," I assured her. "She'll be with us soon."

Bronagh closed her eyes and snuggled Beau.

"I love our family."

"I love *you, pretty girl*."

"I love you too, fuckface."

"Let him go, Georgie," I said, my mind snapping back to the present.

"He has me phone, Da!"

"Let him *go*," I repeated, sternly. "*Now.*"

Georgie gave Beau's neck one last squeeze before she released him and forcefully shoved him to the floor. I folded my arms across my chest and stared down at my only daughter. She placed her hands on her hips and stared right back at me. I looked at my son as he groaned on the floor, then looked back at Georgie.

"Was that really necessary?"

"Yeah," she answered without hesitation. "He took me phone without permission, Da."

I looked at Beau. "Why'd you take her phone?"

He groaned as he pushed himself to his feet, then straightened up to his full height. He was fourteen, but he already dwarfed Georgie's five-foot-two frame with his five-foot-eight one. When he stood next to her, it always amused me. He was fifteen months younger than she was, and he physically looked down at her. My daughter, however, never let a trivial thing like height stop her when it came to disciplining her brothers or any of her many male cousins. She'd had years of practice on how to harm them when she needed to. Or wanted to.

"I was only messin' with 'er, Da," Beau said before glancing sideways at his sister. "She's a bleedin' psycho."

Georgie kicked Beau in the shin. He yelped, grabbed his shin with both hands, and hopped around on one foot.

"Bo, give your sister back her phone," I ordered. "And George, stop hitting your brother."

I hoped by using their nicknames, the situation would calm to somehow make it playful, but Georgie's antsy teenage attitude refused to cooperate.

"No promises," she said to me as she snapped her phone out of Beau's outstretched hand. "Next time, Bo, I'm breakin' your bloody leg."

She turned and stormed down the hall and into her bedroom, the door clanking shut behind her. Beau shook his head, then his leg, before he lowered his foot to the ground and trained his eyes on me.

"Ye' need to send 'er to a mental institution, Da," he said, his face the picture of seriousness. "She is a bloody nightmare."

I raised a brow. "She wouldn't bother you if you didn't touch her things."

"I wouldn't bother 'er if she didn't annoy the life outta me."

I lifted my hand to my face and pinched the bridge of my nose.

"It's too early to deal with this."

"It's after nine."

I dropped my head. "Exactly. That's early."

Beau snorted as shouting and a bellow from my wife sounded from downstairs.

"Not in this house."

I pointed at my son. "Leave your sister alone. Otherwise, she'll whoop you."

"Only 'cause I won't hit 'er back!"

"I know." I grinned. "When you're bigger and fill out more, she won't be able to grapple you so easily."

"I can't feckin' wait."

"Language."

"Feckin' isn't a curse." Beau rolled his eyes. "And neither is damn or hell."

"The former can slide because it's part of everyone's vocabulary in this country, but if I hear you say the second and third, your ass will be whooped by *me*. Understand?"

"Yes, sir."

"Good." I nodded. "Now, go clean your room. It's Saturday, and you *know* your mom will raise all kinds of hell if she finds it dirty when she makes her rounds."

As I walked down the stairs, Beau asked, "How come *you* get to say hell and not be whooped?"

"Who's gonna whoop me?"

"You've got a point, Da." Beau paused. "You've got a real good point."

I laughed as I jogged downstairs. A glance into the living room revealed Axel lying upside down on the couch as he watched a cartoon on the television. I crossed my arms over my chest and stared at him.

"You're going to give yourself a headache watching the TV like that, Ax."

"No, I won't," he replied, not taking his eyes off the TV. "I always watch it like this."

I had no doubt.

"Just sit up every few minutes; otherwise, the blood will rush to your head."

"Okay, Daddy."

I shook my head in amusement, dropped my arms to my sides, and walked down the hallway and into the kitchen. My eyes found her the second I entered the room. With her back to me as she cooked breakfast, I took a moment to drink her in. In twenty years, nothing about her had changed. Not really, even after five kids. Her body was the same level of perfection it had always been. Small waist, thick thighs, and an ass so fat it still made my knees weak when I looked at it.

Her hair was shorter—it hung just past her shoulders instead of touching her butt—but it was still a beautiful shade of chocolate brown. She had more laugh lines around her eyes, more stretch marks, and a slight tummy pouch from having so many babies, but she didn't look thirty-eight years old. She could easily pass for being in her late twenties, and I told her that often because it was true ... not just because it got me laid whenever I said it.

She was tiny, feminine, and was the greatest love of my life, along with my five children. Children *she* gave to me. I glanced down at my ringed finger, smiling at the reminder that we recently celebrated our thirteenth wedding anniversary. We'd been married for thirteen years, but together for twenty, and I couldn't wait to spend fifty more with her, God willing. I couldn't imagine spending my life with anyone else, and I didn't want to, either.

"Good morning, Mrs Slater."

I knew she smiled without having to turn around. I could sense it on her.

"Good mornin', Mr Slater," she replied. "How did ye' sleep?"

"Before or after you woke me up with your mouth on—"

When she spun around and narrowed her bright green eyes at me, my own laughter cut me off.

"Children," she whispered hissed. "They are present."

I glanced to my left, noting my third and fourth sons, Quinn and Griffin, sitting at the kitchen table on the far end of the room, not paying us a lick of attention. I turned my attention back to my wife and grinned.

"They can't hear me."

She gave me a once-over, her eyes lingering on my groin and torso a little too long, allowing naughty thoughts to enter my mind, but just as I knew she would, she turned back to face the stove.

"I made you eggs, and I'm workin' on your protein pancakes," she said, rustling the pan to flip the pancake. "The boys horsed down the first two batches I made, as well as two ten-egg omelettes."

"Q and Griff?"

"Yeah," she answered with a shake of her head. "Axel and Beau had cereal; Georgie hasn't been down to eat yet. Quinn and Griffin are goin' to eat us out of a home all by themselves. I can't believe how much they can put away. They're just as bad as Locke, and that lad *never* stops eatin'."

"They're growing boys."

Bronagh snorted. "Growin' boys, me arse; they are always feckin' hungry."

"So were my brothers and I growing up." I chuckled. "We still are."

"Oh, I know," my wife answered. "I do the cookin'. I know how much your fat self can gobble up."

I stepped closer to her, pressing my body against hers and sliding my arms around her tiny waist.

"You think I'm fat?" I teased. "My body fat percentage would disagree with you."

"Ye' have the appetite of a fat person and so do your kids. Well, except Georgie, but she *used* to eat just as much." Bronagh shook her head. "I don't know how we afford it. Ye' know, it costs me nearly three hundred and fifty euros a week on *just* food? I don't even shop in Dunnes anymore because it'll easily reach over four hundred in price if I go in there."

I leaned down and kissed her cheek.

"Why are you worrying about this?" I questioned. "I make more than enough to cover our bills. We own the house since Branna signed it over to you, and the cars are brand new since we traded in our others for a steal. We have a fantastic policy on our family health insurance *and* both of our life insurance policies. You set aside money each month to pay our bills on time. You're worrying yourself over nothing."

"I know." She sighed, her body relaxing. "It's just with the football season startin' back up, and the lads all bein' taller with bigger feet, it means we have to buy all new team uniforms and tracksuits, and new football boots, which are over one hundred euros *each* in their sizes, and new clothes since they've no summer clothes that fit. I only realised this when they got dressed this mornin' because everythin' was a little tight on all of them. Don't even get me *started* on Georgie's art supplies. She goes through them so fast that we need to replenish every—"

"Sweetheart," I cut Bronagh off. "We have savings for a reason. *This* kind of reason."

She tensed all over again as she placed a large pancake on top of four others next to the large omelette that I assumed was for me.

"Heat the eggs up," she grumbled. "They've been coolin' while I made the pancakes."

I watched her as she moved around me.

"Bronagh, honey—"

"I'm goin' to get a shower," she cut me off, leaving the room. "I won't be long."

I stared after her, frowning. I had no idea why she was so worried about our finances all of a sudden. Ten years ago, I got a loan from my older brother Kane and bought a broken-down old building in the city centre and demolished it. After rebuilding it from the ground up, I opened Slater's 24/7 Fitness. Every month since it opened nine years ago, it'd turned a considerable profit. I was even considering opening a second gym in Tallaght because the main one was doing so well. I had paid Kane back and had no debt whatsoever.

Bronagh knew all of this, so I had no idea why she was worrying about paying for our children's sports gear or art supplies. I had enough to buy hundreds of football cleats. Hell, we could buy another house if we wanted to. My instinct was to follow her and find out what was truly bothering her, but over the years, I'd learned that she needed her space when she got upset. Normally, I invaded her space and didn't give her a chance to run away when an argument got her going, but right now, something else was bothering her. I had to time when I chose to talk to her about it.

With a sigh, I turned to my plate of food and put it into the microwave as instructed. While it heated, I went to the refrigerator with the intention of pouring myself a large glass of orange juice, but when I lifted the carton and found it was empty, I scowled and shut the door with a little force before I turned to my sons.

"Which one of you morons put the empty OJ carton back in the refrigerator?"

Quinn and Griffin pointed at one another, but when Quinn

scowled and slapped Griffin's hand, Griffin yelped, most likely thinking Quinn was going to pound on him for lying, which I knew he had done.

"Griffin?"

"I'm sorry," he said, his eyes still on his older brother. "I forgot."

"How do you forget the carton is empty when you can feel it's fucking empty?"

Quinn glanced around me, looking for his mom, but when he saw she wasn't there, he kept his mouth shut about my cussing. I rarely cussed in front of my kids, and especially not to them, but sometimes, they irritated the life out of me when they did dumb shit, and it just slipped out. Putting an empty carton of orange juice back into the refrigerator was a dumb shit thing to do.

"I'm sorry, Da."

I sighed. "It's okay. Just don't do it again."

"I won't."

"And I'm sorry for cussing."

Griffin's lips twitched. "It's okay. Just don't do it again."

Quinn laughed but muffled it with his hand while I smirked.

"You'll tattle on me to your mom otherwise?"

"Well, duh, I'm hardly gonna try to *fight* you."

I snorted. "You'll be as big as me someday. You both will."

"In height, yeah, probably, but ye' work out a lot. I don't think I'd be into that. I'm lazy."

Griffin *was* lazy.

If you gave him the choice to go outside to play and get fresh air, or stay inside and play video games all day, his games would win every single time. He was on the soccer team purely out of parental force. Bronagh and I ran out of ideas to entice him to leave the house, so we had to resort to giving him an ultimatum. He either joined the soccer team or picked a different sport or activity to participate in, or all his gaming consoles, his computer, *and* his phone were going in the trash.

He signed up for the soccer team the next day.

Beau, at fourteen, played for the sixteen and under soccer team, Quinn and Griffin, who were twelve and eleven, played for the under thirteen team, and Axel had just joined the under eight team. Griffin tolerated the soccer team, but damn, the kid was good. Luckily, Beau and Quinn were awesome too, but they lived and breathed the sport. It wasn't punishment to make them go to practice or to games; it was punishment to *stop* them from attending. Axel's team wasn't competitive because of the age group, so his games were just for fun, but he loved it.

Then there was Georgie, who was fifteen. My eldest, my only girl ... the only girl out of the twenty-five children my brothers and I have fathered.

Sports were out of the question for her because her passion lay with sketching, painting, and, recently, sculpting. The many years of being in her aunt Alannah's company had rubbed off on her. She started drawing when she was young, and with Alannah's guidance and her own talent, she could draw a lifelike portrait of someone by the time she was thirteen. She loved art; it was her form of self-expression. She attended a local art class on the weekends to gain more experience for the rare time when she wasn't around her aunt. Alannah and Bronagh were always joined at the hip but even more so since she started dating my twin brother, Damien, many years ago.

"You're always gonna be lazy if you don't get your head out of the video games you play all the time."

Griffin rolled his eyes and grumbled something under his breath.

"What was that?"

"Nothin', Da," he grunted. "I just don't wanna hear ye' givin' out to me about playin' on me games again. You and Ma always get on me case about it."

"Because you're always playing a console or on your phone."

"I joined the football team like ye' both said I had to do," he protested. "Isn't that enough?"

"For now, yeah."

He relaxed, then went back to eating his breakfast.

"What time is your game?"

"Eleven," Quinn and Griffin replied in unison.

"Is Mom taking you guys?"

Quinn's lips twitched. "She said *you* could either take us, or ye' could go and get the shoppin' instead."

I paused. "Grocery shopping?"

Quinn nodded, then smiled at my horrified expression. I *never* did the grocery shopping. The one and only time I'd done it in the past was an utter disaster. I apparently got the wrong brand of half of the groceries on Bronagh's list and forgot the rest. She had to go back to the store and get the correct stuff, which put her in a pissy mood for that entire day. It was a horrible experience from start to finish, and I'd do just about anything to get out of it. My kids and my wife knew that.

"I'm taking you guys to the game."

Griffin snickered. "Thought so."

Quinn chuckled along with him before inhaling one of his pancakes. I joined them at the table with my food, and we talked about school, sports, and girls while we ate. Recently, both boys had taken a mild interest in girls. It was nothing explicit; they had just started to develop crushes now that they no longer found girls gross.

"Griffin's got two girlfriends," Quinn announced as we all finished our food. "They fight over 'im."

Griffin's cheeks burned. "Shut *up*, Q!"

I frowned at Griffin. "Is that true, Griff?"

"No," he insisted. "They just like me or somethin'. They follow me around at school and get mad when I talk to one girl and not the other. They aren't me girlfriends, though. I don't have one, let alone *two*."

"Good," I said, firmly. "That's disrespectful to play two girls like that."

"I know." Griffin nodded. "We have to be nice to girls and treat them like we'd want a lad to treat Georgie, or you to treat Mom. I remember our talk."

"Ye' said Mom." Quinn snickered.

Griffin scowled at him. "It's only 'cause I was talkin' to Da! You say words like 'im sometimes, too."

I rolled my eyes.

"It's not a bad thing to say words how I say them. I know you guys are Irish, but you're American, too. That's half of my blood flowing through your veins, and I told you it's important to know your heritage."

"Ma said we don't really have an American heritage 'cause the country was stolen like *forever* ago."

I paused. "Okay, that is true but—"

"We're Irish, but because of you, we have American heritage," Quinn cut me off. "We *know*. Please don't tell us about it again. I feel like we're in school when ye' do."

I had to keep from smiling. He looked pained at the thought of me lecturing him about my homeland.

"Put your dishes in the dishwasher and go upstairs and clean your rooms," I said. "Mom won't let you go to your game if you don't do your chores."

Griffin perked up at the prospect of getting out of a soccer game, so I added, "She'll also confiscate your Xbox, desktop, and phone if she has to keep you home from soccer."

Griffin grunted as he got to his feet. "She's evil."

I snorted as they left the room after taking care of their dishes and mine. I relaxed at the table for a moment, then turned my head when Georgie entered the room, fully dressed in jeans, ankle boots, and a sweater.

"You'll be too warm wearing a sweater and boots today, baby. It's warm outside."

Georgie glanced at me and snorted.

"I'm always freezin', Da. There's no such thing as too hot for me. Not in this country, anyway."

My lips quirked as she moved around the kitchen, cleaning up after Bronagh had made everyone breakfast. That was one of Georgie's chores; she preferred cleaning the kitchen to the bathrooms. The boys would flip a coin to see who got stuck with toilet duty.

"What are you doing today, sweetheart?"

"I have class at the centre at half ten," she answered. "Auntie Alannah is collectin' me on 'er way. Alex and Joey are comin' with me."

"And here I thought you would come to the boys' game with me to keep me company. Some of your uncles will be there with your cousins, too."

The look of horror Georgie shot my way cracked me up. Her lips twitched when she realised I was teasing her.

"Will ye' go and get dressed?" she asked, her brow wrinkled. "You're too old to be walkin' around in your boxers like the lads."

"Too old?" I repeated in outrage. "I'm thirty-eight, you little shit."

Georgie smirked. "That's only two years away from forty."

I scowled. "Evil child."

"I'm gonna be twenty in five years, does that make you feel worse?"

Pain clutched at my chest.

"Yes," I answered, rubbing the spot. "It does. You're my baby."

"D'ye hear that, Axel?" Georgie hollered. "Daddy just called me a *baby*!"

I heard movement, then quick paced little footsteps as my youngest son barrelled into the room. Wrapping his arms around Georgie's hips, he crashed into her, making her laugh.

"I *told* ye'!" Axel said to her. "I told ye' they think we're all babies."

"Ye' did." Georgie nodded down at him. "I think Mammy and Daddy are goin' crazy."

"*Super* crazy!"

"Hey," I teased. "You're *all* my babies."

"He's lost his mind," Axel said with a shake of his head. "We should put 'im in the old people's home ye' said he and Mammy are gonna go to someday."

My jaw dropped, and Georgie burst into laughter.

"Ye' aren't supposed to *tell* them what I said," she tittered, hugging her brother to her side. "They get upset when we call them old."

"Ohhh." Axel nodded. "It's a secret."

"A *super* secret."

Everything was super to Axel when it was being stressed.

"A *super* secret." He nodded and looked like he'd accepted a mission of some kind. "I got it."

"A nursing home?" I blinked at my daughter. "Really?"

She smiled wide, and it warmed my heart.

She was the picture of her mother, and apart from my dimples, no one would ever guess she was my daughter. Bronagh got all the genetic rights to our firstborn; she got those rights with Quinn, too. He was the only one of my sons who resembled his mother more than me. He had her green eyes, her perfect complexion, her nose, her mouth. Everything. The rest of our boys got my genetics, which meant they looked the Slater part. Beau was the spitting image of Damien's firstborn son, and since they were close in age, people often thought they were twins, which amused them greatly.

"I'm only teasin'," Georgie assured me with a wink. "I'd never put you in an old folk's home. I wouldn't be able to carry ye'."

I snorted. "Watch your brother while I go shower."

Georgie saluted me, then ducked out of my reach with Axel, both screaming with laughter when I fake dived for them. A big smile stretched across my face as I left the room and jogged upstairs. I heard music blaring from the bedroom in the attic that we'd converted a few years before Axel was born. It was Beau's room, and ever since he hit his teenage years, I was considering soundproofing the damn thing because Beau only understood one volume, and that was *loud.*

"Beau!" I yelled and banged on the rail of the spiral stairs that led up to his room. "Boy, you better answer me."

The music switched off, and the door to his room opened ever so slightly.

"What, Da?"

"Turn that garbage *down*!" I warned. "We have neighbours, you know?"

"Sorry," Beau said, popping his head out just enough for me to see he was red faced and sweating. "I'll keep it low."

His door clicked then, and just as I was about to walk up the stairs to see what he was doing, I paused. The last time I walked into his room unannounced, I got an eyeful of my teenager jerking off like there was no tomorrow. He couldn't look me in the eye for a week after that happened, and since it only occurred a few months ago, I had to keep boundaries and respect his privacy. I remembered what it was like to be fourteen and hormonal. You got wood from something as simple as sniffing fucking flowers.

The only difference between me and my son was that I didn't have to jerk off. I had paid escorts to take care of my needs. I was sure that was a perk from my past life that Beau would desperately love to avail of. With a grin, I shook my head and walked into my bedroom. I glanced at the closed bathroom door and heard the shower running. I quickly closed the bedroom door, kicked off my boxers, and tiptoed my way into the bathroom.

I hadn't had shower sex with my wife in *months*, and there was no way I was going to miss the opportunity of loving her while she was dripping wet. When I stepped into the room, steam slapped me in the face. I could barely see a thing, but that was typical Bronagh. She had to have her shower water run so damn hot before she'd even consider stepping under the spray. The room was like our own personal sauna.

"Hey, mama."

Bronagh jumped when I entered the shower behind her, but she didn't spin to face me.

"You're so predictable," she said with a snort. "I knew ye'd come up 'ere."

I reached out and palmed her ass when I was close enough to do so.

"Can you blame me?" I asked, leaning down and swiping my tongue over her earlobe. "Your ass makes my cock ache."

"After all this time?" She wiggled her butt against me. "I've still got it, fuckface."

My lips twitched as I looked down and watched as I shifted my hips and began to slowly thrust back and forth. My cock fit snugly between Bronagh's ass cheeks and it felt like heaven. I bit down on my lower lip when she clenched her cheeks together, and it sent a wave of bliss riveting straight to my balls.

"Fu...*ck*."

"D'ye want me arse?"

I pressed my mouth against Bronagh's sopping wet hair.

"*Yes*," I rasped. "Yes, please, baby."

She rarely let me fuck her ass, so when she did, it felt like all my Christmases came at once.

"Get me ready."

Those words sent blood rushing to my already throbbing cock. I dropped to my knees behind her, then when I leaned forward, biting her ass, she sucked in a sharp breath, then laughed.

"Bastard."

I smiled as I slid my tongue over the flesh I bit. Without warning, I spread her wide and plunged my tongue into her asshole. Bronagh's hands flattened against the tiled walls. My arm wrapped around her, flattening against her stomach in an effort to support her in case she slipped and fell. I groaned when Bronagh's hand ran over mine before she pushed it down to her pussy, showing me what she wanted me to do. My fingers found her clit, and hearing the first long moan come from her caused my balls to tighten.

I fucking *loved* when she moaned.

I tongued her asshole and played with her clit until her body trembled. When I stood, I fisted my cock and pumped it twice before I aligned the head with Bronagh's body. I used my left hand to spread her, and when I slowly thrust my hips forward, my eyes fluttered shut. The slickness, the heat, the pulsing tightness of my wife's muscles. It was an ecstasy that only she could give me. I forced my eyes open so I could watch as my cock slipped inside her mag-fucking-nificent ass, and as always, I couldn't stop my eyes from rolling to the back of my head as pleasure licked at me.

"Dominic," Bronagh whispered. "Fuck."

Fuck was right.

"Baby," I lowly groaned. "You always feel so perfect."

"Easy," she whispered. "Go *easy*."

I had to go easy with her. No matter how many times I fucked her ass, I always had to be very gentle with her in the beginning until she was stretched and used to the sensation of being so full. She came harder when I started out easier, so I took my time thrusting in and out of her body. I brought my mouth to her neck and kissed her skin until her head fell back against my chest.

"Mine," I grunted as I scraped my teeth over her skin. "Everything about you is *mine*. I'm going to fuck you into ecstasy, baby."

"Yes," she replied, starting to push back against my body. "Fuck. Yes."

Lazy thrusting soon turned to precise pumping. Bronagh bucked back against me wildly, giving me just as good as I was giving her. The only sounds that could be heard were our laboured breathing, the slapping of skin on skin, and the occasional grunt or groan that neither of us could contain. I picked up my pace and fucked my wife harder. When she played with her clit and groaned, the sound went straight to my balls, and I bucked into her harder, faster, deeper. When she sucked in a sharp breath, held it, and went still as I loved her, I knew she was coming. I hissed when her asshole tightened around me as her muscles contracted.

"Good girl," I praised, running my tongue over her shoulder. "Fuck. You feel so good."

Now that she had come, I had to chase down my own orgasm because in the back of my mind I knew that at any moment, one of the kids was going to call us and put an indefinite pause on our alone time. It took another thirty seconds, but when my balls drew up tight and a shiver danced the length of my spine, I knew I was about to come. My lips parted, and deep groans filled the room as the first spurt shot free. I hissed when Bronagh's muscles contracted a couple of times and acted like a vacuum, sucking the cum out of my cock.

"Baby!"

She chuckled in response.

"I fucking *love* you," I panted, slapping her ass for good measure. "You continue to ruin me."

Bronagh grunted against the wall. "Ye've just about fucked me into a coma, big man."

I laughed as I slipped out of her body and hugged her to me. I spent a few minutes catering to her. I washed her hair and skin because not only did I enjoy doing it, but *she* loved me doing it. After I washed my hair, and scrubbed my body, I looked back at Bronagh.

"Are you going to tell me what got you upset in the kitchen earlier?"

She turned to face me, looked up at me, and my heart thumped against my chest. She was beautiful, so painfully beautiful that I could never get enough of her. This woman had my heart, body, and soul. One look from those big green eyes, and I was completely at her mercy.

"I don't even know what me problem is," she answered with a sigh. "Sometimes, I just realise we have such a big family, and I'm terrified if we suddenly can't provide for them anymore."

"Bronagh."

"*You're* the one who makes the money, Dominic," she cut me off. "I just ... I just—"

"You just take care of everyone and everything else," I finished. "Sweetheart, you are the heart of this family. Without you, there is nothing. You know that."

When her eyes glazed over with tears, I leaned down and kissed her until she relaxed against me.

"Alannah pays you too. You've been working with her for years. You contribute financially as well as me."

She sighed but didn't disagree with me.

"No more worrying," I murmured against her lips. "Okay?"

She nodded. "Okay."

"I love you."

She hummed. "I love ye', too."

I jumped when her nails ran over my softening cock, and it made her laugh as I backed out of the shower with a smirk in place.

"Same time tomorrow?"

Bronagh snorted. "If I can sit down by then, we'll see."

I left our bathroom with a shit-eating grin on my face. I dried myself off, changed into clean boxer shorts, and just as I was about to grab some pants, I thought I heard voices in the hallway. I ventured outside to investigate, and the second I left the room, gasps and giggles could be heard as well as a horrified, "*Da!*"

Georgie was clearly heading towards her bedroom with two of her friends in tow, Alexandra and Joanne, aka Alex and Joey. I had known both girls since they were in kindergarten with my daughter, so seeing them stare at me without blinking freaked me out. I looked down at my boxer briefs then back up to my child's teenage friends, and I think, for the first time in years, I felt myself blush.

"Hi, girls." I smiled as I reached out to grab a towel hanging over the stair rail and wrapped it tightly around my hips. "How are you, ladies?"

"I'm doin' *real* good, Mr Slater," Joey replied with a brow raised and her teeth sinking into her lower lip. "Real good, sir."

Alex giggled, and Joey stared at me without blinking while Georgie's burning face indicated her mortification.

"Can ye' please put some clothes on?" she pleaded. "*Please.*"

I bobbed my head, sprung back into my bedroom and closed the door behind me before anyone could speak another word. Bronagh was in the middle of putting a bra on. She already had socks and panties on, and when she saw me, she raised her brows.

"Alex and Joey just saw me in my boxers." I cringed. "I think Joey licked her lips, too."

Bronagh grinned. "Is Georgie red faced?"

"Yeah," I answered. "She'll be complaining about this for the next week."

My wife giggled as she pulled on a pair of jeans, and she playfully rolled her eyes when she found my eyes glued to her as she got dressed. I grinned, not ashamed in the least to be caught ogling her. I watched her as often as I could, and she and everyone else knew it. My kids weren't bothered by it because seeing me being constantly affectionate with their mother was all they ever knew. I think if I stopped showing that affection, they would find it bizarre.

"Ye'll have to apologise to Georgie," Bronagh said as she put on her socks. "She'll be a nightmare otherwise."

I pulled on jeans, socks, and a T-shirt.

"I'll catch her before she goes to the centre with the girls."

"I'm bringin' Axel shoppin' with me, so ye' just have Quinn and Griffin to bring to their game. Their match is a home game, so ye' only have to go down to the pitches. I wanna stop off at Skechers and get Axel new runners; his last two pairs were ruined from all the climbin' he does at Gravity with *you.*"

I smiled. "He loves it."

"His runners don't."

I walked over, smacked her ass, grabbed her face, and kissed her like I meant it. When I pulled away, my wife swayed into me just like she did when we were teenagers.

"What was that for?"

"Because I felt like kissing you."

She opened her eyes and smiled up at me.

"You're so beautiful."

"Speakin' of *beau*tiful ..." She tilted her head to the side. "Why were Beau and Georgie fightin' earlier?"

"He took her phone; she retaliated."

"That lad constantly tries to find ways to annoy 'er."

"He loves her ... loves to piss her off, too."

Bronagh chuckled as I kissed her cheek and left the room. I glanced over the stair rail and saw Alex and Joey descending the stairs with my daughter nowhere in sight. I made my way to her bedroom, and when I entered the room, I froze in the doorway.

"What the *hell* are you wearing, Georgie Slater?"

She spun to face me, and when I saw her bare stomach, my heart stopped.

"Ye' were right ab-about it bein' hot out," she stammered. "I was just changin' into somethin' ... cooler."

"Cooler?" I blinked. "You're naked."

"Da, *please*." She frowned. "I'm not naked. It's a crop top and a skirt."

Two things she had never worn before. Ever.

"Naked," I repeated. "You aren't leaving the house in *that*. If you lean forward, your ass will be out for the world to see."

I ran from her room to mine, grabbed a T-shirt that I made as a joke the year before, and rushed back to my daughter's room. I pushed it at her and waited outside as she changed into it. When I heard her screech, I felt deeply satisfied with myself.

"Daddy!"

"Don't 'daddy' me," I warned as I re-entered the room. "If you won't dress yourself correctly, then *I'll* do it for you. Put pants on with this."

My child almost snarled at me. "This will put me at the *top* of the loser list, Da! No lad will ever look in me direction if ye' make me wear this!"

Fireworks went off in my mind at her words.

"You're never taking it off."

Georgie stomped her foot on the ground and turned her back to me. She opened her mouth and shouted, "Ma!"

I listened for Bronagh and smiled when I heard her walk towards our daughter's room humming a song.

"What is it, Georgie?"

"Da is ruinin' me entire life, and he's *happy* about it."

I was *very* happy about it.

Bronagh entered the room on a tired sigh, but when her gorgeous eyes fell to the T-shirt Georgie had on, she laughed with glee. Our less than impressed teenager screeched. "It's *not* funny! I'll be slagged to the high heavens if I have to wear this, Ma."

Bronagh folded her arms over her chest. "I thought ye' didn't care what people thought of ye'?"

Georgie shifted her stance. "I don't."

My wife raised a brow. "Then what's the problem?"

Georgie pointed at her shirt and read the words printed in black.

"This is my dad. He will do to you what you do to me. It's even worse with the stupid picture of Da without his shirt on under the writin'."

"That's a nice picture." I frowned. "Don't be mean."

She refused to look at me. Instead, she focused on Bronagh. "I'd sooner walk around school in me *bra* in front of every lad in sixth year than wear this T-shirt, Ma."

My child just described an actual nightmare of mine.

"Do you want me to have your cousins flank you all day at school on Monday?" I growled. "Because I'll call them right now and arrange it."

My stubborn child scoffed. "Go for it."

She challenged me, and she was old enough to know never to do that.

"Fine," I said and took out my phone.

"Fine," Georgie quipped.

I dialled Jax's number and placed my phone to my ear.

"What's up, unc?" he answered on the third ring.

"I need a favour, kid."

I heard a female giggle, then a pained groaned from my nephew. "I'm kind of busy, unc. Can this wait?"

I shook my head as a grin crept its way onto my face.

"It's about Georgie."

I heard Jax instantly hush who was giggling.

"Is she okay?" he asked, his focus fully on our conversation and not the girl he was with.

"She is," I said then growled, "but she is threatening to wear *just* her bra to school come Monday."

"She is threatenin' to *what*?" Jax all but roared. "Is she there with ye'?"

"She is."

"Put 'er on the phone," he demanded. "Now."

He was Kane's kid; there was no doubt about it. I tapped my phone on Georgie's shoulder and held it out to her when she turned to me. She looked at the phone for a moment, and I saw her tough girl act begin to crack. She covered up her near slip, took the phone, and pressed it to her ear.

"What d'ye want, Jax?" she asked, though her tone wasn't as stern as before.

I looked at Bronagh when Jax's voice bellowed through the receiver of my phone. She grinned, and I shook my head. She was enjoying this just as much as I was.

"No!" Georgie suddenly bellowed. "If ye' do that, I'll make sure Daisy Mars *never* looks at ye' again." She gasped at Jax's response. "Ye' wouldn't dare, Jax Slater."

"I would," I heard Jax threaten.

"Go ahead then," Georgie angrily spat and hung up on Jax before turning and tossing my phone back to me.

"Can ye' both leave, please?" she asked. "I want to be on me own."

I opened my mouth to ignore her and continue our discussion, but when a soft hand touched my elbow, I turned my attention from my daughter to my wife.

"Come on," Bronagh said. "Leave 'er be."

I had to be tugged out of the room and down the stairs.

"Georgie will be down in a few minutes," Bronagh said to Alex and Joey who were keeping Axel and Beau company in the living room. Beau, whose focus was on Joey, didn't even notice that his mother spoke. He was too focused on his sister's friend, and it made me snort.

Twenty minutes after our argument, Georgie, who was correctly dressed, left with her friends and went to the community centre when Alannah pulled up outside to collect them. Bronagh took Axel with her when she went shopping, and Beau accompanied me to the boys' soccer game. We didn't get home until after four p.m. After soccer, I took the boys to lunch, then to see the new Marvel movie. When I stepped foot into my house, it sounded like World War III had erupted.

Jax was over, and he and Georgie were knee-deep in an argument in the kitchen. I pushed passed my kids and jogged into the room. My wife was leaned against the sink, pinching the bridge of her nose. I looked at my firstborn nephew and my firstborn child, who were glaring daggers at each other. When my nephew caught sight of me, a deadly grin spread across his face.

"Uncle Nico," Jax said, turning his attention back to his cousin. "Georgie has a boyfriend ... and he's a *Collins*!"

CHAPTER TWO

"Can you repeat that, Jax?"

"*Don't* repeat it, cousin," Georgie pleaded. "He looks like he's about to have a bleedin' stroke!"

I was definitely close to say the least.

"Ye' heard me, unc. Georgie has a boyfriend; he's me cousin. A Collins lad through and through."

I hadn't even realised I was pacing back and forth until my wife approached me cautiously and placed her hands on my biceps. All I could think of was this little Collins bastard touching my daughter in her no-go areas.

"Breathe," Bronagh instructed. "Nice and slow, in and out."

I copied her actions, taking slow, deep breaths, but it was futile. My blood pressure was too high for me to calm down.

"Boys," I barked to my sons who lingered in the kitchen doorway. "Get up to your rooms. Now."

My sons wished Georgie good luck as they hightailed it up the stairs without a backwards glance. Georgie didn't look at them; her narrowed eyes were locked on Jax, and if looks could kill, my nephew would have been dead and buried.

I focused on my firstborn. "As of right now, you no longer have a boyfriend."

Her gazed darted to mine, and she screeched, "But Daddy!"

"No!" I cut her off. "No 'but Daddy'! I'm not letting up on this, no way. You're fifteen; what the hell do you need a boyfriend for?"

Georgie glared at me. "I'm not breakin' up with 'im. I don't care *what* ye' say."

Excuse me?

"Is that so?"

Georgie shrunk under my stare but nodded ever so slightly.

"Everything is going in the trash," I declared. "Phone, laptop, makeup, hair products, your television, your sound system, your iPod. Everything. Trash."

Georgie widened her eyes.

"If you're going to disrespect me in my house, then you're sure as hell not having any of the privileges your mother and I paid for."

"This is all your fault!" Georgie snapped at Jax. "Ye' couldn't keep your big mouth shut. Ye' ruin everythin'. *I hate you.*"

Jax flinched as if his cousin's words had struck him.

"Georgie," he said in disbelief. "Take it back."

"No."

"Take it back, cousin," he repeated. "Now."

"No!"

"Georgie Slater," Bronagh said, her voice deathly low. "Take back those hateful words right *now*."

Georgie looked at her mom, held her gaze for a long moment, then turned and ran up the stairs without saying a single word.

"Georgie!" I hollered after her, but she didn't stop.

Jax stood still, staring up after her. When he turned to face me a moment later, he said, "I had to tell you, unc. I was in The Square yesterday with Indie, and he bought condoms in Boots. I jokingly asked who he was datin' to need them, and he said Georgie's name before he could stop 'imself. I had it out with Georgie last night and only kept quiet because she said she'd tell ye', but when I was on the phone to 'er earlier, it was obvious she hadn't."

Bronagh groaned. "Did ye' hit Indie, Jax?"

"Not as hard as I should have," my nephew grunted.

"Indie Collins," I said with a snarl. "Gavin's boy."

My mind was focused on what my nephew said. Indie was buying condoms for him and Georgie to use. Condoms. Every muscle in my body tensed to the point of pain. The urge to punch something was strong, and my heart was beating so fast I thought it might burst.

"Yeah, he's me uncle Gav's eldest kid."

Bronagh suddenly gripped my arm when I turned and headed down the hallway towards the front door.

"Don't ye' bleedin' dare, Dominic!" She scowled. "Ye' aren't havin' it out with Gavin because our kids are datin'."

"Dating?" I repeated. "They're doing more than that. They're having *sex*."

"Dominic, just listen to me."

I knew that tone, and it meant she disagreed with me.

"No," I said, refusing to look at her.

I wasn't letting her talk me around on this, not a chance.

"Baby," she pressed. "We need to discuss this."

"There's nothing to discuss," I answered. "She is fifteen. Fif-fucking-teen. She is not entering a relationship when she has no idea about how they work. No."

"Dominic—"

"Bronagh, I love you to death, but do not ask me to budge on this. I can't. She is my daughter, and fifteen is too young for a relationship. Sex shouldn't even be on her mind."

My wife sighed. "You're right, but we have to speak to 'er and explain why."

I was too heated to go anywhere near the kid.

"Unless it's for school, she's not leaving this house," I stated. "She's fifteen years of age, and she thinks she's grown enough to have sex? Hell fucking no."

"Okay," Bronagh acquiesced. "If ye' say she is grounded, then she's grounded, but just let me go and speak to 'er before ye' go up there and raise ten kinds of hell. She's underage, we know that, but this is 'er private business bein' discussed with 'er father and cousin, and she isn't down here to defend 'erself."

I jerked my head in response, and Bronagh hustled up the stairs. I lifted my hands to my face and resisted the urge to scream. My entire world had been turned upside down, and I was infuriated that it was a Collins boy who caused it.

"How long have they been dating?"

"Indie says a couple of months," Jax grunted. "It's been a huge secret because Locke didn't even know, and he's *always* with Indie. I feel stupid for not coppin' on to them sooner, but I honestly had no clue before yesterday. I never thought me cousins would look at Georgie in that way because they *know* I'd end them if they hurt 'er."

I resumed paceing back and forth, feeling like a caged lion.

"I'm fucking *furious*."

Jax nodded. "Ye' look it."

"Bronagh will kill me if I kill this kid and get arrested."

Jax nodded. Again. "I'd be more scared of Auntie Bee than prison, if I'm honest."

I couldn't even laugh. I felt sick to my stomach.

"She's fifteen," I said. "Fifteen and having sex."

"In 'er defence, Indie did say he was buyin' them for their first time. He's 'er first boyfriend, so she's still a virgin as far as I can tell."

My heart deflated. "Oh, thank Christ in Heaven."

I felt better but knowing that she was most likely planning on having sex still didn't sit well with me at all. She was a child. Still a young girl whose mind shouldn't be on something as grown up as sex. Fear wrapped around me because I realised that so far, I was handling this situation *very* badly. I reacted with anger, and if I continued to push that anger on to my child, she would rebel, and I'd definitely end up in prison to stop her from seeking out this little Collins bastard and his little dick.

"She has four brothers and twenty male cousins ... you're all supposed to repel any boy from sniffing in her direction. You're all doing a *terrible* job."

Jax snorted. "Thanks, as if I didn't already know that."

I shook my head, then leaned my back against the hallway wall.

"She didn't mean what she said, you know? She's just upset."

"I know." Jax nodded. "I still want 'er to take it back, though. Pain sliced across me chest when she said she hated me. She's never said that to me before."

I knew it hurt him. Jax adored Georgie; she was his number one girl. She was everyone's number one girl, and she knew it. She loved her brothers and cousins more than anyone could explain, so I knew that a tearful apology would be given to Jax later when her anger passed, and regret was all that remained.

"She'll take it back; just give her a second to calm down. She'll come and find you when she realises what she said."

Jax only nodded, then turned his head and looked up the stairs. I spotted a hickey on his exposed neck, and my lips parted slightly. I knew from experience that if kids were taking the time to give each other love bites, they took the time to do other stuff too.

"You *better* not be having sex either!"

Jax's gaze darted to mine. "What?"

"You have a hickey on your neck. A big one."

Heat burned its way up said neck.

"I'm not havin' sex," he answered, then cleared his throat. Twice. "I swear."

I glared at him. "You're sixteen. Not much older than Georgie. You aren't old enough to have sex either, so don't think because you're a guy, you won't get into shit with your parents. You and Georgie are in the same boat here."

Jax swallowed. "Trust me ... I know."

He knows?

I raised a brow. "What happened?"

"Earlier today ... me ma and da walked in on .... y'know what? Never mind. I'm sure me da will tell ye' *all* about it."

I was sure he would, and from how Jax's face was burning red, I knew it was going to be a hell of a story.

"Speakin' of me parents," Jax continued. "I was only supposed to come over 'ere to talk to Georgie. I'm grounded."

"Does being grounded have anything to do with what your mom and dad walked in on?"

Jax nodded, and I thought back to my conversation on the phone with him earlier in the day. When I called him, I heard him hush a giggling girl, and I put two and two together.

"You were with a girl earlier when I called you ... is *that* what your parents walked in on?"

Axel came down the stairs at that moment and grabbed Jax's hand.

"Mammy says I can go to your house to play with Eli if you'll bring me."

Jax smiled down at his cousin, "'Course I'll bring ye', cousin."

When he looked back at me, his smile faded.

"I have to go home, but tell Georgie that's where I'll be if she's lookin' for me. Later, unc."

Before I could reply, he was out the door with my son before I could respond. I knew whatever Kane was going to tell me about what he walked in on was going to be a story that was as rough for him as this situation with Georgie was for me.

"Fucking teenagers, man."

I walked into the living room and fell into my armchair with a deep sigh. I leaned my head back and wondered if I was ever as nightmare inducing as this generation of Slater kids were, then I laughed to myself because me and my brothers were *definitely* worse when we were kids. We didn't live in cosy homes with normal, loving families. No, we lived in a compound where disloyalty or hesitation would get a man killed. Our road to adulthood, and to reach the point we were all at now, was a rough one, and to be honest, I was surprised that the five of us survived it.

God knows there were times were each of us didn't want to.

CHAPTER THREE

Ten years old ...

"Dominic!"

I jumped about a foot in the air the second my name was bellowed. I scrambled out of bed, stood straight, and waited.

"Yeah?"

My dad flung my bedroom door open, and it cracked against the wall with a thud. My heart pounded against my chest, and muscles all over my body tensed with apprehension. I swallowed as my dad, who physically reminded me so much of my older brother Ryder, glared at me with cool grey eyes. Eyes that my brothers and I inherited from him.

"What did I tell you about attending your lessons?"

I jerked my gaze to the black on the clock and winced. I was two hours late for math class. It was Tuesday, and on Tuesdays, we had a day-long math class to get us up to par so when we started working for Dad and his business partner, Marco, we'd have a foot in the door of understanding how they did business. Numbers meant everything to Dad and Marco, so it was vital to them that my brothers and I were smart and knew all there was to know about them.

I looked back at my dad and felt myself shrink.

"I'm sorry, Dad." I tensed. "I forgot to set my alarm."

When he crossed the space between us and backhanded me, my eyes stung with tears, but I refused to let them fall. I stumbled back a few steps but quickly stood upright and tried my best to appear I was okay when all I wanted to do was get back into bed, hide under my covers, and never come out again.

"Get showered, dressed, and get your worthless ass to your lessons. Now."

I bobbed my head.

"Answer me with your words, boy."

"Yes," I squeaked. "I understand you. I'll get to class right away."

He was going to hit me again, I knew he was, so I tensed my body to prepare for it.

"Dad," Ryder's voice suddenly spoke. "I'll deal with him."

Dad, who was in the middle of raising his hand, paused.

"You said that the last time, and here he is, flaking on lessons."

Ryder spoke softly as he stepped into view and walked up behind our father. "He is ten."

"I don't give a fuck if he's five!" Dad bellowed when my brother stopped at his side. He shoved Ryder whose entire body was now rigid. "When I tell him to do something, I expect him to do it. If he slacks on attending lessons, he'll slack when he's on a job when he's older, and that is *unacceptable*."

"Like I said," Ryder said gruffly, his muscles in his jaw rolling side to side. "I'll deal with him."

Dad looked back and forth between us, shook his head, then left the room without a second glance my way.

"Fucking useless pieces of shit," he called back. "You're on thin ice, Dom. Get your ass to your lesson. Now!"

I gritted my teeth. I *hated* when he called me that. He was the only person to call me Dom as a nickname, and I couldn't stand it. I couldn't stand when he called me Dominic either ... He made me loathe my name because of how much hate he poured into it when he spoke it.

"Hey," Ryder said, gaining my attention. "You okay, bud?"

I nodded but winced when he reached out and brushed his thumb over my cheek where our dad had struck me.

"It's swelling already ... How hard did he hit you?"

Ryder was angry, I could feel it radiate from him in waves.

"I'm okay."

I wasn't okay, my face was throbbing, but I had to be strong and show no weakness. I wasn't allowed to.

He grunted. "You don't have to be tough in front of me and our brothers, okay? We talked about this. It's a safe space with us, so you don't have to pretend to be okay when you're not. Not with us, buddy."

I hated when my lower lip wobbled. I *hated* crying. I hated showing any sign of emotion because I knew my parents regarded it as weak, but with my brothers ... they didn't make me feel weak. They made me feel like crying whenever I was hurt or sad was a natural reaction, and it was just one of the many reasons I knew I couldn't live without them. They were my rocks. When I lowered my head, my chin touched my chest, and that was when I began to sob. Ryder quickly hunkered down, put his arms around me, and tugged me against his body. I wrapped my arms around his neck and rested my forehead against his shoulder. I loved hugs, and I think it was because I rarely got them that it made each one from my brothers special.

"Ry?"

He squeezed me. "Yeah?"

"Why don't Mom and Dad love us?"

Our dad was always so mean to us. No matter what we did, it was never good enough for him, and our mom ... she only thought of us as a bother. She didn't like hugging or kissing us; she didn't even like being around us. She'd told us that so much that we'd stopped asking her to spend time with us a long time ago. Our parents weren't like normal parents; they only had me and my brothers so their business had a future. The only love they had was for each other and their empire ... We were just pawns in a twisted game that they played.

Ryder didn't answer me for a long time. He only held me until my tears subsided, and I was no longer shaking in his arms. When my brother leaned back, he moved his hands to my shoulders and looked me in the eye. It was weird, but I could almost feel how sad my question made him. He went out of his way to make me and my brothers smile and feel loved, and I hoped he knew that we loved him just as much as he did us.

"They just aren't like every other mom and dad, buddy," Ryder eventually answered. "But you know that I love you, don't you? Kane, Alec, and Damien love you, too. The five of us are an unstoppable team, right?"

"Right." I nodded firmly. "It's us against the world."

"That's right, buddy." Ryder smiled. "Us against the world."

I returned his smile.

"C'mon," he said. "Grab a quick shower and get dressed, then I'll walk you to your lesson."

"Ryder."

"Hmm?"

"I love you, too."

When my brother looked at me, it was with a bright smile on his face. The very first time I had said I love you to a grown-up, I was met with laughter and rejection, but whenever I said it to my brothers, I felt their love for me returned tenfold. With them, I was never met with heartless laughter or rejection, only love and acceptance. That was why I really believed it was me and my brothers against the whole world. Once I had them, I didn't need anyone else. I would follow the code we believed in, and for them alone I would live my life with love and loyalty because it was hard to find one person to love you for who you are, let alone five.

It really was us against the world.

And you know what? *Fuck the world.*

CHAPTER FOUR

Fifteen years old ...

"Dominic?"

I closed my eyes and placed my hands on the tank of the toilet in front of me. I heaved once more, vomiting into the bowl. I willed my stomach to settle, but I kept puking until nothing else came out. I blindly grabbed some tissue, wiped my mouth, tossed it into the toilet, and flushed it. I stood upright and placed my hands on my hips as I took some slow, deep breaths.

"Bro? Are you okay?"

I opened my eyes, turned, unlocked the door of the toilet stall, and stepped outside. Ryder, Alec, Kane, and Damien were standing in the public bathroom of the fancy club we were in. Each of my brothers were frowning at me. I met each of their gazes and forced a smile that I knew they could see through without having to try. I couldn't look at Kane for too long because I was worried I'd break down and cry. His new job required him to be physical with people, and if he didn't do what he was told, he was severely punished.

On his first job, he couldn't go through what was asked of him, and he was lashed until he passed out. His face ... his face had been marred, along with the rest of his body. In total, he had been whipped with a wire over twenty times, but even though his wounds had been stitched and were now healing, they were still such an angry shade of red. I wondered if they'd ever lighten in colour ... For my brother's sake, I hoped they would. He was never a people person, but I knew everyone staring at him like he was something out of a horror film hurt him.

"Dominic?"

I closed my eyes once more, and in my mind, I laughed. I hated my name. I hated it so much that I only ever answered to anyone when they called me Nico, which I preferred, but my brothers were different. They knew I hated my name because of our father. He never said it, though; he always spat it as if it was something sour in his mouth. When he said it, it was with heartfelt hate behind it, but when my brothers said it, it was with love and acceptance. They were the only ones allowed to call me Dominic, though ... No one else would ever be special enough to call me that.

No one.

"I'm okay," I answered Ryder, opening my eyes to find him staring at me. "I'm just really fucking nervous."

"About the fight?" Alec quizzed. "I've researched this joker, and he won't go toe to toe with you. You're gonna clown him easily."

My shoulders slumped. "I'm not a real fighter, though ... I just lost it when Trent hit Dame. What if I fight this guy, and he beats the shit out of me? I don't care about getting hurt. I care about what Marco will do if I don't perform like he expects me to."

"Listen," Kane said, getting my attention. "When you're fighting this guy, it's just the two of you. Forget about everything and everyone, and focus on *him*. Watch his movements, learn his style, counts his steps, and then counter his moves just like I taught you. I've been practicing with you since we all landed these bullshit jobs, and I *know* how good you are. Believe in yourself because we believe in you."

I knew they believed in me, and I tried to turn that into positive energy, but it was hard.

"Let's just get out there," I said, flexing my hands, feeling how comfortably tight my hand wraps were. "I want to get this shit over and done with."

When we exited the bathroom, my brothers flanked me as we entered the club. Music was blaring, and the dance floor was cleared, the occupants of the club were over at the platform that Marco said would be my base of operations for the next few years. I already knew that Marco had me booked to fight in different countries, but I tried not to think about that. I did what Kane said—I focused on this fight and blocked everything else out.

A bellowing voice announced my entrance to the club, and I was met with booing and obnoxious laughter. I was expecting that. I was a lanky kid, and the guy I was fighting was twenty-five ... the same age as my eldest brother. If I were part of the crowd, I would probably laugh, too. They didn't know that the dude I was fighting was doing so for money, while I was fighting for my brother's life.

When I reached the platform, I saw my opponent up on the surface with his hands on his hips as he shook his head from left to right. I could see on his face he couldn't believe he was fighting me. He thought I was going to be an easy win. I'd have to show him and everyone else just how wrong he was.

"You've got this," Damien said when I turned to him.

He was scared for me, I saw it in his eyes, and I knew he saw my fear in mine, too. I hugged him and my other brothers. I didn't linger with them; instead, I jumped up, gripped the platform, then hoisted myself upwards until I was on my feet and standing across from the man whose name I didn't bother to learn. I decided that I didn't want to know the names of the people I fought. That way, it was easier for me to tune out that they were real people.

"How old are you?"

I didn't want this man talking to me. I just wanted to fight him, then leave.

"Fifteen," I answered. "You didn't know about me?"

He shook his head. "I was just told this morning about this fight."

I had known about it for few weeks.

"Let's get this over with."

The man chuckled. "I don't wanna hurt you, kid, but I'm going to."

I shifted my stance. "You can try."

He laughed again, and it wasn't a conceited laugh. It was a genuine one. He thought this fight was a joke. His relaxed stance told me he didn't take it, or me, seriously. He didn't see me as a threat in any shape or form, so I had to use that confidence to my advantage. I knew how to fight. Kane had been working with me until I could no longer stand in preparation for this match. I knew I could handle a body mass twice the size of my own. I knew I was going to kick this guy's ass ... before I was worried, but standing up on the platform facing him, I knew the only person who should have been worried was him.

"No pain," I said out loud, bumping my fists together. "No fucking pain."

The buzzer sounded without warning, and the man came at me fast. Most likely, he wanted to put me out of my misery. He swung his right fist my way, and he put power behind it, hoping to catch my chin and put me on the canvas. I ducked left and fired two jabs to his liver. His body jerked at the contact, but he swung around, and the surprise in the man's eyes wasn't missed. He stood a little taller, tensed his muscles more, and tightened his guard.

He wasn't playing around now.

When he darted forward, I managed to avoid his first jab, but he caught me around the waist with his free arm, lifted me up, and slammed in against the floor. The breath was knocked out of me, and it hurt, but I didn't lose focus. I wrapped my legs around his torso, then latched onto his arm when he tried to twist out of my hold. I controlled my breathing and applied pressure on his arm. I heard him scream, and the crowd did too. Their cheering became deafening and encouraged me to keep hold of the arm bar I had. I got a fright when a roar came from the man, followed by a pop in his arm that I somehow felt. I quickly let go of him, and he promptly rolled off me, hollering in pain.

I couldn't look at his elbow. It was obvious by the angle that I had snapped the bone. I didn't notice the blood until he turned over and I realised the bone had come through his skin. I didn't want to fight any more at that moment ... I didn't want to hurt other people. I looked at my brothers, finding them with wild eyes, and I focused on Kane when he jerked his head. I knew what he was telling me to do. Marco said I wasn't to stop fighting while my opponent still had fight in him. Damien's life depended on me following orders. One look at the man told me that he wanted to kill me, and my heart dropped.

My stomach twisted in knots.

I shot forward before he could get to his feet, and I dived on him. I punched him until he stopped trying to fend me off, and when I saw he was in no condition to continue fighting, I stood and roared. I let out every bit of pent-up frustration, hurt, anger, and fear that I had, and I released it within that roar. I wouldn't fear my fights anymore. I would trust myself, and what I was capable of doing, and I would knock down anyone in my path. It was a stranger's pride versus my brother's life, and my family would win every single time.

Marco would regret the day he made me his fighter ... I'd make sure of it.

CHAPTER FIVE

Eighteen Years Old ...

"All I'm saying is you both don't *have* to go to public school. I can continue to homeschool you both right here."

I gently banged my head that rested on the kitchen table, making my brothers laugh. All but my eldest brother, that is. Finished with my cereal, I pushed the bowl away and gave Ryder my full attention.

"I don't know what you're all finding so funny," he grunted. "I'm serious."

"Ry," Damien began. "We've been homeschooled our whole lives. We've never been around kids our age ... not normal kids, at least."

Ryder sighed, knowing he wasn't going to convince us to stay at home.

"Look," I continued, "it's a good thing. We'll be around people our age in a natural environment. Haven't you always been worried that we were too sheltered?"

"Yeah," he agreed with a nod. "But—"

"We want to go to this public school, Ry."

Ryder looked at Damien when he cut him off, and though he looked so much like our dad, I knew he was a much better person and wouldn't react violently towards us. He looked at all of us, and as I knew he would, he bobbed his head in understanding. He was clearly worried about us, and I hated that. He always worried about us, but something as trivial as us attending school didn't need to be added to that lengthy list.

"The school is ten minutes away from here, and it has a *max* of three hundred kids. There are forty-five kids in our graduating class, Ry. Nothing is going to go wrong. Not even Dominic can get into trouble here."

"Don't jinx yourselves."

"We'll be fine," I assured him.

Kane was observing us quietly, like he always did, but when we stood from the table, he snorted.

I narrowed my eyes. "What's so funny?"

"You're both matching."

Damien and I looked at one another, then down at our school uniforms, before we looked back at Kane.

"You have to wear a uniform at this school. We can't wear regular clothes."

"I get that, but you're twins, so it's funny to see you match."

I never thought of that.

"Do we look stupid?"

"No," Ryder answered instantly. "You look like regular school kids."

He sounded damn happy about that fact.

I nudged Damien. "We have to be there ten minutes early to get our schedules, so we should get going."

He nodded, and after saying goodbye to our brothers, we grabbed our backpacks and left the house. We decided on walking since every other kid would be walking too. No student parking was just one of the many things that was different about Ireland. We had been here exactly six weeks, and I couldn't help but notice just how different everything was. The people, the accents, the food, the alcohol, the scenery, the currency, the driver's side of a car. Anything you could think of, the Irish did it their own way, and I liked it. I had been to so many countries in a few short years fighting opponent after opponent, and Ireland was the first country where my brothers and I felt very much at home. It was a collective decision to stay here, and I couldn't have been happier about it.

I was from New York but living there never felt like home. The compound where I grew up felt like a prison, but being here in Ireland with my brothers felt very much like home.

"Is it normal that I'm stoked to go to school?"

I laughed at Damien's question.

"Nah, bro. I'm excited too. It'll get boring fast but fuck it. At least we'll be around regular people, and that's all I care about."

The walk to the school was quick, and by the time we entered the school grounds, I was sweating. It was too hot to be wearing the thick fleece sweater I had on, and when I caught sight of other students just wearing their school shirts and ties, Damien and I quickly rid ourselves of our sweaters and put them in our bags.

"Are you worried about your fight on Friday?"

"When am I *ever* worried about my fights?"

"Cut the bullshit," Damien said as we searched for the main office. "It's just me. You don't have to lie."

I glanced at my brother and sighed. "I haven't fought since we were in Scotland. That was two months ago, and my training has been off since we moved here. It took us a while to find our house and get settled. I need to win because these next couple of bouts are it, and then we can finally be rid of Marco. I can't lose. I can't give him any reason to think he can ... keep us."

I couldn't let Marco retain his hold over us. I couldn't.

"You'll be great, Dominic. You always are."

"Aw, thanks, brother."

Damien punched my arm, making me laugh. I stopped laughing when I noticed more than a few pairs of eyes focused on us. Many of those eyes belonging to girls.

"Has your ego just inflated massively too?"

"It's not the only thing to inflate massively." I grinned. "Some of those chicks are hot."

Damien laughed. We found the main office, knocked on the door, and introduced ourselves to the receptionist when she opened the door. The woman's name was Ann, and she took all of sixty seconds to give us a crash course on the tiny school. We got our class schedules with a key, so we understood the abbreviations, and a school map. The school was tinier than I imagined. The school's soccer pitch was bigger than its cluster of buildings.

"Ann explained that homeroom is what they call a tutor class here," Damien said as we left the office, reading our schedules. "Our tutor is the teacher we go to if we need anything. We have registration class for ten minutes with her every morning to get marked in on the attendance role, and other mornings, like today, we have a whole period with her."

"So she's not someone who tutors students?"

"No," he answered. "Each class has a tutor, we just go to ours if we need a bathroom pass or something like that. It's just a title."

That's stupid.

I furrowed my brows. "I thought Ann said we were to go to our year head if we need something, but I don't know what the fuck that is."

"It's the head teacher of our entire grade. We go to her if we get kicked out of class or do something wrong. Her name is Ms. Wall. Our tutor is Miss McKesson."

"Let's not get kicked out of class because I'll probably just walk home out of confusion of not being able to understand who I'm supposed to report to."

Damien laughed, shaking his head. "We'll be fine. Let's just find our registration class so we aren't late."

We found it easy enough, but when we got there, the door was locked.

"Now what?"

"Now we wait," Damien answered. "School starts in—"

"Can I help ye's?"

Damien and I turned to the voice, and when I realised the owner of the voice was a hot twentysomething, I stood straighter.

"We're new here," Damien answered the woman. "I'm Damien Slater, this is my brother Dominic—"

"But I prefer Nico," I cut my brother off.

Damien glanced at me, then back at the woman, and said, "This is our registration class."

"Ah, you're me American lads."

Hers?

"I guess we are." I smiled, and she smiled in return.

"I'm Miss McKesson, your tutor. Follow me and we'll get you settled in."

She unlocked the door to the room, and we followed her inside. She gave us another crash course of the whole tutor and year head thing, then proceeded to go through the school rules with us one by one until we repeated them and understood them. Miss McKesson was hot, and I knew Damien thought she was hot too, but unlike me, he wouldn't try his hand at seeing if something sexual could happen. This pleased me ... until I remembered that I promised Ryder I wouldn't do anything out of place while I attended school here.

That sucked.

Once our tutor had finished, she sat at her desk and began taking textbooks and notepads out of her bag. Damien and I looked at one another, shrugged, then sat at a table right next to one of the windows. I glanced at the green fields that led up to the forest covered mountains and relaxed. I loved it here. It was so peaceful.

"She's so hot, the girl with the black hair."

I looked up at my twin brother when he spoke, and I raised a brow at him in question. I must have zoned out because it wasn't only just me, Damien, and our tutor anymore. The entire classroom was filled with students; a lot of those students were girls, and they kept staring at Damien and me. I straightened up instantly.

"Settle down," Miss McKesson announced. "We have two new

students all the way from America. This is Damien and Dominic Slater. Dominic prefers to be called Nico so remember that when addressin' 'im. Please, be nice to them and show them around to help them get settled. Ye' can use this period to catch up on homework due for other classes but do it silently."

No one listened to our tutor, and the questions flew left, right, and centre at me and my brother. I didn't mind answering them because none of them were personal. They were mostly dumb questions like where were we from, how tall we were, how old we were, were our eyes really grey, did we have girlfriends, and if Damien's hair colour was natural or from a bottle.

I looked back out of the window just as Damien said, "Dibs."

"What?"

"The girl who just walked into class ... I call dibs."

I was too tired to pretend I could concentrate on what he was saying.

"What girl?"

Damien grinned at me. "Bro, to your ten o'clock is a fat ass girl with a *banging* body. I. Call. Dibs."

With my interest thoroughly piqued, I turned my attention to where my brother's eyes were focused, and the second I locked *my* eyes on the ass attached to the girl who turned and nodded her head in greeting to the homeroom teacher, my mouth watered.

"Nuh-uh," I said to Damien without looking away from the girl's ass. "You don't get automatic dibs on an ass like that. Christ, man, *look* at it. It's perfect for me."

My brother snickered. "You'd really jump over the bro code—"

"Brother, I'd sell my *soul* for that ass. Yours too."

Out of the corner of my eye, I could see that Damien was shaking his head as he chuckled to himself.

"I think you're drooling."

I swallowed. "I am. Jesus, I'm in love. I am *actually* in love."

"You haven't even seen her face yet."

"Don't care," I answered. "*Look* at her fucking ass, bro."

Damien clapped me on the shoulder. "I'm bowing out. You look like you're about to cry with happiness. Her ass is perfect for you."

"It's beautiful."

I sat up straight, rolled my neck on my shoulders, and ignored all the stares from my female classmates to focus on this brown-haired goddess. I hadn't seen her face yet, her chin was tucked against her chest and her hair fell over her face like a veil, but I didn't care. I wanted to fuck her. I wanted to fuck her so bad it almost hurt, and for that reason alone, I knew I had to be charming and forward just enough that she wanted me to fuck her, too.

When she turned her head in my direction, and her hair shifted, my pants became ridiculously tight. Not only was her ass fat and her body banging, but her face ... she was beautiful. And not that fake model kind of beauty but a natural beauty. Her skin was fair, her nose tiny, her lips were on the small side, but her eyes were large and bright green. She wasn't even that close to me, and I could see the lumious jade that stared back at me as clear as day.

She lowered her eyes as she came to a stop next to the table.

"That's me desk," she said, her tone flat.

I was a little taken aback by her tone. She already sounded irritated with me, and I hadn't spoken a word to her yet. It rubbed me the wrong way that she wouldn't look me in the eye when she spoke to me. It made me feel like she was speaking down to me, and I hated when people treated me lesser than themselves.

Wordlessly, Damien made a move to get up, but for some reason, I stuck my hand out and placed it on his shoulder, halting his movements. We were new students here, so we didn't know this seat was assigned because our teacher never objected to us sitting here. This girl, no matter how hot she was or how fucking stunning her ass was, wasn't going to order me and my brother around. We took orders from one person too many as it was.

"*Your* desk?" I asked with a raised brow. "Does it have your name on it or something?"

She looked me in the eye, and for a few seconds, she didn't answer me. She was thinking hard about something, but like the flip of a switch, she snapped out of it, and said, "Yeah, it does."

She pointed at a name that was carved into the desk, and I hadn't a single fucking clue how to pronounce it.

"Bro-what?"

The chick flat out rolled her eyes at me. I got a kick out of annoying her, and I had no clue why.

"*Bronagh.*"

"Bro-nah?" I repeated, then to myself I mumbled, "What's the point of the damn *g* if it's gonna be silent?"

Bronagh cocked a brow. "Yeah, that's how ye' say me name, and it is on *my* desk as ye' can clearly see."

Damien snorted. "She has you by the balls on that, bro. Let's just move out of this *lovely* woman's way and sit in the back row next to the pretty ladies."

If the giggling we heard was anything to go by, the other girls in our class were listening to our conversation. They were all clearly interested in me and my brother but not Bronagh. If I was being honest, she looked like she was disgusted at that moment, and I'd be damned if I didn't feel offended. I wasn't used to this. I'd never met a girl who was instantly moody with me upon our first meeting ... not even the ones who I didn't want to fuck. It rattled me a little but excited me even more.

I knew she would be a challenge, and I was *so* pumped for it.

I rose slowly from my seat, and teased, "I warmed it up for you."

"Be sure to thank your arse for me," she said as she moved past me and sat down in the seat I just vacated. She put her bag on the chair where Damien had been sitting and tugged it close. It was obvious she was stating that no one was to sit next to her, and that amused the fuck out of me.

I laughed a little as I turned and followed Damien down to a row of tables in the back of the classroom. Another girl with long black hair was getting something out of her bag and happened to look up at me as I sat down at the table behind her.

"What's her problem?" I asked her, making sure my voice was loud enough for Bronagh to hear.

"Who? Bronagh? Nothin'," the black-haired girl replied. "She just doesn't like attention or people that much. She prefers to be by 'erself."

"She doesn't like people?" I repeated. "Is there something wrong with her?"

If she was a psychopath, there was *no way* I was investing time in her. I didn't care how perfect her ass was. I had enough shit in my life to deal with without having an insane girl put me on her hit list.

"I'm sure there are many things wrong with me accordin' to *you*, but I assure ye' pretty boy," Bronagh said aloud, without turning around. "Me hearin' is perfectly fine."

A few people chuckled, and even I grinned. She was ballsy, I had to give her that.

"Inside voice, bro," Damien teased.

While she amused me, I wasn't about to let her insult me ... She'd probably think I was some pussy assed pushover otherwise.

"*Pretty boy*?" I repeated, my voice gruff. "Who does that bitch think she is talking to?"

"Okay, less of that," Miss McKesson said, standing up once she heard the word bitch. "Bronagh, these lads are our new students, all the way from the United States of America."

Bronagh twirled her finger around in the air. "Go US of A."

Miss McKesson bit down on her bottom lip and shook her head.

"The Slater boys are twins, obviously. It's easy to tell them apart with them havin' different hair colour. Nico has brown hair, and Damien has blond hair, well, more white than blond."

"I'll be sure to remember that miss, thank you."

Miss McKesson introduced Bronagh then.

"And this lovely lady, lads, is Bronagh Murphy."

"It's a *pleasure*, Miss Murphy."

"I *seriously* doubt that, Mr. Slater," Bronagh replied, making the class laugh.

"Okay, back to whatever it was that ye' were all doin' before Bronagh came to class," Miss McKesson said with a wave of her hand.

Not a second later, more questions fired left, right, and centre from the girls to myself and Damien. Every girl except Bronagh and the black-haired girl in front of us. I was about to reach forward so I could touch her shoulder and ask for her name, but Damien was way ahead of me. The girl looked around when he tapped her shoulder, and she raised a brow in silent question.

"I'm Damien Slater," he said. "And *you* are?"

"Alannah Ryan," she replied with a smile. "Nice to meet ye'."

Fuck, she was cute. Damien thought so too, the fact that he blocked out every other girl in the room told me that Alannah would most likely be a girl he had some fun with. I turned my attention from their mundane conversation and focused on Bronagh who was unwinding the wire of her earphones from around an iPod. I watched as she called our teacher.

"Miss?"

When Miss McKesson looked at Bronagh, she shook her iPod at her. The teacher nodded, clearly giving her silent permission to listen to music, and that interested me.

"Shit, you're allowed to listen to iPods here?" I asked Alannah.

"Huh?" she said, as she looked from Damien to me to Bronagh and back again. "Oh no, just Bronagh. She gets 'er work done every day, so she is allowed to listen to it as long as the volume is low."

She was a goody two-shoes, and I'd be lying if I said I didn't want to draw out the bad girl in her. I clasped my hands together at the back of my head and stared at her. Since she sat down, she hadn't turned to look at me, not once. She didn't seem to give a fuck about me, and I liked that. It was a different tune than what I was used to when it came to a girl I wanted to have some fun with, but it didn't put me off her. It enticed me that much more. I wanted her, and I was prepared to do whatever I had to do to have her so she'd willingly beg me to explore her thick body.

"You're being weird," Damien said to me, nudging my shoulder with his. "She doesn't like you, Dominic, so leave her alone. Did you see how she looked at you when she came to the table? She looks like she'll try to kick your ass if you press her."

Exactly. She kept to herself, didn't look at anyone, and put earphones in to block the world out. When she looked at me, it really did feel like she had no interest in me, and stupidly, that excited the hell out of me. I wanted her, and because it appeared that I couldn't have her, my mind and body focused on her entirely.

"My guy." I grinned as I looked at my brother. "I want her, and I *always* get what I want. You know that."

"I don't know, man." Damien sighed. "Something tells me this girl will be a whole lot of trouble for you."

"I agree," I said, my eyes sliding back to her as she sat hunched over her notebook. "That's why it's gonna be so much *fun*."

CHAPTER SIX

Eighteen Years Old ...

I can't fucking believe I thought bagging this girl was gonna be fun.

I glared down at my opponent that I had just beat bloody, and I felt slightly bad for him. He could fight—there was no doubt about that—but I had too much anger and aggression in me thanks to Bronagh Murphy to let him off the platform in anything other than bad shape. The girl had my head all kinds of messed up, and what was worse was that I still wanted her more than my next breath. She was hot for me one minute, then cold the next. It was driving me crazy ... *She* was driving me crazy.

I turned to the cheering crowd, and my eyes found her instantly. She was staring up at me with wide doe eyes and her mouth hanging open. I shocked her with my performance, and that pleased the fuck out of me, so I grinned down at her. It took her zero seconds to snap out of her trance and mouth, "Fuck you," at me. Inside, I was seething that she had so much anger towards me, but on the outside, I winked at her to show her she didn't bother me when, in reality, everything she did bothered me.

After I jumped down from the platform, I checked on Drake, the guy I had fought. Once I was sure he was okay, we hugged to show what happened on the platform stayed on the platform, and I went to the back rooms to shower and change into regular clothes. When I finished, I re-entered the club and found the crowd screaming and cheering for the current fighters on the platform beating the shit out of one another. I rolled my eyes over the bodies of people who came for blood, and I was surprised to find Bronagh and Branna right in the mix, cheering and clapping just like everyone else.

"Interesting," I said to myself as I walked back towards the booth reserved for my brothers and me.

They were all there, and Alec had his nightly conquests on either side of him. A woman and a man who both looked infatuated with him. Kane was sitting in the middle of the booth with his arms folded over his chest and his glaring eyes roamed around the room. Damien was on his phone, and Ryder ... well, big brother had his eyes locked on the eldest Murphy sister, and I could have sworn he wasn't blinking.

Seems I'm not the only one who a Murphy girl has messed up.

"Branna's right hook is better than most fighters I've faced."

Ryder didn't smile or acknowledge what I said as I sat down next to him. My other brothers greeted me, congratulated me on a fight well won, then announced they wanted to go home. Just then, the lights of the club came on, and Kane looked so relieved as he jumped to his feet. Alec's play things kissed him goodbye and left the booth with pouts.

"Why didn't you bring them home?"

"I already fucked them both earlier," he answered with a shrug. "I don't like to double dip."

I laughed and shook my head. My attention went back to Ryder who was on his feet. I followed his eyes and saw they were still locked on Branna and Bronagh who were stumbling towards the exit of the club. I shook my head at the pair of them. They were both trying to hold the other up and were failing miserably.

Without a word, my brothers and I walked towards the exit. Alec was giving invitations to certain people to come to our house for a party. I looked at him as we climbed the stairs, and said, "I hate house parties."

"It'll be fun," my brother replied. "I invited that guy you fought and his team."

"And who else?"

"A few others."

That meant a lot of others.

I shook my head and breathed in a deep breath when we got outside. I searched for Branna and Bronagh, and when I spotted them talking to Drake, the guy whose ass I whooped, I stalked towards them, wondering if I'd have to beat the shit out of him again when he said something to make Bronagh laugh. When I came up behind her, my eyes went to her butt, before I looked over her head and locked eyes with a grinning Drake. I caught the end of their conversation, and my lips twitched when I realised Bronagh was making it known that we hated each other and that she wouldn't be allowed come to the party at our house.

"I'm sure Nico won't mind ye' comin'."

Bronagh chuckled.

"No, seriously," she stressed, "he *would* mind."

"I wouldn't mind at all, pretty girl."

Bronagh froze, then said, "Go fuck yourself, Dominic."

Drake raised his eyebrows, and asked, "Is she your missus, man?"

Bronagh cackled with laughter.

"His missus?" she said with distaste. "In his fu-fuckin' dreams—"

"Yeah," I cut her off. "She's mine."

She *was* mine, and deep down, she fucking knew it.

I hardly noticed when Drake departed because I was too concentrated on the little spitfire who whirled around to face me. She looked like she was trying to glare at me and my brothers, but her drunkenness made it seem like she was just making eyes at me. She lifted her free hand that wasn't wrapped around Branna and pointed it at my face. I folded my arms across my chest, fully aware that she was going to cuss me out.

"Ye' little cock sucker, I am *not* yours," she declared. "I am no-not anythin' to ye', and if ye' so much as hint that I am again, I'll—"

She cut herself off when Branna suddenly heaved. I watched as Bronagh struggled to hold her sister up.

"No, Branna, don't do this," she pleaded. "Don't you pu-puke on me or die. I can't carry ye' home. I'm we-weak as shite!"

When my brothers and I chuckled, she looked up and glared daggers at us.

"Fuck all of ye' ... except you, Damien. You're ni-nice."

Damien laughed, and I rolled my eyes.

"Give me her," Ryder said to Bronagh. "I'll carry her back to the house."

Bronagh stared up at my brother and shook her head. "Eh, no, she thinks you're a pr-prick—as do I—and will punch ye' if she realises you're wi-with 'er."

Ryder's lips twitched as he looked down at Branna as he said, "I'll take my chances."

My brother took Branna in his arms, and it left Bronagh to sway at little, so I stepped forward and steadied her.

"I got you."

She opened her pretty green eyes and stared up at me.

"Let. Me. Go."

"Okay," I did as demanded, only to grab her again when her knees buckled from under her. I chuckled and hoisted her against my body. "It looks like you *need* me, pretty girl."

"I don't even look pr-pretty."

I smiled down at her as I lifted her bridal style and placed a kiss on her forehead as she snuggled against my chest. As I walked towards the parking lot with her in my arms, she was mumbling about my brothers and I cutting her and her sister up into tiny pieces, which made me shake my head. I laughed, however, when she said, "Except Damien. He won't help them because he is nice."

When I climbed into the back of our car, I cuddled Bronagh against me, and I was very aware that having her body snug against mine with her arms around me and her head on my chest made me feel the most content I had ever felt in my life. It didn't take a genius to figure out that I was falling for this girl ... and she fucking hated me.

That summed up my life in a nutshell.

When we got back to our house, people were arriving for the party that Alec invited everyone to. Bronagh was in and out of consciousness. She kept telling me she wanted to sleep in my bed with me, and though I knew it would most likely kill me, I gave into her and brought her up to my room. She fell onto my bed, and I loved how perfect she looked even though her makeup was smeared, her hair was all over the place, and she was as drunk as a skunk.

I didn't dare remove her dress, so instead, I took off her high heels, then settled her under the covers. I removed my clothes and left my boxer shorts on as I climbed into my bed next to her. She rolled over almost instantly and wrapped her body around mine. My cock hardened, but I didn't focus on it. I focused on Bronagh and just how much I loved having her in my bed.

When she suddenly opened her eyes and looked at me, I swallowed. There was no anger or frustration in her luminous eyes, just a vulnerability I had never seen before. At this moment in time, her guard was down, and she looked so damn tired from fighting with me.

"Ye' scare me, Dominic."

I frowned. "I would *never* hurt you, Bronagh."

"Yeah, ye' would." She yawned. "If I loved ye' and ye' left me, it'd break me heart."

I realised she was talking about emotional hurt and not physical pain.

"Is that the only reason you don't want me?"

She nodded and said, "I want ye' so bad it hurts, but it'd hurt way worse if I lost ye'."

"Bronagh, I want you too."

She hummed.

"I dream about ye'," she said just as her eyes drifted shut. "Ye' do baaadd things to me."

"Sweet Jesus," I said as she hooked her leg over my thighs, slung her arm over my torso, and rested her face against my neck. "You're killing me, baby."

She snuggled against me, and I knew she was already on her way into a deep sleep.

I stared at her while she slept, and I was very aware that I felt an enormity of happiness by simply holding her. She was as sexy as she was beautiful but holding her at that moment was nothing sexual, and that scared the shit out of me. I never had an interest in a girl past her looks and whether or not I could fuck her, but with Bronagh, it was so much more than that. I had never gotten stupid butterflies from just holding a girl before. I never held one all night in my bed …. In fact, a girl was never in my bed for anything other than sex.

I reached out and ran the tips of my fingers over her creamy, soft skin.

"What are you doing to me, pretty girl?"

CHAPTER SEVEN

Eighteen Years Old ...

I was a hot-headed asshole.

My entire body was tense as I drove Bronagh to the hospital. I was so mad at myself for acting like a dramatic little bitch when Kane called me and told me Bronagh and Gavin Collins were looking mighty comfortable in McDonald's. Like my brother knew I would, I took the bait, showed up, and fought Gavin for no other reason than he liked Bronagh and had her attention. I was possessive of her, and as I glanced at her, I knew I'd have to change my ways because she had gotten hurt and that was absolutely unacceptable.

"Are you okay?"

She jerked her head in my direction. "Does it *look* like I'm okay?"

No, she looked like she was in pain, and it turned my stomach.

When I didn't answer her, she yelled, "Answer me!"

I sighed. "No, because you're just going to yell at me no matter what I say, so I'm keeping my mouth shut."

She grunted. "That'd be a fuckin' first."

When I didn't reply again, I felt her look at me, and it drew a laugh from me.

"I'm not going to argue with you, babe, so stop trying to bait me."

She sounded murderous when she hissed, "I'm *not* your babe."

A sharp pain jolted across my chest.

"I forgot," I said with a forced smile. "Sorry."

She shook her head at me, then looked down at the hand she had cradled to her chest.

"God, this hurts *so* bad."

One glance at her face told me she was about to cry, and it tore me apart inside.

"Bronagh, please don't cry."

She sniffled. "I can't help it. It really hurts."

"I know, but we're almost at the hospital," I assured her. "I'll make them fix it, okay?"

I watched as she rooted for her phone from her bag, and I exhaled a deep breath when she put it to her ear. She whimpered in pain, and I heard Branna's voice as clear as day as she began shouting.

"Bronagh? Baby? What is it? What's wrong? Did Gavin hurt you? I'll fuckin' kill 'im—"

"Branna, shut up." Bronagh cut her off with a cry. "Gavin didn't hurt me, but I *am* hurt, and I'm on my way to the hospital."

"The hospital?" her sister shrieked. "Why? What happened? Are ye' okay?"

Bronagh managed a snort. "Dominic happened."

I sighed again.

"Dominic?" Branna snapped, then growled, "I'm goin' to *kill* your little brother."

"Not if I kill him first," I heard Ryder bellow.

I groaned out loud and silently hoped I could explain what happened to them before they ended my life. Bronagh finished her phone conversation just as I pulled into the hospital. I found parking near the emergency room's entrance and hustled her out of the car. When we got inside, I stayed right on Bronagh's heels. After she was checked in, we headed inside the waiting area that was absolutely packed with people.

Bronagh took one look around the room and glared up at me. "*I hate you.*"

I nodded. "I hate me, too. We're gonna be here all fucking night."

"Leave then," she argued. "No one is askin' ye' to stay."

I raised a brow. "If you think I'm leaving you here, then you don't know me very well."

"I don't know ye' *at all*."

I rolled my eyes and tugged on her good hand, leading her towards the only spare seat in the room. She didn't like me leading her, so she gave me a little kick on the shin as we passed by people, earning us chuckles.

"Trouble in paradise?"

I snorted at the stranger. "Nah bro, this is foreplay for us."

Bronagh was mortified, and her red face told me so.

"I'm sorry, I was only playing."

I saw her eyes widen ever so slightly when I sat down on the empty seat, then her lips parted with shock when I placed my hands on her thick hips, turned her away from me, and then tugged on her so she fell nicely onto my lap. I adjusted her body so she was resting comfortably on my crotch. I slid my arm around her waist and applied a bit of pressure. When her back was moulded against my chest and her head rested against my shoulder, I relaxed and so did she, though I was sure she wanted to remain rigid.

"You can hit me later. Just relax now and let me hold you until you get seen by the doctor."

After I spoke, I nuzzled my face to hers and kissed her cheek a few times. I was so sorry she had gotten hurt because of my temper when fighting Gavin, and I wished I could take her pain away. I hoped she knew that I never intended her to get hurt because I would honestly rather die than cause her a moment's pain. I cared about her too much not to.

A few minutes ticked by slowly when Bronagh suddenly shifted, sitting up to remove her cardigan. She draped it over her legs, and the action seemed a little odd to me.

"Are you warm?" I quizzed as she settled back against me.

She shook her head and held her injured hand to her chest.

"Then why did you—"

"I was coverin' me legs."

Why?

I was silent for a moment then said, "I'm probably going to regret asking this, but why did you cover your legs?"

She turned her head, and in my ear, she whispered. "'Cause they triple in size when I sit down."

Silence.

I tried to see from her point of view why it would be an issue, but I couldn't.

"God save me from girls and their stupid way of thinking."

She was about to tell me off as I nuzzled my nose against her neck.

"I happen to think you look fucking gorgeous tonight. I've never seen you wear clothes that actually *fit* you before. I must say, Bronagh, I like it *a lot*."

She ducked her head as heat made its way up her neck, drawing a chuckle from me.

"Bronagh Murphy?"

We both looked up, then got to our feet when we noticed it was a nurse who had called Bronagh's name. I followed Bronagh closely, and she didn't say a word. I knew she would never admit to it, but she wanted me there with her. I made her feel better about the situation she was in.

"Bronagh?"

Bronagh nodded at the nurse, then the woman's eyes landed on mine.

"Family or partners only—"

"I'm her boyfriend."

Bronagh remained silent as the nurse smiled and gestured us to follow her into the triage room. It took only a few minutes for the nurse to check Bronagh over before she decided she needed an X-ray to see if her hand was broken. I prayed it would only be a sprain. I'd be sick to my stomach if she broke her hand because of me. When the nurse left the room, I focused on a silent Bronagh.

"What are you thinking about?"

She looked up at me. "I'm thinkin' that you're dangerous, and that havin' ye' in me life would be doin' what Branna always wanted me to do, open up to someone. You're a risk that I'm thinkin' of takin'."

I could scarcely believe what I was hearing, and before I knew it, I nudged my way between her thick thighs and stared down at her.

"You want me?"

I knew she wanted me, she had told me as much when she slept in my arms, but I wanted her to say it when she was sober.

Bronagh swallowed. "Ye' have to work on not makin' me so mad, but yeah, I want ye'."

I lifted my hands to her cheeks and strummed my thumbs up and down all the while keeping eye contact with her.

"I'm not sayin' I'll be your girlfriend right away," she added, a little breathless. "I'm sayin' that I'm open to the idea."

I raised an eyebrow. "So I'm on a trial basis with you?"

She bobbed her head. "Exactly. I just want to feel out how this could work with us before I put a title on us. Is that okay with ye'?"

On one condition.

"Can I kiss you whenever I want?"

She playfully rolled her eyes at me. "No kissin' in school because I'm not ready to deal with any of that drama, especially after what happened with Destiny, which, by the way, I *never* want to talk about. We weren't anythin' over the weekend, so anythin' that happened or didn't happen is none of me business. Apart from that, though, yeah, ye' can kiss me whenever you want to."

She had nothing to worry about when it came to Destiny. I

didn't kiss her or have sex with her. When she hinted that we did things in the PE hall, I let her because I wanted to hurt Bronagh like she had hurt me by rejecting me, but when things weren't so fresh, I'd explain that to her and make it clear that since I'd set my sights on her, no other girl had my body. I knew if I said nothing happened between us right now, she would think I was only saying it to please her, so I kept my mouth shut on the topic just as she'd requested.

"I'm fine with it then."

With that said, I crushed my mouth to hers and forced my tongue between her parted lips. Bronagh gripped me with her good hand and groaned as I deepened the kiss and took what I wanted from her. It wasn't close to what I needed from her, but it was a damn good place to start. I had barely had my fill of Bronagh's lips when I was suddenly yanked away from her. I turned and tensed my body as I saw Branna Murphy's fist hurdling my way.

Shit hit the fan after that.

The police were called, and once they got there, Ryder and Branna were separated from me and Bronagh. I was brought to a separate examination room to receive eight stitches thanks to Branna's ring cutting through the tissue just over my eye. Bronagh had gotten an X-ray, and then the all-clear that she just had a sprain. She returned to my side to make sure that I was okay once the doctors discharged her. While I was being stitched up by a pretty nurse, a pretty police officer came in to talk to me about whether I wanted to press charges against Branna, which I found very amusing.

"He already *told* ye' he doesn't want to press charges against me sister. *Why* are ye' bein' so repetitive?"

Bronagh had been in a foul mood ever since the female officer came in to speak to me. I noticed straight off the bat that the officer was interested in me, and Bronagh seemed to notice it too.

The officer flicked her eyes to Bronagh. "It is me job to ask the victim of attacks these types of questions more than once to make sure they are solid on their decision."

Bronagh leaned closer to me. "Is it also your job to flirt with said victim while his *girlfriend* is sittin' right next to 'im?"

The officer looked from Bronagh to me, then back again, and her cheeks flushed. The nurse who was stitching me up also went silent upon hearing Bronagh's declaration. I wanted to laugh my ass off, but I didn't. She asserted herself as my girlfriend for no other reason than to get these women to back off, and I loved it.

"Listen 'ere," the officer narrowed her eyes at Bronagh, "I wasn't flirtin'—"

"Yeah, ye' were, but ye' may as well give it up. He isn't interested in ye'. Right?"

When she looked at me and found that my eyes were already on her, she licked her lower lip and blood rushed to my cock.

"Right," I answered.

Satisfied, Bronagh looked back at the officer and snidely said, "*See?*"

My body was stiff from sitting down for so long, so when the nurse was finished with me, I stretched my arms over my head, which naturally caused my muscles to flex. I was shirtless thanks to Branna ripping my T-shirt during my beatdown, and as I stretched, I saw three pairs of eyes on my bare torso. I wasn't stupid. I knew what my body looked like, and normally, I loved the attention from women, but right now, I only wanted the attention of one woman, and I had it.

"Your tattoo is gorgeous."

I looked at the nurse when she spoke, then at the officer, who was nodding in agreement.

"Thanks, ladies." I smiled as I slid my arm around Bronagh's waist. "My *girlfriend* agrees with you both."

Bronagh tensed when both women pulled a face at the mention of her being my girlfriend, and to be honest, I got a little pissed off at their silent dismissal of her too.

"Is he finished here?"

The officer and nurse bobbed their heads to Bronagh's question, though they looked saddened by their answer.

"So can we leave then?"

I looked at Bronagh, then at the officer, who looked like she'd had just about enough of Bronagh's attitude.

"D'ye have a problem—"

"Yeah, she does," I cut the officer off with a big smile. "She sprained her hand a few hours ago and hasn't had any painkillers yet. We're collecting them from the twenty-four-hour pharmacy on our way home as soon as I'm done here."

The officer smiled at me, suddenly forgetting that Bronagh existed.

"I'll discharge ye' now."

I watched Bronagh as she rolled her eyes after the nurse spoke and left the room, and it caused my lips to twitch. The attention I was getting from these women was *killing* her.

"I'm done 'ere, too, unless ye' *do* want to press charges. We can take this down to the station if ye' do."

Bronagh's eyes narrowed to slits.

"No, thank you," I said politely. "I'm set on my decision."

The officer accepted that, said goodbye, and then left the room. I turned my attention back to Bronagh, who was brooding in silence.

She sighed after a few moments. "What?"

"You're *so* fucking sexy."

I leaned down and latched my lips onto her neck, sliding my tongue over her flesh. Bronagh groaned for just a moment before she jumped away from me with her cheeks flushed red.

"Stop that," she scowled. "Anyone could walk in 'ere!"

My eyes rolled over her curves. She was so thick it made my mouth water.

"Like I care, you being jealous and possessive of me has me hard as a diamond. I fucking *love* this side of you."

"Dominic," she said, her face aflame.

Laughter bubbled up my throat. "You're going from sexy as fuck to adorable as hell. You're killing me here!"

She raised a brow. "I *am* about to kill ye' if ye' don't cut this out. I don't like it."

"Why are you crossing your legs then?"

She looked down at her body and realised her legs were indeed crossed.

"Shut up."

The amount of willpower I had to use to remain seated was incredible. I knew her pussy throbbed for me, and the tighter she pressed her thighs together, the more her cheeks flamed.

"If you come over to me, I'll take that ache away and turn it into immense pleasure."

She closed her eyes as I spoke.

"I bet you're wet for me. I can practically feel how hot you are for me from all the way over here."

She tried to focus on her breathing. I saw her take calming breaths, and it made me smile. She was trying to block me out, and there wasn't a chance in hell I would let her do that, not when she was finally opening herself up to me.

"Come over here, baby."

Almost instantly, she walked towards me, and I licked my lips as if she was a damn buffet. She opened her eyes when her knees knocked against mine. I grinned at her as I leaned my head down and brushed my nose against hers. She was trembling, and I knew that she was scared, but I wanted to show her that being intimate with me was something to crave, never something to fear.

"What are you feeling right now?" I asked. "*Tell me*, pretty girl."

Her breathing turned laboured as she said, "I feel hot ... and achy."

"Is it a teasing ache?" I whispered, brushing my lips over hers. "Does it throb?"

"Uh-huh."

I sucked her bottom lip into my mouth for a moment, then released it. I wanted nothing more than to toss her down on the exam table, pull her jeans down, part her thighs, and fuck her until she screamed, but I knew that wasn't going to happen, so I put that thought out of my mind and focused on the pleasure I'd get from pleasuring *her*.

"Your body knows what it wants, and the more you hold back, the more that pretty little clit of yours pulses away as it demands my attention. It wants just *my* attention, right?"

Bronagh's good hand shot out and gripped my shoulder. She squeezed it when my hands came around her waist, then drifted south and gripped her behind. I palmed her ass and swallowed down a groan of my own. I *loved* her ass.

"Why are ye' doin' this to me?" she whispered. "I'll kill ye' for this when I'm thinkin' clearly."

After she spoke, she kissed me like a woman starved. Quickly, I took control of the kiss. I kissed her hard and deep, and just as she was focused entirely on my lips, I slid my right hand around to the front of her jeans and flicked my fingers over the front, unbuttoning and unzipping them within seconds.

"Dominic, please."

I knew what she was begging me for, and she didn't have to ask me twice.

"Just relax, baby, and let me take care of you."

I slid my fingers down her stomach, then dipped my hand into her panties. She sucked in a sharp breath when my fingers slid between her smooth, wet folds followed by my thumb as it brushed over the tiny bundle of nerves that pulsed away for my attention. I wished I could take her clit in my mouth and lick and suck on it until Bronagh screamed my name, but fingering her was the best I could do, so I focused on making it good for her.

"Bronagh, baby, you're fucking *soaked*."

When I resumed our kiss, she wasn't responding to it with much enthusiasm, and I knew it was because my finger swirling around her swollen clit had her and her body's full attention.

Her grip on my shoulder tightened. "Oh, God."

I pulled back an inch and stared at her expressive face, feeling myself harden to the point of pain as pleasure washed over her face. When her eyes drifted shut, my cock throbbed. Seeing how much she enjoyed my touch turned me on beyond belief.

"Eyes on me."

She pushed her pussy against my hand, and I knew I had her.

"Yes, yes!" she suddenly cried out. "Don't stop."

"Not a fucking chance," I said, rotating my finger at a faster pace. "Does that feel good, pretty girl?"

Her hips bucked in response.

I smiled, and said, "I'll take that as a yes. Open your legs a little wider for me."

She did so without hesitation and moaned a little out loud when I slid my finger down her folds and carefully dipped inside her hot, wet pussy. A shudder ran the length of my body when I felt how tightly her muscles constricted around my finger. My mouth watered, imagining it was my cock.

"I can't wait to feel you wrapped around my cock," I almost growled. "You're going to be the undoing of me, pretty girl. I know it."

After a few pumps of my fingers in and out, I moved back to her throbbing clit and rotated with a faster pace than before, and it had her making noises that made me fight with my self-control.

"Oh God," she whimpered. "Okay, ye'can stop no-now. Dominic, it's gettin' too much. I ca-can't—"

"You're about to come, baby. That's all that is," I said, cutting her off as I pressed my lips back to hers. "Let me make you come, pretty girl."

Her body tried to move away from my touch as her body approached its climax, and I refused to let that happen. I tightened my hold on her and worked her pussy with my fingers until her limbs trembled. She sucked in a sharp breath, then held it as her lips parted and her eyes squeezed shut. I watched her face contort in ecstasy as her orgasm slammed into her, and it was the most beautiful thing I had ever seen. My chest swelled, knowing I put that look on her face and made her body feel that bliss.

When she blinked her eyes open a few seconds later, I licked my lower lip. "You look so fucking hot when you come, pretty girl," I said as I slowly removed my hand from her panties. I kept my eyes on hers as I lifted my fingers to my mouth and licked them clean. "Hmm, you taste even better."

I watched as she began to freak the fuck out.

"Oh, Jesus."

"Don't do it, Bronagh," I warned with a chuckle. "Don't be embarrassed about what just happened. It was fucking beautiful, and I won't let you play it off as anything but. Do you understand me?"

She didn't speak, and she couldn't look at me, so I put my fingers under her chin and lifted her head until my gaze found hers.

"Do you understand me?" I repeated. "Let me hear you say it."

"How can I *not* be embarrassed?" she asked. "Ye'… ye' just did that to me, and then ye'… ye'—"

"Licked your cum off my fingers?" I finished. "Yeah, I did. So what? It tasted great, and I'm already looking forward to seconds."

If I thought her face was red before, it went beet red now.

"Dominic!" she scowled. "Don't say stuff like that to me. I've never done anythin' like this before, ever. Well, except for the times we almost had sex in your bedroom, but still, this is *huge* for me, and I don't know how to process what I'm feelin'—"

"Baby, you need to take a breath and calm the fuck down. This is natural. You had an orgasm, an orgasm that I made you have. Big fucking deal. It made you feel incredible, so why should you be embarrassed about that? I'm your boyfriend; this is what I'm good for. It's pretty much all I'm good for."

I watched her process my words, and I knew that in her mind, she was talking herself down.

"Besides," I continued, "I'm so fucking happy no one else has done that to you before. And I'm *panting* to be the first to have sex with you. I dream about it, pretty girl."

Her eyes flicked to mine. "Ye' do?"

"Every night," I responded. "Ever since you told me you were a virgin that day in my house after I fought Jason, I can't get it out of my head."

She swallowed. "Is it hard to believe?"

"Only because you're so beautiful. I'm just surprised no one else has gotten here before me." I winked. "I'm glad, though, because your virginity is *mine*."

Her lips twitched. "It's yours, huh?"

"I'm the boyfriend, so yep." I grinned. "All mine."

"I thought I said you're on a trial basis with me before I put a title on us?"

I tugged her closer to me.

"Yeah, well, I'm promoting myself to boyfriend because I made you feel drunk on an orgasm. You're welcome, by the way."

She playfully rolled her pretty green eyes. "I don't know why I bothered even sayin' you're on a trial basis with me. As soon as I said I'd take a risk with ye', ye' pretty much took up root that ye' were me fella, right?"

I shrugged one shoulder. "Pretty much. I was going to let you think the ball was in your court and that you had all the power, but as you already found out, I have all the power in the world right here in my fingertips."

Her eyes widened as I wiggled my fingers at her, which made me laugh. I hugged her to me, knowing we would have a lot of ups and downs in our relationship, but I had her now, and I wasn't ever going to let her go. She fit into my life like a puzzle; she was a piece of me that I didn't know I was missing. The thought of living my life with her by my side made the future that much more exciting, and I knew a relationship with her would be more than worth it.

Nothing could take her away from me.

Nothing.

CHAPTER EIGHT

Present day ...

"**D**addy?"
 I looked at the doorway of the living room where my daughter lingered. Her big green eyes were as wide as saucers, and her hands were clasped together. She was nervous, and I knew it was because her mother had sent her to speak to me. She rarely called me 'daddy', so I knew she was worried. I hadn't sought her out all day, and that went against everything she knew about me as a father. Usually after an argument, I would go and clear the air with whoever I argued with because I hated fighting with my kids. But I didn't do that today because I wanted Georgie to know just how much trouble she was in.

"Come in, baby."

She entered the room, her eyes locked on the glass of whiskey in my hand. It was almost six in the evening, and I felt like a needed a drink. I had never been a big drinker—I was usually the one who watched other people get drunk—but tonight, I needed something to calm my spiked nerves. I heard people say parenting drove parents to drink, and never realised how true that statement was until my babies grew into teenagers.

"Are ye' drinkin' that 'cause of me?"

I set my glass down on the side table.

"No, but I'm not gonna lie, it helps."

"I'm sorry I lied to ye' about goin' out with Indie," she said, her big green eyes glazing over with unshed tears. "We're only goin' out a couple of months. It's just ... ye' love me to death, and I know it's hard for ye' to let me grow up."

"While that's true, Georgie, you didn't tell me about Indie because deep down you knew your relationship with him is not what it should be for kids your age. You're fifteen, and Indie just turned *thirteen*."

Most people probably wouldn't think thirteen-year-olds had an interest in sex, but having lost my virginity at that age, I knew all too well how possible it was.

My kid cringed. "It's just a two-year difference, not even a full two years, just twenty months ... give or take a few days."

I stared at her, and Georgie sighed.

"I talked to Ma, and I understand everythin' that both of ye' have said, and I agree. I don't know why Indie bought those condoms because they weren't for us to use. Maybe he just wanted to be prepared. I'm not stupid, Da. I'm too young for sex, and I know that ... I don't even know how it all fully works. I mean, I know how it works, but at the same time, I don't."

Her face was burning red as she spoke, and while I knew she was embarrassed, the relief in my chest made me almost cry. She wasn't having sex, and she didn't want to have sex. That was all that mattered to me.

"Look." I sighed as I leaned forward and rested my elbows on my legs. "I know you get angry about how differently I treat you compared your brothers sometimes, but you have to understand that the world for a boy and girl are very different places. It's unfair, but that's the way it is, and to protect you from the fallout, I'm going to be overbearing."

Georgie nodded. "I know. I accepted that years ago that all of ye' were goin' to drive me crazy."

Me, my brothers, her brothers, and all her cousins adored her.

I managed a smile. "We all love you."

"I know," she said. "I love ye' all, too."

"Even Jax?"

Georgie looked up at me with raised brows. "Of course, I love Jax, Da."

"You told him you hated him today."

My daughter lowered her head in shame. "I was so mad at 'im, but I didn't mean it. I really didn't."

"I know that," I said, "but you're still to go over to his house this evening and apologise. He adores every hair on your head, and it hurt him when you told him you hated him today."

Georgie swallowed. "I'll make it right with 'im. I promise."

I leaned back in my chair. "I'm sorry that I reacted with anger earlier when Jax told me that you had a boyfriend. I never want to make you feel like you can't talk to me. All the secrets were exactly why I got angry, but I shouldn't have, so I apologise for that."

"Thank you," she said. "I'm sorry for keepin' Indie a secret. I just ... it was just nice to have someone like me even though they know a bunch of lads would kill 'im for lookin' at me that way."

I tilted my head to the side. "He doesn't care about your brothers and cousins?"

"Since some of them are *his* cousins, no, he's cool about it. He's worried about Locke, though. They're best friends, and he didn't tell 'im we were datin' because I told 'im I wanted no one to know. They might fight over it, and then Indie might fight *me* over that." She put her head in her hands. "You're right. Relationships are too much to deal with."

I managed a laugh. "Well, you're in one now, and I've never known you to take the easy way out of anything."

Georgie looked up at me, and for a moment, she looked exactly like Bronagh.

"I thought ye' said that I couldn't have a boyfriend anymore."

I stared at her, and I knew if I made her break up with this boy, it would push her away from me. She wasn't a little girl anymore, and while she was still a minor, she had to have some independence and experience life.

"Listen to me, and listen carefully. You can continue to date him, but the relationship is *not*, in *any* shape or form, to become intimate until you're an adult. That means eighteen years old at the very least. There is more to a relationship than sex. Not everything that is special has to become physical."

Georgie's jade eyes widened as she jumped up and flung herself at me.

"Oh, thank you, Da!"

I caught her and hugged her tightly. When we separated and she was stood in front of me, my damn heart broke in two. She was gorgeous. The purest beauty I had ever seen. She was the spitting image of Bronagh just with my smile and dimples. She was a young woman, and I hated it.

"This is hard for me," I said, my voice rough. "You know that, right?"

"I know, Da, but I promise ye' that I haven't even kissed Indie yet, and I won't be doin' anythin' like what you're scared of until I'm a lot older. I swear."

She said that now, but wait until she was in a situation with this little Collins fucker that made her want to try the things she swore not to do. I knew I would be the last damn thing on her mind when this little punk had her attention.

"I want you to promise me that you'll think very hard about decisions when it comes to kissing and everything that follows. Consider every single aspect of it, okay? And number one, do *not* be afraid to say no. Respect yourself, and do not give any boy the time of day if he doesn't give you the same level of respect. Do you understand me, Georgie Slater?"

"Yes, Da, I do."

I nodded. "I want to meet him."

Georgie's smile vanished, and her already fair skin paled.

"Ye've already met 'im loads of times."

"I never knew he was your boyfriend then, though."

She swallowed. "Ye' won't scare 'im, right? Because he is already wary of Jax, and he hasn't even *tried* to scare him off yet ... except for when Jax punched 'im yesterday. Indie text me earlier that when he was over at Jax's house with Locke, Jax just stared at 'im without blinkin'. It was enough to freak Indie out, and they're *cousins*. And I know Beau, Enzo, and Alby are goin' to lay it on thick with 'im now, too."

I fucking *loved* my sons and nephews.

"I won't scare him, but I won't be his friend either," I said firmly. "I want him to know that you're my life, and if he *ever* hurt you in *any* way, I'd end his. That's all."

"Da!"

I shrugged. "I'm just telling you the truth."

Georgie sat back down and sighed. "Okay, I guess that's fair."

"Tell him to come by tomorrow afternoon. I want to be sad tonight that you're growing up. I'll get over it by then and enter a new stage of parenting that requires me to scare your boyfriends into submission."

"Daaa," she said with a shake of her head but with a smile on her face. "I love ye' so much."

"I love you too, but remember what I said earlier. You're grounded for your outburst this morning and for what you said to Jax. No electronics for a week, and you're to pick up extra chores around the house."

Georgie nodded, accepting her punishment. "Okay, Da."

She hugged and kissed me once more before she said, "I'm goin' to go up to me room and text Indie about tomorrow, then I'll put all of me stuff on your and Ma's bed so ye' can lock it away in your safe. I'll walk over to Jax's then."

I watched her leave the room, and I felt damn proud of her for accepting the situation in front of her with her head held high. I picked up my glass, drained its contents, then closed my eyes.

"What are you thinkin' of, big man?"

I opened my eyes, watching as Bronagh silently entered the room and walked towards me. Her hips seemed to sway in slow motion, and my mouth all but watered. When she sat her ass down on my crotch and snuggled against me, my arms automatically encased her and held her body to mine. I loved the feel of her, the smell of her hair. I loved her.

"I was just thinking about when I was a kid, then about how I met you and our life together so far."

She smiled. "We've had a great twenty years, right?"

"And the best years are yet to come."

She ran her fingers through my hair. "Tell me what's on your mind."

"I love you, that's what's on my mind."

She sat up straight and looked at me with admiration and love in those big green eyes of hers.

"I love ye' too, fuckface."

I snorted. "You better, fat ass."

Bronagh grinned. "How are ye' holdin' up after everythin' with Georgie?"

"I've considered whether or not you and the kids could survive without me if I went to jail."

"And what conclusion did ye' come to?"

"That you guys would miss me too much."

"We would." Bronagh nodded. "I'd prefer if ye' stayed home with us. If ye' don't mind benchin' prison, that is."

Smartass.

I sighed. "If I have to."

She smiled, and my heart thudded against my chest.

"You're so beautiful, Bronagh."

Her cheeks flamed, and it drew a chuckle from me.

"After all this time, you still blush when I sweet-talk you."

"Hush up."

I smiled, tugged her head to mine, and kissed her until her body melted against me.

"Hmmmm." She hummed against my lips. "I'll never get tired of your kisses."

"Good," I said, relaxing. "'Cause I plan on giving you kisses for a very long time."

My wife smiled. "I know our girl hurt ye' today. She hurt me too."

I rested my forehead against hers.

"I'm terrified of her growing up, Bronagh. I'm not ready for it to happen yet."

"I know, love. It's snuck up on us. Yesterday, she was a baby, and today, she is a young woman."

I squeezed her body. "This is fucking *shit*."

Bronagh laughed. "Think of it, though, we get to watch her grow into a woman. We get to see her start a career for herself, fall in love, get married, and have babies of her own. We raised good kids, Dominic. She's gonna do us proud. I know she is."

I nodded and closed my eyes. "She's my only daughter, and I just ... I just want ... I want her to be the best she can be. I want her to make mistakes, but I want her to take responsibility for them, like she did tonight. She's perfect to me, Bronagh. She's an extension of you. All my babies are an extension of you."

Bronagh brushed her fingers over my lips. "They're all extensions of you, too. Our boys look just like you and your brothers. Georgie has your smile and your strength."

My chest warmed.

"D'ye feel better after speakin' to 'er?"

"Yeah," I answered. "But I'm still scared because she says she won't do anything grown-up until she is older, but we both know that can be bullshit. What was I doing to you when I was eighteen and you were seventeen?" I asked with a frustrated shake of my head. "I didn't just kiss you in that hospital room when you sprained your hand. My fingers got very intimate with you, if I remember it correctly."

My wife hummed. "Oh, I remember, husband."

"Not now, wife."

"Ye' made me body *yours*," she continued.

"Exactly," I whispered. "Do you remember what I did to you when we were kids? I touched you, licked you, sucked you, and fucked you so hard you sometimes forgot to breathe. Jesus, Bronagh, I'd have jumped through hoops just to have your body before I even *knew* you. Georgie is shaped like you, so I *know* this little prick will have a mind like I did, and he will want to—God, I can't even *say* it."

"Dominic." My wife chuckled. "Ye' can't really think she will be a virgin forever."

"Christ, Bronagh," I almost whimpered. "You have no idea how much I can't talk about this. She is my baby *girl*. No punk will ever be good enough for her. She is above everyone in this world. I love her more than life itself, and this ... this is just fucking *hard*, okay? She was five yesterday asking me for piggy back rides and telling me boys were icky, and now she has a damn boyfriend. *Fuck!*"

My wife's arms came around my neck, and her head rested against mine.

"Our babies are growin' up."

"At least Axel is only seven." A lump formed in my throat. "I'm going to baby him so much his head will spin."

Bronagh vibrated with silent laughter.

"Georgie passed me on the stairs and said that ye' want to see Indie tomorrow."

I nodded. "I'm gonna scare him but a normal amount. I know if I make her break up with him, it will ruin her trust in me, so I have to let her have this, but I made her promise to keep intimacy out of everything until she is older. She promised, and I can only hope she sticks to it."

"She will, babe. She respects ye' too much to break her word."

I hoped so.

"I'll accept this, I will, but tonight, I want to just be upset that she's growing up."

My wife kissed my cheek. "Normally, I'd suggest ye' go trainin', but I don't think that'll help ye'. Go to the pub with your brothers; they'll make you feel better."

I tightened my hold on her body. "*You* can make me feel better."

"I will make you feel better when you come home tonight." She winked as she got to her feet and walked out of the room. "For now, I'll look after the kids, so you go to the pub and let it all out."

I didn't have to be told twice. I dug my phone from my pocket and dialled Damien's number. He answered on the fifth ring.

"Do you want to hit up a bar or ten with me?"

Damien groaned. "What did you do?"

I frowned. "Why do you automatically assume I did something?"

"Because I know you."

I rubbed my face with my free hand. "Shit has hit the fan, and it's got *nothing* to do with me and Bronagh."

Damien gasped. "The kids?"

"Georgie," I said, defeated. "She has a boyfriend, and Bronagh won't let me kill him. He's Gavin's boy."

"Fuck," Damien swore. "Fuck everything. I'm on my way."

Damien disconnected the call and made it to my house in ten minutes flat. He didn't come inside. Instead, I grabbed my keys and wallet and exited my house. He clapped his hand on my shoulder the second I got into his car.

"Are you okay?"

I shook my head. "I will be tomorrow, but right now, I'm heartbroken."

"*I'm* heartbroken, so I can only imagine how you feel."

"Tonight, my eyes were opened to Georgie being a young woman and not a little girl anymore. The thought of some excited little boy near her makes me murderous."

"I'm itching to break the kid's hands and his dick, so you aren't alone, brother."

I grunted. "Nothing short of his death will please me."

"He's a Collins kid, too?"

I grunted. "Gavin's boy ... You want to know the kicker?"

Damien nodded.

"Indie is the picture of Gav."

"He is a good-looking bastard."

"Don't I fucking know it!" I balled my hands to fists. "I almost lost Bronagh to him once upon a time, and now I'm losing my baby to not only his blood, but his lookalike? Fuck. I want to kill him. I don't even care that he's a child."

Damien snorted. "You'll be hell bound for killing him."

"I'll explain at the gates. Don't worry about me, I always get what I want."

My brother grinned. "A certain Murphy sister is a prime example."

A smile stretched across my face. "Can you believe I married my high school sweetheart?"

"No, considering I called dibs on her first. I'm *still* pissed you messed with bro code for a chick."

I laughed. "What do you think Alannah would do to you if she found out that you wanted to take Bronagh for a round of mattress dancing when we first met her?"

"Don't *ever* tell her." Damien winced. "She wouldn't have given me five sons if she knew, that's for damn sure."

"Don't worry, your secret is safe with me." I laughed. "I'll take it to my grave."

Damien laughed as he pulled away from the kerb and drove towards our local pub. When we got there, we settled inside an empty booth, and I ordered a pint of cider. Damien did too. I stared at the table, then looked at my brother when he clapped his hands on my shoulder.

"We'll get you through this, buddy."

I nodded. "I'll be good tomorrow. I'll take it on the chin ... but now ..."

"You just want to be sad that your baby girl isn't a baby anymore?"

Don't you dare fucking cry.

I leaned my head on my forearm. "Call the others ... I need their bullshit right now."

"I'm on it." Damien chuckled, then he added, "You might regret this by the end of the night."

I'd never regret a night spent with my brothers ... They were the very reason I was the man I was today. I owed them everything, and I knew that they'd help me get through this moment of helplessness, just as they helped me with everything else that stumped me over the years. There was no one on the earth who I'd trust to have my back more than them. I just hoped I didn't get drunk enough to go and find this Collins kid because if that happened, not even my brothers could stop Bronagh Slater from kicking my ass to New York and back again.

I closed my eyes and chuckled to myself. Tonight was a rough one for me, but that was part of life when you had kids, and there was one thing I was absolutely certain of, and that was I fucking loved my life, and there wasn't a thing I'd changed about it.

Not a damn thing.

PART TWO

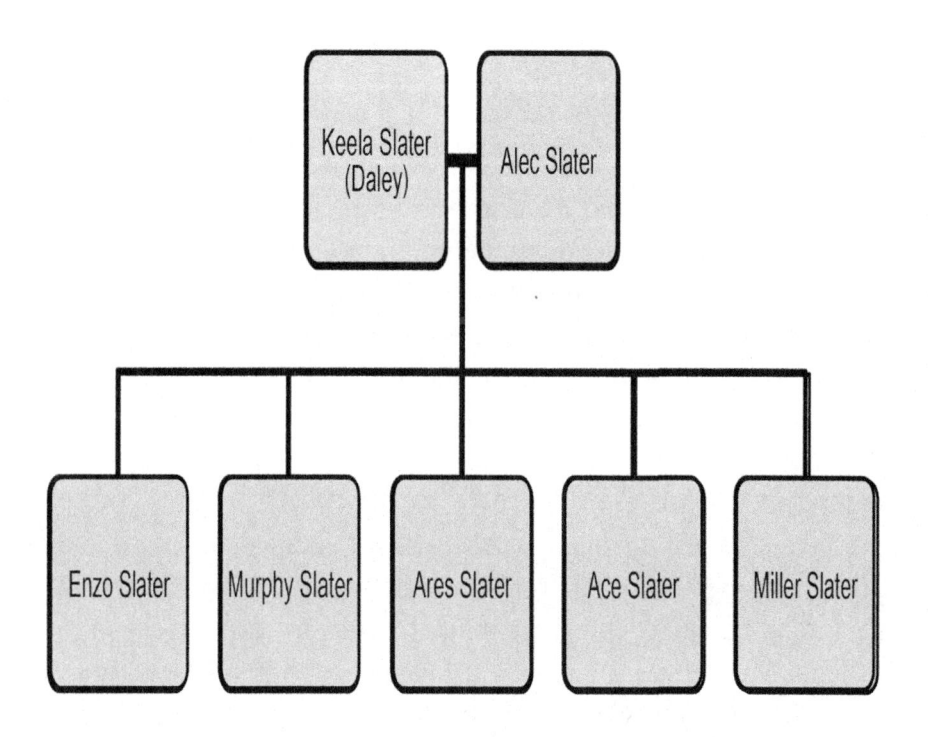

```
        ┌─────────────────┬─────────────────┐
        │  Keela Slater   │   Alec Slater   │
        │    (Daley)      │                 │
        └─────────────────┴─────────────────┘
                          │
    ┌──────────┬──────────┼──────────┬──────────┐
    │          │          │          │          │
┌───────┐ ┌─────────┐ ┌────────┐ ┌────────┐ ┌─────────┐
│ Enzo  │ │ Murphy  │ │  Ares  │ │  Ace   │ │ Miller  │
│Slater │ │ Slater  │ │ Slater │ │ Slater │ │ Slater  │
└───────┘ └─────────┘ └────────┘ └────────┘ └─────────┘
```

ALEC

CHAPTER ONE

Present day...

I woke up that morning to screaming. Loud, terror-filled screaming. I bolted upright and reached for Keela out of instinct, only to find her side of the bed empty. I fumbled with the blanket that covered me and ended up getting my legs tangled, causing me to fall off the bed and land shoulder first on the hard oak floor.

Fuck.

"*Alec!*"

My heart nearly burst with fear as I jumped to my feet and quickly detangled myself from the bed sheets. On my sprint out of the room, I grabbed the first thing I could use as a weapon as I rushed down the stairs, and that just happened to be a Power Rangers umbrella. I ran down the hallway the second my feet touched the floor and skidded into the kitchen. My arms and the umbrella were raised and ready for battle. My eyes darted from left to right, and when I saw no intruders, my body slightly relaxed ... until I spotted my wife on the kitchen table.

"I thought you were being *murdered*!" I glared at her. "What the hell is wrong with you, woman?"

"Just kill it!" my wife pleaded. "Oh, God. *Kill it.*"

Kill what?

I looked at where Keela was pointing, and when I saw the man-eating tarantula gliding towards me, I screamed louder than my wife. I used the umbrella in my hand as if it was a sledge hammer, and I beat the life out of the spider. After a solid minute of blind swinging, I came to a halt and inspected the floor. The spider was there, and it was unmoving.

I exhaled a nervous breath.

"I fixed that problem, didn't I?"

Keela, whose hands were on her hips, shook her head. "Ye' did well, husband."

"I wasn't even scared."

My wife rolled her eyes as I hunkered down to examine the spider.

"Aw ..." I frowned. "I amputated one of his legs by accident."

Keela, who was still on top of the table, said, "I wish ye' had decapitated the little fucker."

I looked up at her. "It seems pointless now that he's dead."

She grunted, clearly disagreeing. I looked back down at the spider.

"It's not even *that* big now that I'm close—OH MY GOD!"

A very manly roar rose from my throat when the dead spider came back to life and ran towards me—no doubt with murder on his mind. He was down one leg, but the loss of his limb seemed to fuel him because he was moving rapidly around the floor, zigzagging from left to right as if trying to confuse me. He was waiting for an opening to spring on me so he could strike a death blow. I knew he was because if I were in his position, I'd do the exact same thing. I sprung onto the kitchen counter just to get away from him. I threw my umbrella at him when I had a clear shot, and it hit the little fucker square on and squashed him.

"Ha! Come back from that, asshole!"

Things were quiet for a moment, then side-splitting laughter came from my right.

"I almost *died,* so what the fuck do you find so funny?"

"*You*," Keela cackled. "Ye' practically leapt onto the counter."

"He was running *at* me. Did you *see* how fast he moved?"

"I thought ye' weren't scared?"

"I thought it was *dead*!" I argued. "Of course, I wasn't scared when I thought it was dead."

Keela continued to laugh.

"How did you even get up there?" I quizzed as I jumped down from the counter. "Did you use a chair to step up on?"

"Nah," she answered as I moved in front of her and lifted her to the ground. "I saw the spider and just hopped on it."

"Oh, yeah?" I waggled my brows, tugging her body against mine suggestively. "I've got something else you can hop on, and it's a whole lot bigger."

"Please," my eldest son, Enzo, gagged as he entered the kitchen dressed from head to toe in his soccer gear. "Don't make me sick before I've even had me breakfast."

Keela pushed my body away from hers like I was scalding hot coal, and it only encouraged me to grope her further. I stepped forward and wrapped my arms around her, pulling her backside tight against me.

"There's nothing sick about a man loving on his woman."

"There is," Enzo said as he searched the fridge. "When the man is me aul' lad, and the woman is me aul' one."

Keela gasped in outrage. "I'm nowhere near old enough to be called aul' one, ye' little shite."

Our kid closed the fridge door, armed with milk, ready-made pancake batter, and a carton of orange juice. He turned to face us but focused on his mother. His grey eyes, which he inherited from me, gleaming mischievously.

"It's just an expression, Ma." He winked. "Ye' know I think you're beautiful."

"Beautiful?" I interjected. "Really, Zo? You think slinging a compliment her way is going to get you off the—"

Keela elbowed me in the stomach and cut me off.

"Ye' think I'm beautiful?" She giggled. "Thanks, son. 'Ere, let me make your breakfast. I'll put chocolate chips in your pancakes."

Enzo leaned his head down and kissed her on the cheek when she moved over to him. "You're the best, Ma."

"Punk," I muttered as he shot a shit-eating grin my way over Keela's head. "Why didn't you come running when you heard your mom scream?"

"'Cause I heard *you* scream not long after, and I heard the word spider mentioned in the midst of that screamin'. I wasn't riskin' me life against a spider for either of ye', I'm sorry."

"I've never felt such betrayal in all my life," I said, placing my hand on my chest. "I have no idea how you came from my angelic loins."

Enzo laughed and nudged by me so he could sit at the kitchen table. I turned to my wife.

"He just had to call you beautiful to get his breakfast made." I placed my hands on my hips in outrage. "I *show* you how beautiful you are with this wonderland body of mine, and I get an elbow in the gut. That's just typical."

"Hush up. I'll make ye' pancakes too."

"With extra chocolate chips?"

"With extra chocolate chips, big man."

I perked up. "You're the best."

"And ye' wonder where Enzo gets it from?"

I grinned. "I am nothing if not a great teacher, kitten."

My wife snorted in response. I leaned down and kissed her neck as she turned to the stove and switched it on. I patted her behind, earning me a giggle, which made me grin. I joined Enzo at the kitchen table and death stared at him as he tapped on the screen of his phone.

"Does your girlfriend still think I'm hotter than you?"

Enzo sighed. "She was never me girlfriend, and she never said ye' were hotter than me. She said ye' were hotter than she *expected* ye' to be."

"That's the story of my life, son. My beauty stuns people; it always has and always will."

Enzo's eyes glinted with amusement. "I'm better lookin'."

"You Slater kids all seem to think that. Jax thinks he's God's gift to women, you walk around like your junk is a foot long, and your other cousins are just as bad. Your brothers, too. I don't know where I went wrong in raising you to give you ugly shits so much confidence."

Enzo laughed at my obvious joke and so did my wife.

"Me sons are beautiful because *I'm* their mother," Keela said as she poured pancake batter into a pan. "Your genes just gave them their height."

And just about everything else.

"I'm thankful for gettin' his height," Enzo said as he leaned back in his chair. "Girls think you're automatically ten times more attractive if you're tall. And ten times ten just makes me the hottest specimen at school. Jax *wishes* he was as sexy as me. Me hair alone makes me stand out."

Enzo was the only one in the entire family to have red hair like his mother. It was curly too, and because it was so wild, he always styled it and kept on top of keeping the length trimmed so the curls only spiralled once. Even I had to admit he was a beautiful little fucker.

"God save me from overinflated egos," Keela mumbled.

"Some of your cousins have white hair; do you stand out against *them*?"

"Yup," Enzo answered me. "I'm the hottest Slater to have ever existed. Period."

The logic of a fourteen-year-old never failed to amuse me.

"Keep that confidence, my boy." I beamed at my son. "A woman will surely cut it in half by the time you're twenty."

Keela snickered. "Did I cut *yours* in half?"

"Woman, you did me dirty when we first met. You dissed *everything* about me."

"Yet ye' wouldn't leave me alone."

"Have you *seen* your legs? You could have waxed me bare and used me for a surfboard, and I wouldn't have gone anywhere. Your legs give me life, and the rest of your fine ass body accompanied with your stunning face is just a major plus."

Keela's ears were red as she made our pancakes.

"Shut up," she mumbled.

Enzo laughed. "I'm goin' to me footie match in an hour. I'll take the boys with me since their match is after mine. Uncle Ry said he'd drive us all in his van. I'll bring them for food on the way home. Ma already gave me the money."

That was no small feat. Enzo was our eldest son at fourteen, Murphy was twelve, Ares was eleven, Ace was nine, and Miller was six. Together, they were a handful for Keela and me to deal with, so Enzo offering to take them all out was a parenting win.

Keela beamed our son's way. "You're such a good boy, always takin' care of your brothers."

"Speaking of your brothers," I quizzed. "Where *are* they? It's entirely too quiet in this house right now for them not to be doing something wrong."

My daddy senses were tingling.

"The four of them are across the road," my wife answered. "I'm surprised ye' didn't wake up when they were gettin' dressed. They sounded like a herd of bloody elephants. Miller and Ace argued for ten minutes about who was shadowing the twins today. They didn't stop until Jules took Miller and Nixon took Ace and separated them. Those two will put me in an early grave with how loud they are, I honestly don't know how ye' sleep through their chaos."

"Sleeping like the dead is a superpower. Many want it, but few have the power to wield it."

Enzo snickered. "You're full of it, Da."

"Thank you!" Keela announced. "I've been tellin' 'im that for years, son."

"The pair of you are haters."

"Can ye' *please* stop usin' terms that are meant for young people?"

I rolled my eyes at my child. "That term was used *before* you took up residence in my left nut sack, so shut it."

"Alec!" Keela admonished as Enzo burst into joyous laughter.

He always got a kick out of me when I ragged on him, and I loved it.

"I'm being honest," I said to my wife. "Kids these days think they own words when they only have them because we dumbed that shit down *for* them."

Keela flicked her eyes to Enzo. "He's right. All the slang *you* say, we said."

"I can't imagine Da callin' anyone an eejit."

"That's different," I said. "If I moved here on my own, I probably would have lost my accent and adapted your mom's, but I'm always around your uncles, so I guess we keep our accent alive … though it's not as prominent as it used to be, I'll say that much."

"Agreed." Keela nodded. "Ye' say the word 'fuck' more like me than ye' use to, and ye' don't say talk in that funny way anymore."

I smiled. "I'm basically Irish."

Enzo snorted. "Yeah, Da, you're *so* Irish."

I ignored his sarcasm and focused on his mother.

"Can we make another baby while the other babies are away?"

Enzo made a noise dangerously close to a squeal.

"Please don't," he pleaded. "Four younger brothers are all I can handle when I have a million little cousins to deal with as well. I beg ye' *not* to do this to me."

Keela laughed at how terrified our son looked.

"Your da is teasin' ye', son," she assured him. "Five is our lucky number, just like your aunties and uncles."

Enzo practically deflated with relief. "Thank Christ."

I snorted. "You love your brothers and cousins, especially Georgie."

"Georgie is everyone's favourite because she is so precious."

"Precious," Keela repeated with a laugh. "She'd kick ye' in the mouth if she heard ye' say she's anythin' other than tough."

Enzo thanked his mother as she placed six pancakes on his plate.

"We know not to say things like that around 'er. She hates bein' the only girl, so we have to make 'er feel like she's in charge."

I rolled my eyes. "Don't kid yourself, son. She *is* in charge. She has you and every other man in this family wrapped around her little finger. She loves being the only girl. She just pretends that she hates it to keep you all on your toes."

Enzo sighed. "I don't know how she does it. Even when she annoys me, I still love 'er stupid face."

Keela chuckled. "She's the only girl, so all of ye' want to protect 'er."

"She can be scary sometimes, like, she knows how to fight really well. I think we all did a bad thing by wrestlin' with 'er growin' up. The only people she can't pin are Jax, me, Locke, Jules, and Nixon. She still gets the better of Beau, but only just. She's a savage, Da. I'm tellin' ye'."

I grinned. "She'll keep trying until she can pin *all* of you."

"I know." Enzo chuckled as he ate. "I think the next time she jumps me, I'm just gonna let 'er win, so she can get it out of 'er system."

I leaned back in my chair and stared at my son long enough for him to stop eating and look at me.

"What, Da?"

"Nothing," I answered as his mother put pancakes in front of me. "Just thinking that I love you. You and that mop of red hair."

"I love ye' too, Da," he replied. "And don't hate on me hair. It's a bird magnet."

I snorted, then bumped fists with him. We ate together, then Keela tidied around the kitchen, joining in on the conversation when something interested her, but for the most part, we talked about sports.

"Zo," Keela said as Enzo finished eating. "If Miller and Ace act up while you're out, phone me and I'll come pick them up. I've warned them to behave for ye.'"

"Jules and Nix will be with me. They worship the twins, so they won't be bad around them."

"We should move the pair of them in here if that's the case," Keela said, making me snort.

When Enzo left the house, it was so quiet I could hear myself think ... that hardly ever happened. I stared at my wife, my eyes roaming over her body hungrily. I thanked God she wore pyjama shorts; her legs were soft, supple, and though she was on the short side, her legs were long, and I loved them. My eyes travelled up to her cute ass next, then her tiny waist, then to her mass of thick red curls.

"How do you get sexier with each passing day?"

Keela looked over her shoulder and locked eyes with me.

"Have ye' been watchin' me again, playboy?"

I raised my brows. "Kitten, I watch your fine self every chance I get. Now come here and give daddy some loving."

She wiped her hands dry on a tea towel and walked towards me, her hips swaying from side to side. She had a grin on her face, and I knew right away that she wanted to fuck me. I straightened up when she gripped the hem of her T-shirt and pulled it over her head. She had no bra on, so her bare breasts drew a groan from me. This was my wife's one insecurity. After having so many babies and breastfeeding them all, they weren't as perky as they were when we first met, and telling her that was perfectly natural wouldn't have worked so I worshiped them just as much as I did when I first laid eyes on them because I loved them just as much now as I did then.

The second Keela was in touching distance, I reached around and snagged her by her waist. She laughed as she kicked off her pyjama shorts and straddled my thighs as I took a rosy pink nipple in my mouth. Her breathy sigh of satisfaction made my cock hard. When her hands slid from my shoulders down my bare back, I hissed against her breasts. When she gently raked her nails over my sensitive flesh, my body involuntarily bucked. My wife knew what touching my back did to me, and she knew it well.

I stood, making her laugh as she wrapped her legs around me. I grinned up at her, but my smile disappeared when I heard a high-pitched cry. Both my wife and I jumped with fright.

"Mammy!"

Keela gasped. "Miller!

I set Keela down and ran out to the hallway with my heart in my throat. I came to a sliding stop when I found my youngest son in the arms of my big brother. Ryder was trying to soothe Miller, but he was too far into his sobbing to calm down for him. When my son locked eyes on me, he cried louder. I took him when he reached for me.

"What happened?"

"He fell and hit the back of his head playing tag with the twins in the yard." Ryder frowned, placing his hand on his hips. "I checked, and he has no cut, just a small bump."

I hugged Miller to my chest and swayed him from side to side to calm him, and I caught the moment my brother looked down at my boxers and used his hand to hide a grin. I looked down and saw the tent I was sporting. Excellent.

"Don't," I warned, looking back up at my brother. "She'll kill you if you make jokes when he's crying this much."

Keela appeared next to me, fully dressed and cooing as she took our son from me. Ryder and I were forgotten as Miller became my wife's sole focus. She wandered off into the living room, and it didn't take long for her to calm Miller down. His crying slowed down until he was just sniffling. Ryder and I leaned against the doorway as we watched Keela work her magic.

"Interrupted playtime, did we?"

"Yeah," I answered. "It's cool, though, as long as he is okay."

I fixed my boxers, glad my erection wasn't an issue anymore. Hearing my son's cry and realising he was hurt killed it instantly.

"I'll call later to see how he is," Ryder said. "I have to take the rest of the tribe to soccer soon."

I clapped my hand on his shoulder. "Thanks, bro."

Ryder left, and I joined my wife and son on our couch. When I sat down, Miller climbed onto my stomach and lay his head on my chest. Keela smiled at him when he sat up and looked at my bare chest. This prompted my son to strip out of his tiny little soccer outfit. I laughed when he was down to his cute little Batman boxers and lay back down on my chest, getting himself comfortable. There were three Slater kids who hated wearing clothes. Miller and my nephews Israel and Rafe *loved* to be in their birthday suits whenever possible. Getting them to keep their boxers on was a challenge.

"Out of all our boys," Keela said, running her hand over Miller's back, "he is the most like you."

I tugged on Miller's hair, earning me a smile. He grew his hair out, so it hung low and brushed his neck just like mine did. He was definitely my mini me; he did everything I did and said everything I said, which had me watching my P's and Q's daily. He was my baby, mine and Keela's last child, so I went out of my way to baby him because I knew these days were numbered. Before I knew it, he'd be a teenager like Enzo.

The front door suddenly opened, and Ryder's middle son, Alfie, strolled in, he too was wearing soccer gear. Nearly all of the Slater kids played soccer. They all played for the same club, just on different teams because of their age differences.

"Cousin." Alfie frowned at Miller lying on me. "My guy, are ye' okay?"

Miller turned his head so he could look at Alfie. "Yeah, I'm okay."

"D'ye wanna come and play *Fortnite* with me?" Alfie asked, then he looked at me as he sat down. "Can he, unc? Me Da said I don't have to go and play football if I came over 'ere and played with Miller."

Alfie loved Miller, I knew that, but right now, my nephew was using my son to get out of playing soccer, and it tickled me. *Fortnite* was the latest craze that all the kids obsessed over.

"Sure." My lips twitched. "Only for an hour, though, okay?"

Alfie nodded, jumped up, then ran out of the room and up the stairs to the kids' game room without a backwards glance.

"Cousin!" Miller shouted as he scrambled off my chest. "Wait for me."

"C'mon then, Mills!"

When both kids were upstairs, I turned to Keela and found her smiling and shaking her head.

"I honestly can't believe they all address each other as cousin."

"I can't even remember how it started, but it's cute."

Keela leaned against me and rested her head on my chest.

"Wanna do somethin' fun?"

I looked down at her. "The kids could come down at any—"

"I'm not talkin' about sex, Alec."

I frowned. "What then?"

"I was thinking of watchin' a film."

I paused. "What movie?"

"I don't know ... oh, I know one of the *Jurassic World* films are on Sky. The second one, I think. What about that?"

"We aren't watching that."

I made a vow to God to never watch that damn movie ever again.

Keela looked up at me. "Oh yeah, I forgot that ye' cried when the dinosaur with the long neck died when we saw it in the cinema."

"You *saw* him, Keela!" I grunted. "He was calling for help; he was asking the humans to stop the boat and help him, but they didn't, and he—" I cut myself off midsentence and took a few deep breaths. "He died," I finished. "It was sad, and I wasn't the only one who cried, so leave me alone about it."

"Everyone else who cried with us was under the age of fourteen, big man."

I glared at my wife. "Then me and the kids are the only ones who aren't pure fucking evil in this family!"

My wife chortled. "What d'ye want to watch then, crybaby?"

I perked up. "I vote *Star Wars*."

Keela groaned and laughed when I said, "I'll eat your pussy until you come later if you watch the new movies with me."

"Ye' better make me toes curl, husband."

I fist pumped the air. "I always do, wife."

I grabbed the remote and turned on *The Force Awakens*. Alannah Slater chose that moment to enter my house like the plague she was. I paused the film before it even had a chance to start, and I glared at her as she walked into the living room. She pulled a face at me when she looked my way.

"That's *way* more of your ugly arse than I need to see on this fine Saturday mornin'."

I stretched my body out. "I'll be naked the next time you enter *my* crib, Ryan."

"I haven't been Alannah Ryan for ten years, and ye' know it."

"You'll *always* be a Ryan, you life-sucking monster. No Slater woman in her right mind would ever be as evil as you."

Alannah sat down on the armchair and snickered. She knew damn well that she was a hellion, and from the look on her too pretty face, she was pleased about it, too.

"Well," I began, "what's good, four eyes?"

Her jaw tensed as I knew it would. Her eyesight had worsened over the years, and she refused to get laser eye surgery out of fear she'd go blind or something, so she settled on getting glasses. She hated them at the start, so I teased her about them every chance I got, and it still bugged her after all these years.

Alannah deadpanned. "Ares and Ace wear glasses, too."

"True, but they're my precious babies. You're a demon from hell."

I blinked when Alannah took her glasses off and rested them on her thigh.

"Why'd you take them off?"

"Because I don't wanna see ye' right now. Your ugly face gives me headaches."

Keela snorted. "That's funny."

Alannah looked in her general direction and smiled.

"Can ye' see me, Lana?"

"Just the outline. All of your features are blurred beyond recognition."

Keela looked at me. "She takes 'er glasses off a lot when she's around *you*."

"It's because I'm so sexy that she's tempted to grope me, so in order to keep my little brother happy, she hides her insane attraction to me by taking her glasses off in my presence. She can't help that she's *wildly* attracted to me."

Keela's lips twitched in amusement.

"Oh," Alannah snorted, "and here I thought I did it because your ugly mug makes me eyes *burn*."

"Nah, that's what you *want* to believe, so you don't feel bad about wanting my sexy body."

Alannah rolled her eyes. "I swear that ye' love the sound of your own voice."

"I'm partial to it," I agreed.

"Remember when ye' had strep last year and lost your voice?" At my nod, she said, "Those were the best ten days of me life."

Keela burst into giggles as I glared at my arch-enemy.

"You're turning my own wife against me, Ryan."

Alannah, looking mighty pleased with herself, put her glasses back on and looked at the television screen and said, "Are ye' watchin' *Star Wars*?"

Keela nodded. "*The Force Awakens*."

"I don't really like them, the old or the new ones."

I tensed. "Get the fuck out of my house."

Alannah didn't move a muscle. Instead, she beamed at Keela when my wife thumped my side. "Ye' can't kick people out of the house because they don't like the same films as ye'."

"You calm yourself." I pointed my index finger at her then looked back at Alannah. "*Star Wars* is more than a movie franchise, and you know it."

She snorted. "*Star Trek* is better."

Keela sucked in a breath. "Alannah, run."

I felt my blood boil. I shot to my feet and put my entire focus on Alannah Slater. She was a pest that I was about to exterminate. Keela's warning was all the head start she got as I made a beeline for her. She jumped to her feet, screamed like a banshee, and ran out of the house at high speed, but that didn't derail me from chasing her. Neither did just being in my boxers.

"Get back here, you little Trekkie whore!"

I could have sworn I heard her fucking *laugh* as she ran from me.

"Help!" She screeched as she sprinted for Ryder and Branna's house.

She made it to the front door just as Ryder and Damien raced outside. When they saw the scene before them, they started to laugh. Damien stopped laughing and widened his eyes when he realised that his wife wasn't slowing down. He opened his arms and caught her as she flung herself at his body and wrapped her short-ass limbs around him.

"Save me," she panted. "He's fuckin' *crazy*!"

"Death!" I hollered as I slowed down to a brisk walk. "Death is what you shall—OW!"

I cut myself off when blinding hot pain shot up my right foot. I reached down, grabbed my foot and hopped around as agony tore through me. It happened. What every parent feared happened ... I stepped on a motherfucking Lego. Right there in the front yard of my eldest brother's home.

"The devil is real!" I hissed as I lowered my foot back down to the ground. "*So* fucking real!"

I heard my brothers crack up, then childlike laughter joined them. I turned to Ryder's van, loaded with his kids and mine, and they were all pointing at me and laughing their little heads off while Enzo was grinning with his phone pointed in my direction. I glared at him until he put the phone away with a rueful smile.

I looked at Damien and Alannah who was standing next to Ryder smiling so wide I knew her damn cheeks had to be hurting.

"Where are *your* demon kids?"

"In our car behind you," Damien answered.

I turned around and waved at my nephews who were laughing at me, too. I think they were laughing at me being outside in just my boxers rather than stepping on a Lego.

Little shits.

"Dame and Ry are goin' to watch their footie games. Don't ye' wanna go?"

"You *know* I'm not allowed at one of their games until my two years are up."

"Oh yeah," Alannah mused. "I forgot ye' got a two-year ban for disruptin'—"

"I disrupted nothing," I stated firmly. "That damn referee was paid off. I could feel it in my bones."

The entire ban was a joke. I was standing up for the club's honour, and I get a two-year ban for assaulting a referee. I barely touched the man. I think I shoved him at best and maybe told him I'd lodge my foot up his ass, but that was *it*.

"That gave ye' no right to attack the man durin' the kids' game, Alec."

I waved my sister-in-law off. "It wasn't *that* bad."

"Ye' made the man cry," Alannah countered. "And a bunch of the kids, too."

I'll admit ... I forgot about that part.

"Bad things happen every day. They needed toughening up."

"It was a nine-year-old's football game, Alec. Not the bloody World Cup final."

My brothers laughed at Alannah, which made me roll my eyes.

"Even if I wanted to go to their games, which I *don't*, Miller hurt his head, so he's staying home. Alfie is in my house too. I'll watch them."

"Ye' sure?" Alannah quizzed. "I won't be there to annoy ye'. Dominic will be there, so will Kane. I'll be at the community centre."

She practically lived there.

"That's a tempting offer, but no. I'm good, love."

Alannah snorted as she walked by me, and mumbled, "*Star Trek* is still better."

"Trekkie whore!"

She ran all the way to her car laughing. She jumped into the passenger side and locked the door, screaming when she looked up and saw me staring through the window motioning my finger across my neck.

"You're *done* when I get you, Ryan."

"I'll have you know she's been a Slater for ten years."

I looked at my baby brother, ignoring the fact that at thirty-eight he wasn't a baby anymore, and glared at him.

"The demon part of her is a Ryan. That's when the bitch comes out to play."

"Don't curse!" Alannah shouted through the window.

"Excuse me, but I am a Christian." I placed my hand over my heart. "I would never speak such vulgar language in front of children."

Alannah rolled her eyes. "It's amazing how ye' become a man of God when you're in it up to your neck."

I scowled at her. "Back off, Satan."

She beamed at me, then discreetly stuck her finger up at me as my brother drove off with my nephews waving and making funny faces at me. Ryder was getting into his van too, so I waved at him, then jogged back across the road to my house, watching my step this time. When I entered my house and closed the door after me, I went into the sitting room and found my wife lying on her side with her eyes closed. I knew she was asleep without having to get close to her to confirm it. After we had babies, she developed the magical ability to fall asleep whenever there was silence.

I sat next to her and put her feet on my lap. Un-pausing the television, I watched *Star Wars* by myself. When an hour passed by, I got up, careful not to wake Keela, and went to check on the boys. They were off their video game without me having to tell them, which pleased me. They were playing with slime that the boys had recently made, and once I saw they had the protective sheets on the floor, I made no mention of reminding them to be careful.

"Are you guys hungry?"

"Yeah," they answered in unison.

"What do you want?"

"I'm feelin' noodles," Alfie answered.

"Yeah." Miller bobbed his head in agreement. "I want noodles, too. Curry ones."

"I'll have chicken, please."

With their orders noted, I went down to the kitchen and made their noodles. I called them down to eat when I dished them up and put them on the table. I jumped a little when I felt hands slide around my stomach. I relaxed when I heard my wife giggle.

"You scared me."

"I know," she mused. "Ye' never hear me when I come up behind ye'."

"'Cause you move like a ninja."

Keela chuckled, and when I turned to face her, my smile vanished when I saw her eyes were red and swollen.

"What's wrong?"

She blinked. "Nothin', why?"

I lifted my hands to her face and gently brushed my fingers under her eyes.

"You were crying."

Keela waved me off. "I just had a bad dream."

"About what?"

She looked away from me. "Those noodles smell *good*."

I turned her head back in my direction and frowned down at her. I hate seeing her upset in any way, and knowing something made her cry, even if it was a dream, made my stomach roil.

"Alec, I'm fine, honey."

"Then tell me what made you cry."

She swallowed. "It's just ... that ... that nightmare I used to have, remember?"

My entire body tensed, and my heart rate picked up its pace. She hadn't had that nightmare in years and knowing that those images were once again in her beautiful mind cut me to the bone. She only had that nightmare because of me. Everything about it was my fault.

"Kitten."

"I'm fine."

She didn't move a muscle.

"Keela."

She closed her eyes. "It was ... I saw them ... touchin' ye' again."

Sickness filled my gut, and my heart just about shattered. I tightened my hold on my wife.

"I have never been touched until you first lay your hands and lips on my body. I have never been touched in any way that matters until there was you. You're the only person on this Earth to own me mind, body, and soul."

Keela began to cry.

"I know," she sniffled. "I know this. I know ye' were forced into what happened. Me mind just likes to torture me. I'm sorry."

It had been a long time since we spoke about our past, mainly because we'd moved beyond it and started a new life together. I knew my wife had accepted what had happened, but knowing it still hurt her, hurt me.

"You saved me," I said, brushing loose strands of hair behind her ear. "You gave me my life, my babies, and my happiness."

She looked up at me, and her beauty stunned me. She had more laughing lines around her eyes, but her energy for life shone brighter than ever within them. We were in our forties now but being with her still made me feel twenty-eight. She was my rock, my heart, and there was nothing on this planet that I wouldn't do for her.

"I wouldn't change anythin' about what happened," Keela said, surprising me. "Gettin' through that got us to today. I love our life together, I love our babies, and I love *you* so much it sometimes doesn't feel real that I am this happy. I don't know why I had that stupid dream, but it means nothin'. It hasn't meant anythin' for a very long time. All that matters is *you*, Alec. You're amazin' the way ye' are, and I would never change anythin' that made ye' the man and father ye' are today. You're my perfect, ye' always have been."

I kissed her the second she finished speaking, and we only broke apart when cheering and fake heaving filled the room as Alfie and Miller came downstairs to eat their noodles. Keela smiled up at me and pecked my lips once more before she turned to the boys and settled them at the table. I watched her as I leaned against the counter, and as per usual, I silently thanked God for blessing me with a woman who gave my life meaning.

My heart was full and happy, but I remembered a time when it wasn't. Things weren't always so perfect for me or my brothers ... but I had a secret that only one brother and one woman knew, and if I had my way, it'd stay that way. There weren't a lot of things I was able to protect my brothers or my wife from in the past, but some secrets were better left unspoken. I'd do anything for my wife and family, and keeping things from her that could never be changed was one of them.

CHAPTER TWO

Fifteen years old ...

When I woke up that morning, I was on cloud nine. I had *finally* lost my virginity ... well, when it came to fucking a guy, at least. Like my older brothers, I had pussy on demand whenever I wanted it. Gang bunnies always hung around the compound and were more than eager to fuck anyone who would let them. I let them fuck me a lot, and they let me fuck them a lot ... but I frequently got an itch that no pussy could scratch. I wasn't exactly sure when I realised I was bisexual, but when I started to like girls in a sexual way, I started to like guys in the same way, too. I just never acted on it because of the homophobes I lived with.

That and I was too terrified to tell my brothers the truth about my sexuality in case they shut me out. Those four were my reason for living, so I could never take the chance and tell them because the risk of losing them was too high. I hated that I thought they would react badly to me liking guys as much as I liked girls when my mind and heart told me they wouldn't give a shit, but the fear of them possibly reacting badly had me keeping it to myself.

I hated keeping secrets.

I entered my family's wing of the compound, and when I entered our kitchen, I found my mom sitting at the dining table.

"Hi, Mom."

Mom glanced up at me. "You're so pretty, baby boy."

I smiled at her, but it didn't come from my heart. I didn't love this woman, and she didn't love me. I had known from a young age that Ryder was my mom and dad rolled into a big brother, and I accepted that. I just wished I didn't have to see my parents and pretend we were anything other than co-workers because that was all they were. Being forced to be around them all the time and pretend I liked them left a sour taste in my mouth.

"Do you have yourself a girlfriend yet, Alec baby?"

She never called me just by my name, everything she labelled me with had to be accompanied by the word baby, and it ground my gears.

I scratched my neck. "No, Mom, I haven't found a girl to take home to you yet."

Not that I'd ever put a girl through the pain of meeting a bitch like you.

She was too immersed in her phone to hear my reply, and she didn't care enough to pretend otherwise. I turned and made myself some cereal, ignoring some of my dad's men when they strolled into the kitchen. They greeted me, and I nodded at them in return. Corbin, my dad's main head of security, leaned down and kissed my mom on the neck, making her giggle. I gritted my teeth. It was no secret my mom had different lovers, and my dad had many of his own, too. They had an open marriage, and I think it was the only reason they managed to remain together. They fucked other people, then they eventually always came back to one another. The only people they loved were one another, but it wasn't real love. It couldn't be.

If I loved a woman or a man, I'd never share them with anyone else, and if they wanted someone other than me, then they never loved me in the first place. That was what I believed after growing up and watching my father allow other men to be intimate with his wife.

"Alec?"

I looked at Corbin when he addressed me, and said, "Yeah?"

"Do you mind if I steal your mom for a while?"

My stomach churned in disgust. I absentmindedly lifted my hand to the rosary beads that I wore around my neck. I wasn't a very religious person, but my beads relaxed me whenever I touched them.

"I don't mind." I turned back to my cereal.

I heard them leave the room, and I shook my head when the sound of a hand slapping skin sent a shiver of repulsion up my spine. I knew Corbin had slapped her ass in anticipation of what they were about to do. My mom was beautiful; she had long dark brown hair, bright blue eyes, and thanks to her plastic surgeon, she had a stunning face and body, but that beauty was only skin deep. I think Corbin knew that as well, but he didn't care about her heart and what was inside it. He just wanted what was between her thighs. It was all any of the men she played with wanted, and she was more than willing to give it up if it made her their focus for a while.

I sat at the now vacant dining table with my cereal, and I had just finished it when my dad suddenly stormed into the room. He looked angry, and when his cool, grey eyes landed on me, I could have sworn I saw them twist in rage. My heart stopped, and fear wrapped around me like a blanket. I knew he was going to beat on me … I knew it in my heart.

"I didn't do anything," I said as I jumped to my feet and tried to run out of the room, but he was bigger and faster than me. He caught me by my hair and slammed me to the ground. I couldn't cry out or make any sound other than a groan of pain. It was like a scream was clogged in my throat and couldn't escape.

"Dad," I rasped when I rolled onto my back. "What'd I do?"

"You're a faggot!"

I widened my eyes just as his boot made contact with my groin and blinding pain attacked my nerves. I cupped my crotch, curled up, and writhed silently in pain. I had never experienced a sensation so agonising as it consumed my body. I felt hot tears sting at the corners of my eyes before they fell in big, fat droplets. I couldn't move, the searing hot agony that spread outward from my groin seemed to paralyse my muscles.

"A security camera tagged you fucking one of the runners after a product drop."

He was circling me now, like a shark stalking its prey. I cried harder when he kicked the base of my spine. I had never been in so much physical pain in my life, but it was nothing compared to the hurt that spread throughout my heart. I knew my dad held no love for me or my brothers, but being on the receiving end of his cruelty hurt me in more ways than one.

"You're a fucking faggot!" Dad spat before he rounded on me and kicked my stomach. "Do you think you can fuck guys *within* the compound, and it wouldn't get back to me?"

I turned my head to the side and vomited at the contact.

"Dad," I choked. "Please—"

He leaned down on one knee next to me and raised his hand. A punch to my face cut me off, and this time, an audible cry escaped me.

"Oh, so now you're gonna fucking *cry*!" Dad cruelly taunted. "You can't take a whooping like a man, so you have to cry like the little bitch you are?"

I gritted my teeth and forced myself not to make a sound. I squeezed my eyes shut and willed my tears to go away. I refused to show him just how much he broke me down. I could never let him know just how badly his words cut me.

"I can take it."

Dad grunted a laugh and hit me again. That punch to the face sent me spiralling into darkness, and I welcomed it. I suddenly felt no more pain as numbness consumed me. Nothing had ever felt better ... until the agony returned. I felt hands on my shoulders, and when they shook me, pain shot up my spine, and caused me to groan.

"Alec?" I heard a sharp intake of breath. "Alec, who did this to you?"

I opened my eyes, and for a second, I jolted with fear because I thought my dad was still hovering over me, but when I focused my eyes, I realised it was Ryder. Fear, worry, and anger shone in his eyes. He turned his head and called for someone. I closed my eyes, and when I opened them next, Kane was in my face.

"Are you okay, Alec?"

I tried to smile to assure him I was okay, but a wince was all I could muster. I wasn't okay, my body was screaming that I wasn't, but for my brothers, especially my younger brothers, I had to hold it together.

"Alec," Ryder's voice repeated firmly. "Who did this to you?"

I lifted one eye, and said, "Dad."

Ryder's eyes flashed with anger.

"Don't ... don't go to him about it," I pleaded as fear filled me. "He'll just come back and beat me again for needing you to defend me."

"You're fifteen," Ryder scowled. "He shouldn't be hitting on you like this. Your entire face is swollen, and I think your ribs may be cracked."

The pain when I inhaled and exhaled told me my brother's theory was mostly correct.

"I'll be fine," I said through gritted teeth as the pain throbbed away. "Just get me to my room, and I'll be fine."

The next ten minutes involved me balling my hands into fists in an effort to cope with the pain as my brothers helped me get to my bedroom. When I finally lay down on my bed, tears were falling down my face. Before I could reach up and wipe them away, Kane did it for me, careful not to press too hard on my throbbing face. I felt my shoes being pulled off and then my T-shirt and jeans. I opened my eyes and realised that Ryder had cut my clothes from my body with scissors, so he could see the damage.

"I'll kill him."

Panic surged through me.

"No, don't," I begged. "Ry, you know going against him will

only make him hurt you and me. Please."

Ryder struggled to remain calm. I saw him flex his fingers before he balled his hands into fists. His body trembled, and I knew anger roared through him for what had happened to me.

"Tell me why he did this to you."

I closed my eyes. "I can't."

My words barely a whisper.

"Why, Alec?" Ryder and Kane said in unison.

"Because you'll hate me," I said, hating when tears stung my eyes. "You'll disown me."

"Alec," Ryder said, his face pale. "Nothing you could ever do would make us reject you. Do you hear me? You're our brother, and we love you."

More tears fell. They slid down my temples and blended into my hairline.

"I ... I got caught having sex on camera," I began, closing my eyes to give me the courage to voice what needed to be said. "With ... with a guy."

Things were silent but only for a moment.

"Okay," Ryder said tentatively. "What else happened for Dad to hurt you so bad?"

I opened my eyes. "That *was* the reason he attacked me."

Kane leaned forward. "Are you telling me Dad beat you bloody because you had sex with a guy? Are you *kidding* me?"

I shook my head and winced. Everywhere fucking hurt.

"Do you think I'm disgusting?"

Ryder and Kane shared a look, then looked back at me with raised brows.

"Because you like guys?" Kane asked. "Alec, I know lots of gay guys. Why would you think something so normal would be wrong?"

My heart slammed into my chest as warmth filled me.

"I ... I was scared you wouldn't think that."

"Being gay is on the same wavelength as being straight. It's not a problem."

I looked at Kane. "I'm not gay. I'm bisexual. I like both."

"I always knew you liked both genders," Ryder commented and surprised the hell out of me. "Your face is expressive when you're around people you're attracted to, little brother. I just waited until you wanted to tell us before I mentioned anything."

I felt my eyes widen. I had no idea Ryder knew I was bisexual. I looked back and forth between my brothers, and there was no anger or disgust in their eyes, just concern. They really didn't feel any type of way about me not being straight. They just accepted it and moved right along to the actual problem—me being hurt. I wanted to sob my heart out. All this time I had been so scared of them reacting like my dad did, and instead, they were supportive and understanding like I knew they would be deep down.

"You guys don't know how relieved I am," I said. "After what Dad did to me, I feared the worst."

Ryder set his jaw. "Forget about him, he's a piece of shit. I'm going to get the doctor to come and look at you."

When he left the room, I looked at Kane, and said, "Do I look as bad as I feel?"

He nodded. "Worse. You look uglier than usual."

When I laughed, I winced in pain, but at that moment I didn't care. My brothers knew me, the real me, and loved me all the same. I didn't need anyone as long as I had them. Ryder was right when he said, 'Fuck dad.' Everyone else who stood against us could get fucked too. We needed no one else. *I* needed no one else.

TRIGGER WARNING:

The following chapter contains details of *rape* and *attempted suicide*. Please skip chapter three of Alec's part in *BROTHERS* if you're are not comfortable with reading the subject matter.

CHAPTER THREE

Twenty-two years old ...

It was only a date. I could handle a simple fucking date.

I shook my head as I stared at myself in the full-length mirror in my bedroom. Tonight was my first night as Marco's hired out escort to a big client, and my stomach had been sick all day about it. I was a confident guy, I knew what I looked like, and I knew how easily I could make people laugh and smile when I wanted to. I rarely got nervous or had any self-doubt, but tonight, I was filled with both. It had been a year to the day since my parents died, and I still felt only relief to have them out of my life. I knew that was horrible of me, but that was just the way I felt. I hated my parents, and I was pretty sure that before they died, they hated me and my brothers too.

Their death hurt Damien, my youngest brother, the most, and like a ripple effect, their deaths caused the death of another at the hand of my little brother. Being an escort was all part of a deal my brothers struck. Marco didn't have to think twice about how he would make me pay off Damien's life debt; he knew from the jump what he wanted me to do, and I didn't give it much thought until now.

"Are you nervous?"

I jumped when Ryder spoke. I lifted my head, and through the mirror I saw that he was leaning against my doorway, his arms folded over his chest. I smiled for his sake because he suddenly looked a lot older than his twenty-five years, and I knew it was because of the deal we made with Marco. He was the head of our family now, officially at least. Ryder had always been the head of our family; our parents just never realised it.

"Nah," I said, uncaring. "I've been on dozens of dates before for Marco in the past year. I've got this."

Ryder didn't move a muscle.

"I'm fine," I pressed. "Don't worry about me."

He snorted. "Easier said than done. I always worry about you guys."

"Well, you don't have to. We have these jobs to protect Damien, and once we meet Marco's quota, we'll be free of him and this shitty life forever."

"That's what I keep telling myself." Ryder sighed.

He entered the room and came to my side, looking into the mirror with me.

"It's weird that we all look so much alike, but none of us are as pretty as you."

I grinned. "God didn't realise what he was doing by making me this sexy. I'm sure he made the four of you so ugly to balance out my beauty."

Ryder laughed and slugged me in the shoulder.

"Asshole."

I snickered as we left my bedroom and headed down the stairs to the foyer. I could hear the twins before I could see them as well as Kane snapping at them to stop fighting, and it made me snort.

"You're the daddy," I said to Ryder. "Go break them up."

He rolled his eyes, but his lips twitched as we entered the living room and found Kane between our twin brothers as they tried to fight one another. I moved to Dominic's side and hooked my arm around his neck. I knew he could break out of my hold if he wanted, but he'd have to hurt me to do that. He struggled a little but sighed loudly and gave up, which made me chuckle. I looked over at Damien and saw both Ryder and Kane had him while Ryder was in his face, talking harshly.

"What happened this time?" I asked Dominic as I released him. "And don't lie."

He brushed his arms and grunted. "That dickhead has been looking for a fight all day. He's been in my face every chance he gets, and it's pissing me the fuck off."

"Come do something about it then!" Damien hollered from the other side of the room.

I grabbed Dominic when he tried to grant his twin's request.

"Shut it!" Ryder snapped at Damien. "What the hell is your deal today?"

"This isn't just today," Dominic bellowed. "He's been like this since Mom and Dad died, since he killed Trent!"

Things were silent for a moment, then Damien shrugged out of our brothers' hold, storming out of the room and then the house.

"He's angry about all of this happening to us," Dominic said, his tone defeated. "He won't say it, but I feel it whenever he looks at me. He wants me to hit him because beating himself up isn't enough."

Ryder placed his hands on his hips, then turned and wordlessly followed Damien out of the house.

"Dominic," Kane said, gaining his attention. "Come and train with me. It'll make you feel better."

It would make him feel better, but Kane had used every free moment he had to help Dominic train. His job was no joke, and he had to be on point constantly or he could be physically hurt. He was only fifteen, so he had to take everything regarding his fighting technique seriously, and Kane knew that, which was why he was the one to help him perfect it.

Dominic looked at me with a raised brow, so I said, "I've got a date. Go with him."

He nodded and left the room with Kane. I looked up at the ceiling and sighed. We were only a year into these damn jobs and already they were putting a huge strain on us. I looked at the doorway when a throat was cleared and found Jenner, one of Marco's men, in the doorway.

"I'm to bring you to the pleasure room."

I pulled a face. "Why?"

"That's where your date is." Jenner shrugged. "It's just a location, nothing more."

I gathered my bearings and nodded. I left the wing of the compound that housed my family, crossed the courtyard, and descended the stairs with Jenner that led to the underground pleasure room. It was where parties were held, ones that ended in an orgy in one way or the other. The journey to the room was quick, and Jenner filled me in on the man who paid for my company this evening. When I entered the room and saw a stout, balding man leaning against the wall across the room with a drinking glass in his hand, I put my game face on.

"Hello," I said, forcing a smile. "I'm Alec ... I'm going to be your dat—"

"Plaything," the man cut me off. "You're going to be my plaything this evening."

My steps sauntered as I crossed the room, and my smile fell.

"I'm sorry?"

"Come in." The man waved. "I only have thirty minutes with you, and I intend to make every single one of them count."

The door behind me suddenly closed, and the sound of its finality made me feel somewhat caged. I turned from the door and looked at the stout man.

"Sir," I said, unsure of myself. "I was informed we were going on a date."

"Well, you were informed wrong."

I froze.

"I've already paid my half for my time with you, so hurry up and get over here."

I turned, and without a word, I walked towards the door but was horrified to find it locked. I yanked on the handle, and when it became apparent the door was locked, I felt sick.

"Get on with it, Alec," Jenner's voice hollered from outside. "Marco's already been paid. He told me to remind me of your family's deal with him in case you want to leave."

Damien.

I thumped on the door. "I was told it was a *date*, Jen!"

"Look." Jenner sighed. "The quicker you fuck the creep, the quicker you can leave."

Fuck him?

"I'm not fucking *anyone*, Jenner!"

Laughter flowed from behind me. "You're right. You won't be."

I spun around and found a second man, taller than the stout man, but fatter and uglier.

"Who the fuck are *you*?"

"I went half with him," he jabbed his finger at the stout man, "to avail of your services."

To avail of my services?

"There has to be some mistake," I said as politely as I could. "I'm not ... I'm not a prostitute."

"Right now, you are."

I stared at the stout man, and sickness swirled within me.

"What's your name?"

"Carl," the stout man replied as he jammed his thumb at the other man, and said, "This is Lewis."

When they looked at me expectantly, I felt tears burn at the back of my eyes. They ... they both expected me to give my body to them, and so did Marco, it seemed. I was about to turn and demand Jenner let me out of the room, but Damien's face flashed across my mind, and I knew I couldn't leave here without him being hurt in some way.

I ... I had to do what these men wanted. I watched as they began to strip out of the crisp suits they wore, and my stomach roiled when

I saw their erections. I damn near pissed myself when Lewis retrieved a whip of some sort from a bag on the floor. I jumped when he cracked it.

"Strip," he ordered. "Get on the foot of the bed, turn your back to us, sit back on your heels, and place your hands on your thighs."

Robotically, I did as asked, and when I was in position, I had never felt more vulnerable in my life.

Don't cry.

"Please," I whispered, my hands trembling on my thighs. "Please don't make me do this. I ... I'm begging you."

Lewis cracked his whip inches away from me, and the sound was so loud, it drew a genuine gasp from me. My reaction caused the man to moan in ... satisfaction. I jerked my gaze over my shoulder and found him standing a few yards away from me with one hand on his whip. And the other stroking his cock. I stared between his thighs, his oddly shaped cock had hardened enough to the point where I could see it visibly throb.

I turned my gaze back to the mattress, and tears stung at my eyes. Something inside me broke at that moment. I realised that my pleading and my begging was turning him on and only adding fuel to the fire that burned within him. These men ... they were going to hurt me in a way I didn't think I'd ever recover from ... and to protect my little brother, I had to let them.

The whip was cracked again, and the sound was, once more, deafening.

"On your hands and knees with them spread apart as wide as you can so I can see your asshole without touching you."

My stomach churned as Carl spoke, and in fear of throwing up, I didn't speak, I only acted. I followed his orders, ignoring a single tear as it slid down my cheek. My body was shaking with fear, and it tensed of its own accord when the man placed his hand on my behind. Each second was agony as I waited, dreaded, to see what he would do next.

When I felt his wet finger touch me, and rub whatever liquid coated his skin, over me, my heart dropped. I knew what he was preparing for, and it killed me.

"Please," I whispered one last time. "Don't do this."

I didn't know what the man was doing because I was too afraid to look over my shoulder to find out, but when I heard him moan, I knew it didn't bode well for me.

"Leave me alone," I choked. "Please."

"Beg us not to, pretty boy," he rasped around another groan as the mattress under me dipped. "Beg us."

A second later, he took a piece of me that I knew I would never be able to get back. I thought of stand-up comedy through the burning pain in my behind. I squeezed my eyes shut and thought joy and laughter instead of the large, sweaty man who was touching me, hurting me. I thought of my favourite films, and music when a hot hand wrapped around my soft penis and squeezed it to the point of excruciating pain. I pretended I was kicking back and shooting the shit with my brothers instead of focusing on the tongue that licked my bare back, and the teeth that bit into my trembling flesh. I thought of everything that ever brought a smile to my face, and when it was over, I prayed to God that I would forget this day and everything attached to it, but I knew I would never forget.

This was a scar no one else but me would be able to see. This was a shame no one else but me could carry. This was a nightmare I knew I would never be able to awaken from. This was the end of my life as I knew it, and the start of a new existence I never wanted.

When I left the room, I was fully clothed, but I still felt naked. Jenner was leaning against the wall outside the room and looked up when he heard me. He shook his head as he looked me up and down, and said, "I'd never love my brother enough to let creeps fuck me."

I didn't reply to him, and he said nothing further. It was dark when I made it back up to the courtyard. I had been in that room for hours, a lot longer than I was told the date would be, and wasn't sure what time it was. I only knew it was late. I was entirely numb as I walked to our family's wing of the compound, and when I entered my home, I was glad to see everything was in darkness and silent. I stood in the entryway for a few seconds before I realised I was crying. I wiped my face and walked up the stairs, heading down the hallway to my bedroom. I didn't look at any of my brothers' rooms as I passed them by. I didn't want to think of them right now.

When I was inside my bedroom, I closed the door behind me and stood still for a minute or two. I reached up to my neck and touched my rosary beads, but for the first time in my life they didn't make me feel better. I pulled them off of my neck, and wrapped them around my hand before hurling them across the room, ridding myself of them.

With tears streaming down my cheeks, I stared at the rope I stole from Dominic's room weeks before. I knew he planned to hang a damn clown from my ceiling to get back at me for stealing a girl he wanted to fuck. Before I could think better of it, I picked it up and threw it over the wooden beams that zigzagged across the ceiling. I tied a knot with the ends and pulled on it as hard as I could. The wood creaked a tiny bit, but other than that, it was solid.

I knew it would support my weight without breaking.

I realised then what I was going to do, and before I could think better of it, I pulled over the chair from my desk, stood on it, put the rope around my neck, and kicked the chair away. Pain and pressure were all I felt, but I could still hear the men's laughter, see their faces, and feel their hands on me. I wanted it all to go away. I wanted everything to go dark and silent.

Black dots spotted my vision, and I couldn't hear anything other than the strangled sounds I made. I thought I saw Damien's white hair and that I could hear his voice, and then suddenly, I was on the floor, and he was over me. I couldn't focus on anything other than sucking in huge gulps of air. When I turned my wild eyes onto Damien, I found that he was crying, shaking, and looked both terrified and relieved at the same time. I tried to say his name, but it hurt. The pain around my neck was immense, and it struck me at that moment what just happened. I had hanged myself, attempted to take my own life, and my baby brother somehow cut me down.

"Alec," he sobbed. "I have to get Ryder."

I panicked and latched onto him, shaking my head.

"No," I rasped. "Please."

The pain when I spoke was unbelievable. My voice was little more than a husky whisper, but I could hear my desperation in my words, so I knew Damien could too.

"Why?" he choked. "Why did you do this? God, I was about to go back to bed instead of coming in to check on you. I heard you cry downstairs while I was in the kitchen getting some snacks. I almost didn't save you in time."

I swallowed, and my entire body jolted as agony tore across my throat.

"Two men," I choked. "They raped me, and I had to let them do it. I had to."

"What?" Damien asked, horror in his tone. "Alec, what?"

"I don't want to be here anymore." I looked at him. "I want to die."

"No," Damien said, his grip on my arm tightening. "I'm not going to let you!"

I did something I have never done in front of him. I cried, and he cried with me as he pulled me onto his legs. He sat on the floor, holding me like a baby, and neither of us cared. He rocked us from side to side and told me how much he loved me and how everything would be okay.

"Is that the date Marco set you up on?"

I jerked my head in a nod, and he was silent for a long while.

"Alec," he sniffled. "You're not going to let those fucking monsters ruin you."

"They've already ruined me," I choked. "I'm not ... I'm not me anymore."

"You're a better you because you're stronger than your hurt," Damien replied. "Look at me."

I did.

"You're still my brother, and the fucking nicest dude I know. That has not changed and will never change."

I didn't understand how he could think that, but I saw in his eyes that he believed it, and that made me break down completely.

"You can't tell the others," I pleaded, ignoring the pain in my throat. "Ryder will blame himself, and Dominic and Kane will want revenge, and they could get hurt. We can't let that happen."

I could see Damien was torn about what to do.

"Damien, please. I ... I don't want them to know."

It took a few minutes, but he eventually nodded, and my body practically deflated with relief.

"Does it hurt?" he asked, looking at my neck.

I nodded. "I'll see the doctor tomorrow."

"The others will see your neck and know something happened, and your voice ... it's not the same, man."

"We'll pretend I'm sick or something. I can stay in bed until my voice is back to normal, and I'll just cover up my neck until everything is healed."

"Ryder will notice. He notices everything."

"I'll have the doctor say I have a bad dose of the flu and it'll take me a couple of weeks to be back on my feet."

My brother nodded then carefully pulled me to my feet, then helped me into my bed. I didn't bother removing my clothing. I just sat and watched Damien discard the rope I used to try to take my life. I couldn't wrap my head around what just happened. Deciding to take my life was a split-second decision. I never thought someone could decide on something so devastating so quickly, but I was wrong. I was surprised when Damien crawled into my bed next to me.

"You ... you're going to stay with me?"

"Yeah, bro," Damien answered. "I love you. I'm not letting you go through this on your own."

I cried again, and I worried I would never stop. I felt broken, no longer like myself, and I knew Damien could sense it.

"I'm so sorry."

"For what?" I asked as I lay down and closed my eyes.

"For everything," Damien answered as I slowly fell into darkness. "I'm sorry that you and the others are hurting because of me … It's all because of me."

"It's because of Marco," I replied. "None of this is your fault."

Marco … he was responsible for everything. Had I successfully taken my own life tonight, it would have been because of what he gave others permission to do to me. Everything, in one way or the other, came down to it being his fault. I hated him. I hated him with every ounce of energy I had, and it still didn't feel like enough. He turned me into a toy for people to play with, a toy that sick bastards used and abused all because he wanted their money.

I was hurting, and I thought that I would always hurt in some shape or form because of what had happened to me, but I'd be damned if I'd let Marco take my mind and heart from me when he already had control of my life. I didn't care what he threw my way. I'd take it on the chin and keep moving forward. I reminded myself that working for him wouldn't last forever, and I swore that when that time was up, I'd get my revenge on him.

When I had the chance … I'd kill the bastard.

CHAPTER FOUR

Twenty-eight years old ...

"I feel lower than low," I said to Kane as I stared down at Branna's friend sitting on the kerb of the parking lot and groaning as she held her face. "She was jumped because of me."

Inside the Playhouse nightclub celebrating Bronagh's twenty-first birthday, we had been having a decent night ... apart from Bronagh accidentally getting involved in a cage fight, of course. That aside, things were moving along just fine ... until a woman I'd previously hooked up got mad it wasn't going to be repeated, and she took it out on Aideen, who just happened to be the woman sat next to me.

Kane rolled his eyes. "You can control what other people choose to do now, huh?"

"Don't be a smartass," I scowled. "You know what I mean; that chick jumped her because of *me*."

"She's fine," Kane said, glancing down at Aideen. "Her friend will be here soon, and she'll be home and tucked in bed before she knows it."

I sighed. "This Keela chick sounds pissed. She damn near shouted my ear off when I called her."

I had been amused with her attitude when I was on the phone with her, but the longer I thought about it, the more I wondered if she would follow through with her threat to kick my ass when she got here.

"I wanna go home." I sighed. "I don't even wanna hook up tonight. I just wanna sleep."

"Looks like we'll be able to leave sooner than you think."

I looked at my brother. "What do you mean?"

"Here comes her friend."

"How do you—"

"Aideen!"

I turned my attention to the heart-stopping siren that ran towards us at full speed. I raised my brows as my eyes scanned over her banging body. Her hair was the colour of a sunset, her skin as fair as snow, and her legs ... Christ above, they were long and looked soft to the touch. My cock hardened with one glance of her, and instantly, I changed my mind about wanting to go home to sleep. I still wanted to go home, but I wanted this woman to come with me, and sleep would be the *last* thing on my mind. She had the tiniest dress on that I had ever seen. The material looked threadbare, and I itched to rip it off her.

Once she was close enough to do so, she dropped down to her knees and pulled Aideen into a fierce hug. I winced on her behalf when I noticed the redness of her bare knees as they pressed against the cold, concrete ground. She either didn't seem to notice or she ignored the pain I was sure she had to be feeling.

"Are ye' okay?" she asked Aideen, pulling back from their hug so she could examine her. "What happened?"

When she pushed Aideen's hair from her face, Keela gasped. I cringed, knowing what she saw. Aideen had a small cut over her eyebrow, and the right side of her jaw was swollen.

"Some bitch jumped me."

"Who?" Keela snapped. "I'll fuckin' deck 'er!"

That drew a smile from me. She was an itty-bitty thing, and I couldn't imagine her hurting anyone in a fight, but she sounded confident in herself. Or maybe that was just her anger on her friend's behalf shining through.

Aideen pulled Keela in for another hug. "I know ye' would, but I just wanna go home now. Can I stay with ye' tonight?"

"Of course, ye' bloody eejit."

Kane and I chuckled, and this seemed to draw Keela's attention. She looked up at us, as if just remembering we were there. Her eyes flicked between us, and then widened to saucers. My lips twitched. I knew what we looked like, and I had no doubt this woman felt intimidated ... until she glared at us.

Keela helped a slightly tipsy Aideen to her feet and hooked her arm around her friend's waist, steadying her just in case she fell.

"This is Alec," Aideen said, but I was too busy roaming my eyes over Keela's body, "and Kane."

I flicked my eyes up to her face and watched Keela swallow as her eyes landed on Kane. She stared at him, *really* stared at him, and I watched as her hold on Aideen tightened. I understood that reaction, and I was sure that my brother did too. All of his scars made eye contact difficult, and it was easy to be afraid of him based on his looks alone.

"Hi," she managed to say.

Kane didn't respond.

"Kane came to me rescue when Alec's girlfriend hit me," Aideen purred at Kane, who smiled right back at her.

"She was my lay from last week, *not* my girlfriend," I said with a grunt. "I also apologised for her actions."

Things seemed to slow down for a moment as Keela let what her friend said process in her mind. I watched as a spark ignited in her beautiful eyes, then a fire blazed. She released her hold on Aideen and all but rushed me. She placed her hands on my chest and shoved me as hard as she could. She caught me completely off guard, so when she pushed me, I lost my balance and fell back onto my ass with a grunt.

"*That* is for your bird hurtin' me friend, and if I find out who the bitch is, I'm gonna do hard time for 'er!"

Aideen pulled Keela back to her side while I looked up at Keela with wide eyes. I looked at my brother, who stared down at me with his mouth agape. A few silent seconds passed until we both burst out laughing like what just happened was the funniest thing ever.

"I told you, bro. She's a fucking hellcat!" I cackled as I gripped Kane's outstretched hand and was helped to my feet. "I can't *believe* this shit."

Kane shook his head, thoroughly amused.

"I wish the twins had seen that!"

Keela wasn't amused by our laughing, not in the slightest.

"Keep laughin', pretty boy, and I'll scratch up that face of yours!"

I stepped forward, a huge grin tugging at the corner of my mouth. "I'm finding myself highly attracted to you right now. Would you like to come home with me since you're already dressed for bed?"

Keela's jaw dropped in shock while Aideen drilled holes into my head with her death glare.

"Give over, Alec! I appreciate ye' both helpin' me, but I won't have ye' treatin' me friend like she is one of your old clients. She is a good girl."

I inwardly flinched at her mentioning my escorting days. It still grated on my nerves that Branna had shared that information with her, but there wasn't much I could do about it. I didn't want that to be the focus on the conversation, so I focused on Keela.

"Oh, I'm betting there's a bad girl deep inside her somewhere. I'll just have to use my fingers, mouth, and cock to bring her out to play."

Keela's lips parted with what I thought was surprise.

"Who the *hell* d'ye think ye' are, mister?"

I grinned. "Alec Slater, your next—or only—great fuck."

She scowled at me, a cute wrinkle creasing her forehead.

"You're about to be Alec Slater—murder victim—if ye' don't shut your filthy mouth!"

Kane cracked up with laughter as he reached for Aideen's arm and pulled her to his side and away from Keela.

"Please, don't interfere," he almost begged the woman. "I've never seen a female, besides Bronagh, backtalk him like this before."

That was true. Bronagh got a kick out of going toe to toe with me. I was staring at Keela, so I saw the moment she noticed that Aideen and Kane were getting pretty comfortable with each other, and she didn't appear to like it.

Her eyes flicked back to mine as I took a step towards her. "Take another step and ye' won't ever be able to have kids. I'm warnin' ye', buddy."

I folded my arms across my chest, thoroughly amused at the turn in events. This woman had a backbone, and even though she spoke with venom and tried to be tough, I could tell she was acting this way because she was unsure of myself and my brother, and her attitude was her go to defence.

"I'd appreciate it if ye' would stop lookin' at me."

I looked from her body to her chest.

"Why would you come outside dressed like *that* if you didn't want people to look at you?"

I was being a dick, and I was fully aware of it, but when she was irritated, she reacted with fire, and I liked that a lot.

"I came outside dressed in me nightdress because me friend needed me. Gettin' dressed didn't cross me mind when ye' rang me to tell me she was hurt, ye' eejit."

I had been called that word a million times since I moved to this country.

"You sound like my bro's girl. She calls me an eejit a lot, too."

"She must be kind 'cause there are a lot of words that would suit ye' much better. Batty boy would be two of them," she quipped, then turned in Aideen's direction and found her *kissing* Kane. Keela walked forward, took hold of Aideen's arm, and tugged her not so gently next to her side.

She not so quietly muttered, "D'ye not remember the stranger danger film we watched when we were in school?"

Aideen sighed. "They aren't dangerous. Kane *saved* me from danger."

Keela jabbed her thumb over her shoulder. "Yeah, and his bird *put* ye' in danger, so let's go, Ado"

"Ado?" Kane's voice purred from my left. "I like that nickname."

"Listen," Keela said directly to Kane, "thanks for helpin' me friend after she got hurt, but she isn't goin' to thank ye' with some personal pole dancin', so give the flirtin' a rest. Please. It's too late for this kind of carry on."

Kane raised his eyebrows as he looked at Aideen, and asked, "You're a stripper?"

"No, I am a *teacher*," she answered a little too quickly. "No pole dancin' means no shaggin'."

Kane blinked. "Your friend is *banning* you from having sex with me?"

"Yes," Aideen and Keela said in unison.

That intrigued me.

"And you're going along with it?" I asked Aideen as I rounded the women and leaned back against our car.

"Yeah," Aideen grumbled. "She is pretty big on no sex with strangers, and ... so am I."

Kane's eyes bore into Aideen's as he said, "Pity."

"Uh-huh," she agreed with a sad sigh. "Such a pity."

Keela nudged her friend, and said, "I'll give ye' some new batteries for your vibrator to get ye' through the night. Ye'll be grand."

"Keela!"

Kane and I laughed.

Keela looked between us, then at Aideen, she said, "Maybe they could apply to Perverts 'R Us. They fit the bill with those stares."

Aideen giggled.

"Excuse me?" I said, confused.

Aideen was grinning as she said, "Keela's neighbour, Mr. Doyle, is a man who stares a lot, so she named 'im Mr. Pervert and imagined 'im bein' the CEO of a company called Perverts 'R Us."

Clever.

"We're leavin'," Keela said to Aideen when she shivered. "I have to go home to Storm."

Who the fuck is Storm?

"Storm?" I quizzed.

"Storm is 'er—"

"Boyfriend." Keela cut Aideen off and gave her a pointed look.

"Storm is pretty protective of 'er," Aideen said, bobbing her head up and down. "Like, *crazy* protective."

Bullshit.

"If he is so protective, then why did he let you come out here alone while dressed like *that*?"

"Storm is very hard to rouse durin' the night," Aideen explained. "He probably didn't even hear 'er leave, but he is still a great ... lad."

"Yeah, he is great," Keela said with a nod, "and he will kick your arse for how rude you're bein' to me."

I leaned to the right, locked my eyes on hers, and said, "I'm a lover, not a fighter."

"Ye' better back off then because I'm tired of your shite."

I bit down on my bottom lip, trying my best not to laugh. She was like a little puppy who thought she was a big scary dog. She had more bark than bite, and I think she knew it. She seemed to know that she amused me greatly, so she scowled at me to show her displeasure, which caused Kane to shake his head. I glanced his way and saw his eyes were lit up with amusement.

"Can we keep her?" he teased. "I like hearing someone put you in your place. The fact that she is a woman is even better. You don't affect her, bro. You're losing your touch."

"We just met," I mused. "Don't shoot me down so quickly, Kane."

"This has been ... interestin'," Aideen said, breaking the sudden tension. "However, Keela is right. We really have to get goin'."

Keela audibly thanked God and blessed herself.

Kane tilted his head to the side as he gazed at Aideen. "I guess I'll see you around, Ado."

"Ye' have to be family or a friend to use 'er nickname."

Kane flicked his eyes to Keela, and after a few seconds of sizing her up, he said, "I like you."

I looked at him, surprised. My brother didn't like anyone. Accepting Bronagh and Branna had been a big deal for him, so for him to say he liked Keela told me that her standing up to us when she was obviously wary of us impressed him. That, in turn, impressed me too.

"Well, I'm afraid I don't like you or your pervy friend—"

"Brother." I cut her off. "I'm his pervy *brother*."

"I don't like you or your pervy *brother*." She continued speaking to Kane as if I hadn't interrupted her. "You're nothin' but trouble. The people ye' pal around with attack women for no reason. You're both very rude, and I don't like bein' in your company. Good night to ye' both."

She turned, grabbed hold of Aideen's hand, and took off walking away from us in the direction of her car.

"What? No goodbye kiss?" I shouted, watching her legs as she walked away. "*Now* who is being rude!"

"I said good night!"

"I'll make the end of your night *very* good, kitten, if you give me the chance."

Aideen laughed as she and Keela got into her car. I stared after the car as it pulled out of the lot and drove off, feeling my heart pound against my chest. That encounter hadn't been long enough for me to have my fill of Keela's body. I knew it'd be a wonderland, and I had a need for her that I hadn't had for anyone in ... ever.

"I want her *so* fucking bad."

Kane chuckled as he clapped his hand on my shoulder. "You say that about anyone who makes your cock stiff."

"Nah." I shook my head. "She's different. I can tell."

"She doesn't seem to like you very much, Alec."

I smiled as I looked at my younger brother.

"Exactly. It'll make the chase all the more interesting if she's repulsed by me."

Kane laughed as he walked towards our car, shaking his head at me. I followed him with a spring to my step and a big ass smile on my face, and it was all because of one fiery Irish redhead. I knew I'd run into her again, and I had never looked forward to seeing someone who loathed me so much in my life. A game had started between us, whether she knew it or not, and little did she know that when I played a game, I *always* played for keeps.

CHAPTER FIVE

Twenty-eight years old ...

"What's the face for?"

I looked up from eating my breakfast, and when I realised Dominic was speaking to me, I raised my eyebrows.

"What face?"

"*That* face." He chuckled. "You look like you've eaten something sour."

I shrugged my shoulders but didn't answer.

"He still feels bad over Branna's friend getting jumped last night."

I turned my head and scowled at Kane, who shrugged, unbothered.

"You don't need to feel bad," Ryder said from the refrigerator as he searched for something to eat. "You can't control what other people do."

"I guess." I sighed. "I just hope she's okay. She has to be sore today."

"Branna called her this morning, and she's okay. Banged up, but okay."

That didn't make me feel better.

"How are *you* this morning?" Kane asked, his lips twitched. "You got beat up last night, too."

Dominic and Ryder's attention snapped my way.

"Who beat you up?" Dominic demanded. "Tell me."

Before I could say a word, Kane said, "A little redhead named Keela."

My brothers shared a looked, relaxed, then laughed.

"She didn't beat me up." I rolled my eyes. "She shoved me because she was angry her friend got jumped. She blamed me because she thought it was my girlfriend who was at fault."

"Doesn't sound like she beat him up," Dominic looked at Kane, grinning. "What else happened?"

I shook my head and continued to eat my cereal.

"She knocked his ass to the ground when she shoved him." Kane chuckled. "And she surpassed Bronagh when she chewed him out as well."

"No way," Dominic said, his lips parted with surprise.

"Yup." Kane bobbed his head. "She insulted him and turned him down multiple times when he hit on her."

"Well, fuck." Ryder laughed. "I want to meet this woman."

Ha, ha, ha.

"You're all fucking hilarious today."

They all laughed and continued to rag on me when the doorbell rang. Ryder went to answer it, leaving me with the two youngest who were talking utter shit. I nodded to them, accepting whatever shit they threw my way, but I stopped when Ryder suddenly shouted, "Alec, a woman is here to see you!"

My eyes widened as I looked at my brothers. They each shrugged as I got to my feet, left the kitchen, and crept down the hallway towards the front door. I kept out of view and to my brother, I whispered, "If she has blonde hair, a mole on her left cheek, and huge tits, close the door right fucking now."

I fucked a woman with that description a few weeks ago, and I guess I fucked her a little too well because she swore she'd find me and make me give her babies. She scared the shit out of me, and I was about to piss myself if she was the woman talking to my brother.

"I don't have blonde hair, a mole on me cheek, or big tits, so it's safe to come out!"

I raised my eyebrows in surprise. I knew that voice, that voice had been the cause of at least six erections since I last heard it the night before. I straightened to my full height and walked to the doorway to stand next to my brother. My eyes landed on Aideen first, and she wiggled her fingers at me in greeting. She looked much fresher, and apart from her black eyes and slight bruise on her jaw, she looked untouched. I grinned at her, then moved my eyes to the little rocket beside her.

My cock jumped in my shorts at the sight of her.

I watched as Keela's eyes raked over my body. I glanced down at myself, aware that I was wearing just shorts that hung low on my hips. I flicked my eyes back up to Keela, and I saw her swallow. In my head, I was doing the fucking cha-cha because I saw that she was attracted to me—or at least to my body—and I knew I already had one foot in the door with her.

"*Keela?*" I said, the shock in my tone not going amiss.

"The Keela who put you on your ass last night?" Ryder murmured to me. "*That* Keela?"

"Yeah, *that* Keela," Aideen answered merrily. "Don't worry, she is calm and won't hurt Alec again. I promise."

Keela bristled and shot her friend a glare, but Aideen paid her no attention. She then turned her attention back to me, took a deep breath, and said, "Can I speak to ye'?"

My eyes dropped to her attire. She had on a cute blue dress that hung just above her knees. It hugged her breasts wonderfully, and even though they weren't big, the swell of them against the fabric of her outfit made my mouth water. My damn knees nearly buckled when my eyes locked on her legs. She had great fucking legs, and I found myself wanting to run my tongue over them.

"Eyes on me face, buddy—me *face*."

Whoops.

I looked up at her face and grinned lazily. "And what a pretty face it is."

"That was pathetic."

Ryder blinked at her, and then to me, he said, "Kane was right. She isn't affected by you. That's a first."

"All in good time, bro." I chuckled.

"I can hear ye' both talkin'. Ye' know that, right?"

I bobbed my head, not really caring that she could hear me.

"Are you goin' to leave two lovely ladies standin' outside on your porch, or are ye' goin' to invite us in?"

Ryder quickly nodded. "Right, sorry, come on in. Branna shouldn't be too long, so you can hang with me and my brothers while Alec and Keela ... talk."

Aideen was happy with that response and headed into the house with Ryder hot on her heels. Keela looked like she wanted to follow her friend but thought better of it and remained in front of me. She looked nervous then, and that amused me.

"You're the *last* person I expected to see today, kitten," I admitted. "How did you know where I lived?"

"Branna told Aideen, and Aideen told me."

Now that Aideen wasn't beside her, she wouldn't look at me when she spoke. In fact, she wouldn't even look in my general direction. I didn't like that, so I reached out, tucked my finger under her chin, and gently turned her head until she was looking up at me.

"Why won't you look at me?"

"Because."

I smiled and dropped my hand. "Because?"

She swallowed. Twice.

"Just because."

"Okay, I'll go along with this," I mused and folded my arms across my chest. "To what do I owe this unannounced pleasure, Miss ...?"

Keela cleared her throat, and said, "Daley."

Keela Daley.

"Miss *Daley.*" I bowed my head, teasing her.

When I straightened, she wasted no time, and blurted, "I need to ask ye' somethin'."

"Okay." I blinked. "But look at me when you do it."

She shifted from foot to foot.

"Look," she began, "it's hard enough to swallow me pride and ask a stranger this question, a stranger who I had an argument with less than twelve hours ago."

She was wound up tighter than a clock, and I decided to tease her to help her relax a little.

I regarded her. "You physically assaulted me less than twelve hours ago as well."

Annoyed, she clipped, "Are ye' tryin' to start an argument, sir?"

I scratched my chin. "You aren't shy when you're frustrated. I'm helping you relax."

She leaned back. "I'm not shy at all."

"Then ask the question you came here to ask me."

She glanced at her surroundings, and said, "Can we not do this *inside*?"

She didn't have to ask me twice. I was more than happy to get her inside my house. I wasn't about to make things easy for her though, so I turned to the side and gestured her in with my hand. She was hesitant for a moment, then turned to her side so she could slide past me. While she carefully shimmied by me, I watched as her eyes locked on my pecs. Her mouth was even height with them, and I could just about feel her breath roll over my skin. She looked up at me, her eyes doe like.

"Hi." I smiled.

For a moment, she stared at my mouth, or more so my cheeks, and I knew she just realised that I had dimples. She was *so* into me. Her behaviour was textbook, though I was sure she had no clue how obvious she was being.

She licked her lower lip, and said, "Hey."

She amused the hell out of me. One minute, she was a boss bitch, and the next, she was a timid kitten who couldn't look me in the eye. She had no problem raking her eyes over my body, though. Once I closed the front door, she visually assessed me, and I didn't interrupt her.

"We can talk here or in my bedroom," I said after a few moments of lingering silence. "Which do you prefer?"

"Right here," she answered in a rushed breath. "Right 'ere is fine, thank you."

She was nervous now. Or more nervous than before.

"I need help with somethin'," she said nonchalantly, "and Aideen told me that you are *more* than qualified to help me with it."

That made me pause, but I tried not to show any reaction to what she said.

"Clarify 'it'."

A tinge of redness flared on her cheeks, and Keela tried to cover them with her hands in an attempt to identify it, but it was futile.

"God." She exhaled. "This is so bloody embarrassin'."

I was patiently waiting for her to get the courage to say whatever it was that she came here to say.

"She told me that you're an escort."

Well, fuck.

"I'm retired," I said after a few moments. "Sorry."

Keela lowered her hands from her face and gnawed on her lower lip.

"Oh," she said. "So ye' can't help me then?"

I wanted to help her. I wanted to do a lot of things *to* her, but anything that involved me being an escort was off the table.

"No, I can't. I don't deal in that business anymore. You will have to find another guy."

I watched her face fall, and I'd be damned if I didn't feel sorry for her at that moment.

"But I don't want your, um, *regular* services. Ye' don't have to do anythin' sexual or anythin' like that, I promise. I just need ... you."

I felt my entire body tense.

"Sexual?" I repeated. "I was an escort, Keela, not a prostitute."

She blinked. "Are they not the same thing?"

Anger rolled through me, but it quickly evaporated when I saw confusion in Keela's eyes, not judgment.

"I'm s-sorry," she stammered. "I didn't mean to offend ye'. I just don't know the difference. I thought escorts—"

"You thought escorts were paid money to fuck people, right?"

I didn't mean to sound so annoyed, but I couldn't help it.

"Um, well, yes, I did."

I shook my head. "Escorts provide companionship to a person. Sex is optional but *not* the baseline. Prostitutes are paid for sex and only sex; that *is* the baseline."

Her cheeks flared with colour once more.

"I apologise for bein' naive."

I shrugged, uncaring. "It's okay, but I still can't help you. I'm not in that business anymore."

She was sad with my response. I saw it in her eyes.

"I understand," she said, lifting her chin. "Sorry again for offendin' ye'. I didn't mean to pass judgment. I know I probably came off as a bitch last night, but I am a nice person, and I wouldn't purposely try to hurt your feelin's. I'm not like that. I'm very sorry."

And just like that, she broke my damn heart.

"Damn, kitten, don't get upset." She chomped down on her lower lip, and the sight was arousing. "Stop biting your lip; otherwise, *I'm* going to bite it."

She released her lip on a gasped breath. I scrubbed my face with my hands, feeling irritated with myself because I was considering helping this woman even though I swore to God, and myself, my escorting days were done with. Something about this woman made me want to help her, and not because she was hot. There was a vulnerability in her eyes, and it made me feel protective of her.

"I'll go and get Aideen so we can leave—"

"Out of curiosity," I cut her off. "What did you want an escort for?"

She cringed. "I'd rather not say; it's embarrassin'."

My heart stopped when a thought entered my mind. "You didn't want me to take your virginity, did you?"

Her eyes widened dramatically, and I knew that I had it completely wrong.

"*What*? No, that is *not* what I came 'ere for!" she stated, her entire face turning crimson. "First, your brother thinks I am pregnant by you, and now ye' think I am virgin? I'm *not* pregnant, and I'm *not* a virgin!"

Ryder thought she looked fucking pregnant?

She didn't wait for a response from me. Instead, she hollered, "Aideen! Move it, we're leavin'!"

She turned away from me and made for the front door. I wasn't sure when I moved, but I was at her back in an instant. I slipped my arms around her waist and brought her to a halt. "Now, wait just a second, kitten. I jumped to conclusions, but so did you. Give me a break here. I'm not being a dick. I'm just trying to understand why *you* would need an escort."

I felt her relax against me, but she tensed again when muffled voices and noises came from the gym to our right. Without a word, Keela stepped out of my hold, walked to the double doors, and opened them. It happened like the snap of my fingers. One second, Keela was standing upright, and the next, she was under three of my fat ass brothers.

"Can't breathe," I heard her wheeze.

I just about had a stroke thinking she might be seriously hurt.

"Get off her!" I snapped, shoving at my brothers. "Now!"

Choruses of the word, "Sorry," were shouted as they rolled off her. I lifted her to her feet and scanned my eyes over her looking for an injury, relaxing when I saw she was okay.

"That hurt," she groaned as she rubbed her hand over her chest. "Jesus."

"Do you think something might be broken?" I asked as I placed my hands on her shoulders. "Does everything feel okay?"

"I'm fine." She nodded. "I just couldn't breathe for a second, and it burned."

Without looking away from her, I said, "You almost smothered a woman."

"Sorry," they said in unison.

I looked at them and scowled. The three bitches must have snuck into the gym while I was speaking to Keela at the front door so they could hear what we were talking about.

"Which brother are you?" Keela asked Dominic.

"Nico," he replied at the same time me and my brothers said, "Dominic."

"What am I callin' ye'?" Keela asked him. "Nico or Dominic?"

His lips twitched. "You can call me whatever you want, gorgeous."

I rolled my eyes as Keela giggled at my soon-to-be dead little brother.

"I'll call you Nico," she replied with a nod.

Dominic was happy with that. He preferred when people called him Nico; he hated his given name because of our father, but myself and my brothers constantly assured him that the man had no influence on him, and his name was his own. That was why we only ever called him it and not a nickname.

"And you are?" Dominic asked, not looking away from her.

"Keela."

He was pissing me off with how he was looking at her, and I couldn't explain why.

"*Kee-lah*," he purred. "Beautiful name for a beautiful girl."

I gritted my teeth as I tugged Keela's body behind mine and locked eyes on my baby brother.

"Boy," I said, my tone threatening, "cut that shit out, or I'm knocking you on your ass."

I didn't look at my other brothers, only Dominic, but when his jaw dropped with shock, I imagined theirs did too. I looked down at Keela when she looked around me and to my brother and said, "Are you okay?".

"We're fine," Ryder assured her.

She moved back to my side and curtly nodded to Ryder, which he frowned at.

"I *really* am sorry for what I said to you earlier, Keela," he stressed. "It was a dick move just to assume something like that. Forgive me?"

I assumed that apology was about him assuming she was pregnant—which I still had no idea why he'd think that, let alone say it—but Keela smiled at him and gave him a hearty nod, forgiving him.

"Were ye' all listenin' to the conversation I had with Alec?"

One by one, the nosy bitches hung their heads in shame and nodded. I found the sight hilarious, but I didn't laugh ... I would later on, though.

"Great," she muttered. "Now I'm even *more* embarrassed."

"What do you need an escort for?" Kane quizzed. "Don't you have a boyfriend?"

At the reminder of the infamous Storm she spoke about last night, I grinned.

"Yeah," I said, folding my arms over my chest. "What was his name again? Thunder?"

"Storm," she answered. "His name is Storm."

"Ah yes, Storm." I chuckled. "Why can't *Storm* escort you?"

She scowled up at me

"Because I don't have a boyfriend," she admitted. "I only said that Storm was me boyfriend last night to stop ye' from chattin' me up because I didn't want to have sex with ye'. I *still* don't want to have sex with ye'. I just need your help, but ye' said ye' couldn't help me so I'll be goin' now. Aideen!"

Aideen walked out of the kitchen. "What's up?"

"We're leavin'. Alec won't help me."

Aideen frowned, and her shoulders slumped. "Crap, who the hell can we get to be your date to that weddin' now?"

"Whose wedding?" Dominic asked Aideen.

Keela gave Aideen what I guessed was supposed to be a stern look, but Aideen ignored her, and the look, and answered Dominic's question.

"Keela's cousin." She clicked her tongue in distaste. "Micah is gettin' married to 'er dickhead of a fella next week. Jason, Micah's fiancé, fucked Keela over a few months ago. Since she *has* to attend the weddin', we wanted someone to go with 'er who would show Jason she can do *miles* better than 'im. I thought Alec was the man for the job, but apparently, I was wrong."

Keela was embarrassed—one glance at her told me so—and it was getting harder and harder to keep from helping her.

"Wait," Dominic said to Keela. "*You're* related to Micah Daley?"

"Yeah, Micah is me cousin. D'ye know 'er?"

"Unfortunately, I do. She was in my homeroom in high school."

My brother leaned forward and really looked at Keela's face. "She was a brunette in school, but I've seen her around town, and she has red hair now. You look similar to her."

"Her hair is *dyed* red. Mine is naturally this colour. I'm not like 'er at all; she is a bitch of epic proportions."

Dominic grinned. "You don't need to convince me that she's a bitch, I believe you."

Keela's lip twitched.

"What did Jason do to fuck you over?" Ryder questioned her.

She rubbed her neck awkwardly.

"He pretended to like me, took me out on dates and so on in an effort to make me think we were a real couple, but really, he was only usin' me to get back at Micah for cheatin' on 'im. It's all *really* fucked up. They worked shite out and are gettin' married, and because we're family, I have to go to their weddin'."

"Why not tell them to shove their wedding up their asses?"

This came from Kane.

"Because me ma would be on me case about it. Goin' to the weddin' and keepin' out of the way is much better than dealin' with me mother if I don't go. She is the devil."

"Amen," Aideen said and made the sign of the cross.

I could feel Keela's disappointment at how the situation had turned out, but she kept a smile on her beautiful face to keep it hidden.

"It was nice seein' ye's again, Kane and Alec, and lovely meetin' you two lads." She nodded at Dominic and Ryder. "Have a nice day."

I moved before she finished speaking. She turned to head for the door, but I was standing in her way. In that split second, I decided to help her. I wasn't sure why I even considered it, but I saw it in Keela's eyes that she needed my help, and I wanted to give it to her.

"Turn around and walk into the kitchen."

"What?" Keela blinked. "Why?"

"Because," I grunted. "I need to iron out some details with you if I'm going to be your escort to your cousin's wedding."

Keela stared up at me with a deer in the headlight look on her face. A few seconds passed by until she found her voice, and said, "But ye' said that ye' aren't in that business anymore, that you're retired and—"

"Do you want my help or not, Keela?"

She sucked her lower lip into her mouth and nodded.

"Then turn around and walk into the kitchen," I requested. "I want to talk to you in private. Just the two of us."

She didn't say word as she turned and walked by everyone on her way into the kitchen. I followed her, keeping my eyes on her body as she walked. I saw her jump when I closed the kitchen door. She turned to face me, and it was obvious she was unsure about what was happening. I wanted to calm her clearly spiked nerves.

"Do you want a cup of tea?"

She stared at me, her eyes unblinking.

"Why do you look like I just asked you to show me your tits?"

Laughter bubbled up her throat. "Because I'd expect a request like *that* from ye', not an offer for tea."

I shrugged. "Bronagh and Branna always tell me to 'put the kettle on' when they need to have a serious conversation, so I figured you might want one before we talk."

"Um, sure." She swallowed. "I'd love a builder's cuppa, please."

"What the hell is that?"

"Ye' know," she said. "A cup of tea with loads of sugar?"

Too much sugar was gross, but if it was the way she liked it, then that was that. I got a cup, popped a teabag inside it, and turned the kettle on. I turned and leaned my ass back against the counter and folded my arms across my chest. My eyes found Keela's, and she appeared not to know what to do with herself.

She shifted her stance a few times, and though she was looking at me, she looked everywhere on my body except at my eyes. I knew I made her nervous, which was the whole reason I was making her a cup of tea. I watched as her eyes moved to my mouth, and I felt my lips quirk upwards into a grin when she licked her lower lip as she stared at me.

"I'm just goin' to sit down."

She moved to the kitchen table and made a huge deal of looking at her surroundings as she sat down just so she wouldn't have to look at me.

"So," she began, clasping her hands in front of her. "What details do we have to go over in order for ye' to escort me to me cousin's weddin'?"

She was looking out to the backyard as she spoke, and it gave me a moment to look at her. She was an enigma to me. Last night, she was hard as nails, and right now, she seemed as fragile as a feather. I wasn't sure how to approach her, and that was new for me, because I normally knew how to approach everyone.

"In order for me to escort you to your cousin's wedding, I need to draw up a contract—"

"Hold up, buddy. A contract? Is this conversation about to get *Fifty Shades of Grey*?"

I raised a brow. "That kinky porn book women love?"

When she nodded, I laughed. I had heard of that book, everyone had heard of it, and the fact that she associated it to our current situation amused me. I turned to the kettle when it made a beeping noise, letting me know the water was boiling, and began making her tea.

"This conversation isn't about to get fifty shades of anything, Keela. Contracts with my clients are routine."

"Alec, I'm not your client. What I am askin' of you is a favour, *not* a business deal."

That was true.

"Why don't you tell me what you want from this favour, so I get a better understanding of things because this is clearly going to be something I'm not used to either."

"Well." She cleared her throat. "Much wouldn't be required of ye'. I just want ye' to pretend to be me boyfriend ... that's it."

With her tea made, I turned and carried it over to the table. I placed it on top of the coaster in front of Keela, then I took a seat across from her. Her eyes focused on my forearms, then they locked on my tattoo. Her eyes rolled over me, and a shiver raced up my spine as if I could feel their touch.

"Can ye' put some clothes on?"

And deny her eye fuck? Not a chance.

"Does my being shirtless make you uncomfortable?"

"Yes, it does."

"Tough shit. It's hot out, so I'm skins for the day."

Keela frowned. "I don't even know what that means."

I teasingly clicked my tongue. "Irish people."

"*American* people."

"So." I snorted. "You just want me to be your boyfriend?"

She played with her fingers. "Yes, ye' just have to make it believable that we are a real couple."

I settled back into the chair. "How would you like me to make it *believable*?"

She shifted. "Please stop tryin' to embarrass me."

"I'm asking a legit question."

"Just act like a lovin' boyfriend; hold me hand, kiss me cheek —"

"Open a door for you, then smack your ass when you walk by me?"

She rolled her eyes. "I'm bein' serious."

"So am I. Deadass serious."

"I just want me family to think we're a real, happy couple. That's *it*."

And I thought this job might be somewhat hard.

I chortled. "Trust me, kitten, this will be the easiest job I've ever done."

"It will?"

I nodded. "Yep."

"So … so does that mean ye'll escort me to the weddin'?"

She looked like she would scream in delight if I said yes.

"If you abide by my conditions, then yes, I will."

Uncertainty washed over her face. "What *are* your conditions?"

I held up my index finger. "Number one, absolutely *no* falling in love with me."

When she laughed, it caught me off guard. I wasn't sure what she found funny. If she knew how many people had gotten attached to me in the past, she wouldn't utter a sound.

"I'm being serious, Keela," I said. "No falling in love with me."

The little witch laughed harder. "I know. That's why … I'm laughin' … oh God. Your face!"

I didn't find her funny.

"Okay," she said, forcing herself to calm down. "So I'm not to fall in love with you. Got it. What's number two?"

I grunted. "Number two, you treat me as a person and not as the hired help."

All traces of amusement fled from Keela's face. "I will always treat ye' as a person. I can't treat ye' like hired help even if I wanted because I'm not payin' ye'."

I waggled my eyebrows. "You could pay me in sexual favours."

Keela tilted her head to the side. "Ye'll get paid with *nice manners*."

Ouch.

"The rest of my conditions might make you a little uneasy then."

She sat up straighter. "What are they?"

I lifted my hand and rubbed the back of my neck. "You sure you want an honest answer to that question, kitten?" At her nod, I said, "I want to fuck you."

She watched me as if she was waiting for me to laugh and tell her I was joking, but when I didn't, fire ignited in her eyes.

"Why aren't ye' laughin'?"

"Because I'm not joking."

"Ye' *better* be jokin'!"

I raised my hands. "I don't joke about conditions for a contract."

She flattened her palms on the table. "This is *not* a contract. This is a *favour*. Ye' don't get paid for it with anythin' other than a *verbal* thank you."

I clicked my tongue. "So I'm supposed to be your boyfriend *without* receiving the privileges or benefits of having a girlfriend?"

"Yes!" she replied, shaking her head. "This is all only *pretend*!"

"Nah, that's a no-go for me. We're going to work that out right now. If you want me to be your boyfriend, then I want some privileges at least. I'm a man—I have needs."

I was milking this, and I knew I was, but I wanted to fuck this woman so bad, I was willing to chance my arm to see if she'd accept it as a condition to me helping her. She probably thought I'd want sex on demand but little did she know that I would make her crave me before I fucked her.

Keela looked defeated. "What exactly d'ye want from me, Alec?"

"I like physical intimacy." I shrugged. "No feelings or emotional bullshit, just the physical stuff. I like holding hands, kissing, cuddling, hugging, and fucking. If I'm going to be your pretend boyfriend, then this is what I want. It's not asking for much."

The woman looked like she was going to kick the shit out of me.

"Shaggin' is *not* on the table at all, so ye' can get it out of your head right now."

My cock jumped at the challenge.

"We'll see, kitten."

"What d'ye mean 'we'll see'?"

"I mean ... we will see."

"We won't *see* anythin'!" She fumed. "I've changed me mind. I don't need your help."

She just about reached the door when my arms wrapped around her. Her gasp told me she hadn't heard me move. "You came to me for help, not the other way around, kitten," I said into her ear. "You don't have anyone else who can help you, or you wouldn't be here ... like it or not, you *do* need my help. You need *me*."

She moved out of my hold and spun to face me.

"I'm *not* shaggin' you. If that is a deal breaker for ye', then so be it. I won't sleep with ye' in order for ye' to escort me to the weddin' as me boyfriend. I don't care how good lookin' ye' are. I'm *not* that kind of girl!"

Hearing her admit her attraction to me made my ego swell.

"You think I'm good looking?"

She glared up at me, and I was sure she thought she looked intimidating, but she really didn't. I liked how she stuck to her guns about not wanting to fuck me, though, and that gave me an idea.

"I want to fuck you, no doubt about it, kitten, but it doesn't have to be a condition since you're so against it. In fact, since you're so dead set *against* it, I'm going to make you a bet instead."

She eyed me. "What kind of bet?"

"A sexual kind of bet."

"*What?*"

I reached up and twirled a curl of her thick, soft red hair around my finger.

"I bet that before anyone says 'I do,' I'll have you on your back with your legs spread wide as I pound away between your thighs."

Keela's jaw dropped.

"And *you* will be the one begging *me* to suck and fuck *you*."

Her eyes dramatically widened. "Are ye' serious?"

At my nod, she laughed.

"Ye' have yourself a bet, laddie."

Her confidence made me smile, but what really amused me was how much she really believed she couldn't be seduced by me.

"My updated conditions are that we sleep in the same bed and that I can kiss you, touch you, and cuddle with you whenever I want."

Keela paused. "Ye' think by doin' all that, I will *willingly* lose our bet and have sex with ye', don't ye'?"

My lips twitched as I shrugged.

"Fine." She snorted. "We can sleep in the same bed, but ye' *have* to wear pyjama bottoms."

Come again?

"I sleep naked," I said. "I always have and always will."

"Ye'll wear pyjamas if you're to sleep in a bed with me. I'm not backin' down on this, playboy."

"Playboy," I repeated. "Really, kitten?"

"Stop callin' me that."

"Nah, I like it. You're small and vulnerable like a cute little kitten."

"If kitten is staying, then so is playboy."

I could handle it. "I've been called worse, *kitten*."

She huffed. "I want to make it clear that I don't like ye' very much."

She only thought that because I didn't bend to her will.

"Give it time and you'll like me plenty."

She ignored me, and said, "Ye' *must* wear pyjamas when you're in the same bed as me. D'ye understand me?"

I licked my lower lip. "I like you giving me orders."

"Does that mean you'll follow them?"

I laughed. "Let's not get too hasty, kitten."

Keela's shoulders slumped. "I'm not backin' down on this. Wearin' pyjamas is a condition of *mine*."

I regarded her. "Is that so?"

"Yes, it *is* so."

Her chin lifted in the air, and I liked how fierce she seemed at that moment.

"Fine, pyjama pants in bed."

Keela beamed in triumph. "And as for the kissin' and touchin' parts of your conditions—we will have to build up to that. I don't know ye', and I refuse to get intimate on any level with a stranger even if it *is* fake."

I could deal with that. "Okay, that sounds fair."

"So, you'll be me pretend boyfriend and escort me to Micah and Jason's weddin'?"

I guffawed at her obvious excitement. "Yeah, kitten. You've got yourself a fake man."

She clapped her hands together. "I can't *wait* to see Jason's face. This is gonna be so feckin' good!"

She returned to her seat at the table, lifted her cup of tea to her lips, blew on it, took a sip, and groaned as she swallowed the hot liquid. Her eyelids fluttered shut, and that was all it took for my erection to spring to life.

"You make the *perfect* cuppa tea."

"All that sugar will rot your teeth."

"I need this. This is how I stay sane."

I sat back down, and discreetly adjusted my cock in my shorts, but my attention turned to the doorway when I heard a thumping sound. Keela heard it too, and she stood and walked towards the door and pulled it open without a word. She leaped backwards when Dominic fell forward and crashed onto the ground. I cracked up with laughter as he hit the ground with a resounding thud.

What a dumbass.

"I *told* ye' she had super hearin'!" Aideen's voice shouted from down the hallway.

Dominic cursed under his breath as he pushed himself to his feet.

"Are ye' okay?" Keela asked him. "Ye' hit the ground hard."

"He's fine. Don't worry about him. It serves him right for eavesdropping."

Dominic's eyes found mine. "I wasn't eavesdropping. I was coming in to get some water—"

"Explain why you were pressed up against the door and fell when she opened it then?"

He opened his mouth to speak but closed it a second later and settled on glaring at me instead.

"Get your water and leave, little brother. I have things to discuss with my *girlfriend*."

Dominic's eyebrows shot up so high they got lost in his hairline.

"Girlfriend?" he spluttered.

Keela glared at me. "He means *fake* girlfriend."

I blew her a kiss. "I'm getting into character, baby."

"Don't call me that."

"Fine," I mused. "Just kitten then."

She placed her hands on her hips.

"How about callin' me Keela since that's me name?"

Dominic chuckled, and said, "Just call her Keela. I never hear the end of it if I don't call Bronagh by her name."

"What do you call her if not 'er name?" Keela asked.

Dominic gently clocked her chin with his knuckles, and said, "I call her my pretty girl."

Keela looked like she just about melted into a damn puddle.

"That is the cutest thing I have *ever* heard in me entire life."

"Besides Bronagh and her sister, you're the cutest woman I have ever seen in *my* entire life."

I gritted my teeth together and flexed my fingers before I balled my hands into fists. I got up, crossed the room, and put my body in front of Keela's. Dominic looked at me with bemused eyes.

"Five-second warning to back off or I'm putting you on your ass, *little* brother."

"Bro, what the hell has gotten into you? Since when do *you* threaten *me*?" he asked me. "Since when do you threaten *anybody*?"

"Stop flirting with her," I growled. "I don't like it."

"Jesus, Alec, calm down," Keela said. "He was only messin' with me, ye' weirdo."

Dominic blissfully laughed, and said, "I like her."

"I like her more and more each time she insults him," Kane's deep voice suddenly spoke as he entered the room and headed straight for the fridge.

"Fucking hell ... déjà vu," Dominic muttered.

I was about to tell both of them to get there asses out of the room when I felt nails gently rake over my back. A shudder ran through my body, and blood rushed to my cock. The erection that fell when Dominic entered the room was back and throbbed. I turned to Keela, pulled her body against mine, and bent down, placing my mouth at her ear. "If you touch my back again, be prepared for a hard fucking, *kitten*."

She gasped, but from the way her pupils dilated, I knew she liked the sound of that.

"If ye' say anythin' like that to me again, I'll ... I'll ..."

"You'll what, kitten?"

She didn't answer me. She just glared up at me.

"She'll kick your ass from the looks of things," Kane commented, then left the room with the food he'd gathered from the fridge.

I swallowed as I stared down at her. She was stunning. Big green eyes, pink lips, a juicy fuller lower lip, and snow white skin that had light brown freckles sprinkled across it. Her hair looked the colour of a summer's sunset, and the contrast of it against her fair skin was beautiful.

"You're a real man, ye' know that?"

"I'm *all* man, baby."

"No," Keela said with a shake of her head. "I mean you're a *man*. Like a caveman."

I had never been called that before.

"Is that a bad thing?"

"Yes and no."

"I don't understand what you're saying. Is it bad or is it good? Be straight with me."

Dominic laughed, and said, "Wrong thing to ask a woman, big bro."

I spared him a glance. "What the hell do *you* know about women?"

"More than you."

I had more notches on my bedpost than this little shit times two.

I smiled. "Be serious, Dominic."

"*I'm* the one who has an actual girlfriend out of the pair of us. You have just fucked your way through an endless line of pussy since you were fifteen. You've never had to deal with a woman when it hasn't come to sex ... not when you weren't working anyway."

Well, he had me there.

I regarded him. "Fine. Since you know so much, enlighten me, Yoda."

Dominic rubbed his hands together. "I'm giving you a crash course in what I like to call The Man Bible. It contains all the secret meanings to what women actually mean when they speak. So listen to me very carefully," he stressed. "It is almost impossible for men to understand it, but a lucky handful of us know the true meanings of words women use as weapons, and I am about to impart this wisdom to you, bro."

Well, he had my complete and utter attention now.

"The first word is 'Fine.' When a woman says this during an argument, she knows she is right and that you are very wrong. She is *not* fine —you're *not* fine, *nothing* is fine."

I frowned. "But what about if she is wrong—"

"No," Dominic interrupted. "Do *not* talk back when she says something is fine; wait until she is calm to mention that she might be wrong. I usually wait a week before I mention things about past fights."

"Okay, fine doesn't really mean fine. Got it." I waved my hand. "What else, love doctor?"

"Second word is 'Nothing.' By the might of God, when a woman says nothing is wrong, *something* is definitely fucking wrong."

I looked at Keela. "I'm starting to believe *that* one."

"The third word is 'Whatever.' This is another way for ladies to say fuck you."

Keela giggled, making my brother grin as he popped up an extra finger. "The fourth is a sentence. When a woman says 'It's okay, don't worry about it,' you *do* worry about it. You worry a lot because she is thinking of a way to make you pay for whatever you did wrong."

I was perplexed. "Why would they say that if they don't mean it?"

"I think it's some sort of mind trick." Dominic shrugged. "They use that sentence as an illusion that things between you are okay, but when you least expect it, they strike like a viper and wound your soul."

This was fucking confusing.

"Why can't they just say what they mean instead of giving words a double meaning?"

Dominic shrugged again. "I know the real meaning of certain things women say, but I don't understand *why* they give them a double meaning. *That* is beyond my area of expertise, bro."

I looked down at Keela, eyeing her. "I don't like this."

She looked innocent, but I had no doubt she could mind fuck me should she choose to do so.

"Okay, listen very carefully to this two-word sentence. I'm serious, Alec. If you're going to remember *any* of what I just said remember this—it might just save your life."

I leaned forward, suddenly desperate to know this piece of information.

"When a woman tells you to 'Go ahead,' you do *not* under *any* circumstances go ahead. You retreat to a safe distance and observe the situation *very* carefully. She is daring you to do something, *not* giving you permission."

Keela cracked up laughing, and it made me chuckle, and say, "I guess you laughing means all of that was bullshit?"

"No, the opposite." She wiped under her eyes. "It was spot-on, and that's why it's so funny."

I stared down at her, and it struck me at that moment just how little experience I had with women when it came to everything but sex. Dominic was right; if sex wasn't on the table, I never had any kind of relationship with a woman. Now that I had a fake girlfriend, I needed to be on my A game. I didn't want to fuck things up for Keela when she was showing this asshole Jason up. I wanted to be the best fake boyfriend she ever had. With my mind made up, I focused on Dominic, and said, "We need to have a *serious* conversation, little brother."

CHAPTER SIX

Twenty-eight years old ...

Brandy Daley turning out to be Keela's uncle was the biggest kick in the teeth I had received in a long time. The man was cold-blooded, vindictive, and not someone you fucked around with. Ryder had worked with him many times when he ran deals on this side of the world, and each time, my brother prayed it would be the last. Brandy knew we were Marco's puppets, and he knew exactly what each of us did for him ... he knew what I did. That was why I wasn't surprised when he wanted to speak to me on my own without Keela present. He was going to warn me to stay away from her. He was going to do something so severe that it would keep me away from the woman I had fallen in love with.

I knew he would.

If there was God, he hated me. I had been through so much darkness that broke me down in my life, and I never even considered having someone who I could feel so deeply for. It was some cruel twist of fate. The unthinkable happened. I fell in love with someone so beautiful, so pure of heart, and now she was going to be taken away from me because someone else said so.

"Ye' know what I'm gonna say, don't ye?"

I lifted my chin. "I have a decent idea, yeah."

"This is nothin' personal towards ye', kid," Brandy said, leaning back in his chair. "Ye' understand how important family is, which is why me niece isn't remainin' involved with the likes of you and your brothers."

The likes of me and my brothers? We did a warlord's bidding because we were trapped by him. Brandy did the things he did out of his own freewill. He was *exactly* like Marco, maybe even worse, and he thought *we* were someone Keela shouldn't have in her life? The fucking hypocrite.

"She loves me," I said, my chest warming. "And I love her, too."

"I thought maybe she did." Brandy sighed. "I've been watchin' 'er, and how she looks at ye'."

"Can we not just come to some sort of arrangement—"

"I've already decided what's goin' to happen, Alec."

My heart dropped to my stomach.

"You simply leavin' 'er won't cut it. I know two of your brothers are in relationships with the Murphy sisters who live in Old Isle Green. The eldest sister is pals with Aideen Collins, who just happens to be me niece's best friend. If ye' cut and run now, your paths will cross again, and I'm *not* riskin' a reconciliation."

Dread flowed through my veins.

"So what do you want me to do?"

"I want you to devastate her."

Fear shot up my spine. "What?"

"Me soon-to-be son-in-law has an odd relationship with me daughter, but she loves the little prick, so I've stepped back and let them live their lives. However, I do know that Jason was involved with Keela for a time and played 'er. While he was punished for that and won't hurt 'er again, I know she hasn't recovered from that hurt he instilled within 'er."

I felt like I was going to be sick.

"Keela trusts you even though she knows with your background that ye' could hurt her worse than Jason ever could, and that is what you will be doin'."

My lips parted, but no words left my mouth.

"She knows ye' serviced Everly when ye' were an escort, and she knows ye' fucked Dante when the thought tickled your fancy. Both of them have already been informed of the playdate the three of ye' will have."

I jumped to my feet. "No!"

"Sit back down," Brandy said, his tone turning dangerous. "Now."

I wanted to rush to his side and slam my fist into his jaw, but I didn't. I was rigid as I lowered myself back to my seat. I looked at the two men who had been leaning against the wall on the far side of the room, and when I saw they had guns in their hands, my pulse quickened.

"I can't do what you're asking, Brandy," I said, focusing on him. "I can't."

"Sure ye' can." He tilted his head to the side.

I gritted my teeth. "And if I just *don't* do this?"

"How much d'ye love your brothers, Alec?"

I froze. "My brothers?"

"Your brothers." Brandy nodded. "How much d'ye love them?"

"More than my life."

"I'm glad to hear that," he said with a sinister grin. "I'd hate for somethin' to … happen to them if ye' weren't to follow a direct order from me."

The threat was plain as day, and it caused my insides to crumble. If I didn't hurt Keela, the woman I loved, in a horrid way, then my brothers would pay for it with their lives. I wanted to scream until my throat went raw. This wasn't a choice; this was as death sentence for me. No matter what decision I made, I would be heartbroken with the result, and Brandy knew that. I thought of Keela and how much she had come to trust me, and hope flared within me.

"She'll realise that I would never do this willingly," I assured Brandy. "When she thinks about it hard, she knows I would never

ever do this to her."

"Oh, I know that, Alec," Brandy acknowledged. "But the damage will be done by then. Whenever she knows ye' were forced or not, she'll still have the visual in her head. Always."

For the first time in a long time, I wanted to cry.

"Please, don't make me hurt her like this," I pleaded. "I'll leave her life, I swear I will."

"No," Brandy answered. "This way will ruin your relationship and her trust in ye'."

My body began to tremble.

"I don't like havin' ye' raped like this, Alec," Brandy commented. "Marco bragged on how people have used and abused ye' over the years, so ye' don't have to have *actual* sex. I'll settle for oral, either giving or receivin' on Dante, and that will hurt me niece just as bad."

Bile rose up my throat.

"Why not on Everly?" I asked. "Why Dante?"

"Because she'll question whether ye' could be attracted to 'er when you're intimate with a man as pretty as Dante. I know me niece, Alec. She is a beautiful girl, but she doesn't have self-confidence."

I felt like the walls of the room were closing in around me.

"You're her blood," I pressed. "*Why* do you want to hurt your blood?"

"To save 'er pain and heartache in the future," Brandy answered, his voice rough. "You ... your family. You're tainted by Marco, and ye' always will be. Me niece deserves better, and she'll get it."

"Please, sir," I pleaded. "Don't make me do this to her. I'm begging you."

Brandy dismissed me when he stood.

"Time's wastin', kid." He turned and walked towards the exit. "Do what ye've been told, or ye'll return to Ireland from this sunny trip to the Bahamas to bury four people. The choice is yours, Alec.

Make the right one."

I already knew what choice I would be making, and that was why when the doors closed behind Brandy and his men, I lowered my head and cried not only for the pain I would have to bring to Keela, but for the agony I would bring to myself in hurting her and letting her go. I had found my forever in her, and that forever would be ending far too quickly ... and all because another evil man took my choice away from me.

CHAPTER SEVEN

Present day ...

"Dinner is on the tabl—what are ye' thinkin' so hard about?"
I looked up at my wife as she entered our bedroom and crawled up onto our bed next to me.

"A lot of things," I answered. "The good, the bad, and ugly."

Keela sat on her behind, cross-legged, and took my hand in hers. There was a hint of worry in her eyes but understanding and compassion shone within them too.

"Anythin' ye' want to talk about?"

I shook my head. "No, because we already got through everything that we once needed to talk about."

Keela frowned. "Is this because of the nightmare I mentioned earlier?"

"Maybe." I shrugged. "I was just thinking of the shit I dealt with when I was younger, then when I met you and all that ... poison happened."

"Hey." My wife squeezed my hand. "Ye' can't change the past, and if we could, we probably wouldn't have the present. We probably wouldn't have our sons or our life together. Hell, ye' probably would have never come to Ireland."

I reached forward and pulled her on top of me so her body was lying on mine. Her cheek rested against my chest, and I closed my eyes, basking in her scent and presence.

"You're right, of course," I mused. "Sometimes when I think about everything, I just have a moment of disbelief that we went through everything thrown at us and made it out to the other side. It seems so surreal that we've lived the life we have."

"We survived it, though." Keela raised her head. "You, me, and the others got through all the bad things we encountered, and d'ye wanna know why?"

I nodded.

"Because we're strong, and nothin' can or will come between us."

The knot that had formed in my chest over the memories flooded through my mind faded until only warmth and love remained.

"How did I get so lucky to find someone as perfect as you to marry me?"

Keela's lips twitched. "Alannah says I was dropped on me head as a child and that I don't know any better."

When I laughed, I quickly covered my mouth and widened my eyes.

"Don't tell her I found that funny," I pleaded. "She'll think she's a god or something."

My wife chuckled. "I'll take it to me grave, playboy."

I hummed and slid my hands down her body until I palmed her ass.

"What do you say we finish what we started in the kitchen this morning and—"

I was cut off by a large, fluffy monster as he dived onto the bed and rolled around, thinking it was playtime.

"Junior," I scowled. "Down."

The spoiled dog didn't budge. Instead, he just rolled on his side and licked my face, making Keela laugh.

"He is *exactly* like his daddy."

I grimaced as I wiped my face dry. "Storm learned his boundaries, though; Junior jumps over them without a care in the world."

Keela chuckled as she reached over and scratched his belly. "I miss your daddy, baby boy."

I placed my hand on my wife's thigh when she straddled me so she could reached Junior easier. I looked at her face as she smiled down at our dog. There was hurt in her eyes whenever she looked at him, but that hurt was fading as time passed. Two years ago, the first member of our family passed away. Storm lived until he was seventeen years old, and he led a good life for a dog. He had survived being shot ... and attempted murder by Aideen Collins on many occasions.

Not long before he died, we decided to see if we could breed him. He had been our only pet, and we had never wanted to add more of them to our family once we had so many kids. We had always planned to get Storm neutered, but we never got around to it, having always been busy with our children, our jobs, or both.

It took one try with a breeder we found. Storm sired a litter of four full-breed German Shepherds like himself and as we had pick of the litter, we chose the only male. Junior earned his name because he was a carbon copy of his father. There were no differences between them, so much so that Aideen Collins believed Storm was born again and that his bloodline was cursed. He was two years old and was already as big as Storm was when he reached adulthood.

"Junior!"

Junior's head shot up when he heard Murphy's voice holler from downstairs. A second passed before he scrambled off the bed, out of the room, and zoomed down the stairs. I heard my second born yelp, followed by heavy laughter.

"Murph loves him somethin' bad," Keela said as she turned and looked down at me. "He still misses Storm."

All of our kids loved Storm, but Murphy had a close bond with him, and had formed a brother-like connection with Junior not long after he was born.

"He'll always miss him, we all will, but we had a long time with him. We have a lot to look back on and smile when we think of the beast."

"Yeah." Keela smiled fondly. "He was pretty great."

I tugged her down until her face was an inch from mine.

"If I get you out of those clothes, *I'll* make you feel pretty great."

She chuckled. "Ye' promised the boys yr'd bring them to laser tag today."

"I did?"

"Ye' did." Keela nodded. "Enzo reminded me about it when they got back from their football games."

As if on cue, Enzo shouted, "Da, hurry up! The next session starts in half an hour."

Keela laughed when I closed my eyes and sighed deeply. She rolled off me, then pulled me out of our bed with her. She got a kick out of me keeping her close as we descended the stairs of our house. We both looked at Miller when he met us at the bottom of the steps.

"I don't wanna go play laser tag."

I frowned. "Why not?"

"I wanna stay with Mammy."

"Why?"

"'Cause she said she'd give me a big cookie after dinner if I did."

I scowled. "You'd ditch me for a cookie?"

With a straight face, my son said, "Every single time, Daddy."

Keela burst into giggles and lifted Miller up into her arms. I steadied her when she struggled slightly in hoisting him up, and it made her huff.

"You're gonna be a little man before I know it, baby."

Miller put his forehead against his mom's, and said, "No, I won't."

"That was cute," I said. "If the other women were here, they'd be hounding my brothers for more babies."

Keela snorted after she kissed Miller's cheek.

"Not likely. We all agreed that five is our number. We're too old for more kids."

I raised a brow. "You're forty-one, and I just turned forty-six. I don't think that's old."

"It's not," Keela agreed. "But me body can't carry any more babies. It would break me back."

I placed my hand on her lower back and massaged it, making her melt. She went into the living room with Miller while I went into the kitchen, looking for my other sons. I slid my arm around Ace's waist when he reached for the refrigerator, making him laugh.

"You're always eating," I told him when I released him.

"'Cause I'm always hungry."

I snorted and looked at Murphy, Enzo, and Ares, who were sat at the kitchen table eating their dinners. Junior was lying at Murphy's feet, relaxing. I quickly reheated my food and joined them.

"Eat fast," Enzo told me. "We don't wanna be late this time for tag."

I rolled my eyes. "Last time was an accident."

"Ye' mixed the slot times up by four hours, Da."

"It could have happened to anyone."

"No, it couldn't." Ares chuckled. "It only ever happens to *you*."

Little shit.

"Well, we won't be late this time, so eat up."

I started eating my dinner just as Ace huffed and puffed from across the room as he tried to open a jar of carrots. Keela walked into the room, saw him struggling, and tried to help, but it wouldn't open for her either. I stood and took charge.

"I've got this."

She handed the jar to me, and when she realised I was having difficulty, she smiled, but said nothing ... Ares did, though.

"Da, relax. You're goin' to burst a vessel."

I didn't let up on trying to open the damn jar.

"You don't understand, son," I huffed and puffed. "Opening sealed objects is one of the perks of having me as a husband. As a man, I can't leave this bastard of a jar unopened. I'll never get an erection again with it hanging over me."

"Oh. My. God." Murphy laughed from the table. "Auntie Alannah is right; you're out of your bloody trolley."

My ego breathed easy when the lid of the jar finally loosened, but somehow as I pulled my hand away, the wrapping of the jar gave me a paper cut, adding further insult.

"Ow!"

It stung. It stung like a *bitch*.

"Let me see," Keela cooed as blood rose from the slit on my thumb.

Ares took the jar of carrots from me as I focused on my wife. She got some paper towels and dabbed at my thumb, wiping away the blood, but it kept on coming.

"Ow, woman." I hissed when she squeezed my thumb. "Be careful."

Her lips twitched as she lazily patted at my wound.

"Oh, sure," I said. "Take your time, it's not like I'm bleeding to death or anything, so please, go at your own pace."

Keela rolled her eyes.

"Am I being passive-aggressive?" I asked. "I'm sorry, it must be a side effect of, you know, dying."

"Alec, it's a bloody paper cut!"

"Don't you *dare* try to lessen the pain I'm feeling! It may as well be a bullet hole because it stings like *fuck*."

Keela laughed. "Don't be a sissy."

"A sissy?" I admonished. "*Sissy?* Do you really think stinging pain from a paper cut is something to joke about? If you do, then I've truly married a monster."

Keela laughed as she got a Band-Aid, wrapped my thumb up, and sealed it with a kiss. "You'll survive."

"Smartass."

She left the room with a grin.

In record time, me and my kids had consumed our dinner, left the house, and headed to the Leisure Plex to have some fun. When we arrived there and I had parked the car, we headed inside, paid, and got suited up to kick some ass. Laser tag was only a new addition to the building, and even I had to admit that it was insanely cool. Each player was fitted with a vest that delivered a body tingling shock when a person was 'shot' and knocked out of the round. The guns were all black, and the styles were wide in variety. The tag room itself was a maze, and the lights were dim and the place was utterly silent during a round of tag, causing the players to play the game at full calibre in order to be aware of their surroundings as they hunted each other.

My kids and nephews loved it.

"It's over for you little turds," I said, stroking the barrel of my plastic gun. "I *run* laser tag."

"We'll see about that, aul' lad."

My eyes locked on Enzo. "You're on my hit list."

"That's not the first time I've heard that. Girls tell me it *all* the time, and not in the way *you* mean it."

Ares and Ace shared a look, rolled their eyes, then took off in opposite directions and got lost in the maze. I gave Enzo the finger, he gave it back to me, then we parted ways and waited for the buzzer to sound. Within the maze were large boulders to hide behind, as well as large plastic tubes that a grown man could crawl through to get to a different side of the room. I chose to hide behind one of the boulders until one of my offspring walked into my line of sight. I shot at Ace when he appeared, but he rolled on the ground and avoided the hit.

"Da's campin'!"

"I'm not. I'm just lying here!"

"That's what campin' *is*!" Enzo's voice hollered from somewhere to my right. "Move around, don't sit and wait for us to come to ye'!"

God's sake.

"Fine!"

I turned and zigzagged my way around as quietly as I could, and when I came up behind Enzo who was crouched as he shuffled forward, I felt a smug smile stretch across my lips. Without a word, I aimed my gun and shot my son in the back like a fucking marksman. Enzo grunted as his vest lit up red and delivered him a tingling shock. The red returned to blue, but Enzo only had two lives left, and he knew it.

"Who's your daddy?"

Enzo slowly got to his feet and turned to face me.

"Wow." He shook his head. "I can't believe ye' shot me, Da."

My smile slowly slid from my face. "That's the game—"

"You're me father," Enzo spoke over me. "I trusted ye'. I trusted ye' to love and protect me, and 'ere ye' are, shootin' me in the back the second it's turned."

Shame filled me.

"I'm sorry," I said, my shoulders slumping. "You guys told me not to do the camping thing."

"This is a betrayal I've never felt before," Enzo continued, sighing. "This brings me pain, Da. Real pain."

"Son." I stepped forward. "I didn't mean to—"

I jumped when my vest vibrated then turned from bright blue to red indicating that I was now out of the game. As an adult, I only got one life so I had to wait for one of my sons to win this round before I was back in the game. I looked up at Enzo and found him smiling.

"Good job, Ace!"

Ace cackled from behind me as he ran away in search of his next victim. I stared at my eldest son who looked so much like me but had the heart of a hell dwelling monster.

"You played me."

"Ye' played yourself by thinkin' we wouldn't gang up on ye'."

"You little bastard."

Enzo winked. "Who's *your* daddy?"

He turned and ran off, and I glared after him, considering putting rocks in a sock and beating him with it when he least expected it. Like when he was in the shower or sleeping.

"Little punk," I said, shaking my head as I chuckled.

I took my phone from my pocket when it rang and answered it when I saw Damien was calling me.

"What's up, Damien?"

He sighed, long and deep. "I'm in a bar with Dominic."

"Okay," I began. "Are you both having fun?"

I wasn't sure what he expected me to say.

"No." He snorted. "Dominic plans to drown his sorrows, and he wants us to help him."

I paused. "What's got him down?"

"Are you sitting down?"

I looked around and lied. "Yeah."

"Georgie has a boyfriend," Damien grunted. "And the little fucker is Gavin Collins' boy."

I fell. I dropped to the ground like a sack of potatoes when my knees gave way from under me. I managed to keep a firm grip on my phone as I brought it back to my ear and snapped, "Murder. We have to *murder* the boy!"

Damien laughed. "We can't. Bronagh forbid it."

I sucked in a sharp breath. "Why would she do such a thing?"

"I don't know," my brother replied. "She's not my favourite person right now."

Mine either.

"What are we gonna do?" I demanded. "Georgie is our precious little flower cup. She can't like *boys*. She's ten!"

"She's fifteen."

Pain sliced across my chest.

"I refuse to believe that. She is ten years old and always will be!"

Damien laughed. "Are you coming to Croughs or not? I still have to call Kane and Ryder and give them this shitty news."

"I'll be on my way soon," I said as I continued to lie on the ground. "I'll finish up this game of tag with my boys soon. I'll be there with fucking bells on."

I hung up on my laughing little brother and stared at the darkened ceiling above me.

"Are ye' havin' a stroke, Da?"

"No," I answered Enzo. "At least I don't think I am."

His face came into view as he stood over me. "Are ye' still sulkin' cause Ace shot ye'?"

I had more pressing matters to worry about.

"No." I sighed. "I'm sulking because Georgie has a boyfriend."

I watched as fury blazed within Enzo's eyes.

"She has a *what*?"

"A boyfriend," I repeated. "An evil being that we failed to protect her from."

Enzo stared down at me, then without a word, he joined me in lying down on the floor.

"I've a pain in me chest," he said.

I nodded. "That's your heart breaking, son."

"I'm gonna kick 'er arse," Enzo suddenly warned. "She never told me she had a boyfriend."

"I doubt she would have advertised she's dating a Collins kid to you Slater kids."

"A ... a Collins kid?' Enzo repeated on a whisper. "She's goin' out with one of Jax's cousins?"

"Uh-huh," I answered. "Gavin's boy, the eldest I imagine. What was his name?"

"Indie," Enzo all but growled. "His name is Indie."

"Indie," I repeated. "This little shit has infiltrated our family."

"I'll take care of this, don't worry."

I snorted. "Bronagh said no one is allowed to hurt him, so I assume that means we aren't allowed to break them up either."

"So what the heck is gonna happen? She's just *allowed* to have a boyfriend?"

"Looks that way."

Enzo was silent for a moment, and said, "Are ye' gonna go and make sure Uncle Nico doesn't go and beat on Indie?"

"Yeah," I said with a laugh. "He's in a bar, and I'll be joining him and the others after I take you guys home."

My son didn't respond. However, he remained lying on the floor with me while the laughter and screams of his brothers sounded around us as they shot at each other and continued the game of tag, blissfully unaware that our family had just been turned upside down. I turned my head and looked at Enzo. He had his eyes closed and looked both irritated and defeated at the same time, making me want to laugh.

I looked back up at the ceiling and smiled.

I knew my younger brother would be heartbroken that his baby girl was growing into a young woman—I was too—but knowing that all of our kids were healthy and happy enabled me not to dwell on it too much. I had my sons, my wife, my sisters-in-law, my nephews, and my niece. Life was good, and I knew we'd deal with this curve ball that was thrown at us just like we dealt with everything.

As a family ... and if all else failed, I'd scare the shit out of the Collins kid, so he wouldn't look in my niece's direction again. Either way was cool with me.

PART THREE

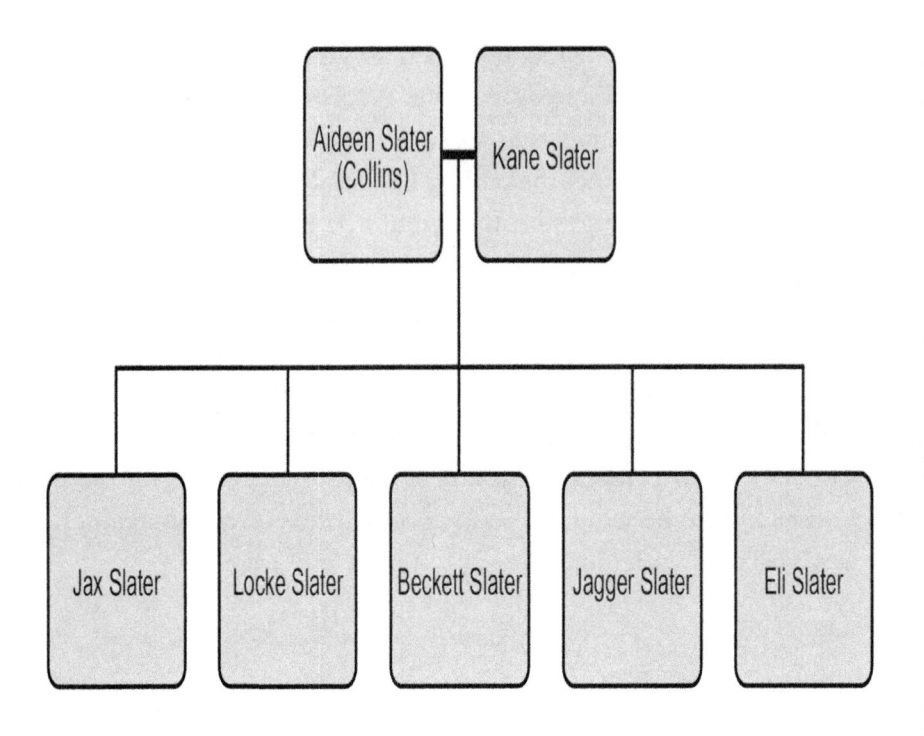

```
        ┌─────────────────┬─────────────┐
        │  Aideen Slater  │ Kane Slater │
        │    (Collins)    │             │
        └─────────────────┴─────────────┘
                         │
   ┌──────────┬──────────┼──────────┬──────────┐
   │          │          │          │          │
┌──────┐ ┌────────┐ ┌─────────┐ ┌────────┐ ┌────────┐
│ Jax  │ │ Locke  │ │ Beckett │ │ Jagger │ │  Eli   │
│Slater│ │ Slater │ │ Slater  │ │ Slater │ │ Slater │
└──────┘ └────────┘ └─────────┘ └────────┘ └────────┘
```

KANE

CHAPTER ONE

Present day ...

Nothing was more sickening than a stranger being in your home. I gestured for my wife to be silent as I nudged her behind my body. Aideen and I had just gotten home from grocery shopping. It was a rare time when we didn't have any of our kids with us. They were down in their uncle's apartment a few floors below ours, which gave us time to quickly get some errands done. When we exited the elevator and entered our penthouse apartment, I heard muffled voices coming from one of my son's bedrooms.

I quietly reasoned with Aideen to return to the lobby and contact the building's security, but of course, she didn't listen to me. We both lowered our bags to the floor as silently as we could. My wife remained rooted to my side, her hands gripping my waist as we investigated the noise. I grabbed a steel baseball bat from the hallway closet that I had just in case of a situation like this. I gripped it firmly.

"How did they get up 'ere?" Aideen whispered, a tremor of fear in her tone. "It's impossible without our code to the elevator."

I had no idea how to answer her question because no one *should* have been able to get into our apartment without the code. Many years ago, after Aideen pleaded with me not to buy a house as she loved our home, I decided to convert the five apartments on the top floor of our apartment building into a penthouse for our family. The elevator opened into our living room, and only our family members had the code to reach this floor. The fire stairwell was designed as an exit, not an entryway. Then there was the added security of the lobby entrance password, the patrolling security guards, and the cameras that pointed at every entrance and exit.

No one should have been able to reach my apartment ... unless they knew the codes.

"Be quiet," I said to Aideen as we approached Jax's bedroom. "They're in here."

"Oh, God."

Her hold on me tightened. I exhaled a breath, raised my hand, and pounded on the door.

"You have two seconds to get your asses out here so I can put my foot up them!"

I heard a female scream, and a male curse.

"Wait!"

I froze, then choked out, "Jax?"

Aideen rounded on me and flung the door open once she realised the intruder was our eldest son. It took two seconds for me to realise just how fucked the situation had rapidly become. My wife screamed, then the teenage girl who was hiding her naked body with my son's bedcover screamed, then Jax paled as I roared, "Are you fucking *kidding* me?"

He was naked as the day he was born, and the only thing saving his mother from dropping dead with shock was the fact that he cupped his meat and nut sack. It did a shit job considering his penis was erect, no doubt from the activities myself and Aideen had clearly interrupted.

"Mama, I'm sorry!"

Aideen didn't reply. She gripped the handle of the door and pulled it shut.

"Ye' call 'er mama?" the girl asked Jax in a panic.

"Me da is American and so are me uncles," Jax said in a hurried breath. "I've picked up on some of their terms, but I rarely call 'er mama ... just so ye' know. She's normally just ma to me."

I looked at Aideen, and we shared a 'bullshit' look. All of our kids, and my brother's kids, called their mother 'mama' when they wanted something, or when they realised they fucked up. It was something me and my brothers did when we were little, too.

"Ten seconds, Jax," I warned him. "Ten fucking seconds."

I pounded on the door in anger.

The girl shrieked. "Where are me knickers?!"

Aideen placed a hand on her forehead. "Omigod."

I resisted the urge to kick the door open.

"It'll be okay," I told my wife.

"She has no knickers on," Aideen scowled. "What part of that is okay?"

Not a single fucking syllable of it.

"He was havin' sex," she whispered. "Kane, what if he wasn't wearin' protection?"

My heart dropped as the two teenagers rapidly dressed on the other side of the door.

"Daisy," Jax said. "I'm so sorry about this."

Aideen and I looked up when the door to the bedroom opened and stood the black-haired girl, now fully dressed, but had a face so red her skin looked crimson. She looked at Aideen, then at me, and for a moment, she didn't look in shock about what was happening. She looked at me like she was checking me out, and I didn't know whether to laugh or shout at her, but she didn't give me a chance. Instead, she ran by us without a single word and fled our apartment. Aideen and I focused on Jax whose face was still pale as he sat on the edge of his bed. He had jeans on but remained shirtless with his hair wild.

"What d'ye' have to say for yourself, Jax Daniel Slater?" Aideen demanded. "*Well?*"

Jax frowned. "What d'ye want me to say, Ma?"

"I want ye' to man up and tell me if I need to ring that girl's parents so they can bring 'er to get the mornin' after pill."

"No, please." Jax choked. "Both of 'er brothers will kill me. They're in their mid-twenties."

I cut in. "Not if I kill you first."

Jax ducked his head and tried to avoid what I knew was a murderous gaze that I shot his way.

"Look." He swallowed. "Ye' both came home before I could ... *ye' know.*"

"Thank God." Aideen breathed, placing a hand on her chest. "Oh, thank you, Jesus."

The relief that fell off my shoulders was instant.

"Good," I clipped. "You don't deserve to know what it feels like yet, you little fuc—"

"Kane." Aideen shook her head.

"Give me five minutes with him. I'll break it so this won't happen again."

Jax leaped to his feet, rushed forward, and hid behind his mother.

"Ma!"

Aideen turned and raised her eyebrow. She looked up at Jax who was already four inches taller than her at sixteen years old.

"I'm *very* disappointed in ye'," she said, her voice thick with emotion. "Ye' promised me ye' would tell me when ye' started to take a physical interest in girls. Ye' *promised.*"

At that moment, Jax wasn't sixteen anymore. He was a little boy who realised he'd upset his mother.

"Mama," he said softly. "I'm ... I'm sorry, I wasn't thinkin'."

Aideen shook her head and looked away from our firstborn, tears glazing her eyes. "I'm goin' to go and tidy up before the boys get home from Harley's."

I frowned as Aideen turned and walked away.

"Ado?" I called after her.

Her sniffles were audible then, and it tore me and, from what I could see, my son apart.

"I oughtta kick the shit out of you, you selfish little asshole!" I lowly bellowed at Jax when Aideen was out of earshot. "You've made her cry."

Jax didn't flinch. "I hate me too right now."

"I *don't* hate you, and neither does your mom," I scowled. "We're just furious with you. What the *hell* were you thinking?"

"I was thinkin' about losin' me virginity to the hottest girl in school. You *or* Ma didn't enter me mind in there, Da."

I wanted to throttle him. "You're my son, but you can't keep it in your pants like your uncles when they were your age!"

Jax raised an eyebrow in question. "Which ones?"

"The twins," I grunted. "Obviously."

Jax looked a little proud, but only for a second before he glanced down the now empty hallway were Aideen retreated.

"I really hurt 'er."

"Yeah," I replied, "you did."

"And you?" Jax looked at me. "I hurt ye', too?"

Like a sucker punch.

"Yeah." I nodded. "Me too."

Jax looked distraught. "I'm sorry, Da."

"I know." I sighed. "But you understand why we're upset, right? Firstly, you're our baby, and you're doing things you shouldn't be doing at your age. Secondly, we told you how your mother got pregnant with you. You're one of five of the best things that have ever happened to us, but you weren't planned, and we struggled coming to terms with there being an 'us' and 'family' and we were in our late *twenties*! Do you think you could handle a surprise baby at sixteen?"

Jax looked visibly sick. "Jesus. No."

"Then think with the head on your *shoulders*," I roughly stated, then softened my tone. "Look, I know what it's like, *trust* me. I've been where you are, but you have to be smart about this, Jax. You can't just go around having sex with different girls no matter how hot they are. Pregnancy isn't the only worry. There are nasty STIs you can catch, too."

"Shite," Jax groaned. "I'm so sorry. I know all this ... it's just ... hard. Literally. All the damn time."

Any other time, I would laugh and tease him, but not now, not about a situation as serious as this one.

"You're grounded for a month," I stated. "You'll pick up more chores and extra nights to babysit your brothers and cousins. No phone. No laptop. No iPad. No Xbox or PlayStation. No soccer games or practice. I'll deal with your coach. Unless it's for school, you don't leave this house, do you understand me?"

Jax looked gutted but took it like a man. "Yes, sir."

"And bottom line, no sex in this apartment. Ever." I raised an eyebrow then. "From now on, I'll keep a box of condoms stocked in the bottom drawer in the bathroom for you. Put one in your wallet and replace it every single time you take it out for use. This isn't permission to go out and have sex with every female in sight. It's a precaution, a safety net so if you ever get into a situation where you're going to do something where you know you'll need it, make sure you use it. Be smart. Be safe. And for God's sake, kid, make good decisions. Please. I'll go old school and beat you bloody if I find out you're playing girls and breaking hearts. I don't respect a man who has no respect for women. Do you understand me?"

"Yes, sir." Jax straightened. "I understand."

"Good," I said, then gestured Jax closer. "Now give me a hug and go comfort your mama. She works herself into a fretting state because of you and your brothers."

Jax moved closer to me and gave me a quick hug before slapping hands with me and bumping fists.

"Hottest girl in school, huh?"

Jax's lips twitched. "You saw 'er. What *d'you* think?"

"I think she forgot about you the moment she walked out of the room. Did you not see how she stared at your old man?"

"I'm better lookin'." Jax glared. "I look like you, me Slater uncles, me Collins uncles *and* me ma. I'm a genetic marvel."

I laughed and shook my head.

"God really didn't want me to have sex today," he then said with a sigh. "First Uncle Nico phones me earlier when I was kissin' Daisy then you and Ma come bustin' in like the guards on a raid."

I snorted but said nothing.

"Can I go to Uncle Nico's house? I need to speak to Georgie. It's important."

I mulled it over for a moment, then said, "Go there, talk to her, then get your ass home. I meant it when I said you're grounded."

Jax nodded. "I got it."

"Get dressed then."

He disappeared into his room, rapidly finished dressing, then went in search of his mother. I leaned against the doorway and looked into my son's room, glaring at the messed-up bed and shaking my head before I scrubbed my face with my hands. I used to think when my kids were toddlers and kindergarten age that they wore me out, but that was only a taste of the stress that the teenage years brought.

After I went to the bathroom, I found Aideen in the kitchen. She was cleaning the countertops even though they were already clean. I slanted against the wall and folded my arms across my chest. Watching my wife, I knew she was hurting without having to ask her. I was in tune with everything about her. I always had been.

"Baby doll."

Aideen burst into tears, then turned and rushed into my arms. I hugged her body to mine, waiting until she was all cried out to lean down and plant kisses on her face. She clung to me like she needed me to get through this moment.

"If we didn't interrupt 'im, he'd have lost his virginity. I heard 'im say that." She sniffled. "He's too young, Kane."

"I know," I said, smoothing her hair back from her face. "He knows he fucked up."

"I couldn't even look at 'im when he came to apologise to me,"

Aideen cried. "I'm so mad at 'im. Doesn't he realise how easy it is to catch a disease? Or to get a woman pregnant? I don't want his life to be—"

"Baby, relax," I said, squeezing her tight. "He knows he messed up, and he's grounded for it. We can both sit down with him later and discuss it, but please, don't worry about him. We caught him before anything could happen."

Aideen's shoulders slumped. "He told me he'd tell me when he started likin' girls. I had it all figured out in me head. You would have a one-on-one talk with 'im. Not the brief facts of life ye' gave him a few years ago, but somethin' proper so he would be aware of the responsibilities that come with havin' sex."

I sighed. "He's aware of the dangers of sex now, trust me."

Aideen used her hands to wipe away her tears. The movements caused my eyes to shift to her arms. The burn scar on her forearm always made my chest hurt whenever I looked at it. It was a constant reminder that I once came close to losing her and Jax, who was in her belly at the time, when she was attacked by Big Phil, a nightmare from my past. But I eventually got revenge by taking his life.

"The boys are still down in Harley's apartment," she said, retaking my focus. "I'll go get them. It's almost dinnertime. They probably have me brother's head melted."

My brother-in-law had looked after my sons for close to two hours, so I had no doubt he needed a break from them. He did us a solid, though, taking our kids when he already had two of his own to look after. Game days were always a little crazy because we only had two sons in the same age group, but we somehow made it work. Jax was on the sixteen and under team with Locke who was fifteen. Beckett at eleven was on the under twelve team, Jagger at nine was on the under ten team, and Eli, who was seven, played on the eight and under team.

They had been like a herd of elephants just after seven in the morning, which baffled me because the first match, Eli's game, didn't start until after ten. Once they were all dressed in their gear and had their own soccer bags with all the essentials inside, we left our home and met up with my brothers and nephews down at the soccer fields next to the team clubhouse. As usual, Alec wasn't there because he was banned from attending any of the kid's games, home or away, for two years.

Damien and Ryder filled us in on the bullshit he pulled that morning with Alannah, and it started our day off with laughter. An hour later, the older boys won their games, and the younger kids lost theirs, which led to a lot of arguments about who was at fault and many unhappy faces. Our families split up afterwards, and Dominic took his boys out to see a movie and to eat after they showered in the clubhouse.

After Damien's boys washed the grime and sweat away, they left to go and collect Alannah, who was finishing up her Saturday art class at the community centre. Ryder, the poor fucker, didn't have time to make sure his kids and Alec's kids were washed and dressed. Instead, he hustled them in his mini bus and drove home, no doubt dying for some peace and quiet. My three youngest, however, refused to shower because Jax and Locke made them believe the water was tainted with the sweat of dead soccer players who roamed the clubhouse grounds angry with whoever lost a game.

They stunk to hell and back, so much so that I opened all the windows in my car as I drove them home. After we got home, and they showered, all five of them went down to Harley's apartment. He was the only remaining Collins brother to live in my building. Not long after the kids went down to his place, Aideen called him to send them back up because we had to go grocery shopping, but Harley was cool with them being in his home, so we went shopping without them.

Jax obviously took this opportunity to try to get some with his female friend.

"Hey?"

Aideen looked up at me.

"It'll be okay, you know?"

She nodded. "I know, I think I'm just in shock at what we saw if I'm bein' honest."

"It'll pass," I said. "We'll tease him about this when he is older."

"A *lot* older."

I chuckled and slapped her ass, making her jump then laugh as she left our apartment to retrieve our tribe. When I was alone, I preheated the oven, then got all the food I planned to cook out of the freezer. As I waited, I walked into the living room, pausing to look at the many photos on the wall. I looked at my wedding photo, and I could remember that day like it was yesterday. I had worn a black suit, and Aideen had worn a beautiful plain white dress for our courthouse wedding.

She looked so beautiful; it still took my breath away. My eyes slid to the pictures of our kids, then pictures of me and my laughing brothers. I lingered on my brothers for a moment and felt myself smile. I wasn't sure if they knew it or not, but they were the reason I had a wife and kids to love and adore. Growing up in a family with loveless parents would have completely ruined me had it not been for my brothers. We had been through the wringer, each of us hurting in our own way, but we came out on top.

Nothing could keep us down for very long.

Nothing.

CHAPTER TWO

Sixteen years old ...

"I don't want to go with him, Dad."

My dad reached out and smacked me upside my head as soon as the words left my mouth. I hissed, lifting my hands so I could rub the painful spot. I lowered my hands after a moment but remained tense. I was angry, so fucking angry, but I knew if I voiced my dislike for my current situation again, then my dad would do far worse than simply smack me.

I remembered how badly he beat Alec when he was fifteen for having sex with another dude, so I knew my dad would have no issue beating on me if I displeased him just like he did to my brother. He didn't treat us like a father was supposed to treat his children. He treated us like cattle that he constantly whipped into shape.

"You'll do as I say, Kane," he warned. "Am I understood?"

I didn't answer him, so he looked in my direction and leered at me. I set my jaw as I regarded him. I hated, fucking *hated*, that the eyes that glared at me were the very eyes that I had inherited from him. I looked like my dad, all of my brothers did, but no one more than my eldest brother, Ryder. He was a carbon copy of our dad, but his heart was a world away from the block of ice that sat within my father's chest.

"I said," Dad sneered, "am I understood?"

Fuck you.

I reluctantly nodded. This drew a sinister chuckle from my father as he turned forward so he could continue talking to the man who was interested in having me working with him for the day. I felt cheap, lower than the ground I stood on as I listened to my dad talk about me as if I wasn't standing next to him. Big Phil, a cold-blooded plague who worked for my dad and his business partner, Marco Miles, looked bored as he listened to my father give him instructions, but he paid attention because he knew what being disrespectful to my dad would result in.

"Mr Slater," Big Phil said. "I'll make sure he gets the full experience when he's with me today. He'll be aware of his future role within our little family."

Dad snorted. "Don't go easy on him. If he had his way, he'd stay with his brothers all the time and never talk to anyone else."

I resisted the urge to curse. My dad was always on my case because I didn't like being around people I didn't know, nor did he like my preference to stay in our home rather than hang out with Marco's nephews. It wasn't that I was scared or anything. Being around so many people just fucked with my head. I couldn't explain it, but I simply didn't like being around people who I didn't care for. I couldn't endure the presence of my parents, only my brothers. Everyone else got on my nerves.

"Like I said." Big Phil grinned. "He'll get the full experience. By the end of today, he'll be a changed boy."

Dad laughed, clapped Big Phil on the shoulder, then without a word or even glancing my way, he left the courtyard. I watched him as he walked away, before my attention turned to Big Phil who was staring at me. He looked pleased that I was in front of him, and I didn't want to know why.

"How old are you, Kane?"

"Sixteen."

He snorted. "Old enough to learn your role in this business."

"What role?" I asked. "What are you talking about?"

"I'm talking about what is expected of you when you turn eighteen. Everyone has a job around here, even if their last name is Slater."

I gritted my teeth. "I thought I could pick my own job?"

"At your size, Marco and your father think you'll suit my field perfectly."

I froze. "I don't … I don't want to be an enforcer."

I knew what Big Phil did, and it was one of the reasons he disgusted me so much. He hurt people, ruined lives, and ripped families apart all because Marco or my father said so. I didn't want to do that. I didn't want to hurt anyone for anybody.

"Tough." He laughed. "It's already been decided. You're sixteen, and you already weigh one-eighty and are nearly six-foot. Marco and your dad have noticed that you've bulked up. You're an intimidating boy, so just imagine how much bigger you'll be when you're a man."

I felt like I was going to be sick. I had noticed over the past few months that my dad had taken an interest in my exercise and diet plan. I liked to work out—I didn't do much else—so I gained muscle easily enough. Had I known that my appearance would land me in this trap, I'd have remained skinny.

"What's today about?" I asked, shifting from foot to foot. "What's going to be happening?"

"You going to accompany me on a collection run. Think of it as an unofficial ride along. You'll get to see how I operate, and you'll learn what is expected of you through me."

I felt like I was going to puke. "Where are we going?"

Big Phil didn't answer me. Instead, he walked out of the courtyard, and I had no choice but to follow him like a dog. When we left our compound, I looked around, noticing just how alone we were outside the high walls. Marco and my dad owned a lot of the land our compound was built on, and for miles in every direction, there were empty fields. We lived in North County, New York. The city was a few hours south, but it might as well have been a world away.

"Kane," Big Phil hollered. "You have shotgun."

I turned to him and looked at the black Cadillac he climbed into. I swallowed down bile, and walked towards the car, sliding into the passenger seat. A quick look in the back told me I was on my own with Big Phil, and I hated that. We drove in silence for what felt like an hour, and when we came to a town, Big Phil drove onto a street and stopped in front of a small house.

"Follow me," he said. "And don't speak unless I say otherwise."

That suited me fine. I didn't want to speak anyway.

"Come on."

We left the car, walked up the pathway to the house, and instead of knocking, Big Phil tried the door handle. When it opened, he stepped inside, and shouted, "Kade!"

There was movement upstairs, then a man wearing just boxers shorts appeared at the top of the stairs. I heard a baby cry, then watched as a woman rushed by behind the man and entered a bedroom, closing the door behind her. I could have sworn I heard a lock click into place, but I wasn't sure.

"Big," Kade said, looking more than a little surprised. "I wasn't expecting you until the end of the week."

"I know." Big Phil nodded. "Things have changed, though, and Marco needs his payment. Right now."

I watched as Kade's face paled. "I don't get paid until the end of the week. Marco knows that."

"As I said, things have changed."

Kade reached the bottom of the stairs, and said, "I don't know what to tell you, Big. I have fifty bucks until payday."

"What about your girl?"

Kade froze. "She doesn't work. She stays at home and takes care of the baby."

Big Phil rubbed his hand over his face, and said, "This is a sad situation. You know Marco doesn't like to be left high and dry when he's expecting money."

"But he *said* the end of the week," Kade stressed. "He promised me."

Big Phil considered this, then looked at me, and said, "Kane, what do you think I should do?"

He's asking me?

I looked up at Big Phil and said, "Why're you asking me?"

"'Cause I want your opinion."

I looked at Kade then back at Big Phil.

"If Marco gave him a deadline, then he should stick to it. I think you should leave him alone."

Big Phil grinned. "Is that so?"

I nodded.

He looked at Kade, and said, "You can have your original deadline back. I'll see you on Friday."

Kade looked like the weight of the world just fell off his shoulders. He thanked Big Phil, said goodbye to me, then locked his front door behind us when we left his house. I followed Big Phil back to the car, and when I was buckled into my seat, I turned to look at him. I sucked in a strangled breath when he reached out and swiped something across my face.

He grabbed my head and forced it down to my knees with one hand while the other went to my neck. It took a few seconds for pain to register, and for me to realise that Big Phil had just slashed my face and cut up the back of my neck. I pressed my hands to the wounds, then looked at them to find them covered with blood. I quickly removed my T-shirt and pressed it against my cheek, applying heavy pressure, while I flattened my palm on the back of my neck.

"Why?" I choked. "What'd I do?"

"You sided against me in there when you shouldn't have. That was a lesson, and you just learned it the hard way. You need to be reminded who owns you, boy."

His demeanour and tone was so calm. He didn't act like he just cut me; in fact, he looked as if that action was part of his daily routine. Knowing him, it probably was.

"The bleeding," I said, feeling my body tremble. "It won't stop."

"We'll get you patched up back at the compound."

He drove us home then, and just like the drive to Kade's house, it was entirely silent. Tears stung at my eyes, but I refused to let them fall. I held my breath whenever I thought a sob would escape, and eventually, the urge to cry passed, but the pain remained and stung terribly. When we reached the compound, I got out of the car, and without a word to Big Phil, I ran towards my family's wing. I ignored him when he shouted after me, but I did turn to face him when I stepped inside my home.

"What?" I demanded, tossing my bloody soaked shirt at his feet as he came to a stop in front of me. "What the fuck do you want from me?"

"One day, Marco will give you to me." Big Phil sneered. "You're going to be my little puppet, and when I say jump, you'll say how high. I'll make you bleed worse than you are now before you ever disrespect me again, boy."

I glared at Big Phil as I reached out and gripped the door handle.

"That may be true," I spat. "But until that day, you can go and fuck yourself."

I slammed the door in his face and hearing him kick the door and curse made me smile. I knew that I had just made an enemy out of the man, and he would most likely make me pay for it, but at that very moment, I got the better of him, and it made me as happy as a pig in shit.

"What the fuck is going on?"

I turned to face Ryder when he jogged down the stairs. He came to a stop at the end of the stairs for just a second before he widened his eyes and rushed towards me. He grabbed hold of my chin when I turned to look at him, and when he examined my face, and my wound, his eyes darkened. He turned me so he could see my neck, and I heard his sharp intake of breath.

"Who did this to you?"

Big Phil had already stormed away from our home, and I was glad because I didn't want him to attack my brother.

"What's wrong with my neck?" I asked, ignoring the question. "It's just cuts."

"It ... it spells a name."

My heart stopped. "What name?"

"Marco."

You needed to be reminded who owns you, boy

Hate filled me. Hate for Marco. Hate for Big Phil. Hate for my father for not protecting me from them like he was supposed to do.

"It doesn't matter," I said, stepping away from him. "Nothing can be done about it, so there's no point in talking about it."

Ryder followed me into one of the downstairs bathrooms and watched me as I retrieved a first-aid kit. I hadn't realised until then that my hands were slightly shaking. My brother stepped forward and silently held his hand out for the kit. I sighed and handed it to him as I jumped up on the counter and sat beside the sink. My brother shook his head as he cleaned the blood from my face, and it made me swallow.

"Does it look bad?"

Ryder didn't have to speak for me to know the answer to my question. His eyes told me everything I needed to know.

"Fuck," I said, forcing a smile. "Alec will definitely be the prettiest brother now."

My brother didn't smile, and it made me lose mine.

"It's only a cut, Ry."

"Only a cut?" he repeated, his voice rough. "It's over four inches in length, and it's deep enough that you'll not be able to hide the scar it'll cause. This is your fucking face, Kane. Tell me who did this to you?"

I felt Ryder's anger for the one who hurt me, but nothing could overshadow the concern and worry that I knew he felt. He was only three years older than Alec, five years older than me, and ten years older than the twins, and he held the weight of the world on his shoulders when it came to me and my brothers. He took care of all of us, he always had, and I couldn't begin to imagine how hard that was for him. He was only twenty-one, and he had the responsibilities of a grown man with four kids in a world where crime was our way of life.

"Ryder, you can't do anything to him."

"To who?"

"Big Phil."

Ryder's lips parted with surprise. "Why the fuck did he slash your face and carve Marco's name into your neck? Why were you even around him?"

"Dad made me go with him for the day. Big Phil said my future within our family was to be like him." I looked down. "I don't wanna do what he does, Ryder. He hurts people."

"Did he make you do something you didn't want to today?"

I shook my head. "This man, Kade, owed Marco money. He didn't have the money yet because Marco gave him a deadline of the end of the week. Big Phil asked me what I thought about it, and I told him that Marco should respect a deadline if he gave it. He cut me because I sided against him. He said it was a lesson I had to learn the hard way. He put Marco's name on me to remind me who owned me."

When I looked up at my Ryder, his face was passive.

"Big Phil said one day I'd be his puppet. That Marco would give me to him, and that he'd make me bleed before I ever disrespected him again."

My brother looked like he was about to explode.

"I'll kill him."

I didn't react to Ryder's threat because I knew it only came from a place of anger. He knew that he could never touch Big Phil.

That man was too deep in with our father and Marco; he was a right-hand man, so he was virtually untouchable. I remained silent as he cleaned up my face. I winced a couple of times, but once he stuck on a few paper stitches, I relaxed. He cleaned up my neck, then placed a large gauze over it and secured it with medical tape.

"Those might come off when it starts to swell," Ryder said, nodding towards the paper stitches, as he cleaned away the items used to clean away my blood. "We'll have to call the doc if that happens or if you get an infection."

I nodded, and Ryder regarded me for a moment.

"I'm going to do what I can to keep Big Phil off your back, okay?" he said. "I'm not going to let him hurt you again."

I knew he believed that, and I knew he would go to any length possible to keep me safe, but I wasn't stupid. I saw the look in Big Phil's eye when he threatened me. He said one day I would be his puppet, and I knew that day would eventually come to pass. Evil outweighed good in our compound, and when someone who was cold as Big Phil marked you as his, then he owned you, one way or the other.

"I know, Ry." I smiled. "That's why I'm not worried."

If I had to smile and lie to appease my brother to save him some worry, then I would. Big Phil had said to my dad that by the end of the day I would be a changed person, and he was right. I saw evil up close and personal and knew that evil would find me one day. I couldn't be ignorant and think staying away from the people my dad did business with would keep them away from me forever. I had to be sensible and prepare for the day when the life Big Phil led would become my own.

There was no escape once you reached the pits of hell. No one came to help you out, but plenty of hands where there to keep you down.

CHAPTER THREE

Twenty-years old ...

"**K**ane!"

I jolted awake, sat upright in my bed, and stared at the figure by my bedroom door. Suddenly, the light in my room was switched on, and I lifted my hand to block the beam.

"Get up," a rough voice demanded. "We have work to do."

Once my eyes adjusted to the light, I lowered my arm and squinted my eyes at the intruder in my room before my eyes narrowed to slits. I said nothing as I threw the bed covers away from my body and quickly got dressed. I felt his eyes on me as I pulled on my boots and tied the laces. I stood, lifted my head, and looked Big Phil in the eyes.

"Where are we going?"

"To settle a score."

My heart stopped. For a few months since I'd become his personal monkey, Big Phil had been showing up at random times throughout my day and night to enlist me into bullshit schemes. I never had to do anything, just shadow him for no other reason than he made me, but tonight ... this was the first time I had to actually do anything since I had become an enforcer for Marco.

Four months ago, my parents had double-crossed him in a bid to make some extra money, and they paid for that with their lives. I didn't care about their deaths when I first heard about it, and I didn't care about it now. The only thing I cared about, the only thing that kept me and my brothers from fleeing this godforsaken life, was the threat over my brother Damien's head. Having killed Marco's nephew in a fight that turned deadly, he had a life debt to repay, and me and my brothers were the ones working it off.

"Who's coming with us?"

"It's just me and you tonight."

Fuck.

I followed him out of my room, out of the house, then down to the lower floors of the compound. I never came down here, not even to attend parties in the pleasure rooms. We walked down lengthy halls and suddenly came to a stop in front of a set of large black doors. Other than hearing the night watch laugh and joke around, it was completely silent. It gave me a bad feeling, but there wasn't a damn thing I could do about it. Big Phil entered the room without a word, and I followed him. I came to an abrupt halt when the coppery twang of blood filled my nostrils. My eyes locked on the person in the centre of the dimly lit room, and my heart pounded against my chest.

"Jesus Christ."

The man's hands were bound with a rope and hoisted above his head. Hanging from the ceiling was a large chain and the rope was tied to the end of it. To my left was a table with knives and other devices coated with blood. I fought the urge to vomit. The man had deep lacerations all over his naked body, there was a puddle of blood under him, and his skin was so pale I knew he was minutes away from dying in front of me.

"What the fuck is this?"

"This," Big Phil said, "is Hector Gomez. Hector is a narc for the feds, and you know the punishment for that."

I wanted to run away.

"Yeah," I said, "death, so what the fuck is *this*?"

"Marco just told me to kill him. He never told me in what way."

Big Phil's grin was sinister, and it disgusted me.

"You're a sick cunt."

He laughed, unbothered.

"That may be so, but I still have a task that I've yet to complete."

When he looked at Hector, I froze. "So complete it."

I felt so unbelievably heartbroken for the man before me, but in his current condition, I knew that death would be a mercy for him. He was mortally wounded, and though he was unconscious, I knew he was in severe pain. Big Phil had tortured him for his own sick amusement. I thought I couldn't possibly think worse of the man than I already did, but he proved me wrong.

"Finishing this job is what you're here for."

I stepped back, my eyes widening to the point of pain.

"I'm not killing anyone," I stated. "I'm just supposed to—"

"You're supposed to do what I say," Big Phil interrupted. "And I say you have to kill him."

"No." I shook my head. "I can't. I won't."

"Do you know what the difference between choking and strangling is?"

I blinked. "What?"

"You heard me."

I hesitated, and Big Phil grinned.

"Choking is when something is stuck in your throat, and strangling is when you forcefully restrict a person's ability to breathe by wrapping something around their throat."

I didn't move an inch.

"Being strangled is an awful way to die, I presume, and that experience will be one your little brother experiences if you don't fall in line and do what you're told."

My body went rigid. "*Don't* threaten my brother."

"Don't threaten him?" Big Phil repeated in disbelief. "Son, I'll take his life in front of you if you slack on a job again."

Fury flowed through my veins quickly followed by frustration and helplessness because there was nothing I could do to Big Phil without it hurting my brother.

"Are we clear?"

"Yeah," I grunted. "We're clear."

"Kill Hector ... with your bare hands."

I felt tears well in my eyes, but I turned my head so Big Phil couldn't see me. I knew if I asked for a gun, he would think of a more brutal way for Hector to die. I slowly approached Hector who began to regain consciousness. He opened one of his swollen eyes and looked at me. He rasped something in Spanish that I didn't understand.

"He's begging you to kill him."

My tears fell and splashed onto my cheeks. Hector saw them, and his body relaxed as much as it could considering its current state. He smiled at me, or at least I thought he did. I felt his acceptance at what was about to happen, and I believed that he saw in my eyes that I didn't want to hurt him. He closed his wounded eye and exhaled a long breath.

"I'm so sorry, sir," I whispered. "I'm doing this for my brother. Please, forgive me."

I closed my eyes as I started the beating. Through the crunching of bones, and the screams of agony, I forced my mind to retreat to a safe place. One where I wasn't the evil thing ending someone's life. Somewhere where I could pretend I was a good man and had a good life. When the screams stopped, I turned away and promptly vomited onto the floor. Big Phil laughed at me.

"You're a man now, Kane, my boy."

"I'm *not* your boy," I snarled as I frantically rubbed my hands on my clothes to rid myself of Hector's blood. "I'm nothing to you."

"That is where you're wrong," he answered. "I own you."

I didn't reply.

"One more task, and you can hop back to bed."

I closed my eyes when the doors to the room opened and a

woman's screams could be heard. Those screams intensified when she entered the room. It was a scream filled with so much agony, I felt it seep down into my bones. A chill ran the length of my spine when the women wailed, "Hector!"

She spoke rapidly in Spanish, and when Hector didn't answer her, she cried until she made no sound.

"This is Hector's wife," Big Phil said. "Also a narc for the feds."

I lowered my head.

"You know what I'm going to tell you, Kane."

I did. He was going to ask me to take a woman's life.

"I can't hurt a woman," I choked. "I can't. I won't."

"Kane—"

"No!" I snapped. "I'm not hurting her!"

There was a moment of silence, then Big Phil sighed and said, "Do you remember what happened the last time you disobeyed me?"

He cut my face, and carved Marco's name into my flesh.

"I don't care," I said, shaking my head. "I don't care. I won't hurt her."

Big Phil was the picture of rage as he jerked his head to his men. They dragged Hector's silent wife, bound her wrists, and strung her up next to him. When the men grabbed hold of me, I didn't even fight them as they did the same to me. My heart pounded into my chest as my sweater and T-shirt were cut away from my body, leaving my torso bare. I struggled against the ropes, and they burned my wrists. I closed my eyes, not wanting to look at Big Phil or his men as they moved about the room. I tensed when they moved behind me, and I could no longer see them.

"You'll learn not to disrespect me, boy," Big Phil hissed. "On my life, you will learn."

There was a sickening crack in the air, then something searing hot licked my back. I sucked in a strangled breath but didn't have time to focus on the pain that tore across my back because whatever was used to hit me, slapped into my back repeatedly. When the woman beside me had her shirt removed, and the crack sounded, her body jerked, and she screamed so loud it made me choke on words meant to comfort her. She received lash after lash, and so did I. Eventually, my screams blended with the woman's until I didn't know where hers ended or mine began, but in the end, her screams faded to nothing as her life left her body while mine echoed throughout the silent compound.

As my body broke down, my mind strengthened. Big Phil had proven that he could do what he wanted to me once I disobeyed him. He proved that I was his puppet, that he owned me ... that was all true, but one thing he would never own was my spirit. He could rip my body apart, but he would never break me. I swore on everything that I loved that he would never get the chance, and that was a promise I intended to keep.

CHAPTER FOUR

Twenty-five years old ...

"S later, are ye' listenin' to me?"

I looked to my right and stared at Joe Riley blankly.

"I'll take that as a no," he chortled. "This piece of shite says he wasn't at the docks tonight. Can ye' believe that?"

I looked at Kevin Marshal, a dumbass gang member who crossed his boss for a stack. If it wasn't for him, I could have still been with my brothers, kicking back, drinking beers and talking shit.

"You're made on CCTV footage, Kevin."

His face paled. "I am?"

Joe snorted. "Yeah, ye' are."

Kevin looked from Joe to me, then back to Joe.

"Please, don't kill me."

Joe burst into manic laughter that was purely for Kevin's benefit. Kevin was Brandy Daley's best friend's son, and Joe, one of Brandy's puppets, was instructed to scare the shit out of him for helping himself to Brandy's money. I didn't hurt people anymore, but if someone paid me to scare the shit out of someone who was in the wrong, I'd happily do it. I scared people every day when they looked at me for free, so this worked in my favour at least.

Not that I needed the money, but a little extra to line my pockets was always nice.

I folded my arms across my chest and narrowed my eyes at Kevin, who honestly looked like he was about to piss himself. He was bound to the chair he sat on with his hands behind his back, and sweat pumped out of him. His face was a little busted up thanks to Joe's men who picked Kevin up for our little chat. He was rightly roughed up, and from the look of fear and regret in his eyes, I doubted he'd steal from his father's friend ever again.

Joe didn't say a word to his men as he motioned for them to remove Kevin from the room, and just as I was about to leave, two other men dragged a battered man into the room and sat him on the chair Kevin just vacated. They tied his hands behind him and pulled the black sack that was covering his head away.

"Shane." Joe smiled. "How are ye', son?"

Shane, a man I had never met, had an eye so swollen it was sealed shut. Blood dripped from his nostrils, and his lip was fat and busted open. Someone had roughed him up good.

"Fuck you, Joe."

I raised an eyebrow and looked at Joe, who wasn't bothered by Shane's outburst.

"Kevin's friend." He shrugged. "Helped him steal the money and was involved in a shipment goin' missin' tonight."

I stepped back. This man wasn't going to get a warning beating like Kevin. He would most likely die for what he did. No one stole from Brandy Daley and got away with it. Kevin was lucky he had a father who was close to Brandy; otherwise, he would mostly have the same fate as Shane. Joe asked Shane a few questions about the location of the shipment that was lost, and he answered none of them.

"Remainin' silent will only lead to more bad shite happenin' to ye', Shane. Do yourself a favour and tell me where the shipment is. I know ye' tried to jack it. I've eyes everywhere along the docks."

Shane laughed, then spat in Joe's direction. "If ye' have eyes all along the docks, then why did none of them see where your shipment got to?"

Joe took out a handkerchief from his jacket pocket and wiped his face. "I don't have time for games. Tell me what I want to know or me friend 'ere will break your legs. Your choice."

Still, he remained silent. One of the men who brought Shane into the room didn't wait for an order from Joe before he advanced forward and threw a punch at Shane, who couldn't defend himself. There was a lot of shouting, cursing, and screaming that followed in the next twenty seconds, and I looked away from the beating just as the other man who brought Shane into the room opened the door, and a gasp sounded.

"I took a wrong turn. I'm so sorry."

My heart stopped because I knew who that voice belonged to. Just before the man could go after Aideen Collins, I stepped forward and moved in front of him.

"I've got her."

He shrugged and turned back to Shane getting his ass handed to him. I looked at Joe, nodded and then left the room knowing I would never take another job offer from him again. I didn't want to be involved in people getting hurt anymore. That part of my life was over, and I wasn't revisiting it for no one. I jogged out of the room and followed the sound of heels clicking against the floor, as well as laboured breathing. I turned onto a hallway and silently walked up behind Aideen, who turned and walked head first into my chest.

"Ow!"

She lifted her hand to her forehead and rubbed it.

"You should watch where you're going."

I watched as she recognised my voice, and I wanted to laugh when her fear fled, and annoyance took root, but then I was reminded where she was and just how dangerous things could have been for her if I hadn't been the one to come after her.

"What the hell are *you* doing back here?"

Aideen swallowed and looked from left to right. "I could ask *you* the same thing," she replied with confidence I knew she didn't feel.

I set my jaw. "No, you fucking can't. This is *no* place for someone like you."

"Someone like me?" she asked, offended.

I walked forward, and she backed up towards the wall. "Yeah, someone like you."

When her back pressed up against it, she blurted, "What's *that* supposed to mean?"

She sucked in a startled breath when I surged forward and gripped both of her arms with my hands.

"It means." I leaned in close to her face. "That good girls don't belong here. Understand me, baby doll?"

Her eyes were wide, and her plump lips were parted. She was scared, but she was trying her hardest not to be, and I admired her for it.

"What makes ye' think I'm a good girl?"

I allowed my eyes to roam over her and felt my lips twitch. "I don't think you're a good girl, baby doll. I know you are."

"That just goes to show ye' really don't know me because I *do* belong 'ere … I'm 'round 'ere all the time. I've actually hung out in Darkness since *before* ye' even moved here. I'm practically an OG of this place."

I wanted to laugh.

"Oh, really? Then tell me something, OG, why do you look lost walking down these hallways?"

She opened her mouth to speak, but quickly closed it because she had no clue how to answer me because she *was* lost. She was too stubborn to admit that, though, so instead, she said, "I don't have to justify meself to *you*, Slater."

I did chuckle then. "That you don't, baby doll."

She tried to pull free of my hold, but my grip tightened on her.

"Let go of me!" she demanded. "And what the hell is with this baby doll crap?"

I hadn't realised I had called her baby doll, but I looked at her from head to toe and shrugged. "You need babying, and you look like a doll so ... baby doll."

"Is that your way of implyin' that I'm fake like a doll?"

I tilted my head. "Uh, no, you little weirdo."

"Now you're callin' me short?" She huffed. "You're a real—"

I surprised her when I began to laugh. She went completely silent, and I concluded it was because she never heard me laugh before.

"You need to calm down," I said. "I'm not insulting you. First, all I'm saying is you need looking after. You being here proves my point, so that's what I meant by babying. Second, you look gorgeous, fucking unreal, so that is what I meant by a doll. Put them together and you get baby doll, *baby doll*."

Her voice was soft as she said, "And little?"

I grinned. "You're a little bitty thing, what can I say?"

Her cheeks flushed a pretty pink, and she couldn't look me in the eye. She was pleased with what I said, but her damn pride wouldn't allow her to admit it.

"Your observations and sugar sweet words won't get ye' anywhere with me, so ye' can let go of me arms."

The challenge in her tone amused me. "Make me."

She scowled up at me. "I don't have time for this. I just saw somethin' I shouldn't have, and I have to leave before they find me—"

"I already found you," I interrupted.

Her jaw dropped. "*You* were in that room?"

I shrugged in response.

She placed her delicate hands on my chest and tried to push me away. "Get away from me."

She looked scared of me then, and I hated that.

"It's not what you think. I was more of an observer than an active participant in that room."

Her eyes widened. "So ye' *watched* a helpless man get attacked? How fuckin' noble of ye', Kane."

"Aideen, you take people at face value too often."

She regarded me. "I clearly do because I thought *you* weren't into anythin' bad. Looks like I was very wrong."

She rounded on me then and turned right, trying to find her way out of the club. I followed her.

"I'm not a bad man, Aideen."

She scoffed. "What are ye' doin' back 'ere then?"

"Working."

She stopped midstride and turned to face me. "What type of work?"

"It's nothing that concerns you, babe—trust me."

"Bite me, Slater."

I took a step closer to her. "Tell me where and I'll be happy to oblige."

Her pupils dilated a fraction, and her breathing became audible as I moved closer to her. She stared up at me with doe like eyes, and said, "Kane?"

I lowered my face to hers. "Aideen?"

Her lips parted ever so slightly, and her eyes locked on my lips. "What're ye' doin'?"

I wanted to kiss her so badly it hurt.

"Call it an act of impulse."

She shivered. "Ye'... ye' better not be thinkin' what I *think* you're thinkin'."

"I bet our thoughts are pretty identical right now, baby doll."

"Get away from me," she said with no conviction. "Lose the stupid nickname, too."

She didn't want me to do either of those things. Her cheeks were flushed, her body was leaning into mine, and she was all but panting before me.

"Not a chance in hell on either count, *baby doll*."

Before she could yell at me, I pressed my lips against hers. I waited for any sign that she truly didn't want me. I had it planned out in my head, and I'd let her smack me if she wanted to, and then I would apologise profusely if she wanted nothing to do with me. But the possibility of that vanished when she opened her mouth and flicked her tongue against my lips. She moaned when I kissed her back as she slid her hands up my arms to my shoulders where she pressed her fingers firmly into my flesh.

I pressed her back against the wall and moulded my body to hers. I slid my hands to her sides, then around to her ass where I roughly palmed her behind and drew a hiss from her parted lips. I positioned my hands under her butt and lifted her so I could kiss her without bending down. I pinned her in place with my hips, hooked my right hand under her ass to support her, and cupped her face with my left hand as I kissed her. Her legs moved around my hips and squeezed me. A groan left me as she rolled her pelvis against mine, sending a shudder throughout my body. My already aching cock throbbed.

Without a word, I broke our kiss, lowered her to the ground, grabbed her hand, and tugged her along behind me.

"Where are we goin'?"

I didn't answer her, the need to push her back up against the wall and fuck her screamed at me. I refused to take her in a place so tainted. She was worth too much to be degraded by the likes of Darkness. Aideen had to practically run to keep up with me, and I appreciated it because if she slowed down, I was more than tempted to toss her over my shoulder and start running.

"*Where* are we goin', Kane?"

Her patience with me was running out.

"My house."

"Why?" she demanded. "There are plenty of rooms right 'ere that we could use."

I didn't stop walking, nor did I look over my shoulder at her.

"I *hate* this place; the last thing I want to do is fuck you in it."

When we reached the main doors that led back into the club, I gripped the handle and pulled it open. Aideen winced when the volume of blaring music flooded into the once silent hallway. She pulled her hand from mine and covered her ears.

"Fuck!"

The noise didn't bother me; the only thing that did was my cock. I took hold of Aideen's arm and led her through the club. Some people moved out of our way, and those who didn't, I pushed aside, not caring who they were. I snapped at a couple of people, and once their eyes landed on my face, they scattered like roaches. Just as I got into a stride, I was suddenly pulled to a stop by Aideen. When I turned and looked at her, she shouted over the music, "Skull is expectin' me to be in a room in the back waitin' on 'im."

I felt my body go rigid. "I don't fucking think so."

I bent down, pulled her over my shoulder, stood, turned, and continued walking out of the club. I could hear Aideen scream with laughter, but I couldn't laugh. I wanted her too much to even consider it. As I jogged up the stairs, she hollered, "Me tits are goin' to pop out!"

I did laugh then as I smacked her ass and ran up the stairs faster.

"Bastard!"

Her laughter didn't stop as I zoomed through the bouncers and people who were still trying to gain entry to the club even though it was nearing closing time. When I reached the car, I set Aideen down on her feet and steadied her by placing my hands on her shoulders. She was looking at the ground, so I tipped her chin up with my fingers until her eyes found mine.

"You seem nervous."

She swallowed. "I *am* nervous."

"Because I'm going to have you or because you're worried Skull will find out?"

I didn't care about Skull, but I didn't want Aideen to care about him either, and it baffled me as to why I felt that way.

"Skull and I aren't together, Kane. We decided that for good tonight. He just put me in the back room because I wanted to go home, but he couldn't leave to bring me home. He's still workin'."

I deadpanned. "I'd bet my life that he would have fucked you when he got back to the room."

Aideen shook her head. "He respects me. He wouldn't take advantage of me if he knew I didn't *want* to have sex with 'im."

I pressed her body against my car with mine.

"Do you *want* to have sex with him?"

She placed her hands on my chest. "I don't know what I want."

"I do," I said. "Me."

I kissed her again, and she melted against me, and it was too much for me to bear.

"Get in the car," I growled against her kiss swollen lips. "Now."

When she slid into the passenger seat, I slammed the door shut and sped around to the driver's side. When I jumped inside, I had my belt buckled, the engine started, and the car reversing in a matter of seconds.

"Oh, my God!" Aideen screeched when I put the car in gear, then took off out of the parking lot. "I want to survive this ride. Slow down."

"The only thing you will be riding tonight, baby doll, is me. Now, sit back, shut the fuck up, and let me drive."

Out of the corner of my eye, I saw Aideen's jaw drop, but no words left her mouth. She regarded me for a long moment, and I could almost hear the gears in her mind turn. Normally, she would cuss at me or demand an apology ... but not tonight.

"Ye' know I don't do what I'm told, Kane."

I took a sharp left turn. "You will when I fuck you."

"That looks really uncomfortable."

I looked at her and followed her gaze to between my thighs.

"It is, but you can make me more comfortable in less than five minutes, so just shut up and let me get to where I'm going."

She didn't respond. Instead, she leaned over and moved her mouth over my cock.

"Aideen!"

I felt the heat of her tongue through my jeans, and the urge to buck my hips up into her face almost killed me.

"Unzip me," I implored. "Fuck, Aideen, unzip my jeans and put your mouth on me."

She grabbed my zipper with her teeth and tugged it down. She used her hand to pull it fully down when it wouldn't budge anymore. "Say please," she murmured and kissed the tip of my erection through my boxers. I would have done a handstand naked at that moment had she asked me to.

"Please!"

She tugged my boxers down but lost her grip, causing the band to snap against my balls. I hissed more in shock than in pain.

"My bad."

I just about whimpered when I felt her hot breath over my cock.

"Just blow me, please."

She gently kissed the tip of my erection and coated her lips with the pre-cum that seeped from the head. She wasted no time in sucking my cock into her mouth and bobbing her head up and down. When she sucked me, my eyes threatened to cross.

"God, *yes!*"

Just as she got into a good rhythm, she backed off, sat back in her seat, and wiped her mouth with the back of her hands.

"Wh-what?" I stammered. "Why did you stop?"

She shrugged. "I figured I'd do a better job once we get into a bed. It's a little awkward givin' head in a fast movin' vehicle, knowin' I'm seconds from dyin'. Plus, me seat belt was diggin' into me side."

I floored the accelerator on the car.

"Kane!"

I ignored her for the remainder of the drive, and when I pulled onto my driveway, I looked at her and barked, "Out. Now."

I tucked myself back into my jeans as I jumped out of the car and slammed the door shut. I wasted no time in rounding on Aideen's side, but she was moving *way* too slow for me. I opened the door, reached in, unbuckled her seat belt, and hooked my left arm under her legs and my right around her back. I wordlessly lifted her out of the car, turned us around, and kicked the door closed with my foot. Aideen giggled and put her arms around my neck. She leaned into me and planted kisses along the base of my neck until her lips touched a spot that made me shudder.

"Damn it, Aideen!"

She laughed when I set her on the ground next to the front door of my house.

"Out of all the times I've been 'ere," she mused. "I never thought I'd be stoppin' by for some midnight sex with *you*."

"Who else would you have sex with here if not me?" I asked as I dug my keys out of my pocket.

She snickered. "Damien could come back here at any time."

Oh, hell no.

I glared down at her. "You're *not* sleeping with my little brother."

"Why not?"

She was teasing me, but I still leaned forward, placed my mouth to her ear, and whispered, "Because after tonight, you'll be mine. Only ever mine."

She burst into a fit of giggles, and I had to bite my lip to keep from laughing.

"Be quiet. Everyone is in bed."

That shut her up.

"Branna and Ryder are home?"

I grinned at her when I saw the worry in her eyes.

"If you run, I'll chase you and catch you, babydoll."

Amused, she said, "I'll smack the shite out of ye'."

"I'm holding you to that."

She smiled at me, and my stomach erupted with those stupid butterflies that my brothers talked about getting whenever they looked at their girlfriends.

"Ry and Bran are on the second floor," I assured her. "I'm up top in Dominic's old room. They won't hear us."

She swallowed. "Just ... just don't say me name."

Pain sliced across my chest, but I refused to let it show.

"Are you embarrassed?"

I wouldn't have blamed her if she was. I was disgustingly ugly, and she probably didn't want people to know she wanted to fuck me.

"*No*, I just don't want to be the butt of jokes," she replied. "Ye' know everyone will tease us if they knew we ... well, ye' know."

I opened the door and stepped inside my house. I turned, waiting for her to follow, and released a breath I didn't know I was holding when she stepped inside. I locked the door behind her and stepped close to her.

She didn't move a muscle. "Ye' aren't goin' to let me leave, are ye'?"

I slid my hands around her waist. "For now? No."

"And later?"

I nipped at her neck and nudged her into a walk. "Ask me later."

She wasn't moving quick enough for me, so I picked her up again.

"I can *walk*, ye' know?"

I squeezed her ass. "Not fast enough."

I took the stairs two at a time and didn't stop until I was inside my room with the door locked. I dropped Aideen on my bed, and she gasped at the contact. She lifted her head and watched me as I removed her high heels, dropping them onto the floor with a thud. With my eyes locked on hers, I slid my hands up her legs until I reached her hips. I gripped the hem of her panties and slid them down her legs. I flung them over my shoulder just as Aideen's eyes widened. She scrambled up onto her knees before me.

"Kane."

I leaned my head down and kissed her. When she tried to deepen the kiss, I pulled back, and clicked my tongue.

"Arms up first."

"What—?"

"Arms up first, both of them. You can kiss me when you do that."

She lifted her arms above my head and froze when I fisted the fabric of her dress and pulled it up her body and over her head. Aideen slowly lowered her arms and blinked. I tossed her dress over my shoulder, reached behind her back, and unclasped her bra. The straps fell down her arms, then before she could blink, the material joined her other clothes on the floor of my bedroom.

"Ye' know, ye' could have just asked me to strip, right?"

My eyes feasted over her naked form. I only had the moonlight that shone into my room to see, but as it cascaded over Aideen's fair skin and supple curves, I felt like the luckiest son of a bitch on the planet. I gripped the back of my T-shirt and pulled it over my head.

"I could have, but what's the fun in that?"

Aideen's eyes dropped to my chest, and it was then I remember about the scars. I wasn't sure how I forgot about them, but I did, and knowing she could see them made my chest hurt. My gut tightened as I stared at her face, waiting for disgust to fill her warm eyes, but it never did. My heart pounded against my chest, and for the first time, I wished that she couldn't see me because I was embarrassed of my appearance.

"Do you want me to put my tee back on?"

If she said yes, I knew that the pain I felt in my chest would intensify.

"No," she answered, flicking her eyes up to mine. "Why would I want ye' to do that? I'm naked, so I want *you* naked."

She was being nice to me and didn't want to hurt my feelings. It made me want her that bit more.

"My body … It's ruined, baby doll. It's not pretty to look at or to feel. I won't be offended if you want me to stay clothed."

I wouldn't be offended, but later, when I was on my own, I'd feel the hurt I felt whenever anyone looked at me like I was a monster.

Aideen locked eyes with mine, and said, "Your body is not ruined; it's unique."

I held my breath as she reached out and ran her fingers over a lumpy scar that curved from my neck down the centre of my chest. I kept my eyes on her face, waiting for a hint of revulsion, but all I could see was acceptance, admiration ... and lust.

"You're the hottest man I've ever laid me eyes on." She smiled, and she leaned into me. "I'll deny ever sayin' that in the mornin'."

I surprised us both when I laughed.

"Are you just saying that so you can get in my pants?"

Aideen grinned. "I could say a lot less and get in your pants, but no, I'm bein' honest. You're perfect the way ye' are. Your scars don't bother me at all, honey."

I couldn't tell if she was lying or not, but I desperately wanted to believe her. She roamed her eyes over my body and bit down on her lower lip. She wanted me, she couldn't fake that kind of attraction. I saw it in her eyes that she really wanted me ... scars and all. A sound rumbled up my throat, and Aideen shuddered.

"I *love* when ye' make that noise."

I snaked my hands around to her bare behind and squeezed her flesh.

"I'm going to fuck you so hard you'll see stars."

"Yes," she whispered. "Yes, please."

"Turn around."

"Okay," she answered and turned her back to me.

I placed my hand against her neck and slid it down to the base of her spine.

"Bend over."

She didn't move.

"Aideen," I growled. "Bend. Over."

Her body trembled as she bent forward and flattened her palms against the soft mattress beneath her. I licked my lips at the arch of her spine and the curve of her rounded ass. I stepped back, and my eyes locked on her pussy. My mouth watered, and my cock jumped.

"I'm going to fuck you right here." I reached forward and lazily rotated my finger in circles around her entrance.

"And if you can take me here," I grunted and moved my finger to her asshole, "I'll fuck you here, too."

Her body tensed, and a smirked curved my lip. I wasn't certain, but something told me she had never had her ass fucked before. I itched to be her first.

"Aideen?" I said, sliding my finger inside her hot, wet, tight pussy.

She moaned out loud when I added another finger, and my lips twitched.

"Oh, so you *are* awake."

Her body jerked.

"Ye' thought I fell asleep positioned like this while you're doin' *that*?"

I continued to slowly pump my fingers in and out of her body. "Stranger things have happened."

Her muscles tightened ever so slightly around my fingers.

"Please."

I licked my lips. "Please what?"

She groaned. "Please, fuck me already."

I had to use every ounce of willpower I possessed to remain still.

"I don't know ... you don't seem to really want me to fuck you."

"Kane," she growled. "I'm *very* ready for ye' to fuck me."

I hummed. "It doesn't seem like it."

She pushed back against my hand, taking my fingers deep inside her tight cunt. I smiled and slapped her ass. "That shows your enthusiasm, but not quite enough for me to be bothered enough to take my cock out."

"I'll show ye' enthusiasm," she muttered under her breath.

I watched her with raised eyebrows as she rolled to the side, got off the bed, and approached me.

"What are you—offt!"

She ran at me and threw her body at mine. I caught her but fell back onto my bed. She pushed me back and ordered, "Move up the bed."

My cock throbbed, but I'd be damned if I wasn't turned on. I shimmied up the bed and then clasped my hands behind my head and waited.

"What now?"

Aideen didn't reply. Instead, she moved down my thighs and grabbed my jeans. She unbuttoned them and forcibly yanked them and my boxers down to my thighs, letting my cock spring free. She didn't ask for permission, nor did she let on to what she was doing. She simply moved back up my body, reached down, grabbed my aching cock in her hand, and guided it to her pussy and sank down. Bliss flooded me.

"*Fuck!*"

My hands instantly went to her hips and her hands went to my chest as her pelvis touched mine. I was buried inside her, surrounded by her heat, her wetness, her tightness. I was surrounded by *her* completely, and I never wanted to leave.

"Don't stop, Aideen."

She wasn't moving, and I *needed* her to move.

"Give me a second," she pleaded. "It's—you're big, okay? Just … let me adjust."

My eyes almost crossed. "I'm big? You're tight as *fuck*. That inch-by-inch thing you just did is a no-go. Jesus, I'll fuck you into next week if you continue to torture me like that."

"Okay," she exhaled and looked at me. "Are you ready?"

I slapped her ass with both hands. "Ride me, baby doll."

She didn't wait a second. She used my chest for leverage to lift herself up and sink back down on me. I didn't know where to look as Aideen fucked me. My eyes flicked between her expressive face, her bouncing tits, then to her pussy where I could see my cock slide in and out of her perfect body. I leaned my head back against the mattress and groaned as sensation flooded me.

"Just like *that*, baby doll."

Aideen locked her eyes on mine, and though her face was twisted with pleasure, I saw her see me. All of me.

"You look like an angel," she said. "A real angel."

My heart slammed into my chest as I moved my hands to her waist and bucked my hips up against her.

"That'd be you, darling."

Aideen suddenly cried out. "Right there!" she shouted and bore down on my cock. I didn't have to look at her face to know she was about to come. I could feel her muscles tighten around her, and I felt her body buck wildly against me, searching for its release. I thrusted my hips as hard and as fast as I could in my position, and when I became frustrated, I rolled her body underneath mine and pounded between her thighs with no restraint. I felt the moment the first spasm of her orgasm hit her as her vaginal walls contracted around my cock. I looked up at her face and forced myself not to blink so I could remember everything about her face. How her eyes were tightly shut, how her wet, swollen lips were parted, how her cheeks were flushed, and how her teeth bit down on her tongue as the sensation overcame her.

Her hands flattened over my back. Her fingers danced over my scars, touching them, loving them.

"Kane."

"I want to watch you come over and over again." I lowered my face to hers. "You're perfect when you're coming around my cock. Fucking. Perfect."

She whimpered. "Please, just don't stop."

I couldn't. I didn't just want to fuck her, I *had* to. Being inside her was rapidly becoming my favourite place, and it scared me to realise that. As I continued to fuck her, Aideen arched her back and exposed her neck to me. I moved my lips over her flesh and kissed and nipped at her skin with my teeth until she gasped. When she suddenly dug her nails into my back, the painful sting of it brought back an unwanted memory.

"When I tell you to hit a woman, boy," Big Phil bellowed as he drove a hair thin needle, no longer than a pin, in and out of my back. He didn't stop until I screamed. "You fucking do it!"

"What's wrong?"
I blinked my eyes at Aideen's question and forced all memories from my mind so I could focus on her, and her alone.
"Nothing ... ju-just be careful with my back," I stammered. "You aren't hurting me, but it just reminds me of something I don't like when you dig your nails into me."
She blinked up at me. "I'm so sorry."
"Don't be sorry, baby doll."
I kissed her lazily and slowed my pace all the way down. I wanted to come so badly, but I didn't want to stop what I was doing. I had never been in a moment that was so perfect before, and I doubt I ever would again. I wanted to make it last as long as possible.
"Kane," Aideen groaned.
I put my mouth against her ear. "You're close again. I can feel your pussy tightening around me."
"Keep talkin'!" She gasped and bucked my hips. "*Oh!*"
"You like it when I talk to you?" I growled. "Do you like it when I fuck your pretty pussy and make it mine?"
"Kannneeeeee."
My name came out in a hiss.
"Tell me what you want," I demanded and sucked her earlobe into my mouth.
"Fast. Hard. You. *Please!*"

I instantly obliged, and just as Aideen's body sent her over the edge, mine threw me over after her. My balls drew up tight, and the pulsing pressure deflated as it released itself in the first spurt of cum. I groaned so loud I wouldn't have been surprised if I woke the neighbours. I had never come so hard before, and it caused me to black out for a moment. When I opened my eyes, I was all but crushing Aideen. I quickly rolled off her body and lay on my back next to her.

"Sorry."

"S'okay."

I reached over and placed my hand on her bare stomach.

"Give me a few minutes."

She looked at me. "Huh? For what?"

I turned my head, and said, "For round two."

"Round two?" she asked, wide-eyed. "I'm knackered."

My body vibrated as I chuckled.

"You don't know the meaning of that word yet, but you will when I'm finished with you."

Aideen laughed when I dove back on top of her body and nudged my way between her thick thighs once more.

"You're supposed to be *ill*," she reminded me. "Ye' can't have too much sex ... Ye' might die."

How shitty I had been feeling lately was the *last* thing on my mind.

"I don't feel sick when I'm with you," I teased. "Maybe *you're* the drug I need to get better."

"I'm not a drug, Kane."

I rolled my hips forward, my hardening cock sliding between Aideen's wet pussy lips.

"I don't know about that, baby doll," I hummed as I angled my hips and sunk back inside her body.

Aideen moaned and reached for me as I lowered my head to hers. "Feeling you wrapped around me, having you so close to me, breathing in your intoxicating scent, wanting to taste you for as long as I live ... I'd definitely say you're my addiction. You're *my* drug."

"Kane."

"Aideen." I nipped at her earlobe. "You're *mine*."

I had never said that to a woman before in my entire life, and I knew there and then that I wanted Aideen, and for a hell of a lot longer than a single night tangled up in my bed sheets. She would make things difficult, her stubbornness would allow for nothing less, but I was ready to go up against anything she threw my way just so I could have her.

I needed Aideen, and no matter what, I was going to take everything about her and make her mine..

CHAPTER FIVE

Twenty-five years old ...

Waking up in a strange place always sucked. Always. Waking up in a hospital with no clue as to why I was there? That sucked even more. Having been feeling unwell for a long while, I assured myself that I was in the best place to get better. I had no clue what was wrong with me, and from the look on the doctor's face when he entered my room, I knew it wasn't something I could simply brush aside.

"Just give it to me straight, doc," I said. "What's wrong with me?"

The doctor, flipping through pages in my patient chart, looked up at me when I spoke.

"I had the nurses gather information from your family members while ye' were sleepin' last night. The nurses then filled me in on your health over the past year. Based on the symptoms ye' were presentin', I had the night staff draw blood so it could be sent down to the lab for testin'."

Before I could speak, Aideen said, "What type of tests were performed on his blood?"

The doctor looked at her. "Glucose and haemoglobin A1C."

Aideen's eyes widened a fraction.

"Diabetes?" she questioned. "Ye' were testin' for diabetes?"

Surprise registered on the doctor's face. "Are ye' studyin' in the medical field?"

Aideen shook her head. "No, no. I'm a primary school teacher. I just read a book before about diabetes, and it had different types of testin' that can be run to get a positive result. The tests you mentioned were two of them."

The doctor bobbed his head. "Well, yes, you're correct. I wanted to see if Mr Slater has diabetes."

"And?" Dominic pressed.

"And my theory was correct," the doctor said, then looked at me. "Ye' do indeed have diabetes, Mr. Slater. Type one to be exact."

Of all the things I was expecting the doctor to say, that wasn't one of them.

"Are you sure?" I quizzed. "I mean, my blood could have been tainted in the lab, right?"

The doctor nodded. "That is a possibility, but I had the tests done three times for confirmation, and nothin' changed. The result was the same all three times. You're a diabetic, Mr Slater."

Well, fuck.

"I'm a diabetic?" I repeated to myself.

The room was quiet again, but not for long because Aideen had a few questions that she wanted to be answered.

"Type one is the one that requires insulin, right?"

The doctor looked at her, and said, "Yes, that is the very one."

Aideen tilted her head to the side. "Isn't that a children's disease, though?"

"Normally." The doctor said. "It was dubbed with the name juvenile diabetes because it's most commonly diagnosed in children, teenagers, or young adults. It can occur at any age, though."

Aideen blinked. "Oh, I see."

"I don't understand," I interrupted. "Wouldn't I have known if I was diabetic? I mean, I would have had some signs, right?"

No one just suddenly becomes diabetic.

"Your brothers mentioned to the nurses last night about your extreme fatigue, weight loss, vomitin', and so on over the past twelve months. It is very easy to look at these symptoms as a case of influenza, a vomitin' bug, or even a simple head cold," the doctor explained. "There are many different symptoms for type one diabetes. Some people suffer from all of them, and others have no signs at all. It varies from person to person."

That shut me up.

"Your body is a special case, Kane. With a lot of people, the symptoms can start like the click of my fingers, and things can progress quickly. Then there are cases like yours where people can be ill for a long period of time but not need treatment straight away. Your body managed to get by with what little insulin it produced for the past year, but the strain has started to show, and it's not enough anymore. Your collapsin' last night is a prime example of that. Your body needs more insulin to survive than what it's currently producin'."

My stomach felt sick, and my mind raced.

"The bad news about type one diabetes is that there is no cure for it. Ye'll have it for the rest of your life. The good news is that it *is* manageable. Ye'll need to take a daily injection of insulin, startin' today. Ye'll have a standard daily dose, and it can be adjusted dependin' on your sugar level. While ye' were sleepin' earlier, we sampled your blood sugar level, so it will be a low dose today as you're not actively movin', or consumin' a lot of calories. That is the trick with your injections. The more active ye' are or the more calories ye' consume, the higher your dose needs to be. Don't worry about that right now, though. We will develop a scale."

The doctor went on as a nurse opened the door and wheeled in a trolley with a yellow bucket and other medical equipment on a large tray.

"Weekly appointments and check-ups at your local medical clinic will be set up until ye' have a handle on your doses. It will become routine for ye', and I doubt it will be difficult for ye' to get a grasp of. Ye' look like a man who knows about diet and exercise. Ye'll just have to follow a new program to balance your body's glucose level. Does that make sense?"

It made sense, but at the same time, I had no clue what the hell was going on. My eyes moved to the tray the nurse brought in, and my body went tense when I saw what looked like to be a needle.

"What's that?"

"Your first insulin dose," the doctor replied. "I'll prescribe an insulin pen just because they are more convenient than dealin' with a separate needle and bottle of insulin."

Fear washed over me like a cold shower, causing me to jolt upright in the bed.

"You are *not* sticking a needle in me."

The doctor jumped a little, startled at my shout, and he looked at my brothers for a moment before returning his eyes to mine.

"Your insulin must be injected under the skin, Mr Slater. It cannot be taken orally because the acids in your stomach will destroy it."

No. No. No.

I frantically shook my head. "I don't care; you're not sticking a needle in me. I don't give a *fuck*."

"Shit," Ryder said from my right. "Kane, you need this medication, or you don't get better. Period. You have to take it."

I looked at my brother, and when he looked into my eyes and frowned, I knew he saw the terror that I felt.

"Not a needle, Ryder. *Please.* Anything but a needle."

I felt everyone's eyes on me, especially Aideen's, but I couldn't look at her.

Dominic moved closer to the doctor. "He's had some ... bad experiences with needles in the past."

That was putting it fucking lightly.

The doctor frowned. "It has to be injected daily. I'm sorry, he has to receive this medication or ... or he will die."

The women in the room gasped, but I didn't care. I wasn't allowing anyone to stick a needle in me ... I refused.

"I'll do it," Aideen suddenly announced.

I jerked my head in her direction and stared at her as she focused on the doctor.

He blinked. "I'm sorry, but that isn't protocol—"

He wasn't going to let up on sticking me with a needle, and my reaction was to bolt. I made a move to get out of the bed and out of the fucking hospital when Aideen suddenly came to my side and took my hand in hers. She didn't seem to care that it was slick with sweat. She gripped it firmly and looked me dead in the eye. I couldn't hold her gaze, my mind was too focused on being stabbed over and over and over.

"Hey," Aideen said, squeezing my hand. "Look at *me,* Kane."

I managed to look at her. "Not a needle," I begged. "Please."

Her pretty eyes shone with unshed tears.

"Ye' trust me not to hurt ye'," she said just as tears slowly spilled over the brims of her eyes and splashed onto her cheeks. "Don't ye'?"

I hesitated. "Aideen ... I can't ..."

"Ye' trust *me* not to hurt ye'," she repeated. "Don't ye'?"

I wanted to scream.

"Yes," I said. "I know you won't hurt me."

She reached out and placed her palm on my cheek. "Then let me help ye'. Let me do this and get it out of the way. It'll be over before ye' know it. I won't ever hurt ye', Kane. I promise."

I looked into her eyes and saw no deceit or malice. I only saw the compassion she held for me. We weren't friends—not even close. We argued and got under one another's skin, but Aideen wanted to help me, and I knew she was the only person who I wanted to do just that.

I exhaled a shaky breath, and said, "Okay."

"Okay," she uttered with a small smile. "We've got this, okay? Me and you?"

"Me and you."

I kept my eyes locked on hers, just so I didn't have to look at her hands and see what she was doing.

"Give her the damn needle," Dominic hissed. "He will only let her do it, so *give it to her*."

I blocked out everyone but Aideen then. I would lose my nerve if I listened to what was being said. My heart just about stopped when she said, "Close your eyes for me."

"Aideen, please," I choked. "Don't stab me with it."

She looked like she wanted to hug me, but she didn't move.

"It's going to be one little prick in your thigh," she said. "That's all."

One little prick. I could handle that. I hoped.

"You promise?"

"I promise, sweetheart."

I held her gaze for a moment longer, then I wordlessly put all my trust in her as I closed my eyes. Seconds ticked by. I felt Aideen's hands on my thigh after the bed covers were pulled back from my body. I focused on her touch and thought back to the night I had experienced more of her than just a simple touch. I thought of how she looked bare before me, how her face twisted in pleasure as I moved inside her body, and how she cuddled against me in her sleep. I thought about that night all the time, and I wondered if she did too.

"All done."

I opened my eyes when Aideen spoke, and my lips parted with shock.

"I didn't feel anything."

She smiled. "Told ye'."

Gratitude flooded me, and before I realised what I was doing, I reached out and pulled her against me, hugging her tightly.

"I'll come back later to discuss a check-up appointment date for next week. I'll also go through everything with 'im, and with you all, about what to expect with his diabetes. We'll keep 'im overnight again, and if he is respondin' well to the injections, he can go home tomorrow."

My brothers replied to the doctor, but I tuned them out once more and focused on Aideen.

"Are you okay?"

I squeezed her. "Yes."

I rested back against the pillows on my bed, suddenly feeling drained.

"What the hell was *that?*" Bronagh demanded of Dominic. "I've never seen 'im like that before."

My little brother looked at his girlfriend, and I saw the moment he knew that he was going to end up in an argument with her because he sighed. "It's not my place to explain *that*, Bronagh. It's up to Kane if he wants to tell you."

Not fucking likely.

"I don't want to *tell* anything because we're done speaking about *that*," I said firmly. "And we're done discussing injections of any type. I am not doing that shit again. No fucking way."

The amount of fear that consumed me at the thought was too much for me to bear. I could never do that on a daily basis. I wasn't strong enough.

"It's not up for discussion, Kane," Branna interjected. "Ye' *will* be takin' the injections. I'll do them for ye'—"

"No!" I cut her off. "Just ... *no*."

Ryder stepped towards Branna. "Stop pushing him."

She turned to him and glared. "*One* of us has to. Otherwise, he will get sick again. Is that what ye' want?"

Ryder didn't respond; he only looked away from her.

"She's right, Ryder," Bronagh commented. "He needs to take them. Ye' can't baby 'im."

Alec's face became hard as he looked at Bronagh.

"We aren't babying him, Bronagh. We're being considerate. He doesn't like needles. End of fucking story."

"Hey!" Alannah snapped at Alec. "Don't talk to 'er like that!"

"Don't shout at 'im, Lana," Keela sighed, clearly not wanting anyone to argue.

Alannah glared at Keela. "Tell 'im to back off Bronagh then."

I wanted to punch a wall.

"It would help if you all stopped talking about me like I'm a fucking invalid. I *can* hear what you're all saying, and I can make my own damn decisions when it comes to my body."

Branna moved to the opposite side of the bed and stared down at me.

"D'ye want to die?" she bluntly asked. "Because that's what will happen if ye' don't take the insulin daily."

"Branna," Ryder shouted. "Fucking *stop*."

Aideen jumped with fright, and that irked me because it meant Ryder had frightened her, and I didn't want her to be scared of any of my brothers.

"No!" Branna bellowed right back at him. "I love 'im! I don't want 'im to get sick again!"

Everyone began to talk at once again, couples arguing, and friends snapping at each other.

"Kane?"

I looked at Aideen and tensed. "I know what you're going to say."

"What?"

"Kane, you need to take the insulin. You'll get sick if you don't," I mimicked her.

When she smiled, my heart thumped against my chest.

"Yep, that was pretty much it."

I swallowed. "I don't do needles, Aideen. I just don't."

Ryder suddenly moved past Branna and leaned down to me. "What can we do to get you to take the insulin shots?"

"I. Don't. Do. Needles," I repeated.

"*You* don't," Aideen butted in, "but *I* do."

The room went silent.

"What?" I balked. "What are you saying?"

Aideen leaned forward, and said, "I'll give ye' your injections every day. Ye' let me do it once; will ye' let me do it every other time, too?"

Everyone in the room looked at Aideen, then I felt their gazes turn to me as they awaited my answer.

"Why would you want to help me?"

She hated me.

Aideen's lips twitched. "I enjoy arguin' with ye', and I need to keep ye' around for that, so I guess I'm doin' this for me own selfish needs. Sue me."

The tension in the room eased when people chuckled, and I grinned.

"Aideen," I said. "Thank you, but I don't—"

"Hey," she interrupted with a beaming smile. "Me and you?"

I wondered if she knew just how deeply those words rooted in my heart.

I exhaled a deep breath and said, "Me and you."

"We got this."

I stared at her for a long time. Every part of my mind screamed at me that no matter what way I looked at the situation, I was still going to be stabbed with a needle, and that scared the life out of me. I tried to assure myself that when Aideen injected me minutes ago, I felt nothing once I focused on her entirely. I wondered if I kept her in my mind's eye, then maybe, I could get through daily injections. Once it was her handling the needle, I knew I would be in good hands. This fear was rooted in me because of Big Phil, and it shamed me knowing that he had power over me when I swore long ago I wouldn't allow him to have it. I focused on Aideen and decided then that through her, I would beat this fear and shatter Big Phil's control over me once and for all.

"Well," Aideen pressed. "What d'ye say?"

She had no way of knowing, but she just intertwined her life with mine, and I intended on keeping it that way.

"I say okay, *baby doll*."

CHAPTER SIX

Twenty-six years old ...

"**K**ane."

I looked at Ryder as he drove. We were on our way home from a job—a job neither of us wanted to do. My brother looked like a broken man. I knew it was breaking his heart to lie to Branna, but he had no choice in the matter. My heart went out to him. We had been out of the game for a few years now, but unfortunately, our past with Marco had caught up with Ryder and landed him neck deep in shit with the feds.

My brother had been given two options, help the feds by spying on Brandy Daley or be tried for murder and if convicted, go to prison without the possibility of parole. He was the only one of my brothers who the feds contacted, and I knew that was probably because of a deal Ryder had worked out to keep me and my other brothers safe. He was always protecting us, protecting Branna, and never once thought about protecting himself.

"Yeah, man?"

"I appreciate you helping me today," Ryder said with his eyes locked on the road ahead. "This is the first and last time I'll need your help with this bullshit, I promise."

"Don't sweat it, bro. I got you."

"No," Ryder said firmly. "This is the *last* time. You're about to become a father, and nothing about that part of our lives is tainting that."

I didn't respond to him. He looked like he was beating himself up enough for needing me to help him. When he called me this morning and told me that Brandy wanted him to run a deal in Wexford, he knew he needed someone to accompany him. No one went to do deals on Brandy's behalf without having some muscle to watch their back. Ryder didn't trust any of Brandy's men, and since I used to be an enforcer, I was his obvious choice.

"It's over and done with now," I said. "You got the deal and earned Brandy a hell of a profit. Put it out of your mind."

I knew it was easier said than done, but my brother nodded. I looked at my phone for the millionth time and was frustrated to find it was still dead. Ryder's phone was out of battery too, so I couldn't check in with Aideen throughout the day to make sure she was okay. When we pulled into the parking lot of my building, we both got out and headed up to my apartment. The elevator opened on my floor just as I heard my girlfriend scream. My heart dropped, and I broke into a run and barrelled into my apartment, the door slamming against the wall.

"Aideen!"

Branna's voice shouted, "In the bedroom!"

Ryder and I wasted no time. We rushed down the hallway and burst into the room. I took in the scene before me. My three brothers were pale, Aideen was naked from the waist down and in the birthing pool, and Branna was next to her and holding her hand. I focused on Aideen, and it took a second to realise what was happening. She was in labour ... and I was missing it.

"Strip down and get into the pool with her," Branna ordered me. "She needs ye'."

Aideen bellowed, "Where the *fuck* have ye' been?"

I didn't answer her, so she picked up two colourful balls and squeezed them. While she was focused on that, I looked at my brothers and said, "How long has she been in labour?"

"Most of the day," Dominic answered. "We tried calling you guys."

His words hurt like a knife twisting in my heart. I hurriedly stripped out of my clothes until I was down to my boxers and quickly moved over to the pool. I stepped inside and lowered myself on my behind. I spread my legs and moved up behind Aideen. I reached forward and gripped her waist before I leaned in and planted kisses along her neck and shoulder.

"I'm here, baby doll."

Aideen began to cry, and it broke my heart. I felt the relief she experienced now that she had me with her, and I couldn't begin to imagine how scared she was at having to go through labour on her own, wondering where I was and if I would make it in time to see our baby being born.

"I'm sorry," I whispered to her and kissed the side of her head. "I'm *so* sorry."

She turned to me and pressed her face to mine. "I can't do this."

"What are you talking about?" I smiled. "You're doing it, and you're doing it fucking awesomely."

"Hell yeah, she is," Branna agreed.

I interlocked my hands with hers, and I didn't make a sound when she squeezed me to the point my hands went numb. It was a small price to pay for the woman who was going through hell so she could bring my child into the world. She was so brave. I couldn't fathom ever possessing an ounce of the strength she had.

"God, it *hurts!*"

She moved our joint hands under her stomach and wailed in pain.

"Spread your legs as wide as ye' can, honey," Branna instructed. "As soon as ye' get another contraction, bear down and push, okay?"

Aideen gripped my hands even tighter as she listened to Branna and did exactly as she said. It didn't take long for a contraction to hit, and when it did, my girl did exactly what Branna had said and pushed with all of her might. My blood ran cold when Aideen screamed. I had never heard that type of wail leave her body before, and it scared me half to death. I flicked my eyes to my brothers. Dominic, Ryder and Damien were staring at Aideen with their jaws slack while Alec had his hands covering his eyes as he recited *The Lord's Prayer* out loud.

Aideen noticed none of this.

"Branna," she whimpered. "It's burnin'."

She leaned her head back against my shoulder as the contraction passed for the moment, and I wasted no time to kiss her and tell her how proud I was of her. She was panting, sweating, and moaning as pain consumed her.

"Push through that sting. D'ye hear me, Ado?" Branna said. "Push through it with everythin' ye' have."

For close to thirty minutes, that was exactly what Aideen did. She pushed, pushed, and pushed some more. I felt absolutely helpless. I found myself wishing I was feeling her pain just so she would have a moment's peace.

"The baby's crownin' so that means the head is almost out, Kane," Branna whispered. "You're about to deliver your baby."

Fear struck me.

"Branna, help him," Aideen pleaded, most likely fearing I'd let our baby fall.

"I'm ready," I said and kissed her shoulder. "I've got this, baby doll, trust me. Push as hard as you can one more time."

Aideen had to adjust her position until she was in a squatted position, and I was behind her, with my hands between her thighs. I pressed my hands against her vagina and felt my baby's head. I could feel hair, lots of hair, and a sob caught in my throat. This was my baby, and the woman I loved more than life was bringing him or her into the world. An abundance of love, adoration, and happiness flooded me, and I had never felt so lucky as I did just then.

My brothers flanked Branna on either side and reached out to Aideen. She grabbed one of Ryder's arms and one of Alec's to steady herself. Their eyes were solely on her face, and my heart was filled, knowing they were here for such a special moment. I never thought I'd want them here when my girlfriend's half naked, but there was nothing sexual about birth.

It was beautiful, scary, and an incredible thing to witness.

"Let's do this, Ado." Alec smiled. "You've got this."

She bobbed her head, sucked in a huge breath, and with all her might, she bore down and pushed like her life depended on it. My eyes widened as more of my child's head became visible. I could feel tiny ears, then chubby cheeks.

"Good girl, baby doll," I praised. "Keep pushing ... keep pushing."

"The head is fully out," Branna whooped a few seconds later.

Aideen screamed as she continued to push. Dominic moved to the side to get a better view and laughed. "Nothing but dark hair. That baby is a true Slater." He tried to high five Damien, who pointed at his own mop of white hair, causing Dominic to wince and say, "My bad, bro."

Aideen screamed loudly as our baby moved through her body.

"Shoulders are out." I beamed. "Chest ... Torso ... Butt ... Legs ... and toes. You *did* it, baby."

Aideen slumped forward against my brothers who supported her. I adjusted my baby in my arms, my heart slamming in my chest as I carefully looked between the chunky thighs. I blinked three times before I realised what I was looking at.

"It's a ... boy!" I announced. "It's *definitely* a boy."

Aideen gasped and tried to look, but she couldn't turn to see because I was behind her, and the cord was still attached to her and the baby.

"Are ye' *sure?*"

Branna carefully helped Aideen sit down, she leaned over the pool and lifted her leg so I could wind the umbilical cord under her so she didn't hurt Aideen or the baby. Aideen turned her head, locked eyes on our child, and burst into tears. She was smiling but only for a moment.

"Branna," she said. "Why isn't he cryin'?"

"It's normal. Give 'im a second," Branna said then reached over and took the baby from me without asking.

My happiness fled, and overwhelming fear consumed me as I stared at my child, willing him to cry.

"Oh, please," Aideen screamed as panic struck. "Please, make 'im cry, Branna."

Aideen tried to stand, so I grabbed her shoulders to keep her still. She shoved my hands away and tried to move closer to Branna, but I wouldn't let her. Branna had to focus, and Aideen could have hurt herself so I wrapped my arms around her body, and held her against my chest.

"Come on, baby boy," Branna cooed to the baby as she rubbed him roughly with one of our baby towels. "Give me a nice big cry."

Time slowed down, and every moment felt like an hour ... until magic. The loudest wail you could imagine from a newborn filled my apartment, and it was the best sound I had ever heard in my entire life. Aideen cried with relief and so did I. I pressed my face against Aideen's hair as I silently thanked God for helping my child.

"Ye' little brat." Branna tearfully laughed as she finished wiping the baby's face. "Givin' your mammy and daddy an awful fright like that."

"Your fucking uncles, too," Alec stated and bent forward, placing his hands on his knees, panting like he just ran a marathon.

Branna moved over to us and leaned down. She lowered her arms and gently rested the baby on Aideen's chest. Both women adjusted Aideen's T-shirt until our son was underneath it and resting against his mom's chest. Aideen adjusted him so she could see between his legs.

"It *is* a boy," she cried with happiness. "We have a son."

I wrapped my arms around both of them and kissed the side of her face. "Thank you so much, baby."

"For what?" She sniffled, looking back at me.

She was sweaty, her cheeks were flushed, and her eyes were red and swollen from crying, but I had never seen her look so beautiful in all the time I've known her.

"For giving him to me," I answered and kissed her lips.

Aideen rested her forehead to mine, then we both looked at our son when he cried.

"Shhh," Aideen cooed and gently rocked him. "Mammy's got ye'."

My heart burst with love at that moment. I was a father, and my girl was a mother.

"He looks just like ye', Kane." Branna sniffled. "He's your double."

"No way," I murmured, looking at the baby. "He's beautiful, so that's all Aideen."

My eyes roamed over his face. He had a cute button nose, chubby cheeks, a head full of dark brown hair, and plump pink lips. He was gorgeous, and he was ours.

"I love you," Aideen whispered to him. "I love ye' so much, baby boy."

I repositioned myself behind her by putting my legs on either side of her hips and then pulled Aideen and our baby back against my chest. I leaned my head against Aideen's, and we both continued to stare at our little piece of heaven. We had waited so long to meet him, and a huge part of me couldn't believe he was here.

"I can't believe we made him," Aideen murmured. "He is perfect."

"He is," I agreed.

Aideen rested against me as Branna got her medical bag. I watched her approach the pool but said nothing. She silently placed a clamp on the baby's umbilical cord, then placed a second one about a couple or so inches from my son's belly. Branna watched the cord, and I found myself watching it with her. I watched until there was no visible pulse on the cord, and when Branna checked it, and confirmed it, she got a scissors from her bag, smiled, and handed them to me.

"Cut between the clamp and my fingers."

She pointed at the exact point. It was tougher than I expected it to be, but it was an experience I would always remember.

"Ye' might want to claw me eyes out, but can I have 'im for a few minutes? I'll dry 'im off and wrap 'im up nice and warm."

Aideen looked up at Branna and said, "Why?"

Branna chuckled. "I have to help ye' deliver the placenta, babe, and I want to weigh 'im."

"Okay." Aideen sighed, and carefully handed our son to Branna.

"He will be back in your arms before ye' know it."

Branna weighed and measured the baby, and he was ten pounds even, and twenty inches long. After weighing him, Branna then cleaned him up, put a blue hat on his head, and wrapped him in a thick blanket then placed him in his bassinet. My brothers gave us their congratulations and left the room then to give us some privacy. Over the course of the next ten minutes, Aideen delivered the placenta.

"All done," Branna announced then reached into the water and lifted the clump of bloody placenta, placed it into a plastic bag next to her, and sealed it. Branna removed her gloves, lifted our son from his bassinet, then gave him back to Aideen. She held her arms up to make sure the blanket the baby was wrapped in didn't touch the water of the pool. I glanced up when I heard a soft click. I noticed Branna had left the room, so it was just Aideen, our son, and me.

"I was so scared there for a second."

"Me too, sweetheart." I kissed her shoulder. "My heart stopped."

Our son wailed, and it made Aideen chuckle when I said, "I love your cry, little man."

Aideen gazed down at the baby, and said, "Ye' don't think the smoke from that night hurt 'im, right?"

"No," I replied. "Look at him; he is healthy as can be. Pink and big all over."

His little face was pressed against his mother's chest, and his instinct took over. He tried to suckle on her skin, so Aideen nervously repositioned him under her breast. I reached around and adjusted her breast and nipple with my hand until it was close to the baby's mouth. It took about a minute of adjusting and brushing Aideen's nipple against our son's lips, but he eventually latched on and began to suckle.

"Ow."

I tensed. "Are you okay?"

Aideen nodded but continued to wince. "It hurts a little, but it's okay. Branna said that some pain was normal."

I pressed my face to the side of hers, and we both looked down as our son fed for the first time. I heard a little click but didn't look up. I heard some movement, then the sound of a shutter caught my attention. I looked up and saw Branna smiling apologetically as she tucked her phone into her trouser pocket.

"Sorry, it was too perfect of a moment not to capture."

I smiled and looked back down at my son.

"How is everythin'?" Branna whispered.

Aideen smiled. "Perfect."

"Branna," I murmured. "He latched on."

"Brilliant." She beamed as she moved closer. "Are ye' feelin' okay, Aideen?"

Aideen silently bobbed her head. I looked down at the baby and noticed he unlatched and smacked his lips together a few times, before just lying on his mom's chest in a baby drunk daze.

"Your colostrum must taste good." I chuckled. "Look at him."

Aideen brushed a finger over his nose. "I love 'im so much."

"Me too, babydoll."

"Put 'im in his Moses basket," Branna instructed me, "and we'll get 'er out of the pool. I want her dried and into warm clothes as soon as possible. I don't want 'er to catch a bug; she's very vulnerable right now."

I sprang into action as I climbed out of the birthing pool. I very carefully placed our son in his bassinet that was by Aideen's side of the bed. I walked back to the pool, and with Branna's help, we got Aideen up and out of the birthing pool. She could walk, but she was tender, so I supported most of her weight to ease some of her discomfort. Branna went and got a basin of hot water and both of us washed Aideen down with a sponge. It was only brief, but it made Aideen feel better. She rested against me when I wrapped a large towel around her and gently rubbed her dry.

I quickly dried off, then pulled on clean boxers and a pair of sweatpants. Aideen lay on the bed so Branna could thoroughly check her vagina for any signs of tearing, and I was glad to hear that there was none. Aideen groaned as she stepped into an unflattering pair of granny panties that had a large maxi pad attached to it, and it made me chuckle. After that, I helped her into a fresh pair of loose pyjamas. I got her a hair tie and held her hips as she tied her hair up into a bun that sat on top of her head. Each action was so simple, so mundane, but I found it incredibly sexy, and I had no idea why.

I could only put it down to her strength. She had just pushed a human being out of her body, and while she was exhausted, she looked like she could take on the world. I was blown away by her. She wanted to rest for a while, so I helped her up onto our bed and tucked her in. I heard voices outside, so I opened the bedroom door and saw my brothers, their girlfriends, Aideen's brothers, and her dad lingering in the hallway. I laughed and shook my head.

I looked at Aideen. "Are you up for some visitors?"

She blinked. "Who's 'ere?"

"Your father, your brothers, my brothers, and all of the girls."

A smile stretched across Aideen's face as she bobbed her head. "Of course, they can come in. They've waited to see 'im as long as we have."

I left the room, walked down the hallway and into the living room where everyone had moved to. The men were either sat down or leaning against a wall. All the women were huddled together, wide smiles on their faces as they spoke a mile a minute.

"Kane!" Bronagh squealed when she caught sight of me. "Congratulations!"

She rushed at me and threw her body at me. I caught her just as her chest collided with mine, and I was carefully of her pregnant belly as I set her gently on the ground. I gave her a warm hug, but she did not release me, and it was then I realised that she was crying. She was always crying, my little bumble bee. Her hormones tortured her.

"Do you ever stop with the waterworks?"

"No," she replied on a sob.

I laughed, and so did my brothers. Dominic was thoroughly amused by her. I looked at him and found his eyes on Bronagh, and there was so much warmth and love in his gaze that I found myself giving Bronagh another squeeze because I was thankful she was the person to make my brother so happy.

"You're a daddy!"

"I'm a daddy."

When she released me, she leaned up on her tiptoes and gave me a big, wet kiss on the cheek.

"I'm so happy for you and Aideen."

Everyone echoed Bronagh's congratulations, my brothers hugged me, Aideen's brothers did the same and clapped their hands against my back. Aideen's father gave me the longest hug and thanked me for making his daughter so happy, but I assured him that she made me happy.

"Do you all want to meet my son?"

Big smiles and loud squeals were my response. I chuckled as I led everyone down the hallway and into the bedroom. Branna was leaning over my son lying on the bed, dressing him as Aideen watched her every careful move, storing the information away.

"Omigod," Keela whispered from my right.

We all watched silently as Branna gently put a vest on him followed by a blue onesie, mittens, and a white cardigan. She adjusted his hat, and she smiled when he yawned and made a squealing noise. I looked from Branna to Ryder and found his eyes solely on his woman. He watched her every move with so much intent I was surprised Branna's skin didn't catch fire.

He was harbouring great demons over his involvement with the feds and Brandy, but what he struggled with most was lying to Branna. He knew he couldn't tell her anything because any involvement from her should things go badly would have bad implications. He knew that, and I knew that, but Branna could never know. He confided in me that their relationship was in trouble. Ever since he was approached by the feds, he found it difficult to look at her, to kiss her, hold her, or make love to her because he felt like dirt knowing what he was keeping from her. He was scared she was going to leave him ... and to be honest, so was I.

I turned back to Branna as she lifted my son, kissed his cheek, then placed him gently in Aideen's waiting arms. She lifted her gaze to our family, and though she was exhausted and sore, she smiled widely. She took my breath away, and I had to force myself to remain still just so I wouldn't cross the room, take her face in my hands, and kiss her senseless.

"Aideen," Keela blubbered as she scurried forward to her best friend's side. "Well done, honey."

I glanced at Alec who was transfixed with his girl as she stared at my son with so much love it radiated from her. I saw love in my brother's gaze and want. Want for a child that he and Keela could call their own.

"He is perfect," Keela said, tears falling on to her cheeks. "So perfect."

Aideen's smile told everyone that she agreed.

"Darlin'."

Aideen looked up when her father spoke, and she beamed at him, "Hey, Granda."

Keela quickly moved over to her place in front of Alec, and my brother wrapped his arms around her, then leaned down and nuzzled his face against hers. I looked at Aideen's father whose resolve shattered as tears fell from his eyes. He sat on the side of the bed, next to his daughter, and he wrapped his arms tightly around her.

"He looks just like ye' when ye' were a baby," her father murmured. "So beautiful. I'm so proud of ye', baby. Ma would be too."

Tears filled Aideen's eyes as she said, "D'ye want to hold 'im?"

Her father nodded and stood. He reached down and gently picked up his grandson, holding him protectively against his chest. Aideen rubbed her eyes with her fingers as she watched grandfather and grandson get acquainted. For a single moment, I thought of my own father and how he missed out on a moment such as this, but then I remembered he was a cruel man who would hold no love for my son or any child fathered by his sons. I was glad that Mr Collins would be the only grandparent my children would know.

"Hey, buddy," he whispered, his eyes welling up. "I'm your Granda."

That was all that needed to be said for all the ladies to crumple to tears, making us men chuckle.

"Well done, baby sister."

Aideen looked at her eldest brother, JJ, and gestured for him to go to her. When he moved to her side, he leaned down and hugged her so tight I worried he might break her. Aideen's other brothers followed suit. Gavin held onto her the longest and whispered something in her ear that made her laugh.

"What's his name?" This came from Bronagh.

Aideen looked at me, and I shrugged my shoulders. We had discussed lots of names for boys and girls, but we never agreed on any, so we decided to wait until the baby was born to pick one.

"No idea yet."

Everyone chuckled at us.

Aideen hugged my brothers then, and she thanked and apologised to Dominic, Alec, and Damien for any harm or discomfort she brought to them during her labour. They smiled at her and waved it off like it was no big deal. I could tell they were just happy they got to be a part of such a special moment.

When it was time for the women to hug Aideen, they all cried uncontrollably, even Alannah who was usually the best of them for controlling her emotions. I was thoroughly amused but touched because I felt the love of every person in the room for my son, for Aideen, and for me. I watched as every person fell in love with my child, and it only caused my love for them to grow.

I didn't know how long everyone stayed, a few hours or so, but by the time they left, even Branna after she checked on Aideen and the baby once more, my girl was close to falling asleep sitting up. She had just finished feeding the baby again and settled back into our bed when she was suddenly lost in thought. She locked eyes on me as I folded up the birthing pool having drained it earlier, and I froze.

"Kane?"

"Hmmm?"

She tiredly blinked. "Where were ye' all day today?"

I stopped moving, stopped breathing.

"Kane?"

I felt every muscle in my body tense as worry flooded me.

"What?" I asked as if I hadn't heard her.

"Alec was callin' ye' for ages, Ryder too, but neither of ye' answered. Where were ye'?"

"I was in the gym for about two hours."

Aideen's voice was soft when she said, "And for the other hours?"

I placed the birthing pool back in its container just to give me something to do before I turned to face her. The picture before me was one I had come to long for after I fell in love with Aideen and waited for my son to grow inside her body. She was the very definition of perfection as she sat on our bed under the covers with our son nestled against her chest.

"I was helping Ryder move ... some stuff."

Tears welled in her eyes, and my heart broke knowing I was hurting her.

"Kane."

I took a step forward. "I swear if I knew you would be having the baby today I wouldn't have left your side."

She held my hand up in the air. "Stay where ye' are."

I wanted to disregard that demand, but I didn't. I remained where I was.

Slowly, Aideen said, "Ye' were movin' drugs or weapons ... weren't ye'?"

I opened my mouth, prepared to lie to her, but I closed it when no words came out. Tears fell onto her cheeks at my silence, and I had to ball my fists to keep from moving to her side.

"Please let me come to you."

Aideen shook her head. "I was in labour all day ... and ye' were out helpin' Ryder with that horrible stuff."

I swallowed. "I'm—"

"Your brothers held me hands, listened to me scream and curse at them, and did everythin' in their power to help me. They never left me side the entire time. They were scared shitless, but they were there for me."

"Aideen," I whispered, feeling my own eyes well with tears.

I was ashamed, and I needed her to forgive me for not being there when she needed me most.

"Ye' almost missed him comin' into this world, Kane."

I couldn't hold her gaze anymore, so I looked down to my feet instead.

"I'm disgusted with myself for not being here for it all."

She was disgusted with me too. I knew she was.

"What did I tell ye'?"

I looked up at her, feeling confused.

"I told ye' I wouldn't be with ye' when you're attached to that life."

Panic rose within me, and I suddenly felt faint.

"Please," I pleaded. "Please forgive me. I won't do it again. I won't help Ryder ever again. I swear on my life."

Aideen's expression was blank, and it scared me half to death.

"I think ye' should leave," she said, her jaw tight.

She was breaking up with me.

"Aideen," I choked and stumbled forward until my knees knocked into our bed. "Please, I'm begging you, don't do this."

Please, don't do this, baby doll.

"I didn't do anythin'. *You* did," she replied with a shake of her head. "I've asked ye', no I've begged ye', repeatedly, to tell me what you and Ryder were up to, and I've pleaded with ye' not to be involved with it ... but ye' completely ignored me. Ye' said it wouldn't take ye' from me, but it has. Ye' almost missed the birth of your son for it ... was it worth it?"

No.

"I'm so sorry," I cried. "I'm *so* sorry, sweetheart."

Aideen remained cold towards me, and it made me want to scream.

"No, *I'm* sorry, Kane," she said with a shake of her head. "I'm sorry I let this go so far. I truly thought your love and respect for me would be enough for ye' to do the right thing, but I'm obviously not worth it. Ye' chose somethin' dangerous, illegal, and plain disgustin' over me."

She looked down to her left hand, wiggled the engagement ring off her finger and threw it to the end of the bed where it landed before me. With my heart in my throat, I looked from the ring to Aideen in what I knew was disbelief. She was breaking up with me. She was *really* breaking up with me.

"Please, don't leave me," I begged her, not caring how she would perceive me for pleading. "I'll die without you."

She looked at our son and swallowed.

"If ye' don't put me first, what's to say ye' won't put *him* first?"

Terrified, I grabbed her ring and crawled up the bed until I was face to face with her.

"I'm begging you not to do this. You and that precious boy are my everything, I swear to you."

Aideen frowned, but I saw something flicker in her eyes. "I don't know if that's enough for us to work."

"Baby doll," I breathed and placed my hands on her cheeks. "I'm willing to do whatever it takes to make this work. I don't want to lose what I live for; you and our son. I never thought it was possible to love two people as much as I do you two. I love you both so much it hurts. Please, don't take away my reason for living."

Aideen's eyes swam with tears as she leaned her face into mine.

"Ye' swear on his life that you're done with *everythin'* related to your old life?"

Hope flared within me.

"I swear." I frantically nodded. "I swear to God."

Aideen regarded me for a long moment before she nodded and said, "Okay."

I could hardly believe what she was saying. She was giving me a second chance when we both knew I didn't deserve one. I crumpled before her and pressed my forehead against hers. I pressed my lips against her, and when I felt her kiss me back with hunger, my heart thumped with relief.

"I love you so fucking much."

Aideen put her arms around my neck. "I love ye' too, sweetheart … now give me me ring back."

I wiped my face free of tears before I placed the ring back on her finger and kissed it.

"Ye' have me heart, Kane," she said to me when I looked into her eyes. "Don't *ever* forget that."

"I won't," I assured her. "Not ever."

When she kissed me, I kissed her back without reservation. I quickly got under the covers with her and moved as close to her as I could.

"Lie down," I urged. "I need to hold you."

I helped her get settled on the bed before I stretched out next to her exhausted body.

"Baby doll?"

She snuggled back against me and murmured, "Yes."

"I say it all the time, but I really do love you with all of my heart. You know that, right?"

"I know, babe." She hummed. "I'm sorry about bein' so horrible. I never want to hurt ye' or make ye' cry."

"You had every right to be furious with me. I almost missed our son being born over Ryder and his stupid deals."

She put her hand over mine. "Let's not talk about it anymore. It's done now, and your decision has been made. Ye' made it for his birth, and that's all that matters."

I hugged her and lowered my hands to her smaller but still rounded stomach.

"It's all flabby."

I found myself chuckling. "It's weird that your stomach isn't huge and hard. I can still feel a smaller bump, but Branna said that will go down in a few days as your womb starts the process of shrinking back to normal."

Aideen glanced over her shoulder at me. "Ye' talked to 'er about stuff like that?"

Every chance I got.

"All the time." I nodded. "I wanted to know what you're going through."

Aideen smiled, then returned her gaze to our son in his bassinet. "What will we name 'im?"

I blew out a breath. "I don't know. What do you like?"

"Promise you won't laugh?" I gave her a squeeze, so she said, "Jax."

I broke my silent promise and laughed, lowly.

"Hey."

"Sorry."

Aideen sighed. "Ye' don't like it."

"I actually do. I was just thinking of how Jax Teller brought us together that fateful day in Ryder and Branna's house."

Aideen giggled. "Through Jax Teller all things are possible."

I smiled. "Jax Slater … that sounds cool."

"Jax Slater," Aideen repeated. "I love it."

"So we're settled on his name being Jax?"

"Yeah," Aideen said, then paused. "But what will his middle name be?"

"I was thinking it could be your father's name."

Aideen gasped. "Really?"

"Of course." I nodded. "Your dad is awesome, and the look of admiration and love he holds for you and Jax fills my heart. He is a good man and will be an awesome papaw."

"Papaw," she repeated. "That's so cute, I love that."

I was elated. "So his name is Jax Daniel Slater?"

"Yes! Wait, Jax Daniel … is it just me, or does that sound like Jack Daniels?"

I repeated it under my breath and found it was similar and laughed.

"We can't change it now. We already agreed."

Aideen vibrated with silent laughter. "Me da will get a right kick out of this."

I sat up on my elbow and leaned up so I could see into my son's bassinet.

"I love you, Jax."

When I looked down at Aideen, she had rolled onto her back and stared up at me.

"Me and you?"

"Me and you."

Her smile was the last thing she did before she fell asleep in my arms. I held her body against mine for a long time. I stared at her, blown away by how much I loved this woman, and amazed by her strength and patience as she brought our son into the world. I flicked my eyes to Jax and smiled when he pulled a cute face in his sleep. I lay down beside Aideen, held her tight, and sighed in utter happiness, knowing that I had my family and they had me too. I fell asleep knowing that I had the whole world in my woman and son, and I knew then that I was the luckiest son of a bitch on the face of the planet.

CHAPTER SEVEN

Present day ...

"Unc?" I looked over my shoulder when Georgie walked into my kitchen.

"Baby," I beamed and opened my arms when she neared me. "I didn't know you were coming over."

She wrapped her arms around my waist and gave me a tight squeeze that I returned before she stepped back.

"I came over to talk to Jax," she said, and lowered her head. "I fought with 'im earlier and said somethin' I really didn't mean, so I've come to apologise."

Ah, now Jax's sulking around the apartment made sense. When he returned from my brother's house earlier, I knew something had happened because when I asked if he was okay, he said he didn't want to talk about it. I knew he was still embarrassed at being caught almost having sex by his parents and mostly likely bummed that he was grounded and had all his electronic devices taken away, but he seemed genuinely upset, and now I knew why.

"He's in his room, George."

Georgie hesitated. "What if he doesn't forgive me?"

I flipped on the kettle, knowing from experience that this conversation would require a cup of tea. My niece looked concerned about the talk she needed to have with my son, and I wanted to do what I could to settle her nerves; otherwise, no amount of tea would calm her.

"Forgive *what* exactly?"

Georgie looked down at her feet. "He was bein' really overbearin' and tellin' me parents me business when he shouldn't have, and I just got *so* feckin' mad at 'im. He is always actin' like he is years older than me when he isn't. I'm the second eldest cousin; there is a few months between us, but he treats me like the youngest, and today, I just had enough of it. I ... I told 'im I hated 'im, and when he asked me to take it back, I wouldn't. Now I feel like dirt on the ground because I don't hate 'im. I love 'im to death, but I don't know if he'll forgive me for sayin' it. I was pretty mean to 'im, so I wouldn't blame 'im if he never spoke to me again. The look on his face ... I hurt 'im."

Well, shit.

"Look," I said, quickly making her tea now that the kettle had boiled. "I can see it in your pretty green eyes and hear it when you speak that you are sorry. People make mistakes and say things they don't mean when they are angry, especially to the people they love most. Jax loves you, Georgie. You're his number one girl. He'll forgive you."

I knew my son, and there was nothing he wouldn't do for his cousins, especially Georgie. He would forgive her for upsetting him. He'd probably make her sweat a little before he did so—just to teach her a lesson—but in the end, he would accept her apology and they would move on with their lives.

"Thanks, Uncle." She sighed, her shoulders sagging as she sat at the kitchen table. "Today has been a shitty day."

I agreed wholeheartedly.

"Well, we're guaranteed that today will end, so it's up to you whether you want to drag your feelings into tomorrow or leave them in the here and now and start fresh come sunup."

Georgie looked up at me and smiled. She was the picture of her mother, but I saw my little brother in her smile, and those dimples on her cheeks were definitely Dominic Slater to the *T*.

"Ye' sound like Alec when he gets all philosophical."

I grinned. "I make sense, though. Your uncle sounds like Yoda having a bad day when he starts rambling."

She laughed, lifted her cup of tea, blew on it, then took a sip and hummed.

"I love that ye' know how many sugars I take."

"Learning how you and your aunties take their tea was wired into me years ago. I realised quickly how a good cup of tea can resolve the most hostile of situations."

My niece giggled. "I can imagine ye' makin' Aideen a cup of tea just to get in 'er good books."

"Guilty," I said as I took a seat across from her. "So are you going to stay here with me and keep stalling or go talk to Jax?"

Georgie scowled. "I hate that ye' know what I'm doin'."

"Baby girl." I chuckled. "You are your mother's daughter."

She leaned back in her chair and sighed before she nodded, took another gulp of her tea, then got to her feet.

"Wish me luck, unc," she said. "And if ye' hear shoutin', just let us argue. We have to fight before we make up. It's a ritual I have with all me cousins. If ye' hear a whole lot of silence, that's when ye' should come runnin' because we're probably stranglin' each other."

I snorted as she left the room with her back straight and her chin lifted.

"Good luck," I said as she left, but I wasn't wishing her luck, I was wishing my son it.

I poured the remainder of Georgie's tea into the sink, then washed the cup and set it aside on the draining board.

"Was that Georgie?"

"Yeah," I answered my wife without turning around. "She and Jax argued, so she's here to apologise."

"I was wonderin' what he was sulkin' around for. I knew what happened this mornin' wasn't bummin' 'im out *that* much."

I turned around and leaned my butt against the countertop. I watched my wife as she opened the fridge and removed her almond milk as she moved to the kettle and flipped it back on. My eyes roamed over her, lingering on her endowed chest and rounded behind. I grinned when she clicked her tongue at me. I looked up at her face, and said, "You're hot."

She giggled. "Shut up."

I moved away from the counter and came up behind her, my hands going to her hips.

"Make me."

Aideen laughed. "In other words, play fight me until we have sex."

"Basically."

Aideen shook her head, amused. "The children are home."

"We'll be quiet," I assured her, scraping my teeth over her neck.

My wife looked over her shoulder at me. "When am I ever quiet when we have sex?"

I paused, then grinned. "Never."

"Exactly," she replied. "The boys will come in and fight ye'. D'ye remember last month when we were havin' sex and Locke screamed from his bedroom that he was on the phone to Childline to report emotional trauma?"

I tipped my head back and laughed. My second born severely disliked whenever I touched his mother. Out of all my sons, he was the mommy's boy, and he wore the title with pride.

"I'll settle for cuddling with you then."

Aideen turned in my arms and looked up at me.

"What's wrong?"

I smiled. "Why does something have to be wrong for me to hold you?"

"It doesn't," she replied, "but ye' seem very hands on with me today. Always touchin' me in some way whenever I walk into a room … why?"

I hadn't realised I had been doing that.

"I don't know." I shrugged. "I went down memory lane earlier. My mind navigated through the good, the bad, and damn ugly, and I guess I subconsciously just want your comfort."

Aideen's arms slid around my waist as she frowned up at me.

"Anythin' ye' want to talk about?"

I shook my head. "It's just memories we've already talked about before. I just was blindsided when I started thinking of my past, that's all."

Aideen slid her hands up to my shoulders, then onto my face where she cupped my cheeks.

"You're still the bravest, strongest, and most amazin' man I have ever met," she said, her love and adoration for me shining within her eyes. "I wake up every single day in disbelief that *you* are me husband. I love ye' more than words could accurately describe. Always know that. Okay?"

My response was a kiss, a toe-curling, mind-numbing kiss that drew a soft moan from my wife. I hugged her tightly to my body and slid my hands over the curves I knew so well. I had had many years of loving and protecting this woman, and knowing I had many more ahead of me made me love my life that little bit more. She was my rock, the mother of my children, and the reason my heart beat. She was the reason for everything that was good in my life, and I loved her.

"Ye' have *two seconds* to back away from me mother, good sir."

Aideen suddenly giggled against my lips while I sighed and stepped away from my wife just so I could turn and stare at my second eldest son.

"We've talked about ye' gropin' her in public," Locke said. "It's got to *stop*."

"We aren't in public. We're in the privacy of our home."

"A home ye' share with five dashin' and very impressionable young lads."

Aideen said, "He's got ye' there, handsome."

Locke grinned because she agreed with him, then crossed the room and put his arm around his mom's shoulder. He was a couple of inches taller than her at fifteen which amused me and baffled my wife. She slid her arm around his waist and hugged him. We didn't have favourite children, but Locke was the only son who let his mother fuss and be affectionate towards him whenever she wanted. Even our youngest son set boundaries but not Locke. He loved her attention.

"How was your match earlier?"

"We won," Locke replied. "I scored. Twice."

I bumped fists with him because his goals *were* pretty good.

The three of us looked towards the doorway when Beckett and Eli suddenly tumbled into the room, limbs tangled together and fists swinging. Beckett was eleven, and Eli was seven, and even though Beckett was clearly trying to restrain his baby brother, it was proving difficult. Eli was the baby of my sons, and because of that, he constantly wanted to prove that he was tough and was, of course, not an actual baby.

"Stop!" Aideen screeched. "Stop!"

They didn't stop.

"Your mother said stop, so *stop*!"

My sons listened to me instantly. They rolled away from one another and got to their feet as Aideen rushed over to them, fussing. They tried to push her hands away, but she wouldn't allow it this time. Locke shook his head at his brothers as though their antics were childish, and I had to agree.

"What are ye' both fightin' for *this* time?"

My sons looked at one another, then at Aideen, and in unison, they said, "*He* started it."

"Did not!" Eli hissed. "You did."

"Me?" Beckett scowled. "*You* came into me room and took it from me."

"Because it's mine, and *you* took it first.

"Took *what*?" Locke demanded, irritated. "What the hell are ye's wafflin' on about, ye' dopes?"

"Language," I warned him, then turned back to my sons. "Answer his question."

"I was playin' COD when Eli came into me room and took me controller right out of me hands, then he got mad when I ran after 'im for it. He's *always* takin' me stuff, and I'm sick to death of it."

Eli opened his mouth, ready to yell at his brother, but Aideen raised her hand, and it shut him up before he even started speaking.

"Which controller?" she asked Beckett. "Be specific."

"The blue one ye' bought me last week."

Eli's eyes widened. "Ye' bought him a blue one?"

"Yes," Aideen answered. "His black one broke."

Eli's cheek flushed red, and he suddenly looked nervous. "I didn't know that. I thought it was *my* blue controller that he had."

"Ye' didn't give me a chance to tell ye'. Ye' just took it and ran." Beckett glared. "Like ye' always do. Ye' never listen. Ye' just do what ye' want, and ye' get away with it 'cause you're the baby."

"I'm *not* a baby!"

Jesus Christ.

"That's enough!" I interjected. "Eli, give Beckett back his controller and use your words before your actions the next time something like this happens. And Beckett? Stop implying he's treated differently because he's the youngest. You *know* he's not."

Beckett didn't look at me, which told me he disagreed with me.

"Fine," he said.

"Okay." Eli sighed. "I'm sorry, Beck."

"Don't worry about it," he grumbled, took his controller, and walked back down the hallway towards his room. Eli went in search of his own console controller, enlisting Locke's help, which left me alone with my wife.

"He's always annoyed with someone."

I raised a brow. "Who?"

"Beckett." She sighed. "He's always grumpy."

"He's eleven, and he's the middle child. He probably feels as if he's always getting the short end of the stick."

Aideen nodded. "You're probably right."

"Probably?"

My wife looked at me. "Just because you're right most of the time does not mean you're right at this very moment, so don't push it."

I held my hands in front of my chest and grinned. "Is Keela coming over tonight?"

"She'll probably swing by when she's out walkin' that fat bastard she owns."

I snorted. "Junior is a good—"

"Don't ye' *dare* compliment 'im. He is tainted, look at who his father was!"

"You cried more than Keela, Alec *and* the kids when Storm died," I reminded her. "You didn't even cry that much when Tyson and Barbara died a few years before him. Admit it, you loved Storm."

Aideen's eyes narrowed to slits. "If ye' ever tell Keela, or Alec, I'll smother ye' in your sleep."

I bit the inside of my cheek to keep from laughing.

"I wouldn't dream of it, baby doll."

"Anyway," she huffed. "It doesn't matter how I feel because that bloody curse is hangin' over me."

Here we go.

"I'm not crazy, so don't look at me like I am," she warned. "Storm hated me, and now his son hates me! Will this cycle ever end?"

"Probably not. The curse will remain in place unless something breaks it."

"Somethin' like a blood sacrifice?" Aideen perked up. "I volunteer Junior."

I laughed. "Alec's family would rain down on you harder than a downpour if you harm their baby."

"I know." She sighed. "I'll just have to live with the curse and hate Junior as much as he hates me."

"I'm sorry for your suffering," I teased.

"Don't be." My wife grinned. "I enjoy me arguments with 'im, and yes, before ye' say it, I know we don't *really* argue, but in me head, I know he is cursin' at me when he barks, so I curse back at 'im so he knows he can't talk to me that way."

"You've lost your damn mind." I laughed and pulled her to my chest. "I still love you, though."

"I love you too, germinator."

I smiled and kissed the crown of her head. I used the moment to tug the shoulder of her sweater down so I could see the writing that still brought a smile to my face after so many years.

"I still can't believe you put my name on your body."

Aideen leaned back, and said, "You love and cherish this body, so it's as much yours as it is mine."

I kissed her, and we parted when my phone rang from the living room. The sound suddenly stopped, then one of my kids began shouting.

"Da," Jagger, my second youngest, yelled, "Uncle Damien is on the phone."

I sighed. "God doesn't want me to have some alone time with you."

"Come bedtime, ye' can have all the alone time ye' want with me, big man."

My blood heated, and my jeans tightened. "I can't fucking wait."

Aideen laughed, then left the room just as Georgie stormed by.

"Georgie," she called after her, but my niece didn't stop.

"Let her go," Jax shouted from his bedroom. "She's in a pissy mood. We made up, but then she got angry with me all over again. I'll never understand women. Never!"

"Your uncle has a Man Bible for that."

I stared at my wife. "What do you know about our Man Bible?"

Aideen looked away. "Nothin'."

She knew something, but before I could pry it out of her, Jagger shouted and reminded me that my brother was still on the phone waiting for me. I smacked my wife's ass as I left the room, making her laugh. I entered the sitting room and found Jagger, my nine-year-old, lying on the couch with my phone to his ear as he spoke to my brother. Jagger reminded me very much of my mother in appearance, but the kid's heart was made of pure gold. His normal white hair—Damien took credit for some of his nephews having the same hair as him—was neon green this week. Ever since he discovered that he could dye his hair a crazy colour and have it wash out after a few showers, he'd tried them all. I hadn't seen his natural white hair in months, and to be honest, I kind of missed it.

"Here, Da," Jagger said into the phone. "Talk to ye' later, Unc. Yeah, I love ye', too."

I smiled as I took my phone from my son's outstretched hand and sat next to him on the couch. He repositioned himself to rest against me, his head leaning on my shoulder as he watched an episode of *Pokémon*. I placed my phone to my ear, and said, "What's popping, brother?"

"I need your help."

I tensed. "What's wrong? Where are you?"

"I'm okay," he assured me. "It's Dominic. Jax outed that Georgie has a boyfriend, and that they were planning on having sex."

I sent a silent thank you up to God that I was sitting down because my legs suddenly went weak. My eyes darted to the elevator that Georgie had left in just minutes ago.

"Why would she do that to us?" I demanded. "She was in my home, and spoke to me, and never said a damn *word*."

Damien sighed. "She thinks she's grown ... Dominic is torn up about it. I think he might cry, if I'm being honest, and that's not even the worst part."

There was a worst part to my niece having a little punk fawning after her? To me, that *was* the worst part.

"Don't you fucking tell me that girl is pregnant!" I warned as my heart slammed against my chest. "I will lose my fucking mind, Damien."

"Fuck no," he responded swiftly. "Her boyfriend is a Collins'."

Shit. This was bad.

"Where are you guys at?"

"Crough's pub," Damien answered. "Dominic is planning to get trashed."

"I'll be there as soon as I can," I said, getting to my feet. "I'll call Alec and Ryder, too. We'll all be there."

"I already called Alec," Damien said. "You just get Ryder and get here fast. Alec will just get us drunker quicker."

I hung up the call just as Aideen entered the sitting room. I told Jagger to go and play with his brothers so we could have a moment of privacy.

"What's wrong?"

I began to pace back and forth in front of her.

"Georgie has a boyfriend, and he's *your* nephew! Can you believe that? She was just here and never said a word about it to me, the little demon."

Aideen's eyes instantly averted, and it made me pause, before I widened my own with realisation.

"You *knew*!"

"Don't be mad."

"Don't be mad?" I echoed. "You knew my niece had a boyfriend, and you didn't tell me?"

"Our niece," Aideen corrected. "And no, I didn't tell ye' because she made me promise that I wouldn't until she got the courage to tell 'er ma and da 'erself."

"You knew, and *Bronagh* didn't know? Good luck surviving that argument."

Aideen cringed. "I'll handle Bronagh ... who told on Georgie anyway?"

"Jax."

She scowled. "I birthed a little rat."

"*Aideen.*"

"What?"

"Which nephew?" I demanded. "Dame just said he was a Collins when he called me."

She sighed. "It's Indie."

Gavin's eldest.

I growled. "I'm gonna kill him."

"No, ye' aren't."

She was right. I wouldn't kill him, but it felt good saying I would.

My wife groaned. "How bad is it? Be honest."

"Bad."

"Nico isn't takin' it all that well then?"

"Dominic is in a bar, Dame said he will be trashed before the hour is up."

My wife winced. "Go make sure he doesn't get hammered 'cause if he does, he'll get the idea in his head to hunt me nephew down, and kill 'im."

"I'm on it."

I kissed her cheek, shouted for my sons to behave themselves while I was out, grabbed my keys and wallet, then jogged out of our apartment with only one thought on my mind. I had to help Dominic find a way to break Georgie and Indie up ... a way that would preferably result in my wife not ripping my balls from my body.

We had planning to do.

PART FOUR

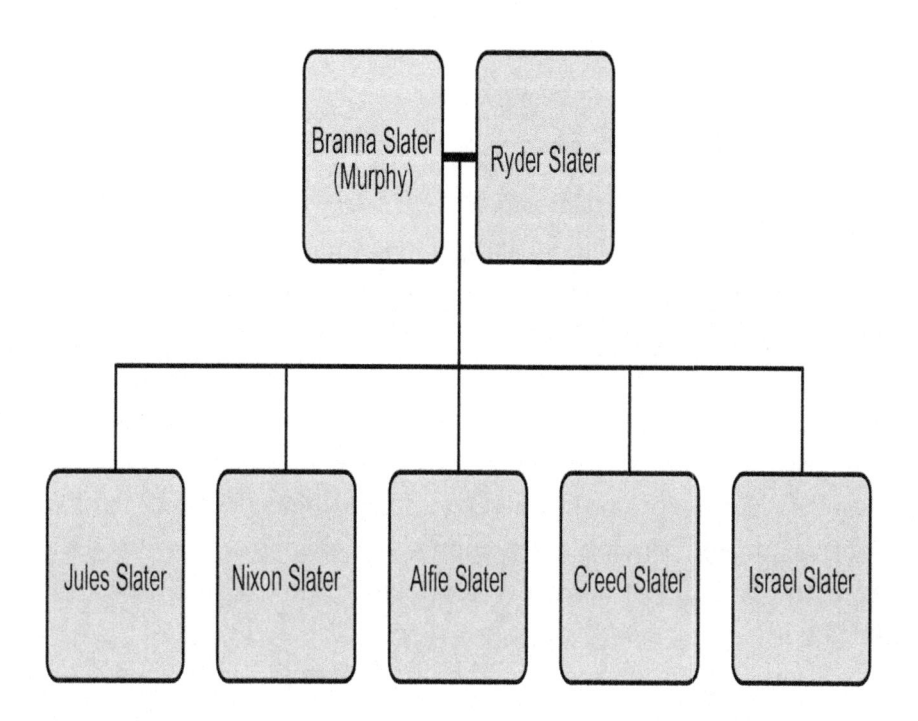

- Branna Slater (Murphy) — Ryder Slater
  - Jules Slater
  - Nixon Slater
  - Alfie Slater
  - Creed Slater
  - Israel Slater

RYDER

CHAPTER ONE

Present day ...

Branna's scream. That was the first sound I heard as I returned home from my son's soccer games. The sound ripped through me like a shard of broken glass. I had my three youngest boys with me—Alfie who was thirteen, Creed who was ten, and Israel who was seven. The three of them jumped when they heard the scream, and before I made a conscious decision to run, my legs were pounding furiously up the driveway of my house. I flung the front door open, and Branna's screaming was then paired with yelling from my two eldest sons, my fourteen-year-old twins, Nixon and Jules.

They had left the soccer clubhouse before me and the others because their game ended earlier, and they didn't want to come along in the car while I dropped Alec's kids home. I ran into the kitchen and found both of them tangled up on the floor as they fought. Branna was throwing cups of water on them like they were dogs in hopes of breaking them up as she simultaneously screamed for them to stop. I looked from my wife to my sons, and bellowed, "That's enough!"

They stopped fighting almost instantly and shoved one another as they got to their feet. Jules had a bloody eyebrow, and Nixon's lip was swollen into a knot and had already bruised. They were both soaking wet, but they didn't seem to notice as they were glaring daggers at one another until their mother got their attention.

"Ye' violent little bastards!" she shouted as she slapped them wildly. "How *dare* ye' carry on like animals!"

My sons had their hands up and easily avoided their mother's flailing hands, but it wasn't her they were worried about; it was me. Their grey eyes locked on me as I approached them, and they tensed the moment I reached in their direction. They grunted when I fisted their T-shirts but didn't struggle as I pulled them over to the kitchen table where I shoved them into the seats.

"You're both grounded," Branna continued behind me as she got the mop to clean up the water puddles on the floor. "You're never crossin' the front door again, and as for your phones, ye' can kiss them goodbye!"

The twins said nothing, only continued to glare at each other so I whacked both of them across the back of the head.

"Da!" Jules hissed at the same time that Nixon said, "That hurt!"

"Good," Branna quipped. "I hope it hurt because seein' both of ye' harm one another hurt *me*! You're brothers. Twins. You're supposed to protect each other, not fight one another!"

Jules looked his mom's way and so did Nixon. I watched as both of their shoulders sagged as what they did registered with them. All my boys hated upsetting their mother, but none more than the twins. They adored her and seeing her so upset because of them made them feel like crap. I could tell by the solemn expression on their identical faces.

"I'm sorry, Ma," Jules said at the same time Nixon said, "Sorry, Ma."

They spoke in unison an awful lot, but we were all used to it at this stage in their lives.

"Sorry isn't good enough!" Branna snapped as she stomped over to the table. "D'ye ever stop to think that ye' could have seriously hurt one another? All it takes is one punch to a certain point on the head and ye' could have *died*."

Jules and Nixon looked at one another, and their anger began to recede as their mother's words sunk in.

"I can't even look at ye's right now. I'm bloody sick of the pair of ye'. Ye' act like babies!"

Branna stalked out of the room, shooing our three other sons away from the doorway where they were eavesdropping. They needed showers because they stunk to the high heavens, apart from Alfie because he didn't go to his game, he spent the day in Alec's house instead. Once Branna gave them their marching orders, they filed up the stairs, and my wife followed to run a bath for Israel who didn't like taking showers on his own yet.

I stared down at my twins, and said, "Do either of you enjoy hurting your mother?"

"Don't be stupid," Jules scowled. "Ye' know we don't."

"So what exactly did you think fighting in front of her was going to result in?"

"We didn't know she was home," Nixon answered. "We thought she was out, and by the time we realised she *was* home, we were already fightin'."

"About that," I said. "What made you guys beat the crap out of one another?"

"Because he," Jules spat, "is *not* me brother."

Nixon didn't answer. Instead, he looked down at the table.

"He's not your brother?" I repeated. "There's another reason you're identical twins then?"

Neither of my boys were amused.

"I don't care if we're twins, and that we look the exact same, he's nothin' to me. Nothin'."

Nixon flinched, and I'd be lying if I said my heart didn't break a little.

"Care to expand on why you're saying such hurtful things?"

"Ask *him*," Jules answered, his tone clipped. "He's the one who mucked everythin' up."

I looked at Nixon and waited.

He glared at his twin, and said, "It was an *accident*."

"Bollocks," Jules snapped. "How d'ye accidentally kiss me girlfriend, Nix?"

"Whoa." I blinked. "You kissed his girlfriend, Nixon? Wait, you have a girlfriend, Jules?"

"Not anymore because she's a cheatin' bitch!"

"It was an *accident*," Nixon repeated. "It wasn't Avery's fault."

"Explain," I said.

"Our game finished about twenty minutes before the others, so that's why we walked home instead of waitin' around with you and the others," Nixon began. "I was waitin' outside the clubhouse for Jules when his girlfriend, Avery, came runnin' up to me. She jumped on me and kissed me before I knew what was happenin'. I lost all train of thought for literally three or four seconds and kissed 'er back until I realised just who she was and what the hell was happenin'. I put 'er down and told 'er I wasn't Jules, and 'er face dropped. She thought I was 'im, I could tell by the look on 'er face. She has trouble tellin' us apart still. She begged me not to tell Jules because it was an accident, but we don't keep secrets from each other, so I told 'im when we got home. He punched me in the face, so I hit 'im back and then ye' got home and stopped it."

Jules stared at his brother, and said, "Why the hell didn't ye' *start* by sayin' she thought ye' were me?"

"I was startin' from the start of what happened, but ye' hit me before I could get to the part that it was a misunderstandin'."

Jules shook his head. "Nixon, ye' made it sound like both of ye' mutually kissed."

"Because ye' swung at me before I could finish me sentence and say it was all an accident," Nixon argued. "Ye' always overreact."

"So ye' didn't wanna kiss Avery?" Jules pressed.

"No, I didn't wanna bloody kiss 'er," Nixon quipped. "She's *your* girlfriend. I've no interest in 'er like that, and even if I did, I'd never act on it because *you* are with 'er. Ye' say I'm not your brother, but I would *never* mess around with a girl you're with. Never. I'm mad that ye' would even hit me over a girl. Ye' didn't even give me a chance to explain it, Jules."

Nixon, who was rightfully upset, got up and walked out of the kitchen, leaving his brother to stare after him. After a minute of silence, Jules looked at me, and said, "I messed up."

"Yeah," I said. "But you can fix it, go and apologise to him."

"I said he was nothin' to me, Da." He swallowed. "Nixon loves that we're twins, he always has. He loves me more than anyone, even Georgie ... well, maybe he loves me the same amount as 'er. She's everyone's favourite."

My lips twitched. "He knows you spoke out of anger."

"Yeah," Jules agreed, "but I shouldn't have said he wasn't me brother. He's right, no one girl should ever come between us. I should have listened to 'im from the jump. I know Nix would never want to hurt me, but I just got so mad when I thought of 'im kissin' Avery, and I lost it."

"Speaking of Avery," I said. "Who said you could have a girlfriend?"

Jules widened his eyes. "I'm *not* allowed to have a girlfriend ... seriously?"

"You're fourteen."

"So?" he pressed. "It's not like we do anythin' sexual. I mean, she only let me kiss 'er for the first time the other day, and I've been with 'er for four months."

"Four months?" I blinked. "Why is this the first I'm hearing about it?"

"I ... uh ... I guess I knew you wouldn't be happy about it."
Damn right.

"Listen to me, and listen well," I said sternly. "Sex is off the table until you're an adult. Now, with that being said, I know my warning may be ignored when the opportunity is presented to you over the next few years, but if you have sex, you better wear a condom or God Himself won't be able to help you. I'll kick your ass if you get a girlfriend pregnant or catch an STI. We clear?"

Jules's cheeks were flaming red, and he said, "We're clear."

"I'm serious, Jules," I said. "Responsibility comes with sex."

"Da," he groaned. "I hear ye', and trust me, at the rate Avery wants to take things, I'll be a virgin until I'm thirty. Ye' *really* don't have to worry about me."

Something in my heart told me that I didn't have to worry about him, so I accepted that with a nod.

"Go clean up your eye, then talk to Nixon," I encouraged. "Bring an ice-pack with you for his lip. Tell him what you just told me, and both of you will be cool by the end of the day."

Jules nodded, then said, "Ma will be a harder hurdle to tackle."

I snorted. "I'll handle your mom. You go and find Nixon."

Jules bumped fists with me and left the room armed with an ice-pack for his brother. I went in search of my wife, and after finding Israel playing in the bathtub on his own, I went into my bedroom and found Branna lying on our bed with her eyes closed.

"Tough day, Mama?"

She grunted. "Is it too late to put the twins up for adoption? Because I'm seriously considerin' it."

I crawled onto the bed beside her, chuckling. "I think we're a little passed that, don't you?"

Branna opened her eyes and looked up at me as I settled next to her.

"They scared me, Ryder." She frowned. "Jules almost hit me when I tried to separate them. They are only fourteen, and they're already bigger than me. Can ye' imagine when they're in their twenties and fight? I'll still try to stop them and will probably get a broken nose for me troubles."

"That'll never happen because I'd break their bones before they ever get a chance to break yours."

"I'm not playin'." She shook her head. "Today was the first day that they didn't listen to me when they fought, and it *really* scared me, Ry. I was on me own with them, and all I could think of was throwin' water on them."

I realised then that my wife was crying, so I bundled her in my arms and rested her against my body.

"I've spoken to them both, and trust me when I say they both feel like shit. Expect apologies from them before the day is up."

Branna sniffled. "I'm so mad at them. They could have really hurt each other."

"I know, and they know that now, too. It was a misunderstanding over a girl, but Jules is apologising to Nixon as we speak. You'll be next."

I had barely finished speaking when a light knock sounded. Both Branna and I looked at the open doorway of our room, and found Jules and Nixon standing side by side, their eyes locked on their mom, and an identical frown on their faces. Jules's eyebrow was cleaned and had stopped bleeding. Nixon's lip was still a swollen knot but icing it for a few hours would help.

"Ma." Jules swallowed. "We're really sorry for fightin', we didn't mean to upset ye'."

"Yeah." Nixon nodded. "We were wrong. We shouldn't have fought at all. We're really sorry."

If I didn't know any better at that moment, I'd say my twins were my twin brothers. Their white hair was inherited from Damien, and their mannerisms were most definitely thanks to Dominic. They looked very much like me, but so did my brothers, so in a way, they resembled them, too. It freaked me out for a minute.

"I accept your apology, but both of ye' really upset me. Today was the first day ye' scared me, and it's not a feelin' I enjoyed at all."

The second the words left my wife's mouth, my sons' eyes widened. They walked into the room and crawled up onto our bed. I was pushed aside as my sons replaced me and cuddled my wife.

"We're sorry," Jules said.

Nixon nodded. "We love ye', Ma. We'd never ever hurt ye'. We're sorry we scared ye'."

Branna hugged them both while I was sitting on the edge of the bed completely forgotten about.

"Both of you guys upset me too, if you want to offer *me* hugs."

Branna giggled, making my sons laugh. They both released their mother, turned to me, and without a word, they jumped on me and tried their hardest to pin me against the mattress. They almost succeeded. Almost. I flipped Jules onto his back, which he found hilarious before I shoved Nixon against him and pinned both of them to the bed by lying on top of them.

"Pile on!"

I looked up just as Alfie and Creed barrelled into the room, freshly showered and in clean clothes as they jumped onto my bed and attacked me. It was four against one then, and for a few minutes I was holding my own, until a naked, and very wet, Israel joined us and sat his slippery ass on my head resulting in my defeat almost instantly. My sons and wife, who was recording the chaos on her phone, cracked up laughing, and so did I.

"We win!" Israel announced as he jumped up and down on the bed, not caring that he was naked as the day he was born. "We beat Daddy!"

Jules and Nixon clapped their palms against his, Creed tickled his stomach, and Alfie, who got off the bed, threw him over his shoulder, slapped his butt, and marched out the room with Branna following so they could get him dried and dressed. I sat up, wiped the wetness from my face, looked at my three remaining sons, and said, "If any of you tell your uncles about this, I'm beating your asses."

The three of them left the bedroom, laughing as they went, which meant they would tell my brothers and they'd do it with a smile on their faces. I lay back on my bed, smiled, and closed my eyes. I loved my life, I loved every little thing about it ... even all the bad that it took for me to have it. After years of worry and shouldering the responsibility of raising my brothers for my absent parents, I knew if I had to do it all over again, I wouldn't change a damn thing.

My past brought me my future, and as fucked up as my past was, I'd live it over and over again to get my future because to me, it was my true happily ever after.

CHAPTER TWO

Six years old ...

The shrill sound of a baby's cry woke me.

I opened my eyes, rolled onto my back, and listened. The crying continued, and it got louder and louder. I groaned, turned onto my side, and pressed my hands over my ears to drown the sound out, but it didn't help. I dropped my hands, sat upright on my bed, and shouted, "Mama, Kane is awake!" I waited for her to make some noise to let me know she heard me, but she didn't. I frowned as I pushed my warm, cosy blanket away from my body and slid out of my bed. I rubbed my eyes as I walked over to the doorway of my room, I squinted my eyes to help me see because my nightlight wasn't very bright.

I opened the door and stuck my head out into the hallway. It was dark, and the only light I could see was the moonlight that shone through the windows. I swallowed, and the urge to close my door and get back into my bed was strong, but when my baby brother screamed, my chest tightened. With trembling limbs, and tentative steps, I made my way down the hallway to my parents' bedroom. I opened the door without knocking, and said, "Mama? Daddy? Kane is awake."

No one answered me. Feeling worried, I quickly found the light switch to the room, and flipped it on. My parents' bed was empty; the sheets were still neatly made which told me that they hadn't gone to sleep yet. I turned off the light, closed the door, and ran all the way down to the end of the hallway to my brothers' bedroom. When I opened the door, the room was in darkness, which I knew wasn't right. Alec liked having a nightlight just like I did. He was only three, still a baby, so he needed one. I just liked having one ... I didn't need it or anything.

"RyRy," Alec sobbed when I flipped the light on. "Kane's sad."

I widened my eyes when I saw tears stream down Alec's face. He was next to Kane's crib, trying to climb into it. My one-year-old brother was screaming so loud it made me want to cry too.

"It's okay," I said, rushing over to Alec, pulling him into a hug. "It's okay, Alec."

My brother squeezed me so tight it hurt a little, but I couldn't focus on him. Kane was screaming so loud that I worried something might be wrong with him. I leaned down to Alec, put my hands on his shoulders and said, "Grab your favourite teddy, and go and sit on your bed, okay?"

I had to repeat myself three times before he understood what I wanted him to do. He sniffled as he bobbed his head and did as I asked. I turned my attention to Kane who had tears running down his face as he lay on his side and looked at me. His eyes stared into mine, and I knew he was telling me something, but I didn't know what.

"Hey baby," I smiled at him. "It's okay, RyRy is here."

Kane didn't care that I was there. He continued to cry, and scream, and because of this, so did Alec.

"Alec, it's okay," I said, my throat tight because I was fighting off a sob. "It's all okay."

"Mama," Alec cried. "I want Mama!"

I knew I couldn't search the house for her, or my dad, because I couldn't leave my brothers alone while they were crying. I needed to protect them and make sure they were okay even though I was so scared that I couldn't stop my hands from shaking. I looked from Alec to Kane and tried to pull the bar of his crib down, but I wasn't strong enough to do it, and that was when my own tears fell. I tried my hardest not to cry, but I was scared. I didn't know how to make my brothers stop crying, and I wanted my mama.

I wanted her so bad.

I looked at Kane, then wiped my eyes. He was only a baby. He couldn't even walk yet, and he needed me to help him. I was six, I was a big boy, so I had to be brave and take care of my brothers because I loved them, and they loved me. And when you loved someone, it meant you took care of them. That was what *Barney* said, so that was how I knew it was the truth.

"I'm coming, Kane."

I used all my strength and pulled Alec's toy chest to the front of the crib, then stood on it. I jumped, pulling myself over the bar of the crib, and fell next to Kane. He was still crying, but when I sat up and reached for him, he calmed down, but only a little. I lifted him into my arms, which was a little hard to do because he was starting to get a little heavy. I hugged him to my chest and kissed his face. It made me feel better to do that, so I kissed him a lot. I set him on my legs and wiped his face. I smelled his dirty diaper then, and I realised why he was crying.

"Alec," I called my brother who was sitting on his bed holding his brown teddy bear, watching me. "Come help me. Hold Kane when I give him to you, just until I get out of here."

He climbed off his bed slowly, lowering himself down until his feet touched the floor. He stood on the chest in front of Kane's crib, then he raised his arms and waited as I lifted Kane over the bar. I struggled to lift him high enough, but I knew I made it when Alec grunted, and said, "Got 'em."

I quickly pulled myself over the bar once more and lowered myself onto the chest. Alec was struggling with Kane; I saw his little arms lowering because he couldn't hold him up anymore, so I quickly took him in my arms and told Alec to get back into bed. I carried

Kane over to the bed and pushed him up onto it. I grabbed a clean diaper and the wet wipes I saw our nanny use to clean Kane back when she worked for us. She hadn't worked for us in a few days. She usually took care of my brothers at night-time, but now that Mama fired her for wrestling with Daddy, it meant that Mama should be taking care of Alec and Kane ... but she wasn't here to do it.

I removed Kane's pyjamas and told Alec to play with him so he wouldn't move while I was changing his diaper. Alec put his face next to Kane's and pulled a funny face and made funny sounds. Some of them were so funny that Kane stopped crying long enough so he could laugh. I laughed too ... until I took off the dirty diaper. The stinky mess was so bad that I wanted to cry again. Alec complained of the smell, so I quickly grabbed two handfuls of wet wipes and cleaned my brother's butt and his pee-pee.

There was doo-doo everywhere ... even in his butt crack. When I cleaned it all, I grabbed a fruity smelling bag and put the dirty diaper and dirty wet wipes into it and tied a knot. I put it in the diaper bin, then went back to Kane. Putting a fresh diaper on was hard. Really hard. It took five tries, and a few different diapers until I figured out how to get it on properly. I put Kane back in his pyjamas because they were still clean. He should have been okay, but he started crying again, and that was when I started to panic because I didn't know what to do.

"I'm hungry." Alec sighed.

Food.

"That's it," I said as I looked at Alec. "I think he's hungry."

"*I'm* hungry," he repeated.

I gave him his teddy bear. "Hold teddy, and I'll go get you and Kane food, okay?"

Alec widened his eyes. "No, take Kane."

I frowned. "Alec—"

"No," he snapped and hid under the covers of his bed.

I wiped away tears that filled my eyes. Alec didn't like it when he was on his own with Kane when he was crying. It scared him, and

I knew that. It scared me too, but I had no one to help me, so there was nothing I could do. I had to take him with me.

"I'll bring him with me," I said to my brother. "You just stay here, okay? I'll bring you food."

"'Kay."

Alec remained under his blanket with his teddy as I hoisted Kane off the bed and carried him out of the room. Kane rested his head on my shoulder as he cried, and I had my arms wrapped tightly around him. My heart beat so fast against his chest when I thought of him falling. I was terrified of him being hurt, but I was even more scared of my dad finding out because he would kick me again. He always kicked me when he was mad at me.

My tummy hurt just thinking about it. It was dark as I walked down the hallway, down the stairs, and into the kitchen. I turned on the light, and by now, I was sobbing right along with Kane. I wanted my parents so bad, but I didn't know where to look for them. Everywhere was silent except for Kane's cry. They weren't home; I knew they weren't.

I had to lay Kane down on the cold floor as I quickly got milk and yogurts from the refrigerator. I grabbed one of Kane's empty bottles, filled it to the top with milk, then put it into the microwave for a few seconds. I remembered our nanny making his milk too hot one day, and it took a long time for it to cool down, so I opened the door every five seconds to check how hot it was. When it was nice and warm, I took the bottle out and tightened the top of it. I picked Kane up and hugged him to my chest. I grabbed his bottle and the packet of yogurts and quickly left the room. When I got back into the bedroom, Alec was still under the covers, but he popped his head out when he heard Kane's cry.

I quickly put Kane on the bed, then climbed up next to him. Pulling him onto my lap, I put his bottle against his lips. His hands latched onto the bottle as he drank. The relief I felt that he was no longer crying made me sniffle, but I used my free hand to wipe my face. I watched as Alec broke off a yogurt tub, opened it, and used his finger to eat it because I forgot to bring a spoon. He ate two tubs before he sat back and watched Kane drink his bottle with sleepy eyes.

"Kane's sad."

"He was just hungry and needed his diaper changed. He's okay."

I hoped, anyway.

Alec frowned. "*You* are sad."

His eyes were on my cheeks where I knew some tears still dampened my skin.

"I'm okay." I smiled big just to prove it.

Alec blinked. "I'm scared. I want Mama."

I swallowed. "When you wake up, Mama will be here, okay?"

He nodded and said nothing further. I looked from him, to Kane, then around the room. I wouldn't be able to sleep knowing that they were in here alone, so I looked back at Alec and said, "Grab the rest of the yogurts and come with me. We're sleeping in my room tonight."

Usually, I had to say things a few times for Alec to understand what I meant because he was still only a baby, but right then he didn't need to be told twice. I held Kane in my arms, ignoring that they burned from carrying him, and Alec had a death grip on my pyjama pants as we walked out of his bedroom, down the dark hallway, and into my room. My brother ran and jumped up onto my bed, burrowing his way under the covers. I smiled as I closed my bedroom door and joined him with Kane. When he was finished with his bottle, I fed him some yogurts until he got that sleepy look in his eyes. I wiped his face with my sleeve, settled him under the covers between me and Alec, who was already asleep, and I stared at the both of them for a very long time.

I turned my head and looked at my bedroom door when I suddenly heard voices. The sounds were faint, but then they got loud as footsteps passed by my door. I knew the laughter belonged to my parents, and I waited for them to go to my brothers' room to check on them, but when I heard their bedroom door open and close, a pain spread across my chest. They should have checked on my brothers, realised they weren't there, then run to my room to see if they were with me ... but they didn't.

I looked at my brothers as tears welled in my eyes once more. Our mama and daddy were very mean to me, and sometimes to my brothers, but they should still take care of us. They didn't, though, so I was the one who had to look after my brothers tonight, and they didn't even care enough to see if they were okay. They just laughed and went to bed like they didn't care. I cared, though. I cared about my brothers more than anyone ... even more than I cared about my mama. They were babies, and they needed to be loved and protected, and if my parents wouldn't do that for them, then I would.

"I'll always take care of you guys," I swore as my eyes roamed over my brothers' sleeping faces. "I promise."

CHAPTER THREE

Eighteen years old ...

I jolted awake upon hearing an uproarious thump on my bedroom door. Damien, my eight-year-old brother, was undisturbed by the sound as he slept peacefully beside me. His mouth hung open as he snored and drool dripped down his chin. I lifted the blanket and checked to see if he had wet himself, and I felt a smile stretch across my face when I noticed he was dry. This was the fourth night in a row that he didn't wet the bed, and as soon as he woke up, I was going to praise the hell out of him for it.

Unlike Dominic, Damien's twin, he didn't suffer nightmares that resulted in him having no control over his bladder, but that wasn't Damien's fault. Damien was very sensitive compared to Dominic and our other brothers. He scared easily, and when he was scared, he craved affection. I never minded him crawling into my bed during the night simply because I knew he just needed to be comforted. He never received comfort from my parents, not for his lack of trying, so he always came to me in the end. He never wanted to appear like a baby to his other brothers, so his bed-wetting was our secret.

I looked from my brother to the door when another loud knock sounded. I pushed the blanket away from my body, got out of bed, and walked over to the door, scratching my ass as I went. I opened the door, and when I saw my father standing on the other side, I blinked.

"What's wrong?"

"Nothing," he replied. "I've got a job for you."

"A job?" I repeated.

Dad nodded, but before he spoke, he looked over my shoulder and saw Damien in my bed. He narrowed his eyes at my brother then looked at me and said, "What's he doing in your room?"

"He's sick," I lied. "He was throwing up during the night, so I brought him in here so I could keep an eye on him."

If my dad knew that Damien wet the bed, he'd bash him until my brother screamed. He would view it as a weakness and would attempt to beat that weakness out of him. He'd do the same if he knew Damien slept in my bed with me for no other reason than he wanted to be close to me. He'd hurt him for that too.

"He probably has the flu." Dad grimaced. "Some of the guys he annoys when they're on patrol have it."

"Yeah," I agreed. "He probably does, but he'll be fine once he gets some rest. Dominic snores so he can't sleep in there; in here with me is quiet."

Dad grunted. "Aren't you a regular Mother-fucking-Theresa?"

I tensed. "He's my brother, so it's not a hardship for me to look after him."

Dad snorted. "Get dressed and meet me in the courtyard in five minutes."

With that said, he turned and walked down the hallway. He didn't ask if Damien was okay nor did he check on him himself, which didn't surprise me. There wasn't a paternal bone in the man's body. I closed the door, then went into my private bathroom and took a quick shower. When I was finished, I dried myself and dressed warm. It was winter and had been snowing for the past few days, so that meant I needed to put on layers. Damien woke up as I was tying the laces up on my boots, sitting up in the bed and rubbing his eyes. I looked up at him and smiled; he was so cute. He was in need of a haircut, the long strands stuck up in all directions making him look crazy.

"Morning, sleepyhead."

Damien yawned. "Morning."

He smacked his lips together a couple of times before his eyes widened, and he hurriedly reached down and patted his pants. When he looked up at me, a huge smile stretched across his lips. "I didn't wet the bed."

I whooped, sprung to my feet, then jumped on my brother who was laughing so hard that he stopped making sounds which amused me greatly.

"You're doing great, buddy," I said, ruffling his wild hair.

Damien rested back against my pillow with a smile. "Why are you dressed?"

I looked down at my clothes, then back to my brother, and said, "Dad has a job for me."

Damien frowned. "What kind of job?"

"I don't know," I answered. "I have to meet him in the courtyard and find out."

My brother yawned again. "I'll go back to my room then. Dominic is probably still asleep, so I'll play the PlayStation until he wakes up."

I bumped fists with him. "I'll see you later, okay?"

As we left the room, Damien said, "Thanks for letting me sleep with you again."

His voice was low, and redness tinged his cheeks.

I squatted in front of him, and said, "Bro, I like having cuddles with you, so I don't mind when you get scared and want to sleep with me. Don't even think about it, okay?"

Damien smiled, his dimples creasing his chubby cheeks. "Okay. I love you, Ry."

"I love you, too."

I watched as he turned and ran down the hallway. I straightened to my full height when he entered his bedroom and closed the door behind him. I turned and made my way down the stairs and out to the courtyard, grabbing my coat from its hanger on the way. I zipped it up and shoved my hands into the coat's pockets because it was fucking freezing outside. I could see my breath in the air when I exhaled. I followed the voices and found my father talking to a couple of strange men. I coughed so they were aware of my presence.

The last thing I needed was to overhear something that wasn't meant for my ears.

My dad looked over his shoulder, spotted me, and waved me over. When I reached them, he slung his arm around my shoulder and to the men I had never seen before, he said, "This is my eldest son, Ryder."

"No DNA test required." The grey-haired man on my right laughed. "He's your clone."

My stomach churned. I knew I looked like my dad, and I hated it.

"Let's see if he's like me business wise, too."

I looked at him and said, "What's that supposed to mean?"

He snorted. "I want to see what skills you have, so I can decide where to place you. You're good at numbers, so I'm thinking heading runs will be for you."

I resisted the urge to close my eyes and sigh. A 'run' was what everyone in the compound called when someone was running a drug or weapons deal. I had noticed over the past year that my dad was on my case a lot pushing math my way for me to figure out someone else's runs, but I didn't think I'd actually have to head them myself. Marco and my dad were all about money. If they paid for a product, they wanted to sell it for a decent profit. Falling short was never an option, and I knew a few men over the years who had disappeared after unsuccessful runs, or worse, having a shipment impounded by the cops.

"Can I talk to you?"

My dad nodded, before moving us away from the strange men. "What?"

I cleared my throat. "What exactly am I going to be doing? I … I don't want to mess it up so give it to me straight."

I didn't want to head a run, or participate in one of any kind, but if I was going to do it, I wanted all the information I could get so I could do it correctly. I knew that if I disappointed my father, it wouldn't bode well for me or my brothers. I had to impress him to keep him happy and to do that meant I had to do a good job during my run.

"That's my boy." Dad grinned and clamped his hand on my shoulder. "It's a small run, considering it's your first time. I've about twenty pounds of heroine that I want you to sell." He handed me a folded piece of paper. "This is a list of the weight, amount I paid for it, and amount I expect you to sell it for during your run. Any less than the number on the paper and it's not a job well done, am I clear?"

I swallowed but nodded my head as I read the paper, then folded it and tucked it into my pocket. He said it was a small run, but twenty pounds of heroin could run for over a million bucks.

"Will this just take the day?"

"No," he answered. "You'll be gone a week, at least. Runs take time, you know this."

I froze. "But … but Damien is sick, I need to take care of him."

He wasn't sick, but his nightmares and his bed-wetting might reoccur, and if that happened, then he needed me.

"You need to take care of him?" Dad snorted. "He's not yours, Ryder."

I stepped back and stared at my father.

"He's as much mine as he is yours, if not more."

Dad laughed. "Really? How do you figure that?"

"Because I take care of him all of the time. I take care of the others, too. I always have."

"Bullshit, you had a nanny most of your life."

"Most of my life?" I repeated on a laugh. "Mom fired her when Kane was one because you were fucking her, and Mom never said that you could. We haven't had a nanny since then."

Dad waved his hand in front of me, dismissing the truth.

"Ryder, Damien will be fine. Don't worry about the brat."

Worrying about Damien and my other brothers was all I did.

"You have no clue what it's like to worry about them," I said, my jaw tensed. "You have no fucking clue."

Dad sighed, and checked his watched, clearly done with this conversation but I wasn't … not by a long shot.

"I'm five years older than Kane, but I've always took care of him. I can remember being six and having to go into his and Alec's bedroom because he was crying and neither you or Mom were home to take care of him. I was terrified. I had to climb into his crib and then climb out with him because I wasn't strong enough to pull the bar down." My eyes stung with unshed tears. "I didn't know how to change a diaper, so I stripped him naked and cleaned him as best as I could with wet wipes. I carried him down to the kitchen and had to lay him on the cold floor while I got regular milk and heated it up in the microwave. I cried the entire time and so did Kane. I put the milk in a bottle, picked him up, and carried him up to my room. I held him until he was fed, then I tucked him and Alec into my bed and watched over them until morning. I did that with them a lot, then I did it when the twins were born too. *I* did all that, never you."

My dad shook his head. "Is there a reason you're telling me this story?"

"They're *my* kids!" I hissed, my voice low. "I'm telling you so you understand one thing. I'm sick of you disregarding them as if they're nothing. They're worth a hell of a lot, and I'm not going to work for you if you don't make sure they're taken care of when I'm not here to do the job myself."

"Ryder," Dad glared. "They are my sons—"

"They're *mine!*"

My father raised both of his eyebrows. He didn't care that I was declaring that his sons were mine; he was surprised that I was raising my voice to him, and that infuriated me. He should fight for my brothers because they were worth fighting for.

"I've been everything that you have never been to them. To *me*. They're my brothers, but I'm the one raising them. If they're anyone's kids, they're *mine,* and fuck you if you think otherwise. I'm fucking *done* acting as your puppet. If I'm old enough to work for you, then you better start treating me like a man and respect me, or you can get fucked."

Things were silent for just a few moments until my dad spoke.

"Ryder." He sighed, long and deep. "If you want them, you can have them. I honestly don't give a fuck. All that matters to me is that you and your brothers contribute to our business. It's the entire reason I made your mother have you guys in the first place. I wanted only sons to strengthen our empire. There is a reason she aborted the girl she got pregnant with a few years after the twins were born. I can barely deal with your mother, never mind another bitch."

I felt like the air around me suddenly disappeared. I had never known this piece of information before now, and I wanted to scream and ask if it was the truth. I could have had a baby sister ... but I was robbed of that, just as I was robbed of having decent fucking parents.

"You ... You checked to see what our genders were before you decided whether or not we would be born?"

"Yes," Dad answered, unashamed. "Like I said, I only wanted boys. Girls serve no purpose to me unless they go to work."

I balled my hands into fists because we both knew what 'work' meant for girls who got involved with my father and Marco.

"Listen," I said, gruffly. "I'll do this job, and I'll do it well, on the condition that when I'm not here, my brothers are taken care of."

My dad regarded me for a long moment, then said, "Deal."

I relaxed.

"Now that's we have *that* out of the way, come on. No more bullshit talk about your brothers. From now on, our only conversations are to be about runs."

He rounded on me and returned to the strangers who were talking quietly until my father returned to their circle. I felt my heart pound against my chest, and my palms were slick with sweat, but I didn't care because I had done something I had never done ... I stood up to my father. I made it clear to him that he was nothing to me and my brothers, and that I was the parent he should have been.

He didn't care ... I knew he wouldn't, but he now knew that if he wanted me to head runs and to make them successful, then he would ensure my brothers were taken care of when I wasn't around. It meant nothing to my father, but it meant everything to me. Once I did this job well, it would be extra security for my brothers. Their safety was all that mattered to me, and if it meant I had to run drugs and weapons ... then so fucking be it.

CHAPTER FOUR

Twenty-five years old ...

"Ryder, what are we gonna do?"

I looked from the frosted windowpane to Kane, and said, "Whatever we have to do to keep Damien safe."

Kane swallowed but nodded, agreeing that no matter what, our brother's safety was the most important thing. I looked from Kane, to Alec and Dominic who, like us, sat in a chair in front of a large desk owned by Marco Miles. This piece of shit ... he had my family right where he wanted us. For as long as I could remember, Marco and my scumbag father were grooming me and my brothers for their business. I had been working for them for years—running guns, drugs, and a few times, people ... once the price was right. I shifted in my seat, feeling my stomach swirl with dread.

An hour ago, Damien had gotten into a fight with Marco's nephew Trent. Damien was the only one of my brothers who grieved our parents' deaths, and when Trent taunted him about them, he exploded into a fit of rage and attacked him. The fight turned deadly, and Damien somehow got his hands on a gun and shot Trent. The doctor pronounced the kid dead not long after, and since then, me and my brothers were on lockdown.

"He'll kill Damien," Dominic said, his hands shaking. "I know he will."

I was terrified of that too, but I forced myself to think logically.

"Killing Damien won't benefit Marco," I said, firmly. "Marco is like Dad in more ways than one. He doesn't care about family; he only cares about money. If he can make a profit moneywise out of Trent's death, then he will."

"What do you mean?" Kane asked, perplexed. "How can he make money from this?"

I looked forward. "We work for him. We work off the debt that Damien would have to pay to keep his life."

"You already work for Marco, though," Alec pointed out.

"Yeah," I agreed, "but I think he knew that my intention wasn't to stick around now that Mom and Dad were dead. This worked out well for Marco; if he accepts our offer, then he owns us until we pay off the debt."

"What offer are we making him?" Dominic asked. "And how do you know he'll accept it."

I looked at my little brother and patted his shoulder. "We'll offer to work for him, and he'll accept it because he is a greedy prick who loves money."

My brothers grunted in agreement.

"We'll only make the offer if you're all happy with it," I said, looking at each of them. "I can't make this decision for you guys."

"Ryder." Alec blinked. "Of *course* we're happy with it. If it means keeping Damien safe, then we're doing it. Period."

Kane and Dominic bobbed their heads in agreement to the plan and looked at me as though they thought I was crazy for suggesting otherwise.

"I just can't believe all of this is happening," I said as I rubbed my eyes. "We were supposed to be out of here in a few weeks. I had it all planned."

I had thought about it every waking hour since my parents died. The only thing keeping me, Alec, and Kane under my dad's thumb were the twins. They were still kids, and if I took them, I knew Dad would send a manhunt after us. I was biding my time until they were adults so we could freely leave, but things sped up when Marco had my mom and dad killed for double-crossing him. I had money saved, and I was going to move my brothers to Canada. I was going to get us out of the States and away from Marco completely ... then everything went to hell when Damien killed Trent.

"Plans have changed." Kane regained my attention. "We'll make new plans."

I nodded and looked towards the door when it opened and Marco entered on his own, closing the door behind him. He looked very fucking chirp for a man whose nephew had just been killed, and it made my blood boil.

"I think we need to have a little chat, boys."

He took a seat behind his desk, clasped his hands together, and looked from each of my brothers until his eyes landed on me. He didn't speak for a long moment, and I found myself playing with the ring on my middle finger that my dad gave me after my first successful run. I hated it, but I had to keep it on my finger until I was free of this life.

"Where is Damien?"

"At our place," I answered. "He doesn't need to be here for this."

Marco raised a brow and sat back in his chair. "Is that so?"

"Look." I leaned forward. "Can we get past the bullshit and straight down to business? None of us have time for this."

Marco, who looked incredibly interested in what I had to say, waved his hand, giving me permission to speak.

"We know what Damien did means he has a life debt hanging over his head, but instead of him paying that debt with his life, my brothers and I have decided *we* will pay it by working it off for you ... if you'll agree, that is."

I held my breath as Marco digested what I said.

"Let me get this straight." Marco tilted his head. "You four will work for me, working Damien's debt off, and in return, you just want him to remain unharmed?"

"Yes," the four of us said in unison.

"*Deal*," Marco said almost instantly.

I knew he would like my deal and eventually accept it, but I didn't think he would be so … eager.

"How long?" Alec asked.

Marco looked at him. "How long what?"

"How long will we work for you?"

"Well," Marco began, "Trent had a promising future heading runs for me, but now that he is dead, I'm losing profit he would have brought to me. Let's say once you guys earn at least ten million for me, we can discuss job termination."

Fuck.

I got a decent profit in my run for Marco, but it'd take me years to rake up ten million for him. Trent would have never made Marco ten million bucks, and he fucking knew it. He pulled that number out of his ass, but I couldn't say a word against him on the matter, and he knew it. Not when Damien's life was on the line.

"I'll teach the guys how to head a run and—"

"That won't be necessary," Marco cut me off. "Runs are your thing, Ryder. I've other jobs that your brothers will do for me."

I looked at my brothers then back at Marco, and said, "Like what?"

"You'll find out soon enough," he answered. "I've other shit to deal with, thanks to your baby brother, so before I leave, I want it understood that we are in agreement. You four work for me, and Damien remains unharmed."

"Unharmed and uninvolved in our new operation," I pressed. "We work for you, not him."

Marco nodded. "Good, that's a deal to me."

He left his office then without a word, and for a long moment, my brothers and I remained seated and didn't say a word as silence embraced us. I was relieved that Damien's life was no longer under active threat, but I was all too aware that it would be if my brothers or I didn't do a job well done for Marco. Worry piled onto my shoulders, but I refused to let it show. I had to be strong for my brothers; I had to be.

"Come on," I said, getting to my feet. "Let's go home and get some food. We can talk when we're alone with Damien."

They got to their feet, and Dominic looked at me, and said, "It's gonna be okay, isn't it, Ry?"

"Yeah, bud." I forced a smile. "It is, I promise."

I would do everything in my power to keep that promise to my brother because if I didn't, it would mean the end of my family … and I wasn't going to let that happen. Not a fucking chance.

CHAPTER FIVE

Twenty-eight years old ...

"It's busy tonight," I shouted to Damien as he plonked down next to me.

He nodded, and leaned his head back against the seat. "Kane wants to go home already."

I sighed. "We haven't even been here long."

"He wanted to leave before we even got here." Damien shrugged. "You know him and crowds; they don't go together."

Truer words had never been spoken.

"Where's Dominic?"

"Getting ready for his fight," my brother answered. "Alec and Kane are with him."

I nodded my head in understanding, then raised my brows when Damien got back to his feet. "Where are you going now?"

"I'm restless on Dominic's behalf," he answered. "I need to find a girl and kiss her. I'll meet you ringside when he is fighting."

With that said, he walked away and got lost in the crowd, making me laugh. I didn't get up to go and find Dominic. Once he had Alec and Kane with him, I knew he was looked after. I looked down at my phone and scanned through my messages. I felt eyes on me, so I looked up, and when I noticed two incredibly attractive women standing in front of my booth, staring directly at me, I pushed my phone into my pocket and gave them my full attention. The woman with the stunning breasts stepped forward and smiled while her friend stepped behind her, hiding from my view.

"Hiya," the woman shouted over the blaring music. "I'm Aideen, and this is Branna. We thought ye' might like some company. Ye' look a little lost sittin' over 'ere on your own."

I raised my brow and looked at Branna over Aideen's shoulder, and it became obvious to me and to Aideen that Branna didn't want me to see her. Aideen scowled as she turned to face her friend and roughly pulled her out from her hiding spot. Branna stumbled to her friend's side and knocked her knee against Aideen's, causing her to wince. She was about to reach down and rub her bare knee, but once she saw I was watching her, she froze. Her eyes locked on mine, and I saw her swallow.

"Hello," I said just as the music lowered for the moment before a new track began to play.

She waved at me, and said, "Hey."

My lips twitched at the action. From what I could see, Branna was a ten, *beyond* hot, but pairing that with a cute little wave and hiding behind her friend made her just about the sexiest woman I had ever seen. She was nervous and clearly approached me because her friend made her, and I wasn't used to that. The women who hit on me usually oozed confidence and sex appeal, and while Branna *had* sex appeal, I got the feeling she didn't know she had it.

"Would you like to join me?"

Branna said nothing; she just stared at me. For a moment, I wondered if I didn't speak loud enough for her to hear me, but Aideen suddenly jabbed her elbow into Branna's side and answered for her. "She'd *love* to," she gushed.

Aideen put her hand on the base of Branna's spine and pushed her to the side of the booth where I was sitting, and I wasn't sure why, but she resisted. Her eyes were doe like, her lips were parted, and she turned her head towards Aideen and said something to her in a rushed breath that I couldn't hear. Aideen didn't reply to her. In fact, she completely ignored Branna. Again, Aideen nudged Branna into the booth and to avoid falling, she had to turn to the side and drop into a sitting position next to me. She didn't look at me, she only looked at her friend, and I saw her entire body tense when Aideen took a step backwards.

"I'm goin' to go and get us some drinks," she stated. "You two get to know each other. I won't be long."

Branna gasped and sat up straight as she searched for her friend in the crowd, and when she couldn't find her, she said, "Oh, my God."

I smiled. This was amusing me greatly, but it interested me more than anything. It was obvious that Branna didn't want to hit on me, so I was confused as to why she didn't just get up and leave. When she plucked up the courage to look at me, she relaxed when she found me smiling. She didn't look scared, just nervous as hell.

"Are you okay?"

She shook her head, and said, "I didn't know she was goin' to abandon me like that. I'm so sorry. It was *her* idea to come over 'ere, not mine."

I figured as much. "I'm glad she thought of it."

Branna blinked. "You are?"

"Of course," I replied. "I probably would have never seen you otherwise. I've found over the past few weeks that this club is always wall-to-wall full. You're such a tiny thing; it'd be easy to miss you in the sea of bodies. And *that* would be a true tragedy."

The booth was dimly lit, but I could see Branna blush scarlet.

"Darling, you look like I'm going to eat you up." I chuckled. "I won't bite you, I promise. Not yet anyway."

Her lips parted. She cleared her throat, twice, and said, "I'm sorry."

"Why're you sorry?"

She scratched her neck. "For bein' so awkward."

"It's not awkward," I said. "It's nervousness, which is the part I don't get."

She shifted in her seat "What don't ye' get?"

I lifted my arm and stretched it out on the back of the seat behind her head before I leaned in closer. She smelled delicious. I wasn't sure what perfume she had on, but it made me want to eat her up.

"I don't get why a woman who looks as edible as you do is so shy."

She leaned towards me ever so slightly, and I was sure she was unaware she had done so.

"I don't usually do this." She swallowed. "I'm not one to walk up to men and talk to them, which is why me friend physically pulled me over to ye'."

I regarded her for a moment. "Usually, I'd call bullshit, but I think I believe you."

She remained silent.

"What is your name?" I asked. "I didn't hear your friend very well when she introduced you both."

I heard Aideen perfectly when she spoke, but I wanted her to tell me her name. I wanted her to give it to me freely.

"Branna."

I dipped my head closer, so close I could feel her panted breath on my face.

"One more time, beautiful, I didn't catch that."

"Branna," she said louder, licking her lips. "Me name is Branna."

The way her tongue flicked in her mouth as she said her name caused my cock to harden.

"Branna," I repeated.

"Yeah," she replied, her chest rising and falling.

My gaze was on hers, but out of the corner of my eye, I saw her thighs clench together, and my mind screamed that she was effected by how close I was to her.

"I'm Ryder," I said as I held my hand out to her.

Her small hand shook as she placed it in mine, and said, "It's nice to meet you, Ryder."

I held her hand and tugged her closer to me until our chests touched. "The pleasure is all *mine*, Branna."

"If he says me name in that low, husky seductive tone one more time, I'm gonna to jump 'im in front of all of these people."

I was going to fuck this woman tonight. I could practically feel her wrapped around me already.

"Feel free to jump me at any given time, *Branna*," I said, sliding my tongue over my lower lip. "I'm *more* than ready."

Branna's eyes widened. "I beg your pardon?"

I grinned. "You said you would jump me if I said your—"

"Omigod." She gasped and pulled her hand free of mine and covered her face with it. "I'm *so* sorry," she began. "I didn't mean to … not out loud … this is awful."

She was embarrassed, and I had no idea what for, but she was killing me. Her nervousness, her embarrassment, her desire for me … I wanted to fuck her into next week, but I knew I had to do this at her pace. Like she said, she didn't hit on guys often so I was counting my lucky stars that she wanted to hit on me. I placed my hands on her soft, bare, milky white thigh, and it caused her to drop her hands and look at me.

"Hi." I smiled. "Branna, was it?"

She hesitated. "Hi back … Ryder, was it?"

"Yeah." I snickered. "I'm Ryder."

"Ryder."

I lowered my face to her, and said, "You're beautiful."

Without pausing, she said, "You're beautifuler."

I laughed as her eyes widened, and said, "Who's sweet-talking who here?"

Branna shivered. "You can sweet-talk me. I'll be quiet."

"I don't know," I mused. "I like this. You're saying what you want to say, then you get embarrassed over it. It's very cute."

She cringed, and I noticed it. "Did I say something wrong?"

"No, it's just, I call me sister cute all the time and because we look similar it just weirded me out for a second."

Cute is something you'd call a younger sister.

"How old is your sister?"

"She turns eighteen next month," she said, and then she frowned ever so slightly. "She's growin' up very fast on me."

I raised a brow. "On *you*?"

Branna nodded. "Yeah, our parents died when she was nine. I was nineteen at the time and refused to let anyone raise 'er but me, so I put everythin' on hold and brought 'er up. She's a good kid, too. I think I've done a good job with 'er."

My jaw dropped, and even though the music in the club was blaring, to me, I could have heard a pin drop. I had never met anyone who had to play the older sibling role, as well as the paternal role, like me. Granted, I was much younger than Branna when my roles switched up, but that didn't matter to me. We had something in common, something selfless that told me a lot about her as a person.

"I'm so-sorry," she stuttered. "I didn't mean to take a huge turn in the conversation."

I shook my head. "No, don't apologise. I was just a little caught off guard. So you've raised your sister?"

She mutely nodded.

"All on your own?" I quizzed. "No boyfriend?"

"No one serious," she answered. "I brought a man home once for dinner but me sister—who was eleven at the time—didn't like 'im because he couldn't say 'er name right. He was from Spain, and his English wasn't the best. She ran 'im out of the house while I was cookin', and we never saw 'im again. I stopped datin' after that."

She had barely finished speaking before I tipped my head back and laughed.

"She's awesome."

Branna smiled. "Yeah, she's me whole world."

I moved my arm that was resting on the back of the seat behind her, to rest on Branna's shoulders. I was sure she held her breath as I tugged her closer to me, but she released it when her body moulded against mine. I lowered my mouth to her ear, and said, "Where is she tonight?"

She was trembling.

"At home. She's probably sleepin' now. She had a long week at school."

I hummed. "I'll have to bring you to my place then. I wouldn't want to wake her up. She might do *more* than kick me out."

She tensed, and it made me pause.

"Branna?"

She turned her head, and looked me in my eyes and said, "Look, you're gorgeous, and trust me when I say that I really, *really* want to go back to your place with ye' ..."

She was rejecting me. Damn it.

"But?"

"But ..." She swallowed. "I've never had a one-night stand before, and to be honest, the prospect of it kind of scares me."

I regarded her. "Would you believe me if I said we wouldn't have to have sex?"

Branna furrowed her brows. "Why else would ye' want me to come back to your place?"

Good question.

I laughed. "This is going to sound like bullshit, but I like talking to you and listening to you speak. From what I've heard, you sound like an incredible friend and sister. You're independent, and that's *hot*, but you know what's downright sexy?" I asked, and she shook her head. "Your shyness and nervousness. It makes my dick hurt. You're beautiful and have a sense of humour. I haven't come across all that goodness in a woman in ... ever."

She looked away from me, embarrassed, and it made me laugh.

"Yeah." I grinned. "That shyness is *definitely* hurting my dick."

Branna bit down on her lower lip as she rubbed her thighs together. I stared down at her thick thighs, and I grinned.

"It's only fair," I murmured when my gaze returned to hers. "If my dick hurts, I want your pussy throbbing."

"Ryder," she all but panted. "Don't talk like that."

She wanted me. I could smell her pussy, for fuck's sake. She wanted me, and I wanted her too. Bad.

I brought my mouth to her ear and nipped at her earlobe.

"Why not?" I asked. "Your clit hurts so good right now, doesn't it? It's *begging* to be rubbed, licked, and sucked."

Branna's hand suddenly came to my thigh, and she squeezed my flesh painfully.

"I'm serious," she rasped. "I will do somethin' *insane* if ye' don't stop."

I was dying to find out what.

"Yeah?" I challenged. "Like what?"

She pressed against me, and said, "Like fuck you where you sit."

I sucked in a sharp breath and tried to focus on everything other than how much my cock ached. "How would you fuck me, sweetness?" I whispered after sliding my tongue over her skin. "Would you ride me slow and deep? Or fuck me fast and hard?"

"Let's find out," Branna almost snarled.

I pulled back from her as she moved with intent. She turned, bent her knees and crawled onto the seat. She cocked one leg over my hips and sat on my groin, and it seemed she couldn't resist rocking her pelvis forward. My hands instantly clamped down on her ass. She groaned as she rubbed her pussy over the bulge of my cock, and the expression of pleasure on her face was one I would never forget. She lowered her mouth to mine and let it hover a hair away.

"You're coming home with me," I growled as my hand blindly moved to the table and pressed a button to dim the lights in my booth. "I don't fuck in public, but darling, you're making me rethink that."

Branna groaned and rocked her pelvis against me once more.

"I think I can come from doin' this alone," she said as she snaked her tongue over my lips. "I really think I can."

My hips bucked up into her. "Prove it."

She kissed me, and the second I tasted her, I groaned. She plunged her warm, wet tongue into my mouth, and I growled as she roughly rolled her pelvis against me. She continued to rock against me, panting as the added friction of our clothes rubbed her the right way. Branna broke our kiss to catch her breath, but I wouldn't allow it. Now that I had tasted her, I wanted to have my fill. I lifted a hand from her behind and fisted it in her thick hair and roughly pulled her head back towards mine and covered her mouth with mine once more. I bit down on her lower lip before sucking it into my mouth.

Fuck.

Branna moaned as I thrust my hips upwards and pushed my hardened length against her pussy. She hissed and rolled her hips back and forth until her breathing became laboured. She was nearing her orgasm, I could feel her body tense and twist as her sensation built. She bucked her hips faster, pushed her pussy against my cock harder. Her lips parted, her eyes rolled back, and she sucked in a sharp breath, then held it as she came. It was the sexiest sight I had ever seen, and it made my cock throb harder.

I trailed kisses, and my tongue, along her jawline, and when I gently bit Branna's neck, she groaned out loud. Her body bucked once, twice, then she slowly began to lean to the right with her eyes closed. I moved my hands to her waist and pulled her against my chest. I held her body to mine until she came down from her high and gathered her bearings.

"Holy Christ," she panted. "Jesus."

"You were right," I rumbled. "You *could* come from just grinding on me."

She stared at me, her eyes cloudy as she remained drunk in the aftermath of her orgasm, then reality slammed into her.

"Omigod," she squealed and buried her face against my neck. "What did I just do? Oh, God, you must think I'm some little—"

"Don't finish that sentence," I interrupted, moving my mouth to her ear. "Using my body to give yours pleasure was the sexiest thing I have *ever* seen. That was for me alone, no one else saw. I dimmed the light in our booth. Only you and I know that you just came apart."

Branna leaned back, and with wild eyes, she stared at me, then around the nightclub where people danced, drank, and grinned at each other, oblivious to what we were doing. Her eyes found mind once more.

"I just turned into the girl me parents warned me to avoid hangin' around with when I was younger."

I laughed. "You amuse me, sweetness."

She raised a brow. "Sweetness?"

I hummed. "Your mouth tastes so sweet."

"You're *so* gorgeous," she breathed. "So, *so* gorgeous."

"Sweet-talker."

Branna's lips curved into a smile, and she was about to reply when suddenly wolf whistles and catcalls got our attention.

"Big brother is *getting* some," a familiar voice whooped as the light to the booth was switched back on. "Damn, is her front as nice as her back?"

Branna pulled back from me and looked over her shoulder where my four dumb-as-fuck brothers stood, openly gawking at her. She took her sweet time inspecting each of my brothers, and I was baffled when I experienced jealousy that her eyes were no longer on me, and that freaked me out a little.

"Fuck," Alec said as he assessed Branna's body. "*Definitely* as nice as the back. You're hot, baby."

"Don't even *think* about it, Alec," I snapped.

My brother frowned, and I stated, "She's *mine*."

I felt the words as I spoke them.

Alec groaned out loud. "You're no fun."

Kane looked at our brother, and said, "You fucked that black-haired chick with the big tits in the bathroom not too long ago, so why are you complaining?"

Alec raised an eyebrow. "That was a whole hour ago. I'm bored now that Dominic isn't fighting."

Dominic laughed. "I heard her screaming 'Elec' from outside the bathroom. You didn't correct her?"

Alec deadpanned. "I was balls deep. She could have called me Barney the Dinosaur, and I'd have answered her."

Branna laughed at that, and she got Damien's attention.

"What's your name?"

"Branna."

My brothers all leaned forward, not hearing her, so I said, "Branna."

When Damien smiled at Branna, my hands flexed on her hips. I didn't like how he was looking at her, not one fucking bit.

"Nice to meet you, Branna." He bowed his head. "I'm Damien." He jabbed his finger to the left. "This is Dominic, the perv is Alec, and that guy glaring at you is Kane."

"Am I glaring at her?" Kane asked Alec, his brows furrowed.

Alec nodded. "Just a little bit."

Kane sighed and looked back at Branna. "I don't like crowds." She didn't answer him, and he sighed. "If I glare, stare, or seem pissed at you, I'm not. I'm pissed at everyone else. I don't like crowds.".

"It's cool," she said. "I won't hold it against ye'."

Kane didn't show it physically, but amusement filled his eyes.

"Thanks," he said and glanced at Alec, who was grinning at Branna.

"Can you four go away now?" I asked. "Like, right now."

"No," Kane almost growled. "You said we could leave after Dominic fought. He fought and won, so can we leave now?"

I looked at Dominic. "You fought?"

"And won." He nodded.

I frowned. "I didn't hear the bells or cheering. I actually didn't hear a damn thing."

This was a huge deal. I had never missed one of my brother's fights. Not a single one.

Damien snorted. "I wouldn't hear anything other than the beat of my own cock if Branna was on my lap either."

Branna gasped. "Ye' dirty little bastard."

Me and my brothers burst into laughter, and it surprised Branna who looked at each of us with wide eyes.

"I apologise," Damien said to her, still chuckling.

She eyed him. "Ye' shouldn't say stuff like that around women ... or girls. How old are ye'?"

"Eighteen."

"That's the same age as me baby sister!"

Dominic grinned at Branna. "Is she as hot as you?"

She blinked. "She's beautiful."

Dominic's eyes gleamed. "Maybe I'll get to meet her if Ry lets you stick around."

I rolled my eyes.

"Not if I meet her first," Damien said, nudging Dominic with his shoulder. "I call dibs."

Dominic glared at his twin. "You don't even know what she looks like. You can't call dibs unless we see her at the same time. That's the deal."

Damien jabbed his thumb in Branna's direction. "If she looks like her, I'm calling an early dibs."

Dominic narrowed his eyes. "Fine, whatever. She's probably not even *that* hot."

Branna glared at the pair of idiots, and said, "She is beautiful, and hot, and everythin' in-between, ye' little shites. Don't talk about me sister like that unless ye' wanna go a few rounds with *me*. I'll put ye' on your back before ye' could blink."

Dominic's jaw dropped while Alec and Damien cracked up laughing. Branna looked at me and blushed, but she held her head high.

"I'm not sorry," she defended. "They shouldn't talk about girls like that."

"You're right. They shouldn't," I said and slid my gaze to my brothers. "Apologise."

The twins did almost immediately, but Dominic had a grin on his face that told me he wasn't all that sorry.

"It's a shame ye' said what ye' did," Branna said with a shake of her head. "I thought ye' were cute."

My hands flexed on her ass.

"I'm still here."

Branna looked down at our bodies, and she seemed to realise then that she was still straddling me. I watched as shock filled her pretty eyes, but when she tried to climb off me, I wouldn't let her.

"I hafta get off ye'."

I held her tightly. "Why?"

She glanced at my brothers, then at the rest of the people dancing and walking around the club.

"Because *I'm* in control now," she said. "*Not* me vagina."

I grinned. "Give me your mouth and I'll switch the roles back."

She laughed.

Kane cursed, then said, "Five minutes, Ryder."

I focused on Branna. "I'll only need one."

When my brothers made themselves scarce, Branna brushed her fingers through my hair, and said, "You're all gorgeous, especially Damien. He looks like the real-life version of the animated Jack Frost, and I have a *huge* crush on that character."

Amusement filled me. "You think my baby brother and other brothers are hot? My ego would be shot if it wasn't me you were sitting on."

She giggled. "I like you best."

"Prove it."

Desire filled her eyes. "I think I did that *before* they showed up."

I patted her ass. "I think I need a reminder."

She lowered her face to mine. "A reminder, huh?"

"Just a little one."

She pressed her lips to mine but gasped when I slid my hand around from her ass, up her bare thigh, and under her sexy little dress. I pushed her panties to the side and glided my fingers up her hot, wet slit until they came into contact with her pulsing clit.

"So wet, Branna," I groaned. "Damn, baby, you're *so* ready."

I teased her clit, drawing lazy circles around the hardened bud before I pulled my hand away and brought my fingers up to my lips and curled my tongue around them. Branna watched me with parted lips and hooded eyes.

"You're *definitely* my favourite kind of sweetness," I said as I dropped my hand back to her thigh. "You tasted good, baby."

"Ryder," she rasped.

I stared at her, and in her eyes, I saw her practically scream for me to take her, to suck and fuck her ten ways to Sunday.

"Say it," I demanded. "Say the words and it's done."

A second later Branna all but panted, "Fuck me."

Things quickly became a blur of activity. One second, she was on top of me, and the next, I had a death grip on her hand as I tugged her along behind me. I weaved around body after body and hauled us up the stairs and out of the club.

"Branna?"

"Aideen?"

I glanced at Branna's friend, Aideen, who was laughing and waving at us.

"Have fun, babe!" She whooped. "Take care of 'er, Ryder!"

Without turning around or stopping, I shouted, "I intend to!"

When we reached my car, I dug the keys from my pocket, pressed a button that unlocked the doors, then threw them to Alec who was walking towards me with my other brothers in tow.

"You drive."

I pulled back into the back seat and tugged her onto my lap.

"Oh, Jesus," I heard Dominic grumble. "I'll give you one hundred Euros if you swap seats with me?"

"Not on your life, kid," Kane replied.

Dominic cursed under his breath as he climbed into the car and settled next to us. Kane slid in next to him and slammed the back door shut while the two doors up front closed. Branna turned so she straddled me instead of draping her legs over Dominic. I kissed her the second her mouth was close enough.

"Don't fuck around, Alec," Dominic warned. "He's about to tear her clothes off back here. Put your foot down."

Branna pulled back from our kiss, breathing heavily.

"Your brothers." She swallowed, leaning away from me when I reached for her. "They can see and hear us."

I needed to feel her lips on mine, so I attempted to steal another kiss, but she shook her head, and said, "I'll let ye' do *anythin'* ye' want to me in private, but I'm not puttin' on some live sex show in the back seat of a car for your little brothers. I don't care how hot ye' are. I won't do it."

"I like her." Damien chuckled.

I pressed my face against her shoulder, and pleaded, "Alec. Drive faster. *Please.*"

I leaned away from Branna for my sanity's sake. She smelled good and tasted even better, so I rested my head back against the seat and counted out loud to distract myself long enough not to traumatise my brothers. That plan was soiled when I felt Branna's hot breath against my ear.

"I can't wait to fuck ye' with me mouth," she whispered in my ear. "I can almost taste ye' on me tongue."

"Oh, Christ."

"I want your hands all over me," she continued. "I want your cock or tongue inside me as I scream your name."

My fingers dug into the flesh of her hips.

"Branna," I hissed. "I'm *this* close to traumatising my brothers, so please shut that hot little mouth of yours. They don't want to see my dick any more than I want to pull it out in front of them, but if you keep talking like that, we'll all be in for a big fucking shock."

This prompted three of my brothers to say, "Alec, drive fucking faster!"

Branna laughed, clearly amused.

"You think you're funny?" I rumbled. "You think you'll be laughing when I have you all alone?"

Branna ceased laughing and breathing altogether as her cheeks blushed scarlet. Moments ago, she was telling me, in detail, of all the dirty things she wanted to do to me, and me to her, and now she was blushing like an innocent virgin.

"Seeing you blush hurts *more* than hearing you say you want me to tongue fuck you."

"Damn," Dominic whispered. "I should have found a chick to bring home if I knew I'd have to listen to live porn."

"You and me both," Kane snapped.

"I have phone numbers," Alec rasped from up front. "I'll call a few women who I know will come by just for sex. They're all hot and have *very* willing friends."

Branna's eyes widened the second Alec finished speaking.

"Maybe this is a bad idea."

My heart nearly stopped.

"This is a great idea," I assured her. "The fucking *best* idea."

Her lips twitched. "Your brother just made me realise I'm actin' like a ... like a ... slut."

Alec winced up front. "I didn't mean *you,* Branna."

"But I'm goin' to have sex with Ryder, and I've only known 'im less than an hour. I'm no better than the girls who you're goin' to ring up for sex."

"First of all," Kane chimed in, his voice gruff. "There is *nothing* wrong with no-strings-attached sex, whether you're a man or a woman. If you want to fuck everyone in sight, that is *your* business and no one else's. Second of all, it's quite obvious you don't do this often, so you don't need to feel ashamed or embarrassed. Sex is a part of life, deal with it."

Branna stared, unblinking, at Kane, then her gaze shifted to Dominic when he snapped his fingers in Z formation, and said, "You sure told her, Oprah."

Kane thumped Dominic's shoulder, making him snicker as he rubbed the spot with his hand. Branna looked back to me, so I lifted my hand and brushed my thumb over her soft lips.

"We can just talk," I said, hoping my voice didn't sound as pained as I felt. "If you don't want to do anything else, we won't."

Something flashed in Branna's eyes as she said, "We'll see."

A minute or so later, and we came to a stop at our home.

"Welcome to *casa* Slater!" Alec announced, proudly.

I escorted Branna out of the car and ushered her up the pathway towards the house.

"You live in Upton," she commented, looking around.

"Yes," I said. "Where do you live?"

"On Old Isle Green, it's just ten minutes from here."

Dominic halted next to us. "Old Isle Green, did you say?"

Branna nodded.

My brother peered at her for a long moment. "What's your sister's name, can I ask?"

I wasn't standing around so my brothers could chat to the woman I wanted, so without a word, I picked her up and tugged her securely over my shoulder.

"Omigod!"

Branna's hands latched onto my shirt as I started for the stairs and ran up them two at a time, with her bouncing and grunting against my back along the way.

"Have fun!" Alec shouted followed by Damien's yelling, "Don't break her!"

Dominic then hollered, "I want to be like Ryder when I grow up!"

I laughed and shook my head.

When I entered my bedroom and closed the door behind me, I set Branna's feet back on the floor. I rested my hands on her shoulders, gripping her tightly as she swayed ever so slightly.

"Sorry about that," I said when she locked her eyes on mine. "They would have started a conversation with you, and I didn't want that."

She huffed a laugh. "I could tell."

I reached for the light switch behind her and flicked it on. When I stepped to the side, her eyes roamed around my bedroom, and I silently thanked God that today was the day I changed my bedsheets and gave the room a thorough cleaning.

"Wow." Branna nodded appreciatively. "This looks like it belongs on an episode of *Cribs*."

I rid myself of my T-shirt. "Thanks, I like it."

Branna seemed to forget about my bedroom as her eyes wandered over my chest, stomach, and arms. I watched her swallow, and my ego inflated massively when she licked her lips suggestively. She found me attractive; there was no denying that.

"You'll need to worry about *me* jumping *you* if you keep looking at me like that, sweetness."

She gnawed on her lower lip. "That doesn't sound bad to me."

I took a step towards her. "Are you sure?"

She silently bobbed her head.

"Last chance to run, darling," I warned as I reached for my belt. "Once you allow me to touch you, you won't leave this room until I fuck the shyness right out of you."

I definitely would let her leave if she changed her mind at any point during our time together, but her breathing quickened when I asserted some dominance with her. Being bossed around by me turned her on, and I loved that she liked it.

"I need ye'," she almost whimpered. "Right 'ere. Right now."

I invaded her space as I backed her up against my bedroom door. "I'm going to make you scream, beautiful."

She trembled before me. "I can't wait."

I leaned down and took possession of her mouth with mine, kissing her with a hunger that almost hurt. Almost. She lifted her delicate hands to my biceps and gently scraped her nails against his skin. A shudder ran the length of my spine at the contact. A low growl rumbled deep in my throat, and Branna groaned upon hearing it. She rolled her hips upwards against my pelvis which caused me to tear my mouth from hers and press it against her ear. "One more bump like that, darling, and I'll forget about easing you into *my* way of fucking."

"I can take it," Branna replied, huskily.

She hissed when I sucked her earlobe into my mouth and lowered my right hand to her leg. Her breathing became erratic as I raised that hand farther and farther up her quivering thigh.

"How long do you think you can take of my cock pounding this sweet pussy of yours before you scream my name?"

I brushed my fingers over the lace of her panties, and her body jerked at my touch.

"Answer me," I demanded.

She cried out, "Ryder, *please*."

She was so responsive that it made me chuckle.

"You cried out my name before we've even got started," I teased. "Oh, darling, I'm going to have *so* much fun with you."

I took her hand in mine and led her to my bed.

"You look stunning, Branna, but I want you naked. Now."

Her lips parted. "O ... okay."

I held myself still as she reached down, gripped the hem of her dress, and slowly shimmied it up to her waist, exposing her bare stomach, hips, and thighs. Branna was nowhere near fat, but she wasn't skinny either. Her thighs were thick, her hips curvy, and her stomach looked soft. I desperately wanted to touch it, to run my fingers and tongue over it. I balled my hands into fists to keep from reaching out and aiding her in removing her clothing quicker. When she finally rid herself of the dress and dropped the fabric on the floor, standing before me in a matching black lace bra and panty set, my memory of her burned into my brain.

"I'm going to ruin you."

She sucked in a deep breath, and said, "Yes, please."

With a growl, I ran at her and practically tackled her back onto my bed. Branna instantly parted her thighs for me, and I nestled between them. I leaned down, covered her mouth with mine, and forced my tongue between her lips. She groaned in delight and matched the fierceness of my heated kiss.

"What can I do to you?" I asked, adrenaline flowing through my veins. "I want to know now so nothing I do surprises you."

"I want ye' to do everythin' to me, Ryder," Branna said, her hands gripping my biceps. "Every. Fuckin'. Thing. Don't hold back, *please.*"

Thank you, Jesus.

"Not in my nature, darling."

I tugged her into a sitting position, reached behind her back, and unclasped her bra. The material fell down her shoulders, then away from her beautiful breasts. I tugged the fabric until the straps slid over her arms, then I threw it over my shoulder without looking away from Branna's chest.

"Damn," I swallowed. "Your nipples are mouth-watering. Dusty pink is my *favourite.*"

Branna tried to press her legs together but couldn't because I was between them.

"Ryder," she whispered. "Please, I'm hurtin'."

I looked down to the apex of her thighs. "We can't have that, can we?"

Branna quickly shook her head.

"So what will I do about it?" I asked, looking up at her as I grazed my finger over her panties, making contact with her swollen clit.

She groaned. "Please."

"You have to tell me," I teased. "I know what you *want* me to do, sweetness, but I want to hear you *say* it."

Again, I rubbed my finger over her clit, but this time, I took it a step further and pushed her panties aside, then pressed my thumb against the hardened bud, and slowly rotated it in circles. I knew my movements were slow enough to give Branna licks of pleasure but too slow for her to achieve orgasm, and from the look on her face, it maddened her.

"I can smell you," I growled. "If you want me to have a taste, tell me."

Her eyes fluttered shut, clearly enjoying my touch.

"Branna," I prompted. "Tell me or I stop."

Her eyes opened, and the look she shot my way was threatening, causing my lips to twitch.

"Tongue fuck me," she said through clenched teeth. "Lick me, suck me, then fuck me with your mouth."

I was expecting her to ask me politely, maybe even add a please at the end of her request ... but hearing an order come from her delectable lips sent blood rushing to my already hard cock. It was brass and direct, two things I loved when it came to sex. Branna whimpered when I pulled her panties down her thighs and threw them to the side. I pushed her legs apart as far as they would go, dipped my head, and sucked in a breath that made me hum as I flattened my tongue against her clit. I closed my eyes as I tasted her and decided that sex with Branna wouldn't be a one-time thing. I had to think of a way to convince her to see me regularly. She made me feel alive and carefree, two things I hadn't felt in ... forever.

"Ryder!" She moaned. "Oh, God. Your *tongue!*"

I lifted my arms from under her thighs, moved them around her hips, and flattened them above her pussy, locking my hands together to keep her lower half on the bed. I sucked her clit into my mouth, and her hips bucked upward into my face. I kept the pressure on her body with my hands to keep her still, but she made it hard with how much she wriggled.

"Yes!" she cried out. "RYDER!"

I felt the first pulse of Branna's orgasm as her clit throbbed in my mouth. She sucked in a breath and held it as her back arched and her hands balled into fists. I continued lazy strokes on her clit, then when her body twitched away from me, I placed a kiss on it before moving up her body.

"I could eat you forever."

Her eyes fluttered open at my words. Her chest was rapidly rising and falling, but her breath seemed to catch in her throat when she looked up and her eyes landed on mine. I knew what she saw in them. My desire, my hunger, for her. My *need*.

"That was ... wow."

My body shook with anticipation. "I couldn't tell if you were enjoying it over all your screaming."

Branna grinned, lazily. "That was all just a big act for your ego."

Chuckling, I stood up off of her, undid the buttons on my jeans, and then pushed them down my thighs. Branna's widened eyes brought another grin to my mouth when she stared at my cock and didn't blink.

"Is that wide-eyed look of yours for my ego too?"

She mutely nodded before clearing her throat. "Of course, it is. I'm not impressed in the slightest. In fact, not only is your cock size lackin', but your tongue skills need some *serious* work."

I smiled down at her as I kicked off my shoes and socks, then stepped out of my jeans, leaving me naked as the day I was born.

"Would you mind being my practice partner?" I asked. "I definitely don't want to be a *fucking* disappointment."

"Fine." Branna dramatically sighed. "Have your way with me, but don't be surprised if I fall asleep halfway through."

Not. Fucking. Likely.

I pounced on her, and it had her squealing with laughter. That joyous laughter was quickly replaced by moaning when I zoned in on her neck and locked my lips on her sensitive flesh.

"Fuck," she hissed and bucked under me.

When it became obvious to me that she wanted us to switch position, I pulled back allowing her to roll me under her body. Before I could enjoy the sight of her naked and straddling me, she shimmied down until she was sitting on my knees. She looked up at me and devilishly smiled. I knew what was about to happen, and I was so excited I wanted to scream. But I didn't.

"My turn."

I raised my hands, clasped them behind my head, and said, "Go right ahead, sweetness."

She licked her palm, gripped my cock tightly, and gave it one long stroke as she squeezed and twisted her hand in a circular motion. I bit down on my lower lip when Branna released my cock only to put her hands between her thighs. When she touched my cock once more, it was slick and slid up and down easier.

"There," she hummed. "Does that feel better?"

When she looked my way, she found my eyes already on her face.

"Holy shit." I exhaled. "That was sexy as *fuck*!"

I watched her, my eyes never leaving her hand as she stroked me. Every lick of pleasure I felt played out on my face, and I knew it did because Branna's pretty cheeks flushed as she watched me. She broke eye contact when she lowered her head and sucked the throbbing tip of my cock into her mouth. The sound that left me was a mix of a groan and whimper.

"Brannaaaaaa." I reached down and tangled my fingers in her hair. "Christ. Fuck. You suck me *so* good, baby."

She hummed around my cock, the vibrations sending jolts of bliss to my balls.

"I won't last," I hissed. "I need to come to take the edge off before I fuck you."

Branna went to work and bobbed her head up and down, applying heavy suction each time she let my cock almost fully withdraw from her mouth only to deep throat me at the last moment. It was a method she had on constant repeat, and all I could handle was one full minute, maybe two, before the pressure that built in my balls screamed for release.

"Fuck!" I roared. "Yes, sweetness. Fuck me with that sexy mouth—oh *shit*!"

I tapped the back of her head with my hand, giving her the chance to pull her mouth away, but she ignored me and sucked my cock harder. The pressure in my balls suddenly released as the first jet of cum coated Branna's tongue. I was vaguely aware of her continuing to blow me as I experienced heaven and continued to come in her mouth.

"Thank you, God," I moaned. "Thank you for gifting Branna with the skill of sucking cock. *Thank you so much*."

When she released me and sat back on her heels, I was spent before her.

"Sinful," I panted. "You're downright fucking *sinful*."

She smiled at me. That was all. A simple smile, and I was done for. I sat up, reached for her, and pulled her on top of my body before I rolled her beneath me. Her legs parted, and I settled between her thighs, feeling her heat on my cock as I nestled against her.

"I may lock you up now that I know how good you are at—"

"Suckin' your cock?" she cut me off, giggling.

"Darling, you should add it to your resume because *damn*."

She burst into laughter.

"Hush," I mused. "I don't want my brothers thinking you're laughing at the size of my dick or some shit like that."

She covered her mouth with her hands to muffle the sounds, but she stopped laughing as I leaned down and planted kisses along her neck before flicking my tongue over the spot under her ear that made her body jump.

"Oh, fuck."

I slowly pumped my hips back and forth, and my cock found its way between the folds of Branna's wet pussy. I felt myself harden, and so did the woman beneath me.

"Already?"

"What can I say?" I grinned. "You bring it out in me."

"Lucky me," Branna said, licking her lips.

I reached over to my nightstand and pulled open the first drawer. I felt around for a condom, and when I plucked out a foil packet, I brought it to my mouth and used my teeth to rip it open. I sat back on my heels, and Branna watched as I rolled a condom down my throbbing cock. She licked her lips.

"Fucking hell," I groaned. "You want to blow me again, don't you?"

She looked at me and nodded.

"You'll be the death of me, woman."

Branna devilishly grinned. "Death by head, that'd be a good way to go."

"You have *no* idea," I said before I moved back between her legs.

I placed my left arm next to her head, bending the elbow so I could hold my weight off of her. I used my right hand to fist my cock and rub it against her clit.

"Ryder," she breathed. "Please. Fuck me. *Please.*"

"You don't need to beg me, but I'd be lying if I said I don't like how it sounds."

I licked my lips as I looked down and watched as the head of my cock slid between her glistening pussy lips. I lined my cock to her entrance, lifted my gaze to Branna's, and said, "You ready?"

"Hell. Yes."

With a grin, I thrust forward, and almost instantly, my grin was washed away as sensation filled me. My lids fluttered shut as I pushed inch by agonising inch into Branna's hot, tight, soaking wet pussy until my pelvis touched hers. I could barely move because I was terrified I was about to come again. Branna ... she felt heavenly.

"Why so quiet?" she taunted. "Nothin' to say now?"

"You ... I ... *Fuucckk.*"

Branna looped her arms around my neck and pulled my face down to hers. When I felt my lips press against hers, I kissed her like I had never kissed another woman in my life. Right now, I couldn't remember any other woman. The only one I wanted to remember was the one with me. Branna's hands roamed all over my body, but when they went to my ass and she dug her fingers into my flesh, I growled against her mouth.

"Your pussy is like a vice around my cock," I all but snarled. "Fuck me. You feel like heaven, sweetness."

I began to slowly pump my hips, I had intended to go slow, to build my way up into fucking her like a madman, but she felt too good for me to go slow. Fucking her fast, at the moment, was the only setting my body accepted, so that was exactly what I did.

"Holy fuck!" Branna cried. "Ryder."

Warmth spread across my chest when she said my name.

"That's it, baby." I grunted. "Let me hear you."

I didn't have to ask her to be vocal because with every pump of my hips, she screamed, moaned, or cried out my name and I fucking *loved* it.

"Oh, my God."

"God can't help you now, sweetness," I growled. "No one can."

She lifted her head and latched her lips on my neck and kissed and sucked at my flesh until I hissed. I jerked away from her and placed my head against her chest, listening as her heart beat wildly. I raised my head, brought my mouth to her ear, and said, "Your heart is beating so fast, Branna."

"Just for *you*, darlin'."

I smiled as I brushed my lips over her neck. "Such a sweet-talker."

"Oh, *there*!" she cried out seconds later. "Right. There."

"Here?" I murmured and thrust at the angle I did just seconds before.

"Yes, yes, *yes*!"

I focused to keep my hips angled in the same position as I fucked her, pulling that scream out of her made the hair on the nape of my neck stand up.

"This is *my* pussy."

Branna scraped her nails against my back. "Yes, yours."

When she dug her nails painfully into my back, I responded and bit down on her neck. Branna's cries of pleasure shattered every boundary I set about being careful with her, and I fucked her so hard and scraped my teeth over her flesh so often that I knew it would leave bruises. That sent a thrill up my spine knowing that I would leave marks on her, marks that would show the world that I had her. The thought of her being mine pushed me over the edge, and suddenly I was coming. My movements became jerky and quick as pressure deflated as I came. When my energy fled, I dropped down on top of Branna, and she sighed in content.

I momentarily worried in case she didn't come again, but when I heard her strained sigh, I knew she did.

"That. Was. Amazin'!" She panted. "It's *never* been like that before."

I rolled off her after a moment but kept my arm draped over her chest, my hand cupping her left breast. I gave it a gentle squeeze, and said, "You were never fucked by me before, that's why."

"Can we do it again?" she asked, my breathing still rapid.

My laughter muffled against my pillow.

"Give me a few minutes," I mumbled. "I'm not a machine."

"Ye' sure about that?" Branna asked. "Ye' have a *serious* amount of stamina."

Again, I laughed and gave her breast another squeeze.

We lay in silence for a few moments, then we started to talk. Nothing about sex or anything related to sex—we had a real conversation about the world, about our families, and it felt pretty incredible lying next to a beautiful woman and seeing who she was as a person was just as stunning. As I looked at her, I was very aware that I didn't want our involvement to end after one night, and after Branna fell asleep next to me, I found myself awake most of the time, trying to think of an excuse I could give her that would convince her she needed to spend time with me.

I wasn't letting her go now that I had a taste of her ... not a chance.

CHAPTER SIX

Thirty-two years old ...

It had been three months since Branna and I made up, and four months and one week since all hell broke loose. We were still taking things slow, and by that, I mean *really* slow. We hadn't done much more than kiss one another, and it was the best decision we had *ever* made. The first night we met in Darkness, sex between us was almost instant. There was thick sexual tension from the moment we locked eyes on one another, but this time around, we were trying a different approach. One where we listened to our minds and hearts, instead of our libidos.

After I came clean about the FBI and my involvement with them, I explained that it was because of them that I pulled away from Branna in the first place. I had agreed to help the feds to cover my ass for the death of Trent Miles and a few of Marco's soldiers. To do away with the threat of prison, I spied on Brandy Daley for the feds, and I immersed myself so deep into the investigation that I almost lost myself, and Branna, in the process. Because I chose not to tell Branna about the situation, I indirectly formed a huge crack in our relationship. One we were still healing from. We switched up our tactics this time, and instead of doing everything ass backwards, we took things in baby steps.

That meant date nights with just a chaste kiss on Branna's front porch.

We spent time together, *lots* of time, and reintroduced ourselves to everything we loved about one another, and learned new things along the way. It sounded boring, but it was anything but. When I knew I was going to see Branna, my stomach fluttered with butterflies, my heart pounded with excitement, and I couldn't remove the smile from my face for all the money in the world. We were happy again. I was me, and Branna was Branna. We weren't our old selves anymore; we were new and improved versions. What we endured—not only over the past two years, but from the moment we met—made us better people. *Stronger* people.

It solidified our bond and proved to me that we really could overcome anything.

I stared at Branna as I entered the living room of Alec and Keela's home, and like a bee to honey, I was drawn to her. I moved next to her, reached out and poked my finger into her side, making her squirm.

"What're you smiling about?"

Branna smiled, devilishly. "Just thinkin' about the plans I have for us later."

I was pretty sure I just gulped.

"What plans?"

I slid my arm around Branna's waist when she smirked at me, and it was all I could do not to push her up against the wall and claim her lips with mine.

"One little smirk and I'm already hard for you."

The little terror reached out and rubbed her hand over my thigh. "How hard?"

I gritted my teeth. "Stop, or I might succeed in traumatising my brothers *this* time."

She laughed, most likely thinking back to our first night together when we were so hot for each other that we almost forgot my brothers were next to us, horrified.

"I don't think I can wait."

My entire body tensed. We had been taking things incredibly slow, so slow that a little kiss got my gears turning. I wanted sex with Branna. I wanted it more than my next breath, but because we had been putting it off, I was so nervous about it and felt a little faint. "It's your call, Bran."

"Now." She licked her lips. "I want to feel ye'. *All* of ye'."

"Fuck. Yes."

Leaning down, I covered my mouth with hers and kissed her with hunger ... until a couple of throats were cleared.

"Uh, guys?" Alec mumbled. "I'm all for you both bumping uglies after such a long drought, but we're *still* here. Jax, too."

At the mentioned of Jax, Branna and I broke apart in an instant. "Sorry."

"What're you sorry for, Bran?"

Branna looked over her shoulder when her sister spoke, and she smiled as Bronagh waddled into the room. The woman was so pregnant that simply breathing looked like it made her uncomfortable.

"Nothin'," Branna replied. "We're just talkin'."

"Is *that* what you call it?" Keela snickered.

Branna looked at Keela, amusement dancing in her eyes as she said, "Keela said Dominic is sexy!"

Keela gasped at Branna's declaration. "*You* agreed with me!"

Bronagh groaned. "Don't use any word around me that has sex in it. Sex does *this* to ye'" She pointed at her large, round stomach. "*And* gives ye' stretch marks!"

"Did ye' get many?" Keela inquired, apprehension to her voice. She and Alec were trying to get pregnant.

"Yes!" Bronagh huffed. "On me stomach, thighs, breasts, and even on me arse. Me fuckin' *arse*!"

Dominic opened his mouth to speak, but Bronagh pointed her finger at him dangerously. "Not now," she warned. "I don't wanna hear it. I'm fat, I have stretch marks, I haven't seen me feet in *weeks*, and I forget what regular sex feels like. Don't annoy me more than I already am."

Alec looked like he was about to pass out.

"Pregnancy stops you from having sex?" he asked wide-eyed before looking at Keela and saying, "We're adopting."

We all laughed.

"It's only the past few weeks that it's stopped," Dominic grumbled. "It hurts her a little, so we don't do it."

"Why would it hurt?"

Everyone looked at Branna for the answer to Kane's question.

"Lots of different reasons, but there doesn't have to be a specific one." She shrugged. "When a woman is pregnant, there is more blood flow to the entire pelvic region, and that engorgement is sometimes just too uncomfortable durin' sex. It goes away when the baby is born."

"Praise Jesus for that, at least," Dominic said. "And for anal."

The women cringed while us men snickered.

"Bronagh," Branna said. "Relax on the sofa."

"I can't. Me body is currently experiencin' some technical difficulties."

Branna stared at her sister. "What does *that* mean?"

"It means her ass is sore, and she can't sit down."

"Dominic!" Bronagh screeched, horrified.

Alec slapped his palm against our brother's, and said, "My man."

I shook my head, amused.

"You might as well do all the kinky shit now," Kane mumbled. "After she has the baby, all that stuff only happens on rare occasions … like when you get a babysitter."

Branna tittered. "Don't worry, I'm sure they'll find a way."

"Damn right, we will." Dominic grinned and winked at Bronagh who was shaking her head good-naturedly as she eased down onto the sofa next to Dominic who absentmindedly slung his arm over her shoulder. She said, "Change the subject."

"Oh," Keela chirped. "Then let's play 'Ask Me Anythin'. It's a game for adults where all questions are appropriate. I'll start simple. Alec, who is your celeb crush?"

I tuned out the conversation then as I stared at Branna, feeling like she was the only person in the room. I heard the laughter, the teasing, and even a few cusses here and there, but nothing pulled my attention away from the woman I loved or the smile on her face. I was fully aware that I was head over heels in love with her, and it made me mad to think I almost lost her because of my own foolishness. Never again would I keep a secret. I would always be truthful with her.

Always.

"Ryder, you go next."

I looked at Damien when he spoke, then remembered that everyone was playing a game. I thought about what I wanted to know, then looked at Dominic and said, "What was the first thing about Bronagh that you found yourself attracted to?"

Dominic looked down at Bronagh, and said, "Your eyes. I had never seen eyes so emerald green before. They were, and still are, beautiful. Your ass got my attention, but your eyes held it."

The women awed, and us men chuckled.

"Are all these questions gonna be about sex or a sexual act?" Alannah then questioned when she entered the room and leaned her arms on the back of the sofa beside Bronagh's head. "Because sex is overrated."

Every one of us snapped our attention to Alannah when she spoke. She rolled her eyes at us, and said, "It is; just because *you all* have good sex lives doesn't mean everyone else does."

Meaning her?

Alec grinned. "I know someone who would be *more* than happy to rectify that problem for you, Lana."

The dumbass didn't understand the term 'subtle'.

"I'm going to get some water," Damien said and shot up from his position on the sofa, and briskly walked into the kitchen.

Alannah focused on Alec. "I don't think I need a *someone* when I have a *somethin'*."

"Sex toys?" Keela questioned with her eyebrows raised. "You're full of surprises, Ryan."

I wasn't surprised. Alannah was quiet compared to the rest of the girls, but she had a spark in her. I had a feeling that my baby brother knew all about that spark.

"It's 2016," she replied to Keela. "Vibrators are *perfectly* acceptable life partners."

Bronagh frowned. "We *need* to get you a boyfriend."

Alannah laughed. "Trust me, as long as I recharge me double A batteries, I'll *never* need a man again."

"Right now, as a man, I feel cheap," Dominic teased. "We're more than sex machines. We have feelings too, you know?"

Alannah rolled her eyes. "*Please*, in school, ye' fucked your way through the girls in our year for sport. Their hurt feelin's never made ye' feel cheap, but I can guarantee your actions made *them* feel cheap."

The conversation took a turn from playful to serious in a split second. The room was so quiet you could hear a pin drop.

Dominic frowned. "I was a kid—"

"That doesn't change anythin'," Alannah angrily cut him off. "Ye' were old enough to know what ye' were doin' was hurtful, but ye' did it anyway. Ye' broke hearts and didn't care about it. Ye' were so horrible."

Dominic looked sullen as he said, "I'm not Damien, Alannah. I didn't do those things to you."

Alannah blinked her eyes, then darted a scared look over her shoulder to make sure Damien wasn't in earshot. Her shoulders sagged with relief when she didn't see him. I looked over my shoulder too, and from my angle, I saw he was leaning against the wall outside the living room. There was no doubt from the expression on his face that he had heard *everything* she just said.

"I know," Alannah then mumbled to Dominic, "it's just hard for me to separate the pair of ye' sometimes. Ye' have his face, and when I see it, I hurt all over again."

"Lana—"

"Look, I'm sorry," she quickly stated. "I had a bad start to me day, and I'm takin' it out on all of you, and that's not fair."

"What happened?" I asked, concerned.

Alannah may not be dating any of my brothers, but she was part of our family, and we all loved her.

"Some arsehole rear ended me and I've to fork out a fortune to get me car fixed. It's the *last* thing I need. Shit has just been goin' from bad to worse for me lately. I just can't catch a break," she said and shrugged her shoulders.

Bronagh looked crestfallen with Alannah's announcement.

"Talk to me." She stood and rounded the chair until she was in front of Alannah. "What's wrong?"

Alannah looked at Bronagh, then out of nowhere she burst into tears. "Me da," she cried. "He is havin' an affair, and me ma has *no* clue about it."

"Oh, fuck," Alec whispered when Bronagh folded her arms around Alannah.

"What am I goin' to do, Bee?" she sobbed. "If I tell me ma, it's goin' to break 'er heart, and if I don't, I'll be the worst daughter for keepin' it from 'er."

Bronagh hugged Alannah tightly.

"Are ye' *sure* he is havin' an affair?" she quizzed. "Maybe you're mistaken, babe."

"I'm not," Alannah sniffled. "I went into town yesterday evenin' to get some ink cartridges for me printer, and as I was passin' by a restaurant, somethin' told me to look through the window. I did, and there he was, sittin' with a woman half his age at the table near the window where anyone could see them. I think she might be the same age as *me*! At first, I didn't even consider anythin', then he reached out and took 'er hand in his. One second, they were holdin' hands, and the next, he leaned over, and they *kissed*!"

"*Double* fuck," Alec whispered.

"I didn't know what to do," she said, her lower lip wobbling. "I was scared he would see me, so I just ran back to me car and drove back to me apartment. I rang me ma to see what she was doin' and she said she was preparin' dinner for me da, his favourite because he had been workin' such long hours lately. She doesn't know, Bronagh … How could he do this to 'er? To our family? I hate 'im."

My heart broke for her and for her unknowing mother.

"We'll figure this out," Bronagh said, consoling her friend.

I knew Bronagh was saying what she thought was necessary, but I could see from her face that she had no clue how to help Alannah through this, but I knew she'd do everything possible to help her. We all would.

"About your car," Aideen added, shifting the attention onto her. "I'll ring me da and have 'im book your car into his garage. Me brothers love you. Dante thinks you're, and I quote 'im, a goddess, so I'm sure he will work on it free of charge."

Alannah pulled back from Bronagh's hold and looked at Aideen.

"I'll pay. I don't want them to help me with no charge, but if it could be in instalments, that'd be perfect."

Aideen said, "We'll work it out. Just don't worry about it."

Alannah nodded, but she wore her heart on her sleeve, and I could see worrying was all she would be doing. When I looked at her, the urge to protect her was something fierce.

"Lana." Branna moved away from me and towards her. "Come with me. I want to talk to ye'."

They both left the room, leaving us to wait in silence. No one knew what to say, not even Alec tried to fill the void with a joke. Minutes went by, and when Branna returned to the room, she frowned.

"She's in denial," she told us. "She thinks she can make 'er da stop cheatin' on her ma. She is puttin' pressure on 'erself to keep 'er family together."

Bronagh rubbed her face with her hands. "What are we goin' to do?"

"All we can do," Branna replied. "Just be there for 'er. Tellin' 'er what to do will only result in a fight because right now, what she has decided is the only thing that makes sense to 'er."

Silence fell upon the room until Damien said, "I have to fix shit with her. I heard what she said to Dominic, and I need to fix it. I hate what I've done to her."

"I understand you better than anyone," I said, "and my advice is baby steps. You've said you're sorry multiple times, and you give her space whenever she is around, but what you need to do now is let her know you're here, you're staying, and that you will earn her trust back."

"How the fuck am I going to do that?" Damien asked on a groan. "She barely looks at me."

"I can't answer that. It's something you'll have to figure out for yourself, kid, but it's obvious you do care for her, so just stick to your guns."

Damien nodded, then retreated into the company of his own mind so he could think. We spent the next few hours together, and after Keela made us a big feast, we scattered around the house to digest our food. I went upstairs with Kane and Alec to check out some new weights he bought, then went back downstairs to Branna. I had hoped I could entice her to come over to my house for a nap, but when I reached the doorway of the living room and saw her sitting on the couch with my nephew lying on her chest, my heart tightened. I loved how she looked holding a baby, and I imagined her holding a baby of our very own one day.

Branna locked eyes with me for a long moment, then said, "Ado, take 'im, will ye'?"

Aideen got him and carefully lifted her son, resting him on the growing baby bump of my second nephew, then looked between Branna and myself, and said, "I've a feelin' the drought is about to come to an end, am I right?"

"Yeah, babe," Branna said as I stood, still staring at me. "There's about to be a fuckin' storm."

"Go get 'im, Mama."

I straightened as she approached me, though I tried to appear like my heart wasn't beating a mile a second. When she reached me, I grabbed her hand, and together we turned and rushed out of the house.

"Don't break him, Branna!" I heard a voice shout from behind us then someone said, "I *still* want to be Ryder when I grow up!"

Branna and I laughed until we got into my—no, *our* house. As soon as the door closed, Branna turned to face me.

"I'm movin' back in. Tonight."

"Okay."

"We aren't usin' a condom either because I want us to have a baby."

"Okay."

"From this moment on, bein' a gentleman is *over*. When we're alone, you're to touch every part of me. Every. Single. Fuckin'. Part."

"Okay."

"And I want to get married. Soon. We can figure out a date."

"Okay."

Every time she spoke, she took a step backwards, and every time I replied, I took a step towards her.

"Just okay?" Branna asked. "Ye' agree with everythin' I've said?"

"Every. Single. Fucking. Word."

Branna swallowed. "D'ye have anythin' else to say?"

"Yeah." I shot forward. "I'm going to make you scream."

Branna yelped when I picked her up, put her over my shoulder, and beelined up the stairs, taking the steps two at a time. Like the snap of my fingers, we were in *our* bedroom, and I had her pressed against the bedroom door, pulling her clothes from her body as I dominated her mouth with mine. Branna matched my hunger and kissed me back, hard. Her hands frantically pulled at my shirt, and I heard some of the material rip. I growled against her mouth, grabbed my shirt, and continued what Branna started. I ripped the fabric from my body and blindly tossed it behind me. Branna placed her hands on my bare chest and groaned when she slid them around to my back.

Christ.

"Now," she begged against my lips. "No foreplay, just you inside me. Please, Ryder."

She didn't have to ask me twice.

"I love you, sweetness."

Branna hummed. "I know, and I love ye' too."

"I just wanted to tell you."

She licked her lips. "Why?"

"Because I'm going to fuck you like I don't."

Branna sucked in a sharp breath when I picked her up and moved her over to our bed. When I laid her down, I rid her of her shoes, socks, jeans, and panties. Her T-shirt was thrown somewhere in the room and so was her bra. I stripped out of my clothes so fast that it made Branna giggle.

"You're so eager."

I looked at her. "You have *no* fucking idea."

I was starved of being intimate with her for a long time too, and I was beyond ready to bring that to an end and reintroduce myself to every part of her soft, curvy, perfect body. To show *her* eagerness, she parted her thighs for me as I crawled up her body and hovered over her. Branna groaned when I balanced my weight on my left forearm and used my right hand to grip the base of my throbbing cock and rubbed the head back and forth over her pulsing clit.

"Ryder," she moaned and slid her hands around my waist and to my back.

"I'm here, sweetness," I said, my body shaking. "And I'm not going anywhere. Ever."

"I'm holdin' ye' to that."

I slowly rubbed the head of my cock down her pussy until it kissed her entrance.

"Fuck," I trembled. "I'm scared, and I don't know why."

Branna moved her hands to my face.

"You're nervous, but don't be. It's just us."

"Just us."

Branna nodded. "Watch me as ye' enter me, ye'll feel better. I promise."

With my eyes locked on hers, I slowly slid into her tight, wet cunt. My eyes threatened to roll back as I pushed into her body, inch by agonising inch. Branna's eyes did roll back, her lips parted, her cheeks flushed and bliss contorted her features.

"Beautiful," I murmured.

I leaned down and pressed my mouth to hers, and she moaned.

"I fit perfectly with you," I whispered against her lips. "You're wrapped around me so tight, Bran ... *fuck*."

She returned her hands to my back and gently grazed her nails against my skin, causing me to hiss and begin to thrust into her harder. Branna's moans were music to my ears, but when she moved her hand to her pussy and slowly circled her clit, heat ignited in my balls.

"Yes," I rasped. "Rub that pretty clit of yours, baby. Show me what you've been doing when you didn't have me."

Branna hummed, then surprised me when she lifted her essence-coated fingers to my lips. Her eyes were hooded with desire as she watched me lap away the cream before I sucked them into my mouth. When she returned her fingers back to her clit, her body shook.

"Holy fuck!"

I drove into her harder, faster, and a *hell* of a lot deeper.

"Did you pretend your fingers were my mouth, baby?" I asked, my voice primal. "Did you fuck yourself and wish it was me?"

"Yes!" Branna panted. "Only you."

Jolts of pleasure flooded my body. "Come on, baby. I'm so close."

My orgasm slammed into me just as hard as Branna's did. It consumed me and flowed through my veins, pumping the feeling of ecstasy throughout my body. My spine stiffened, my hips jerked in involuntary motions, and a pleasure so hot and intense spread across my body and soothed me completely. I was vaguely aware as I fell forward, covering Branna's body with mine. She laughed and moved her hands to my sides and began to tickle me. I twitched and jerked in response and rolled to the side, falling off her, and out of her, in one fluid motion.

"*Baby.*"

Branna hummed. "My thoughts *exactly*."

I reached my hand out, and Branna threaded her fingers through mine.

"Can we do that again?" I asked, my breathing laboured. "Right now?"

Branna laughed, again. "After I take a power nap because that orgasm was ... wow."

"I know how you feel." I shuddered. "It wasn't the longest sex we've ever had, but damn if it didn't feel like the best."

"All that foreplay and teasin' over the past three months has finally found its release."

I turned and grabbed her. I pulled her a few inches up the bed until her head rested on a pillow. I covered us with the bedcover and snuggled my body against hers. Every bad thing we had been through over the past couple of years led to this moment, and it was all worth it.

"I love you, sweetness."

Branna squeezed me. "I love ye', too."

Hearing her say those words, but better yet, feeling those words whenever she looked at me or touched me meant everything to me. I had a woman who loved me like I was her whole world, and in my heart, I knew that to her, I *was* her world. Just like she was mine to me. We had spent our lives looking out for our families and always put ourselves on the back burner, but no more. I would take care of Branna, but in return, she would take care of me too. She was my future, and I was happy to say it had never looked as bright or as beautiful.

She was my happily ever after, and I'd be damned if I didn't deserve her.

CHAPTER SEVEN

Present day ...

When I entered the kitchen and found my wife preparing dinner, I snuck up behind her and snaked my arms around her petite body, making her yelp with fright. I laughed, then leaned down and planted kisses on her neck.

"Scared you."

"Ye' bloody well did." Branna chuckled. "Ye' still move so silently. It freaks me out."

I smiled and placed a soft kiss on her cheek. "How are you feeling after what happened with the twins earlier?"

"I'm fine now that they've apologised and are okay with each other," she answered as she continued to peel potatoes. "I often ask God why he didn't give us five girls to raise, then I think of all the hassle Georgie gives Dominic and me sister, and I realise that I'm perfectly happy dealin' with five annoyin' lads."

I patted her behind. "I'd have a lot more grey hairs if we had five Georgies. I love that girl something fierce, but man, she gives her daddy and mama a hard time, and she doesn't even mean to."

Branna chuckled. "She's such a good girl, though, and she has all of you men, young and old, wrapped around 'er little finger."

"Don't remind me."

My wife relaxed back against me. "Can ye' believe the twins will be fifteen in a few months? I can't. It feels like we just met yesterday, and now we have two almost fifteen-year-olds."

I pressed my face against her hair. "I know, I was just thinking earlier about past events and meeting you was one of them."

"What else did ye' think of?"

"This and that," I answered. "Things that brought us to our now."

Branna hummed. "We've had an eventful life together."

"And the best is yet to come."

"I know," Branna chirped. "We'll hopefully have grandbabies in another decade."

"Jesus." I laughed. "Don't saddle me with grandkids when we still have a kid under ten."

"Can't help it. I love babies."

Her occupation proved that.

"Where are the boys?"

"Their bedrooms," Branna answered. "They'll come running when food is ready for them."

"Want to have some fun in the meantime?"

My wife snorted. "If we have fun, then the dinner won't get cooked."

"We can get takeout."

"I already have everything in the oven cookin'. The potatoes are the last thing to be prepared before I boil them."

"Then I'll help you, and we can have ten minutes to ourselves," I mused. "I know you like long, thorough sex ... but a quickie is good for the soul."

Branna's shoulders shook as she laughed. "Help me then."

I sprang into action, and in just a couple of minutes, we had potatoes peeled, washed and placed in a pot of water on top of the stove to boil. When Branna turned to face me, I was already stripping out of my clothes at a rapid pace. She burst into laughter as she rushed over to the kitchen door and shut it. She flicked off the lights so our neighbours behind our house wouldn't see my bare ass if they looked into our kitchen.

"You're worse than a teenager!"

"It's your fault," I stressed. "I hurt for you, woman."

"Aw." She clicked her tongue. "D'ye' want me to make it better?"

"Yes," I almost pleaded. "Yes, please."

Just as she reached for me, the kitchen door opened, and Branna screamed. I grabbed the first thing I could from the counter to cover my groin and did so just in time for the light to turn on.

"It's not what it looks like!" Branna shouted, her hands on her cheeks.

Jules looked back and forth between us, and said, "Are ye's havin' a bleedin' laugh?"

Branna didn't speak, but I laughed, and it drew my son's hostile glare my way ... until he dropped his eyes to my hands.

"Da, *please* don't tell me you've no boxers on behind that cookbook. Please."

"Okay." I smiled at my son. "I won't."

Jules threw his hands up in the air, and to his mother, he waddled his finger, and said, "I'm *so* disappointed in ye', Ma. Messin' around with *him* when your children are home. Had I been one minute later walkin' in 'ere, I could have been scarred for life. For life, I tell ye'. Shame on ye', woman. *Shame!*"

Branna stared after our son after his dramatic exit, then she looked at me and said, "Why do I feel sad at disappointin' 'im?"

"Because he could convince the Devil that he was God, that's why. Now come here and give me some of that sweet loving."

"I can hear *everythin'*," Jules hollered from the hallway. "Every single word, and I'm callin' Childline!"

Branna burst into a fit of giggles, then proceeded to pick up my clothes from the floor and hand them to me, breaking my heart entirely.

"I'm gonna whoop your ass, Jules!" I shouted. "You ruined Mommy and Daddy's alone time."

"I'm diallin' Childline as we speak!"

Branna's laughter brought a smile to my face as I dressed. When I was fully clothed, I leaned my hip against the counter and watched her busy around the room as she checked on the dinner as it cooked. She was the most beautiful woman I had ever seen in my entire life, and she was mine. She vowed to spend her life with me, to love me and stand by me through thick and thin, and she had done just that. She stuck by me when she probably should have run for the hills, and she gave me my children and took care of all of us even though she worked a trying job.

She was the light of my life.

"Do you have any idea how perfect you are, Branna?" I asked, walking over to her and pushing stray hairs away from her face. "I'm not sweet-talking or trying to get you naked. I'm being serious. Do you have any clue how incredibly amazing you are? I can't believe you're my wife, sweetness."

Her cheeks flushed. "Ryder, what's brought this on?"

"Nothing," I answered. "I was just watching you, and it struck me just how in love with you I am. I'm in awe of you, sweetness. I always have been, and I always will be."

Branna's eyes glistened with unshed tears, and before she could say a word, I leaned down and pressed my lips against hers. She turned her body towards mine, slid her arms around my waist, and relaxed against me as we kissed. I loved how she felt against me, how she tasted, how she smelled. I loved every single thing about her.

"I love you," I said against her lips. "I love you so much, Branna."

"I love ye' too, Ry."

I smiled when I heard a long sigh from the doorway.

"I hate to admit it," Jules grunted. "But that was very romantic. Ye' have to teach me that, Da. Everythin' ye' said was gold."

Branna turned her head, and to our son, she said, "What he said isn't rehearsed. He put what he feels for me into words. When *you* fall in love, ye'll say somethin' similar to your partner, I imagine."

Jules rolled his eyes. "Yeah, yeah. How long until dinner will be done? I'm leppin'."

"Half an hour," Branna answered. "Eat an apple if you're hungry in the meantime."

He groaned but grabbed an apple and ventured out of the room. I heard arguing in the living room then which told me Jules wanted the remote control for the television and whichever one of his brothers had it wasn't giving it up. I was about to go and dissolve the argument by taking the remote for myself when my phone rang. I found it on charge on the other side of the room.

"Did you put this on charge?" I asked my wife.

"Yeah," she answered. "It was nearly dead."

I thanked her, picked up my phone, and answered it when I saw it was Kane calling.

"What's good, little brother?"

"Did you know Georgie had a fucking boyfriend?"

I nearly fell over. "A motherfucking *what*?"

"I'll take that as a solid fucking *no*," Kane grunted. "She has one, a boyfriend, I mean. And he's a Collins."

Now, I knew Kane had no quarrels with the Collins family, he was *married* to one for God's sake, but Georgie was our niece, and she was the only girl amongst our horde of boys … and a snot nose Collins boy was her boyfriend. That was a big fucking problem.

"A boyfriend who's a Collins?" I repeated, hoping I heard the entire conversation wrong. "Is that what you just said?"

"Word for word, brother."

"No," I said. "No she fucking does *not*!"

"Trust me, Ry." Kane sighed. "She most definitely does. Damien called me with the bad news."

"Where does he live? Which brother does he belong to?" I demanded. "We'll fix this problem inside of the hour."

"We can't." My brother grunted. "We've been banned from hurting the boy by the highest chain of command."

I sucked in a breath. "Bronagh forbid us?"

"Yup," he replied. "Dominic is Croughs with Damien, and he needs us there to make sure he doesn't do something that will make Bronagh divorce him or land his ass in jail. Alec is already on the way, and I'm good to go."

"Shit, come and get me. I'm ready right now."

I looked at my wife and found her silently laughing as she checked on the potatoes.

"Branna, why are you laughing?"

"Because, accordin' to what I just heard, Georgie has a boyfriend who happens to be a Collins lad, and you and your brothers are havin' a meltdown over it. That's why I'm laughin'."

"This isn't funny," I stated. "This is very serious."

"You're damn right," Kane echoed.

Branna shook her head. "Where's Dominic?"

"In a pub."

She laughed again. "Go on, go with your brothers to help 'im through this. I have to call me sister to get the full story."

I walked over, kissed her cheek, then turned and walked out of the kitchen.

"Kane, are you on the way?"

"Driving toward you as we speak, bro."

I hung up on him, shoved my phone in my pocket, grabbed a jacket, then left my house. My life was great—no, my life was perfect. I had come across some bumps in the road along the way, then some fucking mountains, but I managed to climb each one and get to where I was now, which was happy, in love, and very blessed. I reminded myself of this as I waited for my little brother to come and pick me up. I rehearsed a speech in my head that I hoped would give Dominic some comfort, but I wasn't sure if it would work. Georgie was his baby girl, his firstborn ... I think this would be one of those mountains in the road that me and my brothers would have helped

Dominic overcome together, but I knew in the end that we would get through it because that was what families were for.

We were there in good times, the bad, and the downright ugly. There was nothing we couldn't tackle together as a family ... and this little Collins motherfucker would soon realise that.

PART FIVE

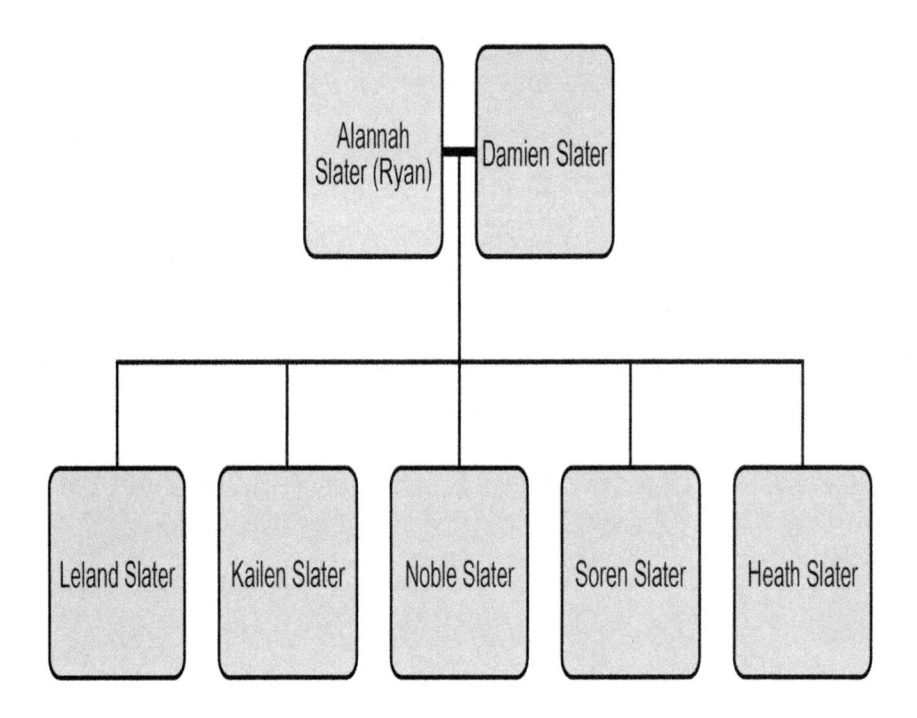

```
        ┌─────────────────┬─────────────────┐
        │ Alannah         │                 │
        │ Slater (Ryan)   │  Damien Slater  │
        └─────────────────┴─────────────────┘
                         │
   ┌────────┬────────┬───┴────┬────────┬────────┐
┌──────┐ ┌──────┐ ┌──────┐ ┌──────┐ ┌──────┐
│Leland│ │Kailen│ │Noble │ │Soren │ │Heath │
│Slater│ │Slater│ │Slater│ │Slater│ │Slater│
└──────┘ └──────┘ └──────┘ └──────┘ └──────┘
```

DAMIEN

CHAPTER ONE

Present day ...

"Damien?"

I had just left the bathroom as my wife called my name.

"Yeah, babe?"

"C'mere," she shouted from the kitchen. "*You* can deal with this disrespectful little shitehead."

Uh-oh.

I jogged down the stairs, down the hallway, and into the kitchen where my second eldest son, Kailen, was leaning against the counter, looking down at his feet. Alannah stood in front of him with her hands on her hips, tapping her foot on the ground. This was becoming a regular occurrence. Kailen was twelve, but his attitude was getting out of hand. He talked back, didn't do what he was told, and I knew Alannah worried herself sick over him.

"What's wrong?"

Alannah didn't look away from our son. "*D'you* want to tell 'im or should I?"

Kailen peeked up at his mom, then looked at me and dropped his head instantly.

"Fine," my wife clipped and turned to face me. "He didn't help me with dinner when I asked 'im to because he was too busy playin' on his phone. I took it off 'im and told 'im to help me, and he told me to piss off and do it meself."

My eyes widened knowing that 'piss off' was another way of telling someone to *fuck* off. Kailen tensed as I reached for him and fisted the fabric at the collar of his sweater. I hauled him out of the room, down the hallway, and into the living room. He didn't say a word, and he didn't struggle. He just walked with me and clasped his hands together and rested them on his knees when I sat him down on the couch across from me.

"Wait," he yelped when he saw me reach for the belt on my jeans. "Please, I'm sorry."

"Sorry?" I repeated. "You're suddenly sorry because you don't wanna get belted?"

Kailen swallowed. "I didn't mean to snap at 'er. I was arguin' with someone, and she spoke to me at the wrong time, and I took my anger out on 'er. I saw the look on 'er face when I said what I did, and I feel like shite, Da. I'm sorry."

I set my jaw. "I don't stand for *anyone* disrespecting my wife. Just because you're my child doesn't mean you get a pass. Get your ass up."

Kailen hesitated but got to his feet and turned away from me before I had to ask him to. He hadn't needed to be whooped in months, but he still knew the drill. He pushed his sweatpants down to his thighs revealing his boxers and balled his hands into fists as he waited. I removed my belt and wasted no time in punishing him. I swatted his backside once, then told him to pull his pants up and sit back down. He did so as I replaced my belt.

"Now," I said, sitting down across from him, "who were you arguing with?"

Kailen didn't answer me.

"I can go and get your phone—"

"It's no one ye' know," he interrupted. "He's just a ... friend."

I raised a brow. "I know all your friends."

"Not this one."

I waited for him to continue.

"Da, I don't wanna talk to ye' about 'im."

That hurt my feelings a little bit because this was the first time he had ever said that to me. Usually, Kailen could talk to me about anything, so this made me think something was really wrong for him to keep it from me.

"Why not?"

"Because I just don't."

I grunted. "Kailen, what aren't you telling me? You haven't been yourself these past few months, you act out, and you constantly have an attitude. What the hell is going on to make you so angry all the time? I can't help you if I don't know what's wrong, son."

My child locked his grey eyes on mine, and seconds of silence ticked by, then out of nowhere, he began to cry.

"Kailen?" I frowned. "Did I hit you too hard?"

I instantly felt sick. I had meant to punish him for being disrespectful to his mother, but I didn't mean to cause him actual pain.

"No," Kailen choked, frantically wiping at his eyes. "It's not that, ye' didn't even hurt me."

I got to my feet and sat next to him, putting my arm around his shoulder.

"Then what's wrong?"

He turned his body to mine and wrapped his arms around me, placing his face against my neck and sobbed. My heart began to beat fast, and adrenaline flowed through my veins. I was sick with worry now, and I had no idea what to do other than comfort my child.

"It's okay," I told him. "Whatever it is that has you this upset, it's going to be okay. I promise."

Kailen cried harder and squeezed me tight. I said nothing further; I just held him and waited for him to calm down enough to speak. This took at least five minutes.

"I'm scared to tell ye'."

I leaned back from him and used my thumbs to wipe away tears from his face. He looked so much like my brother Dominic that it freaked me out. I knew that meant he looked like me, but when I looked at Kailen, he reminded me so much of my brother ... just with my white hair.

"Don't be scared," I told him. "Don't ever be scared to tell me anything, okay?"

Kailen sniffled and he nodded. "It's ... it's about a relationship I'm in."

That was news to me. He was only twelve.

"You're in a relationship?"

He nodded. "Yeah, I am."

"Okay," I said slowly. "Who with? Do I know her?"

Kailen looked down at his intertwined hands. I wondered why he didn't answer me, then it struck me that maybe I didn't ask the right question. I asked if I knew the girl he was dating. I assumed he was in a relationship with a girl when I shouldn't have.

"Or him?" I added. "Do I know him?"

My son jerked his eyes up to mine, and he looked so scared that I wanted to break down and cry myself.

"Kailen, are you gay?"

He shook his head rapidly from side to side.

"Hey, hey, you do not need to be scared," I assured him. "Your sexuality will never change how much me and your mom love you, okay? You're still Kailen, still my pain in the ass son who I love more than life itself. You're perfect the way you are."

Kailen cried again and threw his body at me once more, and I blew out a breath, fighting off tears of my own because I knew I'd be no good to anyone if I broke down. I'd have to call in Alannah if that happened because once I cried, I was a goner.

"D'ye not think I'm straight?"

I looked down at Kailen whose face was still against my chest.

"I've never thought about it, to be honest," I admitted.

My son was silent for a moment, then he said, "Well ... I'm not."

"Not straight?" I questioned.

He nodded. Once.

"That's—"

"I'm not gay either," he interrupted.

He leaned back from me, wiping his face once more. He was shaking, so I reached for his hand and held it in my own. This conversation was huge for him, and he had obviously kept this bottled up inside for a long time, and it made me ill to think that he worried over telling me. That he was probably scared he would be rejected.

I tilted my head. "Are you bisexual or pansexual? Or gender queer? I'm afraid I'm wildly ignorant to what some of those mean, and I know there are a lot of other sexualities, but I will learn them all if—"

"Da," Kailen cut me off, and he huffed a little laugh. "Ye' don't need to learn what they all mean."

"But I want to," I said. "If you identify as one, I want to know everything about it so I can connect with you better."

Kailen squeezed my hand. "Ye' already know every about me sexuality."

"I do?"

He nodded. "I'm bi ... like Uncle Alec."

"Right," I said with a nod of my head. "You're getting the same chat that Leland got. Don't fuck around with a girl's, or a boy's, heart or me and you are gonna have problems. Understand?"

Kailen had a ghost of a smile on his face as he bobbed his head.

"Am I the first person you've told?" I asked.

He shook his head. "Uncle Alec knows. I told him a few months ago, and he has been encouraging me to tell ye', but he said he would respect me decision to tell ye' when I was ready."

That was fair. I didn't know what it was like to be anything other than straight, so it made sense for Kailen to confide in someone he could relate to.

"How long have you known you were bi?" I asked. "I honestly didn't think you would be interested in girls, or boys, yet."

His face flushed red. "Last year, I saw a girl who I thought was pretty, and I wanted to kiss 'er like *you* do with Ma ... then a few days later, I saw a cute lad and thought that same thing about *him*. I didn't know right away, but when I started to like girls, I liked boys in the same way too."

"I'm sorry you felt like you couldn't talk to me or your mom."

"I wanted to," Kailen said, "but I kept backin' out of it."

"Why?"

"I didn't ... I just ... I was afraid ye' would be different with me."

Pain thrummed in my heart.

"Son," I said, firmly. "I love you no matter who you're attracted to. Your sexuality doesn't even come into play. It never has, and it never will."

"I knew that," Kailen stated. "I did, but there was a fear in the back of me head that ye' wouldn't."

"I hate that you've been thinking about and worrying about this for a long time."

"It's cool." He one-shoulder shrugged.

"It's not," I pressed. "I don't want you being afraid to be yourself especially around me or our family."

Kailen cringed. "I don't want the lads to treat me differently."

"Your brothers?"

"And me cousins," he added. "Georgie knows, but I don't exactly know how because I never told 'er. She just started talkin' to me one day about who she fancied and said if I got with 'im, she'd kick me arse."

I snorted. "That girl is a clever one."

"Yeah." He nodded in agreement.

"Is this why you've been so out of character the past few months?" I asked.

"I guess," he said tentatively. "I get mad when I can't talk about who I liked in the way Leland or me cousins do because I was worried they'll laugh at me or not want to be close to me anymore. I think I started to pull into meself, and that's when I started gettin' angry with everyone. Then Rome joined me footie team, and he told me one day after we hit the showers that he fancied me and me heart nearly stopped. Apparently, he was bisexual, and everyone knew it. I started textin' 'im, and then we've got together in secret because he knew I hadn't told anyone that I was bi."

"This Rome is your boyfriend?"

Kailen blushed again as he nodded.

"Are you happy that you're dating him?"

"Yes," he answered. "I am."

"Then I'm happy that you are happy, but you're only twelve, and that's extremely young to be in a relationship. I'm warning you that you're not to enter into anything physical until you're old enough. You may not have to worry about pregnancy when dating Rome, but there are other things that can give you a nasty surprise."

Kailen's face was crimson red. "We've just kissed a few times, and that's it. I swear."

"Good." I nodded. "I want to meet him."

My son's eyes widened. "Jesus, why?"

"Because you're my son, and I want to make sure this dude you're dating is good enough for you. Have you got a problem with that?"

He ducked his head and smiled. "No, I don't."

"Good."

Kailen exhaled a deep breath, and said, "Da, I feel so … light after tellin' ye' this. I love ye' so much for still lovin' me even though I'm different."

"Different?" I repeated. "Everyone likes their cup of tea their own unique way, so in that sense, we are all different."

"Ye' sounded exactly like Auntie Branna just then."

I laughed. "Don't tell your uncle Ryder. He'll rag on my ass if he knows."

Kailen grinned and shook his head.

"Is Rome the only boy, you know, you've kissed?"

"The only person," Kailen corrected. "I've never kissed anyone else."

"Why not?" I asked, feeling offended on his behalf. "You're a handsome kid. You look like me and have your mama's smile. Girls and guys would be crazy not to crush on you."

Kailen sunk lower in the chair as he groaned.

"Please, stop," he said. "This is mortifying."

I laughed. "My bad."

Kailen snickered. "Will ye' come into the kitchen so I can tell Ma? I'd rather ye' were with me."

"I heard everythin'!" Alannah suddenly barrelled into the sitting room, taking us both by surprise as she dived over my body and landed on top of our child. I shook my head and smiled when she started crying, and Kailen looked over her shoulder at me in a panic. He hugged her and comforted her, but she was a complete mess by the time she got to her feet.

"Me precious boy," she cried and kissed Kailen's face. "You're so perfect, and so handsome, and you're gonna be the best boyfriend that Rome or anyone could ever ask for. I love ye' so much."

I laughed at Kailen's deer in the headlights expression. He looked at me and playfully glared as Alannah tackled him with another hug. She didn't let him go for a long time, and when they finally did separate, he tugged her into the kitchen so he could help her with the dinner as he was originally asked to do. I followed them and silently watched them interact. The difference with Kailen was incredible; it was like I could see a weight had been lifted off his shoulders now that he'd revealed his secret to us.

I was proud of him, so damn proud. I walked out into the hallway when one of my other sons ran down the stairs.

"Leland." I sighed when he jumped the last three steps and landed on the floor with a thud. "You're going to break your damn neck. Walk down the stairs like a regular person."

"Da," he beamed, turning to face me. "Just the man I wanted to see."

The boy was thirteen, but he acted sixty.

"What's up?"

"I've a question."

"Shoot."

"Have ye' ever seen a girl so beautiful that she made your heart stop beatin' in your chest with one glance at 'er face?"

I looked at my eldest son and wondered what girl turned my child into a poet.

"Yeah, Leland," I said. "I have, and she is your mom."

"This girl is like Ma." He smiled. "I'm gonna marry 'er."

"Hold your horses." I chuckled. "You're only thirteen."

Leland flicked his grey eyes to mine, and said, "I'll marry 'er when I'm eighteen then. I'm not being stupid and marryin' her after spendin' loads of years in love with 'er like you did with Ma."

My lips parted. "Things were complicated with me and your mom. It wasn't that easy."

"Love is always easy, Da. Once ye' find the right girl, it'll figure itself out."

I watched him walk into the living room, and as I stared after him, I pondered if he was really my son or Alec's.

"Who is this girl that has you madly in love with one glance?"

Leland fell into the couch, and said, "I've no idea, but I still love 'er."

God, give me patience.

"Start from the beginning."

"I saw 'er on the sidelines durin' me match today." Leland sighed. "She's one of me mate's cousins, I know that much, but they left before I could ask 'im what 'er name was. She's from Japan, and holy crap, she's beautiful. She has hair as dark as night, skin like caramel, and she's itty bitty. I'm gonna marry 'er, I know it."

"You're spending too much time around your uncle Alec."

"Da," Leland groaned as he rolled off the couch and onto the floor. "I'm in love, and I don't even know 'er name."

I smiled, shook my head, and said, "Text your friend and ask him her name."

"I already did that," he grunted. "Akio says he won't tell me because I'm not sniffin' around his cousin. He said she doesn't speak English very good either. He's standin' between me and the girl I'm goin' to marry, the shitehead."

I laughed. "Love always finds a way, don't worry."

"I guess," he said just as Alannah hollered, "Dinner's done."

"Thank God," Leland said as he got to his feet. "Bein' in love makes me hungry."

I playfully swiped at him as he ducked out of the room. My remaining three sons, Noble who was ten, Soren who was eight, and Heath who was six, all descended the stairs, talking at once. They walked by me without a word, but when they entered the kitchen, each of them hugged and kissed their mom. I glared after the little turds before I followed them and joined them all at the table as my wife, and Kailen, served us dinner. Once everyone was seated and eating away, conversation about the soccer games earlier in the day became the main topic of discussion.

"I have somethin' I wanna say," Kailen said during a moment of silence.

Noble looked at Kailen, and said, "So say it."

"I will, but before I do, I want ye's to promise me ye's won't think differently of me."

I felt nervous on my son's behalf but so proud of him for deciding to tell his brothers about his sexuality.

"I'd never think different of ye'," Soren said. "So shoot."

The rest of the boys nodded in agreement, so after Kailen looked at me and his mom for support, he took a breath and said,

"I'm bisexual, and I have a boyfriend. Ye' might know 'im. It's Rome Forrest."

Leland, who was next to me, began to choke on his chicken, so I smacked his back out of instinct.

"You're *gay*?" Leland eventually asked, his breathing laboured.

Kailen stared at not only his brother but his best friend.

"No," he said, calmly before he repeated, "I'm bisexual."

Leland stared at Kailen, and Kailen stared right back at him. I didn't realise I was holding my breath until my chest began to burn with pain. I prayed my son didn't say something homophobic because I knew it'd devastate Kailen. They were the closest of my boys, and they were always together.

"I'm not hungry anymore," Leland suddenly said and got to his feet.

Tears filled Alannah's eyes instantly.

"Leland!" Kailen shouted, jumped to his feet and stopped Leland from leaving the room. "Don't be like this, man. Please."

"Be like *what*?"

"Don't be weird about this," Kailen pleaded, his hands shaking. "You're me best friend, me brother, and I don't want ye' to ... to hate me."

"I don't bloody hate ye'," Leland stated. "I'm pissed at ye'."

"Why?"

"Ye' *know* I hate Rome Forrest. He is an arsehole who never passes the bloody ball durin' our matches, and he always talks shite, now I'm supposed to be chilled with ye' just announcin' at the dinner table that you're goin' out with 'im? No, ye' can piss off, Kailen."

Things were silent for a few seconds, then Kailen's laughter rang loud and clear.

"What the *hell* are ye' laughin' at?" Leland demanded, shoving his brother. "This isn't funny."

"You're mad at me about Rome, not about me bein' bi?"

"Are ye' thick?" Leland asked, baffled. "*Obviously,* it's over Rome. Why would I be mad at ye' over ye' likin' a lad?"

Alannah laughed as the tears left her eyes, I practically deflated against my chair, and Kailen wrapped his arms around his brother and hugged him tightly.

"I was shittin' it to tell ye'. I thought ye' might—"

"Want nothin' to do with ye'?" Leland finished, returning his brother's hug.

Kailen nodded and cleared his throat when he and his brother separated.

"Rome's chill, Leland."

"No, he's not, and I'm not bein' nice to 'im," Leland stated. "I don't care if ye' marry the fella. I'm not bein' nice to 'im. Not now, not ever."

"You'll come to the weddin' though?" Kailen asked, smiling. "If we get married, that is."

"Obviously," Leland said with a roll of his eyes. "But I'm not bein' nice to 'im, no matter what, so you're just goin' to have to get over that 'ere and now. Accept it, because I have."

Kailen laughed, shoved his brother, then returned to the table. Leland followed him and returned to his seat. Alannah was wiping her eyes, and I was grinning like a freak.

"This is so weird," Soren said, his brows furrowed. "Why would you like boys? Girls are really pretty. Look at our ma and Georgie."

Kailen looked at his brother, and said, "I can't help it. I just happen to like both boys and girls."

Soren looked around the table, then to his mom, he said, "Do *I* hafta like boys? 'Cause I don't wanna."

His mother laughed. "It's not a choice, baby. Ye' like who ye' like ... ye' just aren't allowed to be mean to someone for who *they* like, okay?"

"Okay." Soren nodded and went back to eating his dinner.

Heath looked at Kailen, and said, "I like dogs. Does that mean I hafta marry one, Kai? 'Cause that'd be *cool.*"

A moment of silence passed before we all burst into laughter. Heath frowned as he looked at us; he was clearly dead serious about his question, and that made it funnier. He rolled his eyes and returned to eating his dinner, ignoring all of us. After we settled down, some of the kids asked Kailen questions about him being bisexual, then it was just accepted, and everyone moved on from it. From the look on Kailen's face, I knew he was happy.

He was being himself and that made me happy.

"Da," Noble said as I pushed my plate away and rubbed my stomach.

"What?"

"When are ye' gonna shave your beard?"

All of my sons looked at me. Alannah ducked her head, but I caught her grin. I reached up and touched the beard I had been growing out over the past few months and frowned. "I wasn't planning on shaving it, son."

"Ye' should," Noble said. "It looks stupid."

"Hey." I frowned. "Don't hate on me beard, ye' little turd."

My son snorted. "It was either slag your beard or your gut."

Have a two-pack was considered a gut according to my children. I growled. "So I don't have a six-pack anymore, sue me."

"Uncle Nico still has *his* six-pack."

"Noble," I growled. "You're on thin ice, princess."

He *hated* being called princess.

"Don't hate on *me* just because *you'll* be fat in a few years and look like Santa Claus!"

I sucked in a sharp breath. "You take that back, you little shit."

My son got to his feet and stomped out of the kitchen.

"Santa Claus *wishes* he was as ripped as me!"

I didn't have a six-pack anymore, but I was still pretty damn toned.

"You're fooling no one with that beard, Da," he hollered back. "You're gonna look like Father Christmas when it gets really thick, and Uncle Alec will *never* let ye' live it down."

I paused and realised my son was right. Once my older brother realised this, he would compare me to Santa Claus because my hair was white ... and that would fucking kill me.

"Clippers," I grunted as I got to my feet. "I need my clippers."

Everyone laughed as I left the room and headed up to my bedroom. I entered mine and Alannah's bathroom, picked up my clippers, and stared in the mirror.

"Can I shave it for ye'?"

I glanced at Noble as he leaned against the doorway. "Does it look *that* bad?"

"Nah," he answered. "I'm just teasin', but I know what Uncle Alec is like, and he'll slag ye' for *sure*."

He was right. I lifted him onto the counter, handed him the clippers, instructed him on what to do, then held perfectly still as he shaved my beard. When he was finished ten minutes later, he looked proud of himself. He leaned in and kissed my cheek, which was so cute I almost forgot about him being a turd.

"Want to watch how I shave with a razor to get the rest of it off?"

Noble nodded and spent the next few minutes watching me shave. He was interested in the whole process, so I talked him through it all. It dawned on me that it would only be a few more years until I would be showing Leland how to shave, then Kailen, then Noble then my other sons. Time was flying by, and there was nothing I could do about it.

"There." Noble smiled when I used a towel to dry my face off. "Ye' look like me da again."

I chuckled as he jumped of the counter and ran out of the room. I looked in the mirror, then left the room, walked over to my bed, and fell on top of it.

"Nice arse."

I grinned into my pillow. "Where are the boys?"

"Leland is in charge of cleanup tonight, so he has recruited all of them to help. Bein' the oldest has its perks he said."

I rolled onto my back, and said, "Get your fine ass over here then."

Alannah approached me, and said, "I think I'll miss the beard, but Noble was right. Alec would end ye' with jokes over it."

"I know." I sighed. "He's a dick."

My wife laughed as she climbed on top of me. She leaned down and brushed her lips over my freshly shaved skin. I slid my hands around to her ass and squeezed. She moved her lips to mine and smiled.

"Do we have sex or take a nap?"

I looked up at her, and said, "We had sex this morning, so I vote for a nap."

Alannah laughed and rolled on her side next to me. She cuddled against me, and said, "I'm so proud of Kailen."

"Me too," I said, hooking my arm around her body. "I had no idea that he was dealing with it, though. Did you have any idea?"

"None," Alannah answered. "I'm so glad we all know, and everyone is happy for 'im because it breaks me heart thinkin' how scared he was that maybe we wouldn't accept 'im."

I kissed the crown of her head. "Me too, but he's happy now. Did you see his smile?"

"Yeah." She relaxed. "He doesn't have to hide anymore."

I sighed, feeling content. "I love you, freckles."

"I love ye' too, Jack Frost."

I smiled. "Can you believe it's been twenty years since I first met you?"

"No, because it feels just like yesterday. Now we're married and have five handsome young men. I love our life."

"Me too, freckles. Me too."

I closed my eyes and relaxed. I loved my wife and my kids more than life itself, but I would be lying if I said they didn't wear me out. It was worth it, though. *They* were worth it. I counted my lucky stars every single night when I slid into bed next to my wife that I led the life I did because things could have turned out very different for me had it not been for my brothers.

I owed everything to them, and I always would.

CHAPTER TWO

Fifteen years old ...

"**D**amien?"

Please, go away.

"Damien, listen to me."

I kept my eyes closed and didn't move a muscle. I pretended that if I stayed still and didn't speak, then no one could see me. I told myself I was trapped in a nightmare, and that at any minute, I would wake up and everything would be back to normal. That was all this was—a horrible dream. There was no way any of it could be real.

"Damien, open the door."

I gritted my teeth and tried to force my brother's voice out of my head. I kicked the door I laid next to, but still, I didn't speak.

"It was an accident," my eldest brother assured me through the white oak wood. "Everything is gonna be okay. Just open—"

"I killed him!" I cut Ryder off with a scream. "I killed Trent! I shot him. He's dead because of *me*!"

I didn't realise I was crying until I felt hot tears slide down my temples and into my hair. I reached up and covered my face with my hands as sobs tore free of my throat. I had been lying on my bedroom floor for what felt like hours, but in reality, it was probably only one. I had run up here and locked myself in when Dominic told me that the doctor said that Trent was dead. I lifted my hands from my face and punched myself in the head as I cried.

I wanted to run away and never look back, I wanted to forget my life and start over somewhere new ... but I knew that would never happen.

"Damien." Ryder sighed, long and deep. "Please, just unlock the door so we can talk."

There was nothing to talk about. Trent was dead because I lost my temper and shot him.

"Just go away!" I shouted. "Just leave me *alone*!"

I heard a commotion outside in the hallway, then Kane snapped, "Open the door or I'm breaking it down. I'm deadass serious."

I believed him, but I simply didn't care. My chest hurt so much, my stomach felt sick, and my mind raced with terror. My brothers were the least of my problems at the moment.

I jumped when an uproarious smack sounded next to me.

"Kane!" I shouted. "Stop!"

"Open the fucking door then. Now!"

I scrambled to my feet, unlocked the door, and pulled it open. My four brothers stood in the hallway staring at me. Dominic was the first to step forward, but I jumped back away from him. Hurt cascaded across his face, but he said nothing. My brothers knew I was upset, but Dominic knew that what happened was killing me inside. He didn't have to ask me; he just had to look in my eyes. We could always tell what was wrong with the other without asking questions.

"Marco's gonna kill me," I said, wiping my face with my hands. "I have to leave before he sends—"

"He's not gonna touch you," Ryder cut me off. "I told you everything was going to be okay, and I meant it."

I sniffled. "Trent was his nephew, and I killed him. Marco won't let me get away with that, Ryder."

I killed a member of our crew, and I knew the punishment for that. I had a debt to pay, a life for a life. Marco wouldn't care that I was a kid. He had killed people younger than me for far less.

My brother stepped forward and placed his hand on my shoulder. "We've taken care of the problem. You're safe."

I looked from Ryder to my other brothers, then back again. "What'd you guys do?"

"We had a meeting with Marco," Dominic answered. "We made him an offer, and he accepted it. You aren't in danger."

I couldn't comprehend what they were saying, and before I could question them, Ryder pushed me over to my bed and sat me down.

"Ask us questions in a minute," he said, sitting next to me. "Right now, tell me what happened."

My mouth went dry. "You *know* what happened."

"I know bits and pieces. I want you to tell me *exactly* what happened."

I looked down to my feet. "I feel sick about it, Ryder."

"It was an accident," Alec stated.

I looked up at him, and said, "But it wasn't."

No one spoke.

"I aimed the gun at his chest, and I pulled the trigger because I wanted to kill him for what he said about Mom and Dad. I wanted … I wanted him to pay for it."

I looked back down at the floor. My mind kept replaying what happened over and over, but I forced myself not to focus on it. I didn't want to relive it.

"I wish I hadn't done it," I said. "I just got so mad, and my chest hurt when he said Mom and Dad deserved to be dead. I couldn't think after that."

I lifted my hands to my face and for a minute or two, complete silence filled the room … until a sick thought washed over me.

"I'm just like him."

"Who?" Dominic asked.

I clasped my hands together to stop them from shaking.

"Dad," I answered. "I always wanted him to love us, to love me, but I knew he was a bad person. I knew he did horrible things, and now so have I. I'm just like him."

I loved my parents much to my brothers' resentment. They did not understand how I could love people who didn't love me back, and neither did I, but I loved them all the same. It shook my entire world when they died, and my brothers knew that.

"No," Ryder said, turning me to look at him. "No, you aren't. He did everything he did because he enjoyed it. He was *happy*. I can see by just looking at you how much you regret what happened, bud. You aren't like him. You aren't even close."

I swallowed and inhaled a deep breath before I started speaking.

"Trent kissed Nala. I knew he had a crush on her, and it pissed me off that he would try to move in on her. I thought he was my friend." I shook my head. "He smiled when I jumped him; it was like he knew I wanted to fight, and I was more than happy to give him what he wanted. I haven't been feeling like myself since Mom and Dad died, so I wanted to take out all of the pain I felt on Trent."

I paused to wipe my nose.

"When he said they deserved to be dead because they were traitors, my mind just snapped. I can't remember much after that. I just know I was holding the gun and pulling the trigger because I wanted to. I wanted to kill him, but when he fell to the ground and I saw the blood, I instantly regretted everything. I'm a murderer."

"Stop it," Dominic suddenly snapped. "Just stop. You're a good person. You didn't plan to hurt Trent; it just happened because he provoked you."

That didn't make me feel better, but I nodded to keep my brothers happy.

"What did you mean when you said you took care of things with Marco?" I asked Ryder.

"We offered to work for him to work off your debt, and he agreed. You won't be hurt."

Dread washed over me.

"What work will you have to do?"

"Business kind," Kane answered. "We don't know all the details yet, but we'll all be in this together, so don't worry about a thing."

Don't worry? How the fuck could I *not* worry? This was all my fault, and they wanted me not to worry.

"I want to work—"

"No," Ryder cut me off. "You're not involved."

"Not involved?" I repeated. "This is all because of me."

"I don't care," my brother continued. "The terms were we work for Marco, not you."

I didn't know what to say. At that very moment, I didn't feel like I was their brother. I felt lesser than them. They didn't treat me like their equal. They treated me like I was a baby they had to protect because no one else would.

"I'm staying in here with you tonight."

I looked at Dominic, and said, "Why?"

"Because I want to," he answered.

I didn't argue with him because I knew I would most likely need him to keep me calm. I wasn't like my brothers; when they got scared, they dealt with it, but when I got scared, I ran to one of them to make me feel better. I always did, and I hated it, but it was something I couldn't change about myself. Maybe that need for affection was why my brothers treated me like a kid under their feet in the first place.

I *was* a kid, but I had a responsibility coming my way that wasn't childlike at all. Nala, my girlfriend of two years, was ten weeks pregnant with my child. She told me a few days ago, and I hadn't talked to her since. I was fifteen. I wasn't ready to be a father because I was still a kid myself. I didn't know the first thing about babies, and I didn't want to. I was terrified to become a father, but I was even more terrified of having a baby and loving it, because ever since my parents died, I had a fear that all the people I loved would leave me.

I had even found myself pretending that I didn't even really love my brothers because I was so scared of one of them dying and leaving me. My mind had developed a fear, and I had no idea how to overcome it ... and what was worse, I didn't know if I wanted to. I killed someone. I took another person's life. Maybe God was punishing me for that; maybe the pain and fear I lived with was what I deserved.

Everything was all my fault.

Everything.

CHAPTER THREE

Eighteen years old ...

"Who are you glaring at?"
I didn't look at Kane when I sat down next to him.
"No one."
He followed my line of sight and chuckled.
"Alannah."
I wasn't glaring at Alannah ... just the pussies who were dancing next to her. Her focus was entirely on Bronagh as they laughed and danced, but the men around within their reach were focused on them. I didn't like it, and I didn't like that I didn't like it. Feeling anything for Alannah was bad news. She was a jewel, someone worth great value, and she was as precious as she was fragile. I messed up people's lives, it was what I did, and I didn't want to mess up her life. Keeping away from her when I was so wildly attracted to her was agony, but I endured it. I also endured her sweet smiles, the sound of her laughter, and the longing look of lust she often shot my way.

I withstood it all from the moment I had met her ... but I was starting to break.

"I'm not looking at her."

Kane laughed and clapped his hand on my shoulder. "A blind man could see that you have feelings for her, little brother."

"Feelings?" I choked. "I don't have feelings for her. I don't even know her all that well."

Lie. Lie. Lie.

Kane raised a brow. "It's more than attraction. You wouldn't give a shit about other guys moving in on her if you only thought she was cute."

I set my jaw. "Leave it alone, Kane."

He looked from me to the dance floor, and said, "Never mind, she's kissing another guy, so you don't have to worry about her."

I jerked my gaze in Alannah's direction so fast I almost hurt my neck. My entire body was tensed to the point of pain, but when I saw Alannah still dancing with Bronagh and not paying attention to any of the guys around her, I looked back at my smirking brother and glared at *him*.

"You're an asshole."

"And you're an idiot," he countered. "You like the girl, so what's the issue? Dominic is in love with Bronagh, and I've never seen him so happy. That same goes for Ryder and Branna. That could be *you* with Alannah."

I rolled my eyes. "Since when do you give a shit about relationships?"

"I don't," Kane answered. "I care about you and the others, and if a relationship is what will make you guys happy, then I'm all for supporting them."

I didn't answer him, and he didn't speak another word. We watched the girls as they danced, and before I knew it, I was on my feet and stalking in Alannah's direction with Kane's laughter echoing behind me. Some punk was dancing a little too close to her and had his eyes on her perfect body too long. He caught my eye as I approached, and when he saw the look on my face, he backed off, then disappeared into the crowd. I reached Alannah and tugged her towards me when I noticed that Bronagh was no longer with her.

She tried her hardest to break my hold as she shouted at me, but she stopped fighting almost instantly when she turned and looked up at me. Her whiskey coloured eyes lit up when she saw me, and warmth spread across my chest.

"Damien!"

My lips curved upwards into a smile as I looked at her. I had the sudden urge to hold her, so I placed my hands on her waist, and without a word, I tugged her body until she was flush against me, and it drew a gasp from her. I couldn't hear it because of the music, but I could imagine it, and it sent blood rushing to my groin. When she gathered her bearings, she placed her hands on my shoulders and bit her lower lip when she rolled her body against mine. My hands flexed and bit into the flesh of her waist.

"I want you so bad it hurts, baby."

Alannah shook her head, and shouted, "I can't hear ye'."

I grabbed her hand and led her off the dance floor. When I turned to face her, Alannah took my breath away when she leaned back up onto her tiptoes, placed her hands on either side of my face, and tugged my head down to hers. She moved in and pressed her soft lips against mine. I held still for maybe two seconds. I had planned to pull away, but the sensation of her lips against mine was all I could take. I wrapped my arms around her petite body and pulled her as close as I could get.

"Alannah," I murmured against her lips.

She pulled back from our kiss and stared up at me with wide eyes. She said something with a dreamy look on her face, but I couldn't hear her over the music and the rowdy crowd, so I grabbed her hand once more and led us over to two large men who stood outside the entrance to the back of the club. One of them was Skull, a bouncer that I had met a few times.

"Can I use an available room?"

Skull glanced at Alannah behind me and grinned as he nodded. "Last room on the left."

I thanked him, and Alannah hid behind me as we were let by, then when the door closed, and the hallway we entered was coated in silence, she looked at me, and shouted, "Me ears are ringin'."

I laughed and silently led her down the hallway to the room Skull said I could use. When we stepped into a huge living area, the first thing Alannah spotted was the huge bed. I closed the door as she walked towards it, and I was about to follow her when I came to a dead stop. Alannah reached the bed, then bent forward and ran her hand over the linen.

"This feels good," she hummed. "It's *so* soft."

I made a sound dangerously close to a gasp as my eyes locked on Alannah's ass. Her dress had ridden up a bit, allowing me to see the curve of her ass cheeks. My cock throbbed painfully, so I adjusted it and swallowed.

"Heaven, help me."

Alannah straightened, without fixing her dress, and turned to face me. Her creamy, thick thighs were on display, and I had to force myself to stay still just so I wouldn't go to her, drop to my knees, and run my tongue over them.

"Did ye' say somethin'?"

I lifted my hand and ran it through my hair.

"I said," I rumbled, "heaven, help me."

"Why d'ye need help?" she asked, tilting her head to the side. "Ye' aren't in trouble."

"On the contrary." I licked my lower lip. "I think I'm in a whole heap of trouble."

Alannah's eyes were locked on my tongue's movement, and it caused her lips to part ever so slightly.

"What trouble would that be?"

"The five-foot-five, black hair, and brown eyes kind."

Her eyes widened. "You think *I'm* trouble?"

Is she kidding me?

"Babe." I chuckled. "I think you're the definition of it."

"I think ye' have me confused with someone else," she said, falling into a sitting position on the bed when she tried to take a step back. "I've never been in trouble in me whole life."

"No, I'm sure you haven't," I agreed, my lips twitching. "But I think you could stir up a lot of it."

"Yeah?" she questioned. "Like what?"

"Like how one kiss has me wanting to touch you in ways you've never been touched."

She audibly swallowed.

"H-how d'ye know what ways I've been touched?" she stammered. "I could have already been touched in every way possible."

She was so cute, so sexy, I almost couldn't stand it.

"*Babe*."

A pretty blush stained Alannah's cheeks.

"Fine." She licked her lips. "No one else has touched me, but *I've* touched me an awful lot."

I locked my eyes on hers.

"Why don't ye' change the former and touch me?"

I was seconds away from tackling her back onto the back, and she didn't even know.

"Be careful, freckles," I warned. "I think we should just cool it and talk—"

"I don't wanna talk." She cut me off. "I wanna kiss ye', to touch ye' ... I want ... I want to get into trouble with ye'."

"My *God*." I put my face in my hands. "You aren't a sex only girl, Lana. You're the flowers, chocolate, cuddle nights in, and steady boyfriend kind of girl. And I love that about you, but I can't give you that."

She frowned.

"Don't look at me like that," I said, flustered. "I'm trying to do right by you. I'm trying to convince myself that you don't really want me like this—"

"I do," she interrupted. "I know your situation, and I'm not a fool. I know it's just sex with you, but I want ye' so much that I'll take it."

Fuck. Fuck. *Fuck*.

She was saying exactly what I wanted to hear, but it still didn't feel right.

"This was a bad idea. I shouldn't have brought you in here." I began to pace back and forth. "I just wanted to talk to you, but *damn*, you look edible, and you smell and taste so good. It's all I can do to stay on this side of the room."

"C'mere to me," she beckoned. "Don't think about the after, think about now. If I'm angry later, it's on me. This is probably a stupid idea, but I've never needed someone like I need you. If this is a mistake, let me make it and learn from it."

Christ, she wasn't making this easy.

"You've been drinking," I said flatly. "I tasted it on you."

"I've sobered up a hell of a lot since ye' told me I was trouble."

"You *are* trouble."

"Prove it," she challenged.

I took a step forward, then hesitated before I said, "Let's just chill and talk for a while. Just … just to see if this is what you really want."

The words were hardly out of my mouth before she turned and scrambled up the bed, flopping onto her back.

"What are you doing?"

"What d'ye mean?" she asked, holding her position. "I'm chillin'."

Amused, I folded my arms across my chest.

"You usually chill on a bed with your thighs parted?"

"This is how I lie on me bed. It's kind of … freein'."

I dropped my gaze to the middle of her legs even though I told myself not to. I quickly crossed the room, turned my back to Alannah, and sat on the edge of the bed. Without turning around, I patted the spot next to me, and said, "Come here and talk to me. I want to hear your voice."

She moved to my side an instant later, and it made me laugh.

"What d'ye want me to say?" she said, a little breathless.

I turned my head and stared into her whiskey coloured eyes, and said, "Say anything. I just want to hear your voice. I love your voice."

"Ye' do?"

I shuddered. "Yeah, I hear your voice even when you aren't around."

"Ye' do?" she repeated.

"I hear you when it's quiet," I said, my eyes lowering to her lips. "Really quiet."

I followed the movement and bit the inside of my cheek to remain still.

"What do I say when ye' hear me voice?"

I huffed a laugh. "You don't want to know, freckles."

She scrunched up her face in displeasure. "Why d'ye call me that?"

I lifted my hand, and with my pinkie finger, I ran the tip over her nose and underneath her eyes.

"You have a splash of freckles right here."

"If ye' say ye' think they're cute," she grunted. "I may slap ye'."

I simpered. "Cute is *not* a word I associate with you."

Alannah leaned toward me.

"What word *do* ye' associate with me?"

"I have a few," I replied. "Smart, funny, hardworking … beautiful, elegant, sexy as sin."

She gasped. "Ye' think I'm funny?"

I almost instantly burst into laughter.

"Hell yes, you're funny." My shoulders shook as I laughed. "Out of all the words I said, you picked funny."

Alannah blushed. "No one has ever said I was funny before."

"Well, you are."

She leaned in a little closer to me. "Ye' think I'm beautiful and elegant?"

"And sexy as sin," I rasped. "Can't forget about that."

Alannah smiled, stood from the bed, and then kicked her heels off before she turned to face me. She groaned and looked down at her feet as she wiggled her toes.

"Jesus, it feels good to take those hell blocks off."

"Hell blocks?"

"Until ye've walked in high heels." She playfully glared at me. "Ye'll *never* understand how much they hurt."

"It's a good thing I'm tall then."

She hummed. "It's *definitely* a good thing that you're tall."

"You're looking at me like you want to pounce on me, freckles."

"I do."

My whole body tensed when she stepped forward, parted my thighs with her knees, and stepped between them.

"Alannah, what are—"

She brought her mouth down on top of mine and kissed me with raw hunger. She lifted her hands, thrust them into my hair, and curled her fingers around the strands as she tugged at it.

"You're playing a dangerous game with me, Lana," I warned against her lips. "I'd walk away if I were you."

Her spine straightened.

"That sounds like a challenge to me."

"Talking." I groaned into her mouth. "We're supposed to be *talking*."

"We are," she replied, sliding her tongue over my lower lip. "We're talkin' with our bodies."

She wanted to have sex with me. I broke our kiss and stared up at her, trying to see in her eyes if this was really what she wanted. I wanted to see a glimpse of doubt, something that told me she was confused, but all I saw was her lust and hunger for me.

"I want you so much," I breathed. "God knows I've dreamed of touching you, kissing you, tasting you."

Alannah's body trembled.

"What will ye' do to me if I let ye' touch me?" she asked, her voice thick with desire. "I need to hear it."

"I'd kiss you. Nice and slow until my lips are all you know. My hands would explore every inch of you until you only knew my touch. I'd love you so good, the feel of me would be imbedded into you for life. I'd make your body *mine*."

"Yes," she whimpered. "Please, I want that."

So do I.

My resolve snapped as I pulled her against me and covered her mouth with mine. I hooked my hands around the back of her thighs and picked her up in one swift motion. Alannah latched her arms around my neck and wrapped her legs around my hips.

"I *love* how tall ye' are," she moaned. "It makes me feel tiny."

"You *are* tiny," I said, pushing her dress up with one hand so I could palm her behind.

I touched my lips to hers once more, moulding them together as my tongue slid inside a kiss so ravenous it caused Alannah's spine to arch, and her skin to flush with heat. My thoughts were scattered with every thrust and slide of her tongue, licking against my own. The kiss was so consuming I didn't know where I ended and Alannah began.

"You're so gorgeous," she blurted against my lips. "And I love your hair. It's so feckin' pretty and soft. What conditioner d'ye use? Actually, never mind. I love your face. My *God,* do I love your face. Your dimples are stunnin'."

She was nervous and saying the first things that popped into her head, and it made me laugh. I moved my lips down to her jawline, then to her neck where I feathered kisses over her fair skin.

"Ye' wouldn't *believe* the things I've dreamed of doin' to ye' and *you* doin' to *me*."

My cock jumped as I imagined all the possible scenarios *she* imagined. I scraped my teeth over her flesh, and it caused Alannah's back to suddenly arch, which pushed her breasts against me. My hands flexed around her ass.

"Why don't you tell me in detail what you've dreamed of us doing?" I grunted. "*I* need to hear *that*."

"Ye' used your m-mouth on me," she stammered. "And when I thought that would kill me, ye' added your fingers and used them both to make me scream."

I lightly bit her neck, encouraging her to continue.

"Your tongue." She hummed. "You'd lick, and suck, and taste me all over until I was putty in your hands."

I turned and dislodged her arms and legs from around me as I pushed her from my body and onto the mattress with a bounce. I rid myself of my shirt with one tug, and Alannah watched me with wide eyes.

"You're perfect," she said, staring up at him. "*Fuck*, you're perfect."

She stared at me like I was something to behold, but if she only knew how beautiful she was, inside and out, she would know that if anyone should be in awe, it was *me*. She was a treasure, something to protect and take care of.

You have no idea what you're doing to me, Lana.

"Perfect?" I repeated as I gripped the hem of her dress and pushed it up to her waist. "No, baby, that'd be you."

Without another word, I gripped the top of her dress, pulled the straps down her shoulders, and tugged the material down until her bare breasts were free. She didn't have a bra on, and I groaned in appreciation as my eyes feasted on her perky breasts and pale pink nipples.

"You're stunning, Lana."

I slid my hands up her thighs, skimmed her stomach, and flattened them over her breasts. I cupped them, giving them a gentle squeeze before I ran my thumbs over the hardened, sensitive pink tips. The small action drew a slight moan from Alannah, her breathing was starting to become laboured and her body rolled slightly from side to side. I locked down between her legs, and when I saw her panties, my brows raised.

"Lace?"

"I like pretty u-underwear."

"So do I." I looked up at her, bare before me. "Christ, I'll never get this image of you out of my head."

"What are ye' goin' to do to me?" she whispered.

Everything.

"What I've wanted to do to you from the first moment I saw you."

"What's that?"

She yelped when I gripped the hem of her underwear and pulled them from her body. If the rustled sound of fabric tearing was anything to go by, I'd say I even ripped them a little in the process. I parted her thighs wide and lowered my eyes to her pussy. I licked my lips and inhaled.

"Damien!" Alannah cried, desperately trying to shut her legs, but my shoulders wouldn't let her. "Why are ye' sniffin' me? Oh, God! D'ye have a weird fetish or somethin'?"

I shook my head, smiling.

"No," I mused. "I'm savouring how you smell because it's damn good."

Alannah's body shook.

"This is indecent!" She hissed. "Ye' can't just ... *Damien*!"

I didn't want to talk to her. I wanted to show her how good I could make her feel, so I parted my lips, and flicked my tongue over her swollen clit.

"Holy Mary, Mother of God."

"Pray to whoever you want, freckles. No one can save you from me now."

I licked and sucked on her pussy lips, her clit, and every piece of flesh I could reach. Alannah's breathing was audible, and I knew she was enjoying my mouth on her just as much as I was. Her hips bucked into my face when my tongue slid up the trail of slick heat and curled it around her pulsing clit. She reached down and tangled her fingers in my hair. She was talking, but nothing she said made sense. She was beginning to fall apart. I applied pressure as I swirled my tongue around the sensitive bud, and the action knocked the air out of Alannah. She couldn't lie still, so I hooked my arms around her thighs and applied heavy-handed pressure on them, which helped to keep her in place.

"*Dame, Dame, Dame, Dame,*" she cried out. "Oh!"

I rapidly suck my head from side to side before sucking her clit into my mouth.

"Oh God!" she screamed. "Oh God, oh God, oh *God*!"

She fell apart, and I looked up so I could watch her face as she experienced heaven. Her swollen lips were parted, her eyes squeezed, her cheeks flushed, and her body quaking. I continued to lick and suck on her clit but lifted my head when she came down from her high. She was very still, only her chest rose and fell when she breathed, and it looked like she was depleted of energy. She looked so perfect, so beautiful ... I had to know how she felt. I undid my jeans and pulled them and my boxers down my thighs. I removed a condom packet from my back pocket, ripped it open, and rolled it onto my cock.

"You're so beautiful, freckles," I said as I moved upward, grabbed my cock, and aligned it with her entrance. "I'm sorry if this is uncomfortable."

Alannah's eyes opened, and her hands flew to my arms as I sunk inside her. She winced slightly, and it made me sick. I tried to focus on her and not how hot, tight, and wet she was, but it was ... difficult.

"It'll pass," I whispered, my voice hoarse. "Give it a second."

I lowered my head and kissed her with tenderness and care. I whispered words of encouragement against her soft lips and brushed the tip of my nose against hers, then rested my forehead on hers and stared deeply into her eyes.

We were one at that moment.

Before long, Alannah wriggled her hips, pulling a pained groan from me as I was trying my hardest to remain as still as a statue. She wriggled once more and from the look on her face, I knew she felt no pain. The second she hummed, I took it as a green light to move. When I withdrew slowly and thrust back in, her muscles tightened. I almost came there and then.

"Relax, baby," I rasped. "You're squeezing me like a vice."

"*You* relax!" she countered. "It feels like a melon is bein' shoved up me."

I managed a chuckle, but when I withdrew and thrust back into her body, a moan left my mouth at the sensation that ran the length of my body. I quickly fell into a rhythm, and I hoped and prayed to God that I could last long enough to make Alannah come again, but I wasn't sure I could. She felt better than I could have ever imagined.

"Christ." I lowered my head and planted kisses along her neck. "You feel fucking incredible."

Alannah was very vocal, so much so that each time she cried out, I fucked her a little harder just to pull another delicious moan from her lips.

"Oh!"

"Yeah," I rasped. "*Oh!*"

"Keep doin' that," she ordered. "Oh, keep doin' *that*!"

"I couldn't stop if you paid me."

Fast and hard poundings replaced the slow and gentle thrusts. Alannah dug her fingers into my flesh, and I was tempted to bite her but held it back. Alannah couldn't, though. She leaned forward and latched her teeth onto my neck and bit down. I thrust into her so hard in response, a resounding *slap* echoed in the room.

"*Fu...ck*! Uh, *yeah*! You're going to ruin me for any other woman."

Alannah moaned in response.

"God, I could keep you forever."

She pressed her forehead to mine. "Will ye' keep me?"

"Yes." I panted, nudging her face with mine. "God, yes. You're mine."

I couldn't think of anything other than sensation as I fucked her, and when she suddenly orgasmed, and her muscles contracted around my cock, I fell apart with her. The pleasure that began to ripple through my body sent small spasms rolling throughout my limbs and left me trembling.

"You promise to keep me?"

"Yes," I shouted. "I promise. *Lana!*"

I closed my eyes, biting down on my lower lip as my movements became frantic. My hips jerked as I came, and my muscles tightened as the pressure deflated. Ten or so seconds later, it was like every ounce of tension that had worked its way into my muscles melted away and spread over my body like a deep tissue massage. Completely spent, I fell forward.

"Damien!"

Alannah's laughter reminded me that I could be hurting her, so I used my elbows to prop myself up, taking most of my weight off her. I focused my vision on her smiling face beneath me, and for a single moment, everything was perfect ... until I realised what I just promised her.

"Hi." She beamed up at me.

"I didn't mean to say that," I blurted.

"Say what?"

"That stuff." I cleared my throat. "About keeping you."

A feeling of sickness began to form in the pit of my stomach when hurt flashed in Alannah's eyes.

"Damien," she whispered. "Can ye' not say that while you're still *inside* me?"

Fuck.

I looked down at our still connected bodies and quickly pulled out of her. She winced, and I apologised. I disposed of the now used condom and quickly began to redress, but my shirt was somehow ripped so I didn't bother putting it back on. Alannah redressed too, and when we were decent, we got off the bed.

"I don't understand what is happenin'," she said as she slid her high heels back on. "Are ye' okay?"

No, I wasn't okay.

"I shouldn't have said that shit."

She flinched. "Don't say that."

"I have to; otherwise, you'll believe it."

"So, what? I'm not to believe that ye' said ye'd keep me?" she demanded. "That ye' *promised* to? What the fuck did ye' say it for then?"

Because I was a fucking dumbass.

"Alannah, I would have agreed to anything at that point during sex," I explained. "I couldn't help it. My mind and body were both focused on the sensation, and my voice took on a role of its own."

She took a step back away from me.

"You're ruinin' this!" she said, her lower lip wobbling. "You're ruinin' everythin' about me first time. Why are ye' doin' this to me?"

I held her gaze. "I'm sorry, but I won't lie to you."

"What's the lie?"

"When I promised to keep you."

Her eyes filled with tears, and I wanted to kick my own ass for upsetting her.

"Damien," she whispered.

I knew I shouldn't have had sex with her, I knew she would regret it afterward. I tried to make it clear, but I mustn't have made it clear enough, so I chose my words carefully so she would stay away from me for her own sake. I broke everything I touched, and I was terrified of that happening to Alannah. I had to keep her away from me.

"It's not that I *can't* keep you, Lana; it's that I don't *want* to."

She stumbled back as if I had struck her. The lie I just told hurt her deeply.

"I'm goin' to get c-cleaned up," she choked out.

"No." I frowned. "Please, we have to talk about this. What I mean is—"

"I don't think anythin' ye' have to say will make me feel better."

"Alannah—"

"It's fine."

"It's fucking *not*," I countered. "I knew this was a bad idea. Just look at how upset you are! This is why I've tried to stay away from you. You're a good girl, and I knew you'd let your emotions take centre stage. This was a mistake!"

Tears fell from her eyes and splashed onto her cheeks.

"Ye' were right. This was a mistake, but I've made it." She swallowed. "And I'll learn from it, too."

I reached for her, but she moved farther away from me and headed towards the door that led to the bathroom.

"I don't want to speak to ye' anymore, Damien," she said as she opened the door. "Just ... just go away. Please."

"Lana."

She closed it behind her, and when I heard the lock slide into place, I turned and punched the mattress. Again, I fucked up. I pressed my face into my hands before I lowered them and stared at the door Alannah just walked through. I hurt her, I knew I had, but it was what was best for her. If I gave her false hope that a relationship was possible between us, I would break her heart in the long run, and I refused to do that. She was too good for me; I didn't deserve someone who was as pure as her. I sat on the edge of the bed and stared down at my shoes.

I wanted Alannah, but for her sake, I wouldn't let myself claim her. She wasn't for me ... no one was.

CHAPTER FOUR

Eighteen years old ...

After Alannah entered the bathroom, I sat on the edge of the bed feeling sick until a hard knock sounded on the door. The knocking was constant, so I hurried to open the door, and when I did, Bronagh stumbled forward.

"Ye' scared me, ye' bastard."

I grinned at her, trying to appear like nothing was wrong and my heart wasn't ripped in two, but she didn't seem to buy it.

"Where is she?"

I raised my eyebrows. "In the bathroom—"

"Did ye' have sex with 'er?"

My hands flexed, and my sadness over Alannah was quickly turning to anger thanks to Bronagh.

I narrowed my eyes. "I don't think that is any of your business, Bee."

Her eye twitched. "It *is* me fuckin' business when it's me friend you're fuckin' over."

She pushed by me to enter the room, but just as quick, I wrapped my hand around her arm and brought her to a stop.

"I didn't fucking rape her!"

Bronagh's eyes widened in alarm, but only for a moment.

"Let go of me arm or I'm tellin' Dominic."

I let her go. "Is that how you deal with problems? You have my brother fix them?"

"Fuck you, Damien." She took a step back away from me. "Ye' know fuckin' well that I deal with me problems meself. I don't need Dominic to defend me from *anybody*!"

I humourlessly laughed. "Jason Bane and Gavin Collins would disagree."

She looked me up and down. "Ye' can go and fuck yourself."

I didn't reply.

"Is she okay?"

I looked at the bathroom door, then back at Bronagh, and said, "She cried because after we had sex, she realised we would never be in a relationship."

Bronagh lifted her arms and shoved me as hard as she could. I locked eyes with Bronagh and willed her to hit, kick me, to physically hurt me in some way to take away from the raw pain in my chest, but she didn't. She looked at me with disgust, and it made me feel sick.

"I was *very* wrong about you. I thought ye' were a good person; I didn't let what Dominic told me about your past change me opinion of ye' because what ye' did wasn't planned or even thought on. Ye' did it to protect yourself, your brother, and Nala, but this? Ye' *knew* how much Alannah liked ye', ye' *knew* she was a virgin, and ye' *knew* she didn't want to be a one-hit wonder, yet ye' *still* pursued 'er and persuaded your way into her knickers all because she rejected ye' and ye' liked the challenge of pullin' 'er."

Was that what I was doing?

"You're no fuckin' better than any other scumbag out there who uses girls, and I hope ye' realise what a cold and cruel person ye' are for doin' this, Damien Slater!" She stepped away from me. "After hearin' a description of your ma and da from Dominic, it looks like the apple didn't fall too far from the tree after all because ye' only think about one person just like they did. Yourself. I bet they are so fuckin' proud."

I couldn't breathe, and it felt like the room was closing in around me. Bronagh's words ran through my mind, and my heart slammed into my chest, pleading for them not to be true. I fled the room without a backwards glance, and before I knew it, I had made my way through the club and out into the night air. I bent forward and placed my hands on my knees. Bronagh's words hit me harder than a train, and they hurt so much because I knew they were true. I was treating women like they were disposable. I made it clear I only wanted sex from a woman, but my attitude towards that was vile.

I could see that now, and it made me want to vomit.

I turned back towards the club with the intention of talking to Alannah and clearing everything up with her. I would beg her for her forgiveness, I would make it clear to her that I liked her more than I had ever liked anyone and that she made my stomach fill with butterflies whenever I looked at her. I was rehearsing in my head what I was going to say when I felt hands on my shoulders.

I looked over my shoulder, and when I saw a smiling Marco Miles, my spine stiffened.

"Damien, my boy. It's good to see you."

Before I could answer, something hard slammed into my head, sending me spiralling into darkness. When I woke up an unknown amount of time later, my head was pounding, and my entire face felt like it was on fire. I groaned and tried to sit up, but my body felt heavy. Panic flared as I looked around the room I was in, trying to figure out where the hell I was. I heard a groan from my left, and when I turned my head and saw Bronagh, my heart stopped.

"Bronagh!"

She stirred

"Bee?" I urged, pulling my aching body towards her. "Wake up, please."

She groaned out loud as she woke up. She sat upright, winced in pain, and lifted her hand to her head. When she looked at her palm and saw there was blood on it, she frowned.

"What happened?"

I pulled myself into a sitting position and put my arm around her waist. She jumped as she looked my way, and she relaxed when she realised it was me, but only for a moment.

"Damien," she whimpered. "Are you okay?"

I nodded as she began to cry.

"I'm sorry for everythin' I said to ye'." She sobbed. "You're still a dick, but what I said was wrong."

I chuckled. "Shut up, Bee. You were right about everything you said, and I only reacted the way I did because I knew it was true, and I hated it. I never want to be like my parents, and the shit I've being doing just proves that I am."

Bronagh frowned at me.

"I don't set out to break hearts. I actually don't set out to have anything to do with hearts at all, but some girls get attached to me. I swear I never meant to hurt Alannah. I know this will make me sound like a prick. I am a prick, but I just wanted to be with her in the only way I know how to be. She's different."

She tilted her head. "Is that your cryptic way of sayin' ye' like Alannah?"

I nodded.

Bronagh sighed, then looked around. "I can't believe I was knocked out."

Neither could I. I lifted my hands to my face and felt how swollen it was. Whoever knocked me out had beat me while I was unconscious and unable to defend myself.

"Tell me about it," I growled. "They did this to me *after* I was knocked out, the fucking pussies."

Bronagh winced. "The back of me head is throbbin'. It's bleedin' as well."

I checked the back of her head. "It's not a deep cut, and it's starting to clot. I can see all the dried blood."

"Thank God for that."

"Who hit you? Marco?" I asked. "I saw his face before I was hit."

She looked at me, her eyes widening. "It wasn't Marco, Damien ... it was Trent."

My heart stopped. *"Trent Miles?"*

Bronagh nodded. "He isn't dead. Marco said he just pretended he was so that he could hold the threat of killin' ye' over your brothers' heads. He lied to you all, Damien."

I felt like I was about to be sick.

"For the past three and a half years, I've seen his face every night when I've gone to sleep. I was convinced he was haunting me for what I did to him, but now I realise it's all just been in my head."

Bronagh touched my arm. "Ye' can let go of all that now."

My mouth was dry. "Is he really alive?"

Laughter from the doorway caused us to look in that direction. I turned my head, and for a moment, I thought I was looking at a ghost until I realise it wasn't a ghost, it was a living, breathing person.

"I'm really alive," Trent announced as he approached me, grinning wickedly. "Did you miss me, buddy?"

A range of emotions flooded me at that moment.

"It looks like I've got to work on my aim."

Trent patted the space between my shoulder and chest. "I'm glad you had a shit aim. Things wouldn't have worked out for me the way they have otherwise."

I pushed myself to my feet but froze when Trent pulled a gun and aimed it at me.

"Oh, déjà vu." He cackled. "Does this scene remind you of something, *bro?*"

Bronagh got to her feet and grabbed my arm. "Leave us alone."

Trent grinned. "Can't do that, baby. Uncle Marco wants to have a chat."

He gestured for us to exit the room with the gun, and we walked where he pointed without question. When we stepped into the hallways of Darkness, confusion gripped me. I kept my mouth shut as

Bronagh and I walked ahead of Trent out of the hallway and into the nightclub. We came to a stop at a booth where Marco Miles was receiving a lap dance. Bronagh looked around the room, clocking Marco's men, but I couldn't take my eyes off him as he sent the woman away.

"You let me believe I killed him!"

Marco nodded. "I did."

I wanted to wrap my hands around his neck.

"Just to keep my family in the business?"

Marco shrugged as he lit up a cigarette, inhaled, then exhaled, and blew the smoke in our direction, causing Bronagh to cough.

"Your brothers were born for this line of work, *literally*," he said, his lip quirked. "I've heard lately that you have a way of getting pussy by just blinking. I could tie you into what Alec does if you're interested? Brothers on Demand, it will be my, or your, next big *hit*."

Marco, Trent, and the two men across the room chuckled at this, so I glowered at them.

"You're nothin' but a scumbag!"

I stood in front of Bronagh after she insulted Marco, and it made him laugh.

"Calm down, blondie," he said to me. "I'm not going to touch your brother's bit on the side."

"He will kill you for this. I hope you know that. Dragging me here was strike one, knocking Bronagh out was strike two, and using her life as a bargaining chip to keep him in the business is strike fucking three."

Marco thought he knew my brothers and what they were capable of, but he had no fucking clue the lengths we would go to to protect one another.

"I can be *very* persuasive, Damien."

I shook my head. "You won't be able to talk your way out of this one or make up some bullshit story like you did with Trent. We aren't the same people you took advantage of back in New York."

The muscles in Marco's jaw rolled from side to side. "You're the men you are today because I fucking made you that way!"

"Which is *exactly* why this is going to blow up in your face," I countered. "We know all the tricks of your trades. Each one of my brothers knows the ins and outs of how you do business. They do all your work while you sit back and reap the rewards. You would be *nothing* without them!"

"Nothing?" Marco roared. "Who the fuck built up this empire? *Me*!"

I laughed. "You *and* my dad until it went to your heads. His head is full of lead now and, trust me when I say, soon, so will yours."

Marco wanted to hurt me—I could see it in his eyes—but just as quick as he got angry, he laughed and calmed himself down.

"I guess this side of him was what that little chinky bitch loved so much."

I stared at Marco, then at Trent when he said, "She only liked him for his hair colour, which is exactly why I put a blond wig in my hole with her. No one can ever say I gave the bitch nothing."

I closed my eyes and dread filled me.

"Who did you bury in Trent's grave if he is here?"

No one answered me.

"Who did you bury if he is alive?"

I opened my eyes when Marco said, "That little Asian chick you were dating or fucking. What was her name? Gala? She came to the house looking for you the day after the 'incident' and walked in on Trent being treated by a doc. Of course, I couldn't let her walk out of there alive. She would have told you Trent was alive, and then I wouldn't have been able to cash in on Dominic's talent. Your brothers running shit for me was a plus, but getting Dominic where I wanted him was my true prize." He chuckled. "After I saw the CCTV footage of him attacking Trent before you shot him, I knew your brother was a born fighter. Another plus was that kid's body was the weight I needed for the coffin that was for Trent. She probably weighed as much as him back then."

I couldn't focus.

"You killed Nala and buried her in Trent's grave?"

"*Nala*, that's her name!" Marco snapped his fingers. "Cute little chick, put up quite a fight."

I rushed forward, intending to kill Marco where he sat, but I wasn't fast enough. From my left, a man blindsided me and rammed the butt of his gun into my face, bringing me to my knees.

"Damien!"

My vision swayed as I stumbled to my feet. I turned and watched as another man was dragging Bronagh away by her hair.

"Let her go!"

The man who had Bronagh pressed her to the floor, and rammed his knee against her neck, pinning her there.

"Matt, I need her *alive*," Marco hissed. "Nico won't be reasoned with if she is dead!"

Bronagh gasped and choked for air when Matt moved his body off her completely. I rushed to her side and helped her to her feet seconds later. She looked up at me and whimpered. I felt blood drip from my nose, one of my eyes was swollen shut, and I knew I had cuts and bruises all over my face. She reached up and ran her fingers over the swelling before whimpering and leaning into me. I pulled her against my chest and swayed her from side to side.

"It's going to be okay, Bee." I gently kissed her head. "He will come for us."

There was no way in hell that Dominic wouldn't come for us. He always protected me, and now, he protected Bronagh, too.

"Are you fucking your brother's girl, D?" Trent asked, chortling. "That would be boss if you were."

My hold on Bronagh tightened. "Don't."

Trent snickered. "Always the protector of females. That particular trait had you swimming in pussy when we were kids. I'm glad to see nothing has changed."

Bronagh tensed in my arms. "He is a good person, you fuckin' prick. He doesn't need a reason to keep people safe!"

Trent's eyes roamed over Bronagh in a way that twisted my stomach into knots.

"Say *fucking* one more time, baby."

Bronagh glared at him. "You're a vile creature."

Trent narrowed his eyes. "You haven't seen anything yet, baby. Let's see what names you call me after I fuck that smart mouth right out of you."

I pushed her behind me. "You touch her, and I will kill you for *real* this time!"

"Oh, I'll be touching her. I seem to have a need to fuck Slater bitches," Trent taunted. "Nala was a fighter, but I'm betting little Irish here will give me one hell of a time."

My body went rigid.

"You said you killed her," I said to Marco.

"I never said that," he answered. "I said I couldn't let her leave my house alive. She did die that day but not by my hand. She died by *his*."

Trent looked proud of himself, happy even.

"I knew you loved her, and after she rejected me, what better revenge could I get on you for almost killing me? Killing your heart, of course. She screamed as well, so loud I almost wanted to cap her before I was even finished fucking her, but I didn't. I got a shot at all her holes before I blew her mind. Literally."

No one was quick enough to stop me from getting to my target this time. I slammed into Trent and knocked us both to the ground. I raised my hand and rapidly punched Trent in the face until hands yanked me off him.

"She was ten weeks pregnant!" I screamed, violently trying to reach Trent again. "I'll kill you for this!"

Trent got to his feet and rubbed the blood away from his nose and mouth. "So I killed your bitch *and* your kid? Fuck me, talk about killing two birds with one stone, or one bullet as it was."

I roared and attempted to attack him again, but the arms around me kept me still. All the focus was on me, so everyone was surprised when Bronagh suddenly charged at Trent. She jumped on him and punched, slapped, and dug her nails into his face, making him scream. Satisfaction filled me as she hurt him. When he knocked her off his body and kicked her in the stomach, I roared for him to stop, but he didn't listen to me.

"I'm going to make you scream, bitch. You will see how much of a vile creature I can fucking be."

Trent attempted to hit Bronagh again, but Marco moved next to him and grabbed his raised arm.

"Enough! I need her *alive*. How many times do I have to fucking say that?"

Trent slowly lowered his arm. "But Uncle—"

"No buts. You can have the other one. This one belongs to Nico, and I need him, and he needs her, so she is off-limits. Do you understand that, boy?" Marco asked Trent, his gaze now a glare.

Trent swallowed. "Yes, sir."

The men who were holding me suddenly released me, and I dropped to my knees, agony flowing through my veins.

"If you keep it together for the rest of this meeting, then you can have this one to play with."

Someone was dragged into the room, and I had no idea who it was until Bronagh screamed, "Alannah!" She crawled over to her body and felt her neck for a pulse.

"Is she alive?" I asked, panicked.

"Yes," she called back as she gathered Alannah into her arms and glared at Marco as if daring him to touch her.

He laughed. "I like you, kiddo. You have heart, but I'm not sure if that makes you brave or stupid."

"Probably both," Bronagh replied.

He winked. "I definitely like you."

"Yeah, well I fuckin' *hate* you!"

Marco snorted. "You wouldn't be the first or the last to hate me, kiddo."

I crawled over to the girls and put my body in front of theirs. Trent was laughing at our little huddle but stopped when he heard the noise of gunshots come from the stairway entrance to Darkness. The doors were slightly open, allowing us to hear them. Bronagh reached for my arm and gave it a squeeze.

Marco grinned. "The Slater brothers are here."

Trent moved into the shadows to my left while Marco's men drew guns from inside their coats. Marco, too, took out a handgun. Twenty seconds passed before the doors to the entrance of the stairway were fully kicked open. I was relieved when Dominic, Ryder, Alec, and Kane all walked in with guns in their hands. They didn't raise and point them at anyone, though, because Marco and his men had their guns pointed at us.

Dominic locked eyes on Bronagh, and I could tell from one look that he was willing to move mountains to make her safe.

"Let my brother, my girl, and her friend go, and I *won't* make you suffer when I kill you."

Marco laughed as he sat down in the booth. "You haven't seen me in months, and that is the greeting you give your uncle?"

"You're *nothing* to us!" Kane growled.

I looked at Bronagh when her body began to droop.

"She's going to go any minute," Matt said to Marco.

"Put her up here then."

I took hold of Alannah's unconscious body as Matt lifted Bronagh to her feet and held onto her as he moved her over to the booth where Marco was sitting. She instantly slumped forward onto the table, and Dominic's roar made me jump.

"Give it a rest, *bro*," Trent's voice sang merrily. "She took a knock to the head, but she is okay."

"Trent?" my brothers said in unison.

"Happy to see me?"

"What the fuck is going on?" Alec demanded.

"I'll tell you," I growled. "Marco lied when he said I killed Trent. He just wanted an easy way to pull you four deep into the business, and when you guys offered to work for him to protect me, it was the perfect opportunity."

"We *buried* the little prick, though," Ryder's voice snapped.

"No," I said, my voice hollow. "We buried Nala. Trent killed her when she found out he wasn't really dead."

The room filled with silence until Trent said, "And the slut was pregnant with his kid as well. Talk about shit luck for her."

"*Pregnant?*"

I nodded when my brothers looked my way.

"She told me the day Mom and Dad were killed."

"That was why you've been distant?" Dominic asked. "Not because of Mom and Dad but because of Nala?"

"I thought she fucking left on purpose with my kid, so yeah, I'd been messed up about that, but now I know she is dead and so is my kid. Having this prick haunting me every night because I thought I had killed him wasn't fun either."

"Does that make me the man of your dreams, D?" Trent taunted.

All focus was on Trent, and again, Bronagh blindsided everyone when she snatched Marco's gun from under his nose and pointed it at him.

"Damn, Irish, you sure know how to play a man."

Bronagh looked close to collapsing.

"Tell your men to back off or I swear to God, I will pull this trigger and kill ye'," she warned. "I'm not afraid to do it."

"Stay where you are!" one of Marco's men growled.

"Unless you want your boss's brains all over the place, I'd advise you to let me go to my girl or she *will* kill him," Dominic said, slowly. "Trust me on that."

Trent moved closer to the booth. "She's bluffing. She doesn't have it in her to pull that trigger."

"I wouldn't put money on that," Kane said.

"Hey, pretty girl," Dominic said as he slid into the booth next to

Bronagh whose hands were shaking.

"I could kill 'im and make all this go away. I could do it."

She kept her eyes on Marco as she spoke.

"I know you can, baby, but this piece of shit isn't worth it."

He reached for her, but she leaned away from him.

"He wants to take ye' away from me, and I won't let 'im." She hissed. "You're mine, *not* his!"

Dominic got close enough to kiss her shoulder, and whatever he whispered made Bronagh cry.

"Give me the gun," he urged. "That's it, good girl."

Bronagh had slowly started to lower her arm when a bang suddenly sounded. She screamed and instinctively pulled the trigger on the gun, causing an even louder bang. I flinched, then rolled Alannah's body under mine when more gunshots went off around the room. Minutes passed, but when everything went silent, I sat up and darted my eyes around the room. When I saw Marco's men were down, and all of my brothers were standing, I nearly collapsed with relief.

"I didn't mean to," Bronagh said gaining my attention. "I got a fright and—"

"Bronagh!" Dominic snapped. "It's okay, baby. It's going to be okay."

"We're going to go to prison. Those men—"

"Will be disposed of, as will Marco and Trent when we're finished with them."

She looked at Kane when he spoke to her.

"We won't get in trouble then?"

"I did a lot more for this scumbag than just hurt people, Bronagh," he assured her. "He is about to get the experience of me *fully* displaying my 'services'."

Bronagh whimpered.

"Nico, Kane ... we can talk about this," Marco said, then cried out in pain when Alec rounded on the booth and pressed a finger into Marco's wound, making me almost vomit.

"Out of all the things on the to-do list, Marco," my brother growled. "Talking to you won't be one of them."

I checked on Alannah, making sure she was breathing as I pushed myself to my feet.

"Bring Alannah to the room I'm putting Bronagh in," Dominic said to Kane who approached me. "They're soundproof, so they won't hear a thing if they wake up."

Kane carried Alannah, and Dominic carried Bronagh into an empty room with a large bed.

"What'd they do to you?" Kane asked, anger in his tone.

"I don't know," I answered. "They did this to me when I was out cold."

"Fucking pussies."

"We can't leave them for long," I said to Dominic. "Bronagh has a concussion, and Lana hasn't woken up since one of those pricks knocked her out."

He cracked his knuckles. "Trust me, bro, this *won't* take long."

"Promise me something."

"What?"

"He killed Nala, he killed my child, and he planned to rape Alannah," I said, my voice a growl. "Leave Trent to me."

My brothers nodded their heads. They knew taking care of the evil that was Trent Miles was what I needed to do. He had ruined my life for the past three years, and he took someone I loved away from me and stole my first child from me. I was going to kill him, and this time, I'd make sure of it.

CHAPTER FIVE

Twenty-one years old ...

"**W**hat's popping, little brother?"

I smiled, just as I always did when one of my brothers called me. I relaxed on my couch, looked around my embarrassment of an apartment, and said, "Nothing much. What's new with you guys?"

"Other than me going to the Bahamas as escort for Branna's best friend's friend, nothing much."

I shot upright. "Hold the fuck on."

Alec laughed.

"Repeat that for me, *slowly*."

"It's as crazy as it sounds, Dame," Alec said. "Branna's best friend, Aideen, has this other friend, Keela, who is *smoking* hot. Little brother, I mean the devil crawled out of hell and sat his ass crack on Earth kind of hot. She has red hair, legs for days, and her mouth ... Jesus."

I laughed. "I get it, Alec, she's hot. Now, why are you her escort?"

"Right." He cleared his throat. "So, she was fucking this dude a while who was actually dating her cousin, and he slept with Keela in a revenge plot against her cousin, but the twist is, him and the cousin made up, and now they're getting fucking married, and Keela has to go to the wedding because her mom is Satan and will make her life hell otherwise. She asked me to escort her, to be her fake boyfriend, so she can get through the wedding in one piece."

I sat back. "Holy fuck."

"Tell me about it," Alec snorted. "It's fucked up, but bro, it's in the Bahamas, and my fake girlfriend is hot. I'm deadass happy."

I shook my head. "Good luck, I guess."

Alec chuckled. "Why do you sound bored?"

"Because I am bored," I said. "There is nothing to do here."

"Damien, you live in Queens. There is plenty to do."

"Nothing I wanna do," I explained. "Besides, someone shot up my block an hour ago. Cops are everywhere, so I'm not leaving this place for nothing."

"You're an idiot," Alec clipped. "You're happy to live in the hood, but not here in Dublin with us?"

"I don't wanna argue with you about this again, Alec." I sighed. "I'm here because I need to be."

I was bad luck. Everything or everyone that I touched was followed by something bad. I shot Trent, which led to Marco on upping my brothers and roping them into a life of hell. I got close to Alannah when I shouldn't have, and she was nearly raped and killed because of her involvement with me. I was a sorry excuse for a person, and I knew it. I left Dublin three years ago because it was best for everyone.

The first thing I did when I got to New York was remove the false tombstone on the grave of Nala and our baby, then I had a new one erected for them. It wasn't much, but it was the best I could do for them both. Since then, I got a shitty apartment in Queens, and a job in a butcher shop and just existed. I missed my brothers, I missed Bronagh, Branna, and I missed Alannah. I missed her a lot. I thought about her all the time, so much that I knew it wasn't good for my mental health.

"Damien," my brother said. "Why did you run away?"

I leaned my head back against the chair.

"I break everything, Alec," I answered. "I wanted to leave everyone because I believe you're all better off without me. The problem is, I'm not better off without you guys."

"You're a dumbass," my brother snapped. "You break nothing! Every shitty thing that has happened to our family, happened to *me*, was never your fault, and if you stopped feeling sorry for yourself for two seconds, you would see that!"

I didn't understand how he could defend me when every problem he and my other brothers faced was because of me. If I didn't shoot Trent, Marco would have never faked his death and took up my brothers on their offer to work off my life debt.

"Are you listening to me?"

"Yes."

"We miss you."

"I miss you guys too," I said. "I won't stay away forever. I'm not good on my own for long, but I just need this time to try to figure shit out in my head, Alec. I always rely on you and the others, I need to do this by myself."

He sighed, but said, "I understand."

Thank God.

"I saw Alannah today."

My pulse spiked. "Is she dating anyone?"

"No," Alec answered. "But if she starts to, I'll drive him away. I'll get super weird and make him uncomfortable. Or we'll just have Kane stare at him until he runs away."

I snorted. "You're a dumbass."

"Says the guy on the other side of the planet asking about the woman he's been trippin' after since he was a kid. Who's *really* the dumbass?"

I grunted. "Point taken, asshole."

Alec chuckled. "She's doing her thing, Dame. Working hard in her fancy art college and keeping to herself. She's with us all the time when she's not in class and has shown no interest in dating anyone. The girls try to encourage her, but she isn't biting the bait."

The relief that flowed through my veins was almost embarrassing.

I closed my eyes. "How does she look?"

"Same as she always does."

"Beautiful?"

"Yup."

I sighed. "I drive myself crazy thinking about her."

"Then come home and claim her."

"Claim her?" I repeated. "Who do you think you are, Tarzan?"

"Bro, the ladies love a bit of dominance. They rub up on me when I get bossy."

"Shut up."

"You wouldn't complain if Alannah rubbed up on you, I bet."

I closed my eyes and thought of her body rubbing slowly against mine, and my jeans suddenly became too tight.

"Don't mention rubbing and Alannah in the same sentence, please."

Alec laughed. "Little Damien suffers, huh?"

"*Big* Damien," I corrected.

My brother cackled, and it made me smile.

"I have to go," Alec said. "I'm moving in with Keela until we leave for the Bahamas. I told her it was because I wanted to make it authentic when we appeared as boyfriend and girlfriend, and that she needed to get used to me, but I really just want to wear her down. She wants me; she's just dead set against it because she thinks I'm a player."

"You are a player."

"Even the best of players have to hang it up at some point. This chick ticks all my boxes, so if I have to be a one-woman man, then so be it. Dominic and Ryder have corrupted me by having steady girlfriends who they love. It almost makes no strings attached sex … meaningless."

I laughed. "Are you telling me you want this Keela chick to be your Bronagh or Branna?"

"Ask me after this trip, and I'll let you know."

He hung up on me because I was laughing. I shook my head and tossed my phone on the cushion next to me. I always felt a little better after I spoke to my brothers, but then my loneliness would scream at me until I dragged myself into my bedroom where I would lie in the darkness until sleep claimed me. It was a miserable way to live, I knew that, but this was what I had to do until I decided it was time for me to go home.

I just wished that I knew when that time would be.

CHAPTER SIX

Twenty-four years old ...

"Damien?" I looked from playing with Jax to Kane when he stepped into the room.

"Yeah, man?"

"I went down to speak to Alannah."

I froze. "What? Why?"

"Because you're making yourself sick by being apart from her, and I'm not standing by and watching it."

I opened my mouth to speak, but Kane held up his hand. "I don't wanna hear it. What I do wanna see, though, is you getting your ass down to her apartment because she wants to speak to you."

I stared at my brother. "What?"

"Alannah wants to talk to you ... right now."

I looked from Kane to the others in the room, then without a word, I kissed Jax, got to my feet, and all but sprinted from the room with everyone's laughter and cheers following me.

"Dame!"

I stopped when Alec called me.

"What, Alec? I have to go to Alannah before she changes her mind."

"I know, just listen," he said, lowering his voice. "That day when Carter made her doubt us, she looked at me with fear, and I still think about it. I love Alannah, and I don't want her to think I'm evil, so I want you to share part of my past with her that only you know."

I was shocked he was willing to trust Alannah with something not even Keela knew.

"Are you sure?" I pressed. "Think about this."

"I have," Alec said. "I want her to know that I do trust her, and she is part of our family. Share what happened that night to her, and she will know we value her."

"Okay," I said. "I will."

"Good luck." Alec smiled. "Go get your girl."

I turned and ran until I reached the stairway, and I didn't stop until I got to Alannah's floor. I stopped yards away from her doorway and took a few deep breaths. My heart was racing, and my mind was scrambled. I had been waiting weeks for her to give me the chance to explain myself, endless days and nights longing to hold her. I missed her more than I had ever missed another person, and I needed things to be okay with her.

I loved her.

I knocked her open apartment door. "Alannah?"

"I'm in the sittin' room."

I entered the apartment and walked into the living room. When I saw her sitting on her couch, my instinct was to go to her, to touch her, to kiss her, to hold her and never let her go, but I knew we had to have a long talk before that could become a possibility.

"Sit down."

I sat on the couch facing her.

"Thank you for agreeing to talk to me," I said, clasping my shaking hands together as I rested my elbows on my knees. "I know how hard it is for you."

"Talkin' to you isn't hard," Alannah said. "It's one of the easiest things to do. The hardest is hearin' what ye' have to say."

"I know, baby."

Her face softened for a moment before she threw her wall back up and lifted her chin.

"I'm goin' to listen to whatever ye' have to say with an open mind, so don't dilute anythin'."

"I won't," I answered. "I told you when you were ready that I'd tell you everything, and I'm going to do that."

She nodded and waited. My heart thrummed in my chest.

"My parents were murdered by a man named Marco Miles," I began, my eyes locked on hers. "My dad was Marco's best friend and had been since they were kids. They started their empire from scratch and grew it from the ground up. They had links to most likely every mafia family in and out of the States, every drug cartel known to man, and others that were unknown, and they had the law in their back pocket for decades."

Alannah didn't say a word, but she looked like she was holding her breath.

"My brothers and I grew up in a lifestyle that was *nothing* like yours. We were treated like princes and got whatever our hearts desired because of who our dad was. Escorts were servicing me and Dominic from the time we were thirteen; the first time was actually a birthday gift from our brothers. Our lives were a blur up until my mom and dad got killed just after Dominic's and my fifteenth birthday."

My leg bobbed up and down as I spoke.

"My dad crossed Marco, looking to get some extra money on a drug deal, so Marco had my dad and mom killed. They were best friends, had known each other their whole lives, but my dad's greed for money and power changed him, made him hollow ... evil. My mom was no better; the only thing she loved was money and materialistic things. I didn't lie to you about that; she and my dad were cold to me and my brothers."

Sympathy filled Alannah's eyes.

"I'm sorry," she said. "I'm sorry ye' were raised by loveless parents. I hurt for ye' knowin' that."

I cleared my throat. "Thank you."

She leaned back in the chair and waited for me to continue.

"For a long time after my parents died." I sighed. "I convinced myself that I didn't love my brothers."

Alannah's lips parted in shock.

"I have always been the affectionate brother," I continued. "I was always the one who craved my parents' love and attention, and when they didn't give it to me, I'd do crazy things to get it. After they were murdered, I was so lost in grief that I was terrified of losing any of my brothers, so I pretended I didn't love them. That way if I did lose them, it wouldn't hurt. I told myself I tolerated them because they were my flesh and blood. It made me a nasty son of a bitch to be around at times. Because of that, I never let anyone close. I had sex with a lot of different women because it was the only connection I could control. I was hollow inside … until I met you, Lana."

She swallowed.

"Back on the compound, we grew up with Marco's nephews, Trent and Carter. Carter was around us a lot, but he was the opposite of Trent. He was a loner and never seemed into anything that happened in the compound. Dominic, Trent, and I were practically best friends at one point. The only difference between us was he enjoyed when people were beat up and tortured. When our dad and his uncle made us participate in punishing someone, he loved it and said it helped build character."

Alannah curled her lip in disgust.

"We hated it too," I said, noticing her reaction. "We didn't want the life our dad had provided for us if it came along with the things we hated. The day our parents were murdered, Dominic and I were going to tell them we wanted to leave, but after they died, I refused to leave. I felt connected to the place since I no longer had them."

Alannah nodded, seemingly understanding my decision at the time.

"Trent was bad for me to be around when I was in the state of mind of wanting to feel some pain, the only person who balanced me out was Nala."

She exhaled a breath. "Nala?"

"My girlfriend at the time," I said, then quickly added, "I don't want to hurt you by talking about her, but you need to hear about her to understand everything. To understand me."

"I told ye', don't dilute anythin'."

I hesitated. "I met Nala when we were ten. She had just moved into the compound with her dad, and we hit it off right away. She followed me and Dominic everywhere, and I never minded because I had a crush on her. I asked her to date me when we were thirteen, she said yes, and we were together up until she was murdered."

Alannah's hand flung over her mouth.

"Oh, Da-Damien," she stammered. "I'm *so* sorry."

I clasped my hands tighter together.

"Before that happened, we were pretty inseparable, but after my parents died, I began to pull away from her, too. I loved her, or at least as much as a thirteen-year-old could love someone. She took my pulling away from her hard, and Trent was there with his shoulder for her to lean on. Two weeks after my parents died, I was having a really bad day, and Trent made the mistake of kissing Nala. I attacked him and beat the shit out of him. He became hostile and brought my parents into the fight, saying they deserved to be dead for what they had done. He wished I was dead along with them, and that caused Dominic to snap. It was the first time I saw him fight, and it scared me how hard and fast he could hit another person."

Alannah's eyes widened slightly.

"I was annoyed with Dominic for stepping in to defend me when I could do it myself, so I got him off Trent and intended to whoop him on my own, but he pulled a gun. If Nala hadn't jumped on Trent's back to distract him, he would have shot me. I saw it in his eyes, and he was going to do it. I got the gun from him, thanks to Nala."

I clenched my teeth together.

"When I think about that night, I can still hear Dominic plead and cry with me to throw the gun away because we weren't our dad, and I wished I had listened to him. Because what I did ruined my brothers' lives. I shot Trent, and when he hit the ground, he stopped moving. Blood was everywhere, and shit passed by in a blur after that."

Alannah lifted her hand to her mouth and began to chew on her nails.

"I knew what I had done would mean I would have to die. That's just how it works—a life for a life. At the time, I was prepared to accept that. I felt so torn up over my parents, over the fact I had turned out just like my dad, that I was willing to die just to escape everything. Ryder met with Marco, and I wasn't dumb as to what it was about. If Marco killed me, he knew my brothers would retaliate, so they both discussed it until they reached a decision."

"The life debt," Alannah concluded. "Morgan said your brothers started to work for Marco to pay off your life debt."

"Yes," I answered. "They cut me out of the deal to protect me."

She raised her eyebrows. "You're disappointed that ye' didn't have a dangerous job?"

"No," I answered. "I was disappointed that my brothers put their lives on the line to protect me and didn't give me a chance to pay off the debt I brought on us myself. That was the day I stopped being a brother."

"What d'ye mean?" she quizzed. "Ye' *are* a Slater brother."

Not in any way that matters.

"On paper, yeah," I said, "but inside, I don't feel like one."

"Why?"

"Because they don't treat me like their equal," I answered. "They treated me like the baby they were stuck with and had to raise.

I hate it; I always have. Dominic is four minutes older than I am, and he knew about everything because he had a job for Marco."

Alannah remained quiet.

"Anyway." I cleared my throat. "I didn't know that Nala was dead until we moved to Ireland, and my brothers wanted out of their deal with Marco because they repaid the life debt and made Marco more money than Trent ever could. Marco wanted to keep my family under his thumb, so that night in Darkness when we were together, I was attacked until I fell unconscious. You were knocked out and so was Bronagh. Marco used us as bait to lure my brothers into his trap. It all went sideways for him. Trent admitted he raped and murdered Nala the day after I shot him. She came by looking for me and walked in on Trent being treated by a doctor. Marco couldn't let her live after what she saw, so he let Trent kill her. He raped her, killed her, and then buried her in the grave that was meant for him. She was ten weeks pregnant at the time; she had told me a few days beforehand, and I began to pull away from her because of that. I was terrified of having a baby, but it scared me more to love it in case I lost it."

Tears filled Alannah's eyes.

"I didn't know it when I was a kid, but I thought Nala's dad packed her up and moved because I could never find either of them when I searched. I always thought she was alive and had our baby, and I was pissed at her for not allowing me to be a part of that. My parents' death sent me into grief, but Nala kept me there, and because of her, I kept everyone at arm's length. I was so angry with her … and all the while, I never knew that they were dead because of me."

"Trent."

I blinked. "What?"

"They died because of Trent, not you." She sniffled. "Ye' have to stop placin' blame on your shoulders when it belongs on someone else's."

"Alannah—"

"No," she cut me off. "Ye' blame yourself for everythin' that happened, but ye' were a baby. Fifteen years old. Ye' had no control over what other people did, so stop blamin' yourself. Marco tricked your family into workin' for 'im. He is to blame for all of this, and Trent is responsible for killin' Nala and your baby. *Him*, not you!"

I stared at her, struggling to allow myself to believe her words.

"Ye' aren't to blame."

I swallowed. "You don't blame me for everything?"

"No," she said. "And I know no one else does either."

I looked down, not believing that.

"We can come back to that," I said, clearing my throat. "I want to keep going."

Alannah nodded and waited.

"After all that happened, everything with Darkness, with us, I decided to leave to better myself, thanks to Bronagh."

"Bronagh?"

"Yeah." I nodded. "When she came by the room we were in, she was straight with me. She told me exactly how she felt, and how horrible I was for sleeping with you when I knew you liked me. She knew how much I never wanted to be like my parents, and she made me realise how I was treating girls, how I treated *you*, was wrong and something they would do. She was brutal, but no one else was going to tell me what I needed to hear. She flipped a switch in me."

"What did ye' do when ye' went back to New York?"

"I removed the headstone for Trent on Nala's grave and had a new one made for her and the baby. I know it was still inside her stomach, but it was still a baby, and I wanted people to know that he or she existed. You know?"

"Yeah, sweetheart, I know."

I exhaled a breath. "Do you hate me for getting Nala pregnant?"

"Of course not," she replied, shocked. "Damien, ye' didn't know I existed when ye' and Nala were together. Don't be silly."

I nodded and looked down at my hands.

"Maybe ... maybe we can buy Nala and the baby a star, just like you bought me," she suggested. "That way when we look up, we'll know they're out there watchin' over us. Would that help ye' in any way?"

I lifted my gaze and locked eyes on the most considerate, selfless, and wonderful woman I had ever had the honour to meet. Here I was, telling Alannah all of my dark past. She listened to horrifying things, and she still wanted to respect a girl I loved in my past along with the child we created but was never born. She was everything that was pure in my world, and I loved her more than I could accurately put into words.

"It's okay to cry," she told me. "You're allowed to be sad and grieve who ye' lost. Ye' don't need to worry about how I feel about it. I'm sad for you and for Nala and the baby, too. No one deserves what she went through."

My eyes stung as I got up and sat beside her. She wrapped her arms around me when I hugged her body to mine. I put my head against hers and cried. I cried for Nala, I cried for our baby, I cried for Alannah, my brothers, their partners, and I cried for all their suffering, and I cried for my own, too.

"I have more to tell you," I said, clearing my throat.

"More of your story or your brothers?"

"My brothers," I answered, pulling back to look at her. "Mine ended after I ... after I took Trent's life."

I waited for Alannah to be revolted with my admission, but it never came.

"I'm glad," she said, taking hold of my hand. "I'm *glad*."

I closed my eyes and rested my forehead against hers.

"Also, I don't want to hear your brothers' stories from you. I want to hear it from *them*."

I nodded and kept my eyes closed, savouring her touch.

"Are ye' okay?"

"I'm just enjoying this feeling of being close to you," I answered as I opened my eyes. "I've missed you so much, freckles."

"I've missed ye' too," she said. "It killed me to shut ye' out, but I needed to. I needed to reach this frame of mind where I was able to hear ye' out."

"I know, baby."

When she kissed me, I was so surprised that I didn't return the kiss for a few seconds, but when I did, it felt like magic. When we separated, I kept my hold on her. I never wanted to let her go again. Without her, I wasn't complete.

"I want to talk to you about Alec," I said. "He gave me permission to tell you this. This is something only I know, and by allowing me to tell you, he wants you to know that he loves and trusts you enough to keep this secret between the three of us."

She reared back. "I don't wanna know. I don't wanna keep secrets anymore."

"This is a secret that you won't want to share," I assured her. "It's only to help you understand my brother and understand the level of love and trust he has for you after everything you have been through with Carter."

Alannah looked torn but eventually nodded, and said, "Okay."

"Alec is in his thirties, and he is happy all the time," I began. "He makes innuendoes, he overreacts about a lot of things, he has shits and giggles about random things that pop into his head. He is different. Have you ever stopped and wondered why?"

She blinked. "No."

"Out of all my brothers," I continued. "Alec is the one who deserves to smile and laugh over dumb shit because for a very long time, the bubbly, happy man you know didn't exist. He was a shell of a person."

"What?" she whispered. "Why?"

"He was heavily abused in his line of work." I swallowed. "He was a prostitute in Marco's eyes, but he considered himself to be an escort. Most of the time, he had consensual sex on the job. A lot of the time, he didn't even have to kiss his dates, but some of the time

… he was forced to do things that I don't want to go into detail about."

"R-rape?"

"Yes."

Alannah covered her mouth with her hand.

"It got bad," I said, my voice tight. "When I was sixteen, a year after the jobs started, Alec was hurt by two men in a way I'll never be able to get over."

Alannah paled.

"He always came home late, and this night, I got some midnight snacks when I heard him come in and go up the stairs. He was crying. I had never heard him cry before, so I knew whatever happened to him was bad. I followed him up the stairs after a minute or two, just to see if he was okay and … he tried to kill himself, Alannah," I said, pain spreading across my chest like wildfire. "He used a rope, threw it over one of the beams on the ceiling, and put it around his neck. What those men did to him made him want to die."

"Oh, God."

"I still don't know how I got him down or got the rope from around his neck. It's all a blur, but I'm just happy I was awake when he came home, and that I followed him to see if he was okay."

Alannah cried for my brother, and I held her.

"He told me everything that had happened to him and made me swear never to tell the others. Not because he didn't trust them, but because he wanted to save them the pain of knowing."

"Like … like you and the others tried to do with me."

"Yes, because some secrets are best left buried, baby."

She nodded.

"I'll never tell," she swore. "I promise, I'll never tell. I won't even speak of it to Alec."

"I know you won't."

"I can't believe he went through that."

"All of my brothers have been through hell."

Alannah was quiet.

"It's my fault," I continued. "I ruined their lives because I couldn't keep my temper in check."

She looked up at me. "Are ye' *sure* he never told Keela about this, though?"

"I'm sure." I nodded. "When I came back, and when I was on my own with him, he explained that it was a part of his life he wanted to protect her from. Since he couldn't protect her from the other parts of his life that had bad implications on their relationship."

"Then why are ye' tellin' *me*?"

"Because he wants you to know just how much he does trust you. He hated how you looked at him the day Carter got in your head; it hurt him to see you scared of him. It's just ... he was silent for so long, but now he has a reason to be heard. Do you understand?"

"I do." She nodded. "I really do."

When she suddenly stood, I looked up at her and frowned.

"What's wrong?"

"Nothin'," she answered. "I want to go up to Kane's apartment so we can talk to everyone else."

I got to my feet. "Are you sure?"

"I've never been surer of anythin' in me life."

When we entered my brother's apartment, it was silent. We both entered the living room, and all eyes fell on us. Everyone's eyes locked on Alannah's and my hands, and they all seemed to sigh a breath of relief when they saw our fingers threaded together. Before anyone spoke, Alannah crossed the room to Alec and wrapped her arms around him tightly.

"I love ye'," she said, her voice muffled against his chest. "So much ye' cup obsessed bastard."

Alec vibrated with laughter.

"I love you too, you cup destroying bitch. You're getting me a new one, by the way. I'm going to be a nightmare until you do."

When they separated, they were laughing. I noticed everyone was looking at the pair of us with grins. Bronagh embraced Alannah next, and she was crying.

"I love ye' so much." She sniffled. "I'm so sorry."

"Don't be sorry," Alannah told her. "Do *not* be sorry. I understand."

They held each other tightly.

"You're me best friend, and I love ye' so much."

When they separated, Alannah looked around the room.

"I apologise to all of ye's," she said, swallowing. "I understand why ye's wanted to protect me from knowin' about your past, and I'm so sorry I called ye' monsters. I hope ye' can forgive me."

"Alannah," Ryder said with a huff. "You were forgiven the second you said it, kid."

She hugged him, and then everyone else in the room, before she returned to my side and slid her arm around my waist.

"Me and Damien have talked, a lot, and he has told me everythin' he needed to," she said. "I wanted your stories to come from each of you, and I know you're all willin' to tell me, but as of right now, I don't need to know any more. If I do, I'll ask. At this moment in time, I just want to leave the past in the past and focus on our futures."

"I couldn't have said it better myself, Lana."

She looked at Dominic when he spoke and smiled.

"I just need *you* four to help me with somethin'," she said, nodding to Ryder, Alec, Kane, and Dominic. "Somethin' important."

"Anything," they replied.

"I need ye' to tell Damien not to blame himself for all the horrible things Marco and those other people involved have put ye's through because he blames himself and doesn't believe me when I say otherwise. He doesn't feel like he is truly a brother to you lads, and it breaks me heart that he feels that way."

I tensed and looked down at her, shocked she had mentioned that.

"I don't know what you want me to say."

"I do," Dominic said, gaining my attention. "Say that you aren't to blame, and that you're my brother."

"I am to blame, though," I replied. "This happened, all of it, because of me. Every job you all had to do, every ounce of pain and worry your women went through, was because of me. I ruined everything."

I remained still when Dominic got in my space, grabbed the collar of my sweater, and hauled me up against him. I saw pain in his eyes, and I wanted to make it go away.

"Whatever you have done or whatever you do, you're still my fucking brother! Realise that, and then fucking accept it. I love you to death, man. I wouldn't change a thing about my life; it's made me who I am and brought me to my family."

"But your life—"

"Wouldn't have turned out like this if our past didn't happen. I'd have never met Bronagh, the woman I'm going to marry, and she would never have given me a beautiful baby girl or be pregnant with my second baby."

I stared at my brother, my twin, and I felt lost.

"But Dominic—"

"No!" He shook me. "You. Did. Not. Ruin. Our. Lives."

"Dominic—"

"Damien!" he screamed, his body shaking. "You did nothing to us. So many people are responsible for the bad shit that's happened to us, but it was all because of one person, and that person was Marco, not you. Never you."

I remained mute.

"Acknowledge it," he pressed. "Out loud."

I squeezed my eyes shut. "I can't."

I felt responsible for everything, and I couldn't just switch it off.

"Damien," Dominic said slowly. "Acknowledge. It. Out. Loud."

I heard Alannah's cry, and it broke my heart that this confrontation was upsetting her.

"Damien," Alec spoke from behind us. "Say it because it's the truth, bro. Everything that happened to us was not your fault. *None* of it."

I didn't know how he could say that to me after what happened to him.

"Say it, kid," Kane urged. "You're not to blame, for fucking any of it."

I opened my eyes and looked at each of my brothers. I looked into their eyes, and a sob caught in my throat when I saw their truth. They truly didn't blame me for anything that had happened to us. They weren't just protecting me because I was their brother; they were telling me the truth because they loved me.

"Come on, Dame," Ryder spoke last, his voice firm. "Say it. You didn't ruin our lives, Marco did."

I opened and closed my mouth twice before I said, "I ... I didn't ruin our lives ... Marco did."

Dominic hugged me, and my brothers quickly followed suit.

"Everyone has demons, Dame," Kane said, clapping his hand against my back. "We just need to be meaner than them because you know what, bro? We *deserve* to be happy."

When we separated, I turned my eyes on Alannah.

"I love ye'," she said for the first time, knocking the air out of me. "I love ye' so much, Damien."

I stood across the way, staring at her for a good ten seconds before I snapped out of my trance and crossed the room to her in two seconds flat. My body crashed into hers, and to avoid falling backwards, her arms instantly latched around my waist, while my hands gripped either side of her face. I stared down at Alannah, hoping she could see in my eyes how much I loved her.

"I love ye', Damien," she repeated. "I have never come close to lovin' another person; it's why I've always been so scared when it came to ye'. I have never loved another person the way I love you. You're me heart, and if ye'll still have me, I'm yours. I've always been yours."

Tears spilled over the brims of my eyes and streamed down my cheeks like a collapsed dam.

"Love, no," she pleaded. "Please, don't cry. Please."

She leaned up and kissed away my tears, pressing her lips all over my face, landing lastly on my lips.

"I love you," she said, pressing chaste kisses to my mouth. "I love you; I love you; I love you."

My forehead fell against hers, my hands dropped to her waist, and I hugged her body to mine so tightly.

"Alannah," I rasped, my voice tight. "I've loved you since we were kids."

A sob tore free of her throat.

"Me too, I just didn't realise it," she said. "God, I love ye' so much it terrifies me, Damien."

"Don't be scared," I said. "I've got you. For as long as you'll have me, I've got you."

"How does forever sound?"

I squeezed her. "It sounds fucking heavenly, freckles."

"Everything about ye', Jack Frost," she said, "is mine."

"Jack Frost?"

"You've just been upgraded from snowflake. Congratulations."

I smiled. "I'm yours, Lana. Only yours."

Only. Mine.

"I've never looked forward to the future as much in me life," she declared. "You're movin' in with me, and we're havin' sex every single day at *least* three times. I want to have babies, five of them, ten of them. I don't care how many. I just want babies with ye'. I want to get married, but ye' hafta ask me da first, otherwise he'll kill ye'. When I want ye', I'm havin' ye', and I don't want to hear a feckin' peep outta ye' on the matter. Are ye' clear on all of that?"

I leaned down and pressed my forehead against hers.

"Yes. Fucking. Ma'am."

When we kissed, it was to the cheers, hooting, clapping, and laughter of our friends, our family. We may as well have been kissing to fireworks at midnight on New Year's Eve because it was just as sweet, just as tender, and just as perfectly perfect as a moment could be. It was the start of a beautiful forever.

"Endgame, freckles?"

"Yeah, Jack Frost." She smiled, rubbing the tip of her nose against mine. "We're *definitely* endgame."

CHAPTER SEVEN

Present day ...

I opened my eyes as immense pleasure pulsed between my thighs, pulling me into consciousness. I sucked in a breath when I lifted my head and locked eyes on my wife as she bobbed her head over me, my cock sliding in and out of her hot, wicked mouth. My lips parted as I reached for her and buried my hands in her thick black hair. I leaned my head back against my pillow and tried my hardest not to moan out loud.

"Christ, baby." I breathed. "*Fuck.*"

Alannah sucked my cock harder, faster, and without warning, pressure built in my balls and deflated as I came. Bliss spread out and covered every inch of my body. Alannah hummed around the head as she milked me dry. My muscles became lax, my breathing remained laboured, and my heart slammed into my chest.

"It's time to wake up," Alannah said. "We napped for over an hour."

I couldn't move. "Give me a minute."

My wife giggled as she righted my boxers and pants, then returned to her spot next to me.

"I haven't done that in a while," she said. "I *love* the look on your face when ye' wake up and realise that I'm suckin' ye'."

"Let me return the favour," I said, reaching for her.

She laughed and shook her head. "I can hear the boys downstairs arguin', so we have to go and parent them. We can have some fun tonight."

"I'm holding you to that," I said and tugged her towards me. "Give me a kiss."

She granted my request, and when I tasted myself on her tongue, I hummed.

"I can't wait to have you."

"I know." Alannah smiled against my lips. "You're obsessed with me."

"Always have been, and always will be. There is a reason you're wearing my ring."

She raised her head and brushed her lips against my nose.

"You've made me happier than I could have ever imagined," she said. "Wakin' up with ye' everyday and tacklin' our horde together … ye've no idea how much that means to me. I'm still so in love with ye', Jack Frost."

I lifted my hands to Alannah's face, and said, "I'll always be madly in love with you, freckles. My life didn't begin until I met you."

My wife smiled and kissed me. We separated when my phone rang in my pocket. I took it out and answered it when I saw it was Dominic calling.

"Do you want to hit up a bar or ten with me?"

I winced. "What did you do?"

"Why do you automatically assume I did something?"

"Because I know you."

Dominic sighed. "Shit has hit the fan, and it's got *nothing* to do with me and Bronagh."

I sucked in a breath. "The kids?"

"Georgie," he said, defeated. "She has a boyfriend, and Bronagh won't let me kill him. He's Gavin's boy."

"Fuck." I cringed. "Fuck everything. I'm on my way."

I disconnected the call, looked at my wife, and said, "Georgie has a boyfriend, and he's a Collins."

Alannah widened her eyes. "Jesus Christ, go deal with 'im before he kills the lad."

I kissed my wife hard on the mouth, jumped up, pulled my sneakers and sweater on, then ran out of the room, and down the stairs. With one shout for my kids to behave, I grabbed my jacket, keys, and wallet, then I was out the door. I reached Dominic's house in ten minutes flat.

"Are you okay?" I asked when he slid into my car.

He shook his head. "I will be tomorrow, but right now, I'm heartbroken."

"*I'm* heartbroken, so I can only imagine how *you* feel."

"Tonight my eyes were opened to Georgie being a young woman and not a little girl anymore. The thought of some excited little boy near her makes me murderous."

"I'm itching to break the kid's hands and his dick. You aren't alone, brother."

Dominic grunted. "Nothing short of his death will please me."

"He's a Collins kid, too?"

I didn't see them often, and if I did, they blended in with my nephews.

I nodded. "Gavin's boy ... You want to know the kicker?"

I bobbed my head.

"Indie is the picture of Gav."

"He is a good-looking bastard."

"Don't I fucking know it!" Dominic balled his hands to fists. "I almost lost Bronagh to him once upon a time, and now I'm losing my baby to not only his blood, but his lookalike? Fuck. I want to kill him. I don't even care that he's a child."

I snorted. "You'll be hell bound for killing him."

"I'll explain at the gates. Don't worry about me, I always get what I want."

I grinned. "A certain Murphy sister is a prime example."

A smile stretched across his face. "Can you believe I married my high school sweetheart?"

"No, considering I called dibs on her first. I'm *still* pissed you messed with bro code for a chick."

Dominic laughed. "What do you think Alannah would do to you if she found out that you wanted to take Bronagh for a round of mattress dancing when we first met her?"

I shivered.

"Don't ever tell her." I winced. "She wouldn't have given me five sons if she knew, that's for damn sure."

"Don't worry, your secret is safe with me." He laughed. "I'll take it to my grave."

I smiled as he pulled away from the curb and drove towards our local pub. When we got there, we settled inside an empty booth, and I ordered a pint of cider, Dominic did too. He stared at the table, then looked at me when I clapped my hand on his shoulder.

"We'll get you through this, buddy."

He nodded. "I'll be good tomorrow. I'll take one on the chin ... but now ..."

"You just want to be sad that your baby girl isn't a baby anymore?"

He leaned his head on his forearm. "Call the others ... I need their bullshit right now."

"I'm on it." I chuckled, then he added, "You might regret this by the end of the night."

I spent a few minutes calling my brothers, and both Dominic and I had drained our pint glasses by the time the three of them got there.

"Okay," Alec said, as they took their seats around our table. "Who is okay with going to prison for murdering a child?"

Every one of us raised our hands.

"Fantastic," Alec continued. "Now we just need to fairly pick who gets the pleasure of sending this little asshole on to be with Jesus."

Dominic sighed. "Bronagh would know it was one of us, and she would kick my ass."

Alec considered this, and said, "We'll just have to accept you as a casualty. Every war has them."

I laughed and shook my head. "How does she have a boyfriend? I don't understand. She's fifteen."

"We had sex a hell of a lot of times by fifteen," Dominic reminded me. "That's why I'm so torn up. I don't want her having sex. It makes me sick."

"Me too," Kane said. "It's not right. She's the only girl of all our kids. She has twenty-four males looking out for her … This little fucker should have been terrified to look her way."

"Maybe he thought being your kids' cousin gave him a pass."

"Yeah," Alec butted in. "This is all Aideen's fault with her stupid family."

I laughed again, and this time, the others joined me. I got a round of drinks in, and halfway through those pints, we still couldn't wrap our heads around what was happening.

"Someone tell me something shitty about their kids so this doesn't seem so awful, please."

Kane groaned. "I've got a fucking kicker."

"Jax mentioned that you'd have something to tell me earlier."

"I fucking do," Kane grunted. "Me and Ado got home from shopping earlier, and we heard a noise coming from one of the kids' bedroom. Everyone was supposed to be out, so I assumed it was an intruder, but it turns out Jax was just getting it on with some girl."

"Get the fuck outta here!" Ryder stated. "For real?"

"For real." Kane shook his head. "We showed up before he could get going, thank God. Aideen was all kinds of upset, but we've talked about it, and he is aware of the dangers of sex other than a pregnancy."

"Man." Alec whistled. "That's rough."

"Tell me about it."

"I don't have anything kid related, but I did save my wife from a man-eating spider that died, came back to life, then died again because I squashed the shit out of it."

We all looked at Alec and laughed. He shrugged his shoulders and grinned.

"I've something kid related," Ryder chimed in. "I came home today from the boys' soccer game to find Branna throwing water on Nixon and Jules in an attempt to stop them from beating the shit out of one another on the kitchen floor. They stopped when I shouted, and it turns out it was over a girl. Jules has a girlfriend who kissed Nixon because she thought he was Jules, and Jules overreacted before Nixon could explain. It all ended in apologies, but fuck, this is only the beginning. I know it."

I shook my head. "That's a doozy."

Dominic looked at me. "Do *you* have a kid related story?"

"Yeah, but it's nothing bad. I got to the bottom of why Kailen has been so out of character these past few months, and it turns out he's bisexual and has a boyfriend who Leland absolutely *hates*."

Alec focused on me. "Did he tell you that—"

"That you know? Yeah, he did."

My brothers looked back and forth between us silently.

"Are you mad?" he asked.

"No," I answered. "I get it. He felt comfortable talking to you about it 'cause you're bi too. I understand that you had to respect his decision on when to tell people. I'm just glad he could turn to you. I feel like crap that he felt scared to tell me."

"He knew deep down you wouldn't care. It's just the initial fear that stopped him."

"I know." I nodded. "He told his brothers at dinner, so all of your kids will be next. He's worried they won't accept him."

"What?" Kane blinked. "Our kids love each other. If anything, they'll protect Kailen just because they'll know other people can be assholes about non-straight people."

"I know." I smiled. "I'm not worried."

"Funnily enough," Dominic chimed in. "I'm not worried about

Georgie either, I trust her."

"It still sucks," Alec said. "Thank God in heaven she was the only girl. I couldn't go through this more than once."

"Amen," we all agreed, then laughed.

We talked about anything and everything then, our stories cracking each other up, our teasing going one step too far when Alec threatened to sleep with all our wives ... once he got Keela's permission, of course, to adding new chapters to Dominic's Man Bible. We simply talked and enjoyed each other's company just as we always had. We had a bond that no one could sever, and those who tried over the years only made the bond stronger. We all came from a dark past, but each of us had bright futures and we all knew it.

"A toast," Ryder announced. "To our wives."

"To our kids," Kane added.

"To our health," Dominic said.

I smiled. "To our happiness."

"To sex," Alec shouted. "And to Manchester United!"

We laughed as we all raised our glasses and together, we toasted to the most important thing in our crazy, blessed lives.

Family.

ACKNOWLEDGEMENTS

This is the first time I've cried while writing the acknowledgments to a book. Not sniffling, or whimpering either, I am currently sobbing like a baby. *BROTHERS* isn't just any book, and deep down I know that. This is the final main book in my *Slater Brothers* series, a series that has completely changed my life.

The series is, as of right now, officially complete. I have THE MAN BIBLE: A SURVIVAL GUIDE to release in December 2018, but BROTHERS is the last story for our Slater brothers. I honestly never thought I would see this day. It took me four and half years to get the eleven books in the series written and published. It took me countless days of tears, endless laughter, self-doubt, fear, stress, and worry to get to this point, and you know what? I wouldn't change it for the world. Not a single second of it.

To my daughter, my sister, and my family, thank you for the support you've given me since the second I told you I wrote *DOMINIC*. If I didn't have you guys in my corner, I don't think I'd be writing these words. You have truly made the difference by not only being interested in the words I write, but for supporting me while I write them.

Mark Gottlieb, thank you for being a kickass agent, and having my back. You found me through KANE, so I truly have this series to thank for our paths crossing. You're awesome. Thank you for all you do for me.

Mayhem Cover Creations, thank you for giving me a series full of covers that reflect my beautiful characters, and their stories, perfectly.

Editing4Indies, thank you for all the hard work and endless hours of scanning through many pages and reading hundreds of thousands of words. You're fabulous, Jenny.

Nicola Rhead, thank you for your thorough proofreads of my books. You're very much appreciated.

My best friends, Yessi and Mary, you ladies are more than just my friends, you are part of my family. From our venting, to our rants, to our uber weird TMI discussions, to our one liners. I love our friendship, and I love you both more.

My readers, you guys are the reason I am able to write these words. From the second DOMINIC released, to now, you have had my back, and encouraged me to write on days when I didn't want to. I love your love for my lads, their ladies, and their babies. This series isn't just mine, and it hasn't been for a long time, it's ours, and I've never been happier to share something so important to me in my life.

Look out for our beloved Slater couples in the upcoming Collins Brothers series and the Slater Legacy series. I'm so glad I have those spin off series' to continue on with this world, because I would honest to God miss the families I have created. I've said this many times before, and I'll say it again, you guys make my world spin.

From the bottom of my heart, thank you <3

ABOUT THE AUTHOR

L.A. Casey is a *New York Times* and *USA Today* best-selling author who juggles her time between her mini-me and writing. She was born, raised and currently resides in Dublin, Ireland. She enjoys chatting with her readers, who love her humour and Irish accent as much as her books.

Casey's first book, *DOMINIC*, was independently published in 2014 and became an instant success on Amazon. She is both traditionally and independently published and is represented by Mark Gottlieb from Trident Media Group.

To read more about this author, visit her website at
www.lacaseyauthor.com

ALSO BY L.A. CASEY

Slater Brothers Series
Dominic
Bronagh
Alec
Keela
Kane
Aideen
Ryder
Branna
Damien
Alannah
Brothers
The Man Bible: A Survival Guide

Maji Series
Out of the Ashes

Standalone Novels
Frozen
Until Harry

Printed in Great Britain
by Amazon